Series Info

Hell For Hire
Hell of a Witch
Hell to Pay
Hell Hath No Fury
Tear Down Heaven

Publishing and Copyright Info

Hell to Pay

Aaron Bach LLC
"Writing to Entertain and Inform."
Copyright © 2025 Rachel Aaron

ISBN Paperback: 978-1-952367-46-5

Cover Illustration by *Luisa Preissler*
Cover Design by *Rachel Aaron*
Editing provided by *Red Adept Editing*

HELL TO PAY

Tear Down Heaven: Book 3

Rachel Aaron

Prologue

~3000 BCE, the fall of Paradise.

The lands of death were dying.

They lay beneath the endless summer sky like the burned banner of a fallen castle. All the glories of Paradise—the green of the Riverlands, the blue rivers of Ishtar, the white city of Anu shining like a beacon in the distance—were now the same uniform black, their timeless beauty reduced to ash by the all-consuming fire of war.

Only the sky-cutting mountain—that most holy place where the eternal gods first appeared to bless this world with their wisdom—remained untouched. Unlike Ishtar's charred fields or Anu's conquered city, it rose above the chaos, the golden temple at its lofty peak still gleaming like a torch of hope through the smoke. It was the last stronghold of Paradise, yet no guards stood upon its walls. There were no shining armies, no volleys of glittering arrows to fall like lightning upon the enemies of divinity. All the great weapons had been used up long ago, leaving only a naked fortress. One final defense between death and the deathless, guarded by a single queen.

The last queen.

She stood tall in her loneliness. Her golden armor still gleamed in the smoke-choked sunlight, and her sacred weapon—a bladed spear even taller than she was—had been polished until it shone like an obsidian mirror. Her dark skin was smeared with darker blood and the ash of her burning homeland, but her proud chin never dipped as she lifted her head ever higher, showing off the crown of her towering horns—the tallest of all Ishtar's daughters—to the enemy army that was marching up the mountain toward her.

Such a pathetic rabble should never have set foot in the realm of the gods. They weren't even proper monsters. Merely humans. Lowly mortals whose ratty clothes were stained garish red from their animal blood. Their bleary eyes did not deserve to look upon such sacred sights, and yet they'd come by the thousands, ragged men clutching their crude, black-stained weapons without fear as the first among them stepped forward.

"Queen of Pride," he said in the language of the Riverlands, smiling at her with the same disarming charm he'd used when he'd walked this path as the gods' favorite rather than their conqueror. "It seems you're the last one left."

The Queen of Pride said nothing. This traitor *deserved* nothing. He didn't even look like one of the gods' chosen anymore in his ugly leather cape stitched with bronze scales. There was no crown atop his dark curling hair, and his lean body was covered in the same simple tunic his soldiers wore.

He looked like a pauper come to beg at the golden gates, but his keen eyes shone with the light of victory almost achieved. Had the situation been different, the Queen of Pride would have feasted on that arrogance, but she had no taste for betrayers.

"This doesn't have to end in tragedy," the human known as Gilgamesh said. "Step aside, and your defeat will not be a bloody one."

The queen's lips curled into a sneer.

"Step aside?" she repeated, her divine voice ringing through air that, even here at the peak of Paradise's most sacred mountain, reeked of smoke and death. "Have you forgotten whom you presume to address? I am the Queen of Pride, Ishtar's Crown!" She lifted her horns even higher. "I step aside for no one."

"I am well aware," the traitor king replied with a smile. "But the gods do not deserve such loyalty. It was they who set themselves up as the infallible masters of creation. If they were truly worthy of the songs they made us sing, they wouldn't be cowering in their final temple. They would be out here facing me themselves, and yet the only one I see is you."

The queen's mouth pressed into a hard line.

"Such cowards are unworthy of your worship," the enemy of Paradise continued, "but I am not." He held out his war-scarred hand and pointed at the stony path between them. "Kneel and accept me as your king, and I will free you from the tyranny of the gods."

The Queen of Pride lifted her enormous spear, swinging the black weapon one-handed until its gleaming point was level with the traitor's nose.

"How about this instead?" she offered. "*You* get down on *your* knees and beg the gods' forgiveness, or I'll make you kneel forever."

She turned the spear so he could see the lowly serpents etched into the blade's long shaft.

"You know what my sacred weapon does. One strike from me, and even the unfathomable hubris of Gilgamesh will shatter like dropped pottery. If you do not wish to spend the rest of your miserably short life crawling on your belly like the worm you are, take your army and leave this place while the gods still have mercy to spare."

"The wounds of Pride are fearsome indeed," Gilgamesh admitted, ignoring the spearpoint aimed at his face. "But do you have the will to inflict them?"

The queen was opening her mouth to say of course she did, who did he think she was?—when the other figures stepped out of the crowd behind the king.

There were seven in total. Each face was as familiar to the queen as her own, but their once-living flesh was now as cold and white as temple stone, and they had no horns at all. They looked like ivory statues, mockeries of the idols that decorated the altars of the gods, but they moved like predators, fanning out in front of the human king to push the Queen of Pride back.

"What did you do?" she demanded, backing away in horror until the heels of her golden boots touched the great vault door that protected the final temple of the gods. "*What did you do to my sisters?*"

"What we asked for," replied the tall white ghost who resembled the Queen of War. "You thought I was the only one who switched sides?" She shook her hornless head. "Stupid, smug Netara, always so stiff-necked, but we weren't foolish like you. *We* knew to take the better deal when it was offered."

"You betrayed your goddess!" the Queen of Pride roared.

"*She betrayed us first!*" War roared back. "Ishtar made her demons to be the dumping ground for humanity's evil, but she couldn't even do us the kindness of removing our ability to feel the trash we were being fed! She created us *knowing* how much we would suffer, and you still want me to kneel at her feet? To call her mother?" Her new white lips peeled back in a snarl. "You want me to be as pathetic as you?"

The Queen of Pride bared her own viper-sharp teeth. "There is nothing more pathetic than a traitor."

"I can think of one," War taunted. "A queen who stakes her life defending a pack of sniveling losers."

Her white arm shot out to grab the shaft of Pride's spear. The Queen tried to yank it back, but War had always been the strongest of Ishtar's daughters. Even this pale shadow was able to rip the weapon from her grasp, throwing it to the ground with one hand while her other grabbed her sister's towering horns.

"Anu and Ishtar are defeated," War hissed as she forced back Pride's head. "Your oh-so-divine gods lost their Paradise to the same mortals they treated as pets. That's like a shepherd being overthrown by his sheep."

"Blasphemy!" the queen yelled, struggling against her sister's hold.

"Truth," War corrected as she added her other hand to her grip on Pride's horns. "Now *kneel.*"

The Queen of Pride dug her golden boots into the mountain's stone, but it did no good. War was too strong, and the others had come to help, grabbing the queen's shoulders as they forced her to the ground, but the real horror came from the hands wrapped around her horns. Her proud crown, the mark of her divine purpose, was cracking beneath the Queen of War's grasp. Another few seconds, and her blessed horns would break like infantry before a cavalry charge. War had always had the power to destroy everything she touched, but Pride had never been one to accept defeat. Ishtar's Crown would *never* fall to such unworthy, backstabbing hands, so the Queen of Pride did what pride has always done and turned her weapon on herself, calling her sacred spear off the ground where her sister had thrown it to strike at her own forehead.

"*No!*" screamed War.

"*No!*" cried Gilgamesh at the same time, but it was too late. The Spear of Pride had already collided with its queen's horns, shattering both into a thousand pieces as the Queen of Pride, Ishtar's firstborn, the last defender of Paradise, removed herself forever from the traitor's reach.

Chapter 1

Downtown Seattle, present day.

"**O**kay," Bex said, holding her giant sunglasses out in front of her so she could check her reflection in the plastic lenses. "Let's do this."

She pulled her black hair forward so that it was hiding as much of her tall, ridged horns as possible before placing the sunglasses back over her glowing red eyes. When all of her demonic features were as hidden as she could get them, Bex shoved her hands into the pockets of her beaten-up black leather bomber jacket and stepped out of the alley where she'd been hiding into the crowded street that marked the official entrance to Pike Place Market.

It was a gorgeously sunny October afternoon. Technically, it wasn't tourist season anymore, but the open-air shopping district was still packed with sunscreen-slathered humans eating street food from paper plates. A few of the shoppers paused taking pictures of the iconic florist stalls to glance at Bex's horns, but the magical scales in their eyes quickly removed the memory and turned their attention elsewhere, leaving Bex free to stroll down the street in search of her next target.

She had a very specific type in mind: tourist, male, not too old or too young, easily distracted.

Fortunately for her, there were always bored dads hanging around in front of the fancy shops that lined the market's cobblestone main drag. The covered sidewalk in front of the original Starbucks was especially good hunting. That line was *insane*, and while true fans wouldn't give up their spot for love or money, the friends and family they'd dragged along with them usually jumped at any opportunity to escape. Bex had already spotted one such likely mark near the line's end: a middle-aged man with a sunburnt face standing at the edge of a large group of teenagers and their moms.

Bingo.

"Excuse me," Bex said, slumping her shoulders to make her already annoyingly short frame look even smaller. "You seem pretty strong. Could you help me move something out of my car real quick?"

"Oh," said the human, his scaled brown eyes sliding over Bex's foot-tall black horns to settle on what was visible of her pale face beneath her giant sunglasses. He must have liked what he saw, because his red face burst into a smile. "Yeah, sure. Give me a sec." He turned his head and bellowed over the crowd. *"Honey!"*

One of the moms at the front of the coffee-hungry pack looked over her shoulder, and there was a brief-but-loud conversation as the man explained he was going to step out of line for a second and help this nice girl. Bex spent the whole exchange trying to look friendly and nonthreatening, something that was usually impossible for demons but worked depressingly well now that she was five-foot-two.

2

Blind fools, Drox grumbled in her mind.

Hush, Bex thought back, covering Drox's black ring with her hand and smiling even more vigorously as her chosen mark handed off his shopping bags to one of the teenagers and stepped over the plastic rope that kept the coffee line from spilling into the street.

"All right, little lady," he said, adjusting his floppy sun hat. "Where's your car?"

"Right over here," Bex said, crooking her finger as she led the helpful human back to the alley she'd just stepped out of.

The man slowed down when he realized she was taking him away from the crowd, but a few more smiles got him moving again, at least until Bex opened an unmarked steel door in the alley's brick wall and waved for him to go inside.

"Your car's in a building?" he asked suspiciously.

"It's a garage," Bex replied innocently, pointing at the graffiti-covered garage door that was, indeed, set into the wall right beside them. "I can't park in the alley."

That must have sounded logical enough, or maybe he just didn't want to chicken out in front of a girl half his size, because the human went in a few seconds later, entering the dark garage like he was stepping into the mouth of a monster, which wasn't actually that far from the truth.

"I don't see a car."

"Keep going," Bex said as she followed him inside. "Just one more step."

The human was looking *really* nervous now, but he took one more step into the dark, which was just enough room for Nemini to close the door behind them.

"What the—"

The man whirled around, fists coming up to defend himself from the mugging or kidnapping or whatever he thought was about to happen, but it was too late. Bex had already taken off her sunglasses, staring at the human with eyes that glowed like burning embers in the dark.

"Sorry about this."

That was all she had time to say before the kick landed.

As ever, the magical boot hit her stomach like a battering ram, knocking Bex away from the terrified human and the scales that glittered like soap bubbles in his wide, frightened eyes. For one breathless moment, she was hurtling through darkness, and then she landed sprawling on her back in the endless gray of Limbo.

"That's always fun," Bex wheezed, sitting up to look for Nemini.

As usual, the void demon was already standing next to her, completely unfazed. Even the glossy black snakes that formed her Medusa hairstyle didn't look alarmed at getting booted out of reality, coiling peacefully above the dark-skinned demon's lovely-but-blank face as Nemini reached down to help Bex off the ground.

"Did you leave the door cracked?" Bex asked as she hauled herself to her feet. "The last thing we need is to come back to a second kick because our dude couldn't find the exit."

"I have no reason to believe he won't be able to find his way out," Nemini replied in her usual monotone. "Humans are generally clever animals, and once Gilgamesh's scales remove us from his memory, he will no longer be afraid and irrational." Her lips pulled down in a slight frown. "Not that he shouldn't be afraid, considering our ultimate powerlessness in the face of an infinite and uncaring universe."

"Good thing he's probably not as aware of that as you are," Bex said, brushing the dust off her blue jeans as she studied the seemingly empty gray landscape. "Okay, same deal as last time. You ready?"

Nemini shrugged. "There is no way to be 'ready' for an unknowable future, but I am physically prepared for exertion."

"Good enough," Bex said, pulling Drox out of his ring and raising him above her head. She went ahead and lit herself up as well, wrapping her body in the raging flames of the Bonfire of Wrath for extra visibility. When she was shining like a signal flare, Bex took a deep breath and bellowed into the nothingness.

"Children of Ishtar!"

She shouted the words in the language of the Riverlands. They didn't sound nearly as good coming out of her mouth as they did when Iggs said them, but Bex was still relearning their old language, and hunger-crazed kick demons didn't care about pronunciation. Volume was what mattered here, so Bex belted out the words, projecting her voice as far as she could while reaching with her fire at the same time to catch her people's wrath.

That part worked almost *too* well. Just like when she'd fought the crazy prince, the anger of her imprisoned demons hit her bonfire like a bucket of gasoline. Her flames flared up so big, she almost engulfed Nemini, but Bex was an old hand at this now. The moment her fire jumped, she wrestled it back, condensing and focusing the inferno until she was blazing like the sun.

"Children of Ishtar!" she shouted again, her burning voice ringing with the command she'd inherited from her divine mother. *"Come to me!"*

The words sailed like arrows through the emptiness of Limbo. Between the endless gray and her own blinding light, Bex couldn't see if they struck true. She must've landed at least a couple hits, though, because a few seconds later, the ground started shaking under her feet.

"Here they come," she said, lowering her sword as she set her stance. "Get ready to catch."

Nemini nodded and darted away at a speed that still surprised Bex no matter how many times she saw it. By the time her eyes caught up, the void demon's elegant hands were already wrapped around the horns of the nearest charging kick demon, turning its rampage into a faceplant as Nemini's emptiness flooded its mind. That was Bex's signal, and she moved as fast as she could, whipping Drox's blade around to point at the spot directly between the kick demon's empty gray eyes. The moment she was sure her aim was true, Bex set her boots and spoke the name her dutiful sword had already placed in her mind.

"Heratex, return to me!"

6

The power required to speak the demon's true name was enough to make even her raging bonfire flicker. That wasn't because the demon in question was particularly strong or ancient—he actually looked about Iggs's age—it was this place. The magic that chained her people to Limbo was backed by the power of Heaven. To break it, Bex had to assert her authority even harder. She hadn't known it was possible before she'd freed Iggs, but she had the trick down pat now. Bex yelled the demon's name with the force of a sledgehammer, knocking him out of Limbo's madness and forcing him into a human form.

That last part always left a bad taste in her mouth. Bex *hated* changing her people before she'd even spoken to them properly, but leaving them in their natural shapes was impractical. She couldn't reach everyone she needed to save if she was surrounded by a wall of gigantic, emotionally overwrought wrath demons.

The one she'd just freed had already fallen to his knees. He was still wearing the bloodstained ancient farmer's clothes that all her wrath demons seemed to have been damned in, but they barely fit him anymore. Though he'd clearly been a big man once, his body was now so thin that his bones showed through his pale human skin. But despite his skeletal appearance, his eyes were bright and red again, and the oxlike horns that rose from his dark hair were now a healthy jet black instead of Limbo's sickly gray.

He bowed them before Bex as soon as he was able, lowering the points all the way to Limbo's gray ground as his skeletal body heaved with sobs. Bex wanted nothing more than to stop and comfort him, but their window in Limbo was short, and she had a lot of work left to do. Nemini had already jumped on top of the next demon, taking the raging female to the ground with a small hand pressed against the back of her gray-skinned neck. Bex got there a few seconds later, pointing her sword in the general direction of the demon's head as Drox slipped the correct name into her thoughts.

"Zargrexa, return to me!"

The command left her like a thunderclap, which was surprising. This demon had looked smaller than the first one, but her name was a mountain on Bex's tongue. Pushing the whole thing out left her gasping, but it was worth it. The moment the command left Bex's mouth, the raging gray kick demon collapsed into an old woman with straight, proud horns that looked like a shorter, more battered version of Bex's.

She's a village chief, Drox informed her.

"Great," Bex panted as she crouched beside her newest free demon. "Zargrexa?"

The old woman raised her shaking head. "My queen," she whispered in the tongue of the Riverlands, her red eyes filling with tears. "Is it really you?"

"It is," Bex replied in the same language. Terribly, admittedly, but it didn't matter. She hadn't spoken a word of Riverlander when she'd freed Iggs, but he'd still understood her because she was his queen. Bex was trying to use more Riverlander these days because it was the language of her people, but translation was a luxury she was running out of time

8

for with Limbo's five-minute timer ticking down, so she gave up and switched back to English.

"Stay behind me and keep an eye on him," she ordered, pointing Zargrexa at the skeletal male, who was still weeping on the ground. "I'll send more your way as I free them."

The old lady said something that sounded like an agreement, but Bex was already running for the next demon Nemini had brought down. She shouted the name as Drox fed it to her, only pausing long enough to make sure the command actually got through before moving to the next target.

As always, the sound of combat brought more kick demons. Soon, they were swarming, but after weeks of doing this every day, Bex and Nemini were a well-oiled machine. They moved from demon to demon, burning them free from Gilgamesh's damnation one after another until Nemini called the warning.

"Ten seconds."

Bex had no idea how the void demon kept such accurate time. She never wore a watch or used the phone that Bex had given her, but she was never wrong. If Nemini said ten seconds, ten seconds was what they had, so Bex pulled her sword back into its ring and looked around to take stock of their situation.

It wasn't nearly as bad as the pileups that used to bury Iggs. Now that they were freeing kick demons instead of merely keeping them back, the area around Bex and Nemini was reasonably clear. More gray demons were still charging in, but ten seconds wasn't long enough to free them, so Bex signaled Nemini to focus on protecting the cluster of terrified demons they had managed to save. The hunger-maddened kick demons were wild, but between Nemini's void touch and Bex's quick kicks, nothing got through. Working together, they held the line as the seconds ticked down, pushing off bigger and bigger crowds of kick demons until, at last, Bex felt the blessed crack of the floor breaking beneath her feet.

"Here we go!" she shouted, turning away from the snapping gray fangs of the demons she hadn't been able to free to wrap her arms around the ones she had. "Get ready to fall!"

The ground was gone by the time she finished, dropping Bex, Nemini, and all the demons they'd rescued back into the real world.

They landed in a heap on the garage's oil-stained floor. Once she'd scrambled off her people, Bex looked for the human they'd used to get into Limbo, but as Nemini had predicted, the man was long gone. Saying a quick prayer of thanks to Ishtar that they wouldn't have to deal with a second kick, Bex turned around to have a look at her catch.

Thirteen demons, Drox reported in her mind. *That's three more than your average and a hundred so far for the day. Well done.*

Bex didn't feel like she'd done well. The crowd huddled on the floor looked pathetically small to her eyes, which was depressing, since, by the old standard of having freed one wrath demon from Limbo in all her lives, thirteen was incredible. A hundred in one day would've been unthinkable only a month ago, yet it was barely a drop in the bucket compared to how many demons she still had left to save.

Ironically, the huge upswing in her success was entirely due to Gilgamesh. Ever since Bex's rebel army had taken over the Seattle Anchor a month ago, the Eternal King had been in full retreat. He'd pulled back his warlocks and sealed his Anchors, cutting off all travel between the living world and the afterlife. Even his princes were no longer showing up, which was how Bex had been able to chain-kick herself into Limbo and spend the full five minutes freeing demons instead of fighting nonstop duels to the death. It was incredible. She should have *felt* incredible, but whenever Bex looked at the people she'd saved, all she could think about was how many more she'd left behind.

Drox estimated there were a hundred thousand wrath demons damned to Limbo. That was only half the prewar population but still a daunting number. After four weeks of getting kicked as many times a day as possible, Bex had only managed to free five thousand and ninety-eight people. If she and Nemini kept up their average of a hundred and sixty demons a day, getting all one hundred thousand wrath demons out of Limbo was going to take twenty months.

There was no way Gilgamesh would leave them alone for that long. Bex wasn't sure why he hadn't sent his princes after her already, but she knew the clock was ticking. She *had* to figure out a way to go faster, to free more demons before—

Now is not the time for that, Drox said, his sharp voice slicing through her frantic thoughts. *Freeing your people from Gilgamesh's gray hell is not your only duty. You can't do anything for the demons you haven't saved yet, but the children of Paradise you have set free need you to guide them. Will you fail one duty worrying over another? Or will you be the queen Ishtar made you to be?*

As usual, her sword cut straight to the point. Duly chastised, Bex made herself stop focusing on how much was left to do and turned her attention back to the thirteen demons in front of her, every one of which was kneeling on the floor with their black horns pressed against the garage's dirty cement.

"Daughter of the most holy Ishtar," said the old demon woman Bex had rescued second, the one Drox had identified as a village chief. "Your unworthy people kneel before you. Despite our failure to defend your lands from the conqueror king and his traitorous war demons, you have still saved us from torment and starvation." She bowed her long horns even lower. "We always knew that you would come for us! We are blessed beyond reason to be in your presence once again. Praise be to Ishtar's sacred daughter!"

All the demons repeated the praises as she finished, adding their voices to the old lady's. Even after Bex acknowledged their words and bid them stand, they refused to stop, making her groan internally. Freshly freed demons were always like this. Iggs had refused to get off his knees for a solid thirty minutes when Bex first pulled him out. She should've been used to it by now, but the flood never got any easier to listen to, and Bex's face began to burn.

"Please don't," she begged when she couldn't stand it anymore, reaching down to help the old lady—

Zargrexa, Drox supplied.

—reaching down to help Zargrexa off the floor.

"I'm the one who's blessed to be here," Bex insisted, bending over instead of crouching since she'd learned the hard way how badly her people took it when she did anything that looked like kneeling in front of them. "You kept faith in me even after I failed to protect you from Gilgamesh's armies or the hell of Limbo. I'm furious at what has been done to you, and I swear on my mother's name that I will set every single one of Ishtar's children free. Before we can do anything, though, you must rest and recover. Lift your horns and rise to your feet, and I will take you to food."

Bex had freed a lot of demons over the last month, and she'd found that nothing got them off their knees faster than the word "food." This group was no different. Even pious old Zargrexa popped to her feet, her red eyes gleaming hungrily as Bex pointed her toward the door Nemini was holding open at the back of the garage.

As always, her people gave the void demon a wide berth. If this bothered Nemini, though, Bex couldn't tell. Her face remained blank as always as she directed the nervous wrath demons through the doorway into another world.

The reason Bex had chosen to do her demon-freeing in a garage was because it wasn't *actually* a garage. The graffiti-covered room was one of many secret entrances into the business side of the Seattle Anchor. This particular garage connected to what had been the Market's dry goods storage area. By raising the metal garage door, Gilgamesh's sorcerers had been

13

able to unload entire tractor-trailers straight into the warehouses beneath the Anchor Market, largely through the use of slaves.

After Bex freed every demon in the Anchor, those same slaves had helped her uncover all the Anchor's secrets, including the door they were using now. The Anchor's back-end office—that architecturally impossible maze of beige hallways Bex had cut her way out of during their first trip into the Anchor—was full of useful features she'd never known about until the freed demons showed her. The best discovery of all, though, was the control room.

Before they'd taken it over, Bex had assumed the Anchor was like her Winnebago: a sorcerously stretched space created and controlled by magic she'd never be able to alter or understand. That was *mostly* true, but unlike the demon's magical RV—which had been made by a single sorcerer for his own amusement—the Seattle Anchor was an official outpost of Heaven. It had been used for decades by lots of sorcerers doing lots of different things. To keep all those competing needs and egos within safe-operating parameters, all the stretched space in the Anchor was managed from a single point. In Seattle's case, that was a room full of cuneiform tablets that controlled every aspect of the Anchor's look, layout, and size.

Once Bex and her team realized this place had a steering wheel, they'd gotten right to work. They couldn't stretch the Anchor any bigger since they weren't sorcerers, but the slaves who used to serve the Anchor architects had watched their masters work the control panels long enough to know how to change the way the existing spaces were laid out.

The very first thing Bex had asked them to do was untangle the Gordian knot of beige cubicles into something that was actually navigable. Once that was unraveled, they'd discovered tons of warehouses, storage lockers, and cold vaults hidden under the offices. It made sense in hindsight—the Market vendors needed somewhere to store all those marble entertainment centers and twenty-person dining sets the denizens of Heaven were constantly buying—but Bex had never realized there were so many. Once the control room team figured out how to unlock all that storage space, they had plenty of room to house their exploding free-demon population.

Since Bex was already busy freeing demons from Limbo by that point, most of that work had fallen to Lys. As usual, they'd done a fantastic job, working with the control-room team to transform the Anchor's cavernous storage space into seven floors of high-density modern demon living.

That was great for the freed warlock slaves who were used to the human world, but thanks to the memory loss caused by the madness of Limbo, Bex's wrath demons were still stuck five thousand years in the past. Culture shock didn't begin to describe it, so Bex and Iggs had put their heads together and redesigned the Market's former fresh-food storage area into a miniature version of the old Riverlands.

Bex had never appreciated just how crazy stretched space could get until they'd pushed it to the limit. Unlike the Anchor Market, with its giant golden statue of Gilgamesh and fake rolling hills, Iggs's rendition of Paradise actually felt like home. The moment Bex stepped through the door Nemini held open at the back of the garage, she was greeted by the sound of flowing water and the sweet smell of river grass. The sunlight was green and dappled thanks to the enormous fig trees that grew like giant umbrellas overhead, shading the growing collection of small buildings built in the traditional way from river stones, reed-mat roofs, and clay-brick chimneys.

As always, the sight filled Bex with a swell of emotion that was difficult to describe. She knew the village was fake because she'd helped Iggs design it, but the sight of so many wrath demons—*her* demons—talking to their neighbors, mending their clothes, and just living their lives in the cool shade of the river trees never failed to bring tears to her eyes. Even more than freeing her people from Limbo, *this* felt like victory, especially when all the demons in the square stopped what they were doing and rushed forward to see if any of the new arrivals were people they knew.

This happened every time Bex brought in a new group. The result was always chaos, but it was also the happiest few minutes of Bex's day. *This* was the moment when all the fighting felt worth it, because this was when Bex got to watch children find their mothers, husbands find their wives, friends, partners, even strangers throwing their arms around each other with wild shouts of joy that the hell was finally over, and they were finally free.

It didn't get any better than that. No matter how many times she saw it—which was a lot given that she'd been freeing demons every waking moment for the last thirty days—Bex never got tired of her people's joy. The only reason she didn't jump in to start hugging and crying with them was because she was their queen, and traditional old demons like hers expected queens to be dignified. Bex was struggling to keep it together when she felt something bump against her arm, and she looked over to see Nemini handing her a tissue.

"Thanks," she whispered, taking the paper and ducking her head so her people wouldn't see their queen wiping ashy tears out of her eyes.

"You're the one who deserves that word," the void demon replied, watching the mob of furiously hugging people in front of them with uncharacteristic intensity. "When you've accepted that you're nothing but a speck of dust drifting through an unfeeling universe, it's easy to forget that sometimes, our actions *do* matter. Even if they're all still doomed to die someday, right now, in this moment, these people are the happiest they're ever likely to be." Her yellow eyes flicked back to Bex. "You did that. You changed the world for these demons, and that is deserving of praise."

"Thank you," Bex whispered, stunned. "That means a lot coming from you."

"All opinions are equally meaningless," Nemini replied with a shrug. "But for what it's worth, I'm glad you finally found a way to free your people."

Glad didn't come close to describing how Bex felt. From someone like Nemini, though, those quiet words were as good as a scream from the rooftops. Bex was still staring at her in awe when the chaos in front of them finally subsided as someone brought out the food.

The whole village fell silent as the platters were laid on the long public tables. By Ishtar's mercy, the former kick demons didn't remember the painful, humiliating details of their time in Limbo, but they all remembered the hunger. Bex had always thought Iggs's habit of eating anything within arm's reach came from him being young. Now, though, she suspected it was due to starvation trauma, because every wrath demon she'd freed ate like they'd never see food again.

Even the demons who weren't partaking stayed quiet to allow the newcomers to stuff their faces as quickly as possible. The food Bex had ordered the kitchens that surrounded the square to keep putting out around the clock was savory oatmeal, a dish Iggs said was the closest thing the modern world had to traditional Riverlands home cooking. Bex liked it because it was gentle on the stomach, easy to prepare in large quantities, and—most importantly for their current situation—consisted mostly of water from the Rivers of Death.

Not *actual* deathly water. That beautiful, blue-glowing liquid only came from Paradise itself, which was why it was so expensive. It was also completely unavailable at the moment thanks to Gilgamesh locking down every Anchor Market on the planet. Fortunately for Bex and her demons, the Rivers of Death still originated in the land of the living, and their stolen Anchor had access straight to the source. Bex had broken the connection to Heaven when she'd cut the chain, but the door leading out to the bridge where she'd battled the Prince of Sorrow was still there, as was the freezing river she'd almost drowned in. It didn't look like a river of Paradise, but the water that flowed past their Anchor still carried the souls of dead mortals to the afterlife, which meant it contained all the wrath her people needed to survive.

It wasn't an ideal solution. The black water was weak and lost potency quickly. Even after Iggs installed a pipe to pump it straight into the fake river that flowed through their village, it took Bex's demons multiple tries to pull out enough wrath to sustain themselves. As wrath demons, wrath was the only sin they could draw from the water. The rest returned to the channel, where it was dumped back into the dark river to go on up to Heaven.

Honestly, Bex was lucky her people were still able to stomach it. Modern demons who'd been brought up absorbing their food from living humans had a hard time with the raw stuff. Even Lys's iron stomach couldn't handle lust taken straight from the river, which meant the rest of their demon population was still stuck feeding the normal way. Seattle was a big town, so it wasn't a problem yet, but with the way their free-demon population was exploding, it might be soon.

That was a problem for the future, though. For now, Bex was content to watch her people eat. The team of demons Iggs had trained to record everyone's name and home village was already moving in to begin their interviews. Iggs used to do it himself before he'd been forced to delegate as their operation here got bigger.

Honestly, Bex thought the old ladies he'd found to replace him did a better job. Having come straight from the fall of Paradise, wrath demons were a very traditional society, and despite being a direct servant of the queen, Iggs was still young, which didn't garner him a lot of respect. Having elders do the asking got the information they needed with much less drama, which meant Bex was free to start working on the next batch. She'd just pulled out her phone to add thirteen more free demons to her running tally when she saw what time it was.

"Oh crap," she said, glowing eyes flying wide as she whirled to Nemini. "Can you lock up the garage? I'm supposed to meet Adrian in thirty minutes, and I've still got to take a shower."

"I don't mind securing our perimeter," Nemini replied, tilting her head. "But why do you need to take a shower to meet Adrian? He's seen you looking much worse than this."

"Because tonight is special, and I don't want to ruin it by looking like a chew toy," Bex said, pointing at her jeans, which were riddled with rips, bloodstains, and claw marks after ten trips to Limbo. "He's finally back in town from checking the other Anchors, so we scraped out some time to have dinner together."

She was doing her best to sound professional, but Bex's voice was giddy by the end. Between the trips to Limbo that took up her every waking minute and Adrian's attempts to break into the locked Anchors so they could cut another chain, Bex hadn't gotten to see her witch in a month. Not since the night they'd kissed, actually, which was a gods damned tragedy. They'd talked on the phone a few times, but nothing like they used to, which was why, when Adrian had texted that he was coming home, Bex had bent over backward to make sure she had time to see him.

It was horribly selfish behavior for a queen who still had demons suffering in Limbo. Bex had been feeling guilty about it for days. When she'd mentioned the problem to Lys, though, the lust demon put their foot down. Bex hadn't taken a night off since they'd conquered the Anchor. She needed a break, and Lys had threatened to go on strike unless she took one.

Since Lys and Iggs were the ones who actually kept things operational while Bex popped in and out of Limbo, that was a serious threat. Bex had caved immediately, even going so far as to agree to let Lys pick out her outfit for the evening. She should've been dreading what she'd find when she got back to her bedroom in the RV, but it was hard to feel anxious about anything when she was so happy.

Even with endless amounts of work to distract her, Bex had missed Adrian terribly. She missed his forest, missed his witchcraft, missed his smiles and his sly looks and the deep rumble of his laugh. She missed how he always found a way to make even the most impossible battles feel winnable. She missed *him*, and now, after a month-long drought, she was finally getting him all to herself for an entire evening!

He'd even offered to fly her back to his Blackwood and cook her dinner just like old times. Bex was still getting used to eating like humans did, but she was already certain that no restaurant could compare to the food Adrian made. She'd rather eat an apple from his Blackwood than any other dish on the planet.

The feeling must've shown on her face because Nemini gave her something that almost, maybe, could have been a smile.

"All joy is temporary," she said as she stepped back through the door that led to the garage. "Go enjoy yours before the moment is lost to the endless void of time. I'll lock up here."

Bex mouthed *Thank you* at the void demon as she dashed away, making a beeline for the exit before any of her demons broke the spell of food long enough to notice their queen was gone.

Since it had started out as a storage room for perishables, the new wrath demon village was just one floor below the Market. It was separated from the rest of the Anchor by a long hallway sealed with a steel security door that required a passcode to open. Officially, this was to protect Bex's Bronze Age demons from accidentally stumbling into the modern world and giving themselves whiplash. In reality, however, the door was there to protect all the *other* demons in the Anchor from them.

Wrath demons had always been true to their name, but thanks to the time they'd lost in Limbo, every one of them was still fresh off the end of the war. Even the children were hardened survivors of Gilgamesh's conquest of Paradise, and the whole tribe harbored a special burning hatred for war demons.

Bex didn't blame them a bit for that. By her people's reckoning, the Queen of War's traitors had been burning their villages to the ground just a few weeks ago, but the war demons who'd joined Bex's rebellion were not the same ones that had sided with Gilgamesh. They weren't even their grandchildren or their great-great-grandchildren. For modern war demons, the fall of Paradise was ancient history. They didn't care about the crimes their queen had ordered their ancestors to commit thousands of years ago. They just knew that they'd been born into the same slavery as all of Ishtar's children, and they wanted out.

There were also a *lot* of them. Bex knew war demons were popular with warlocks, but for all their supposed loyalty, once the Queen of Wrath's rebellion had proven their mettle by taking an Anchor, more war demons had flocked to Bex's banner than any other sort. She wasn't particularly fond of them—ancient grudges aside, war demons were prickly bastards who couldn't take a compliment without turning it into a fight—but they were damn good soldiers. Even her war-demon-hating crew had been forced to admit they couldn't beat Heaven without them, but Bex had still asked the control room to put the war demons' training yard far away from her wrath demon village. Just in case.

Bex was still double-checking the security door's lock when she heard someone shout her name.

It's Iggerux, Drox informed her unnecessarily. *I wonder what he's so worked up about.*

Iggs was panting pretty hard as he jogged down the hallway toward her. As usual now that he was

23

basically leading the largest magical marketplace on the planet, her original wrath demon was dressed to impress in a nice pair of navy slacks and a white button-up. He'd even managed to tame his dark hair, which was something Bex never thought she'd live to see. His tanned face still split into a huge, sharp-toothed smile when he waved at her, though. Proof that her Iggs hadn't been swallowed up by this respectable new demon.

"Hey!" he huffed as he jogged up.

"Hey yourself," Bex said, though a bit more nervously. "Why are you running? Is something wrong?"

"Not a thing," he assured her quickly. "It's just that it's a damn hike up here from the meeting rooms on the sixth floor. I've only got five minutes before I've gotta go back down, but I wanted to check and see if you freed any of my family today."

"Glad it's not a crisis," Bex said as she turned around to reopen the security door for him. "I only broke out a hundred demons, though, so I'm afraid chances are low."

"Any chance is still a miracle," Iggs told her with a beaming smile. "But I'm glad I ran into you. You're spending tonight with Adrian, right?"

The way he said that made Bex jump like a hose-sprayed cat.

"We're just having dinner!" she snapped, face flaming.

"Are you sure?" he asked as he pulled out his phone. "'Cause Lys has you blocked out on the schedule until eight a.m. tomorrow."

"I think I'd know if I was going to be spending the night with Adrian," Bex grumbled as her face got hotter and hotter.

Iggs frowned as if that didn't make sense for a second, then his red eyes went wide as the implications of what he'd said finally dawned on him.

"Ooooh! No, no, no, not like that! I mean, if it *was* like that, that's awesome, and I'm super happy for you. Adrian is great, and, yeah, I think I'm just going to shut up now."

"Good choice," Bex huffed as she turned back to finish punching in the security code. "Why are you asking, anyway? Do you need Adrian for something?"

"Not Adrian himself," Iggs said, rubbing the back of his neck. "But I did want to ask you if you could ask him when he thinks he'll be able to break into another Anchor."

Bex frowned. "Why don't you just ask him yourself?"

"Because I don't want to put more pressure on him," Iggs said, looking really upset now. "I know Adrian's already working his hardest, and I don't want to be *that guy*, but it's been a month since this locked-Anchor situation started, and we're having a bit of a problem."

"What problem?" Bex demanded, turning around. "And why haven't I heard about it?"

"Because I didn't want to pressure you either," Iggs grumbled, glancing over his shoulder to make sure the hallway was clear before leaning down to whisper in Bex's ear. "We're running out of quintessence."

"How is that possible?" Bex whispered back. "I thought we got mountains of it after the Anchor Market fell."

"We *had* mountains of it," he said. "But then we had to make housing for all our new demons." He waved his hand at the long cement hallway they were standing in. "Even with the control panel doing the actual sorcery for us, making all this new stuff still took a ton of magic, not to mention the cost of keeping this much stretched space running. Just the fuel needed for our normal daily operations is burning through our quintessence stockpile fast. Normally, I'd say let's just go steal some more, but since Gilgamesh put the Anchors on lockdown, there's been no new quintessence coming into the system. Everyone's still spending it, though, which means supplies are getting short all over. Rumor has it that even the big sorcerer circles and warlock cabals are starting to run low."

Bex sighed. Any other day, hearing that the warlock cabals were running out of magic would have made her cheer. Now, though, it was just another disaster to manage.

"How much time have we got?"

"Two weeks," Iggs said quietly. "Maybe a few days longer if we start cutting now."

Bex sighed again. "Is there anywhere else we can move people to?"

Iggs shook his head. "Nowhere big enough. You've been spending every waking second running the Limbo circuit, so you haven't been downstairs in a while, but we're packed to the rafters. With the warlocks' control weakened by the quintessence

26

shortage, slaves are running away in droves, which is *awesome*, except that they're all running here. You're the queen. Everyone knows you're the only one who has a prayer of stopping whatever horrible revenge Gilgamesh has planned, and they'd rather stack on top of each other than risk leaving your shadow."

"That sounds like a reason *to* leave to me," Bex argued. "I'm the target."

"You're also the wall," Iggs reminded her. "Also, no one wants to go." His face split back into a grin. "Again, you've been buried in Limbo, so you haven't had a chance to see, but we're doing amazing. We actually have a demon city for the first time in the living world! If we didn't need the quintessence, I wouldn't care if Gilgamesh kept the other Anchors locked forever. Unless we can figure out another way to power this place, though, we're going to be up against the wall soon." He glanced nervously at the cement ceiling over their heads. "We never had the guts to run the RV totally dry, so I don't actually know what happens to stretched spaces when the quintessence runs out. If we get unlucky enough, this whole place could collapse on our heads."

"So what do you want Adrian to do about it?" Bex asked impatiently. "He's not a sorcerer."

"But he *is* working on breaking into the Anchors," Iggs replied. "And there's *always* quintessence in the Anchors! If we got our hands on another windfall, we could keep this place going for another month easy, though that might not even matter if you can cut another chain. I don't know if you've had a chance to review our army lately, but it's looking pretty fantastic. That deal we cut with the goblin princes to trade all the caviar and other fancy crap for guns has paid off in spades. We've got enough weapons to arm every demon in the Hells now."

The huge grin from earlier came back to his face. "Can you imagine what that'll be like? Hundreds of thousands of demons erupting out of the Hells with our guns in their hands! Meanwhile, Ishtar will be back and cutting down princes like weeds with her divine wrath. It'll be glorious! And all we gotta do to make it happen is get you on a chain."

"I don't know if it'll be *that* easy," Bex said with a smile of her own. "But I'll ask Adrian about it."

"I'm sure he's almost done," Iggs said confidently. "Adrian always comes through. Witchcraft's just slow, though if you could ask him if he knows any ways to stretch quintessence, I'd appreciate it."

"I will," Bex promised, holding open the security door for him. "Good luck finding your family."

Iggs gave her a beaming smile and bolted through. After a final wave, Bex shut the security door firmly behind him and started walking down the last bit of the hallway toward the grand staircase at the end.

Like the storage warehouse they'd turned into a Riverlands village, this section of the Seattle Anchor also was completely changed. Bex wasn't sure which part of the old sorcery office it had once been, but there were no more ugly beige cubicles or cheap carpeted hallways. The whole place had been transformed into an eight-foot-wide staircase that ran between the new demon living quarters downstairs and the Market on the street level.

Not just any staircase, either. This thing looked like a relic from the golden age of the gods. The steps were made from huge slabs of granite scored with hatch marks for maximum grip. The walls were dove-gray marble lined with gleaming brass banisters and Art Deco sconces, and each landing was decorated with a carved relief depicting Ishtar in all her six-horned, bewinged glory.

Given what Iggs had *just* said about the quintessence cost of running this place, that might've been a bit much, but it was hard to feel guilty about something so beautiful. Just walking into the elegant stairwell made Bex hold her head higher, and she wasn't the only one. Every demon around her looked prouder, which was the entire point.

The marble carvings and fancy sconces weren't just there to be pretty. The grandeur had been added on purpose to remind the demons of the Anchor that they were not born to be slaves. They were the children of Ishtar, the rightful people of Paradise. They deserved beautiful staircases, especially since every demon in Seattle seemed to be currently using this one.

Thanks to the grand design, Bex could look down the middle of the oval-shaped staircase and see all seven of the floors Lys had carved out of the former sorcery office and turned into housing for their new free-demon population. Each loop was packed with demons of every sort going up and down like rivers. Since the second floor where Bex had come out was right below the Market, this landing was always the most jammed. That usually worked in her favor, but Bex had barely climbed three steps before the crowd of demons on the staircase realized who was walking next to them.

Chaos erupted after that. All over the stairs, demons shrieked and bowed their horns in a panic. Down the center column, hundreds of heads stuck out over the railing to see what the commotion was about only to immediately bow—and sometimes almost fall down the center of the stairwell—when they realized the Queen of Wrath was standing above them.

Bex faced the sea of bowed horns with a barely suppressed wince. She truly was dedicated to rescuing her demons from Limbo, but she'd be lying if she'd said this wasn't also a big factor for why she spent so much of her time inside the wrath demon part of the Anchor. Her people treated her like a queen, yes, but they'd grown up with Ishtar's daughters being a walking, talking part of their lives. Modern demons, on the other hand, treated her like a figure out of legend. She couldn't even walk up a staircase without causing a giant scene. If Adrian hadn't been gone all the time, she would've asked him to make her some more of those forgetting strings he'd used to hide her horns while they were staking out the Anchor. At least then she could've sneaked up to the RV to take a shower in peace.

They pay you homage, Drox said as she began awkwardly climbing the stairs through the empty space the crowd had shoved itself against the banisters to make for her. *Their reverence is your due. Enjoy it.*

30

"Who enjoys being stared at by hundreds of people?" Bex whispered, climbing the stairs as fast as possible with her eyes locked on her boots. "If I was on fire, I'd understand, but I'm not even doing anything impressive."

Her sword scoffed. *You are a queen and the daughter of a goddess. You are impressive all by yourself.*

Bex supposed he had a point, but she still hated it, and not just because being the center of so much attention made her want to sink into the floor. This sort of terrified bowing and worship was what Gilgamesh's warlocks demanded. She didn't want to be part of a system like that, but every time she told the demons to stop, they acted like she was going to burn them alive for failing to please her, which was even worse. There was simply no winning in situations like these, which was why Bex did her best to avoid them entirely. She had to go upstairs, though, so she went as fast as she could, racing up the cleared path into the Anchor Market's main entry hall.

Unlike everything else, this place still looked largely the same as the night they'd taken the Anchor. It was still ridiculously grand with towering arched ceilings, white marble floors, and fancy chandeliers. The only major difference was that now—instead of golden-suited Anchor Guards and fancy warlocks waiting in velvet-roped lines—the entry hall was jammed with vendor tables.

The sheer volume of stuff in her way slowed Bex's progress to a crawl. No wonder Iggs's schedule had been booked with meetings recently. She'd known the demons' new Free Market was doing well—as the

31

only Anchor Market left in the world that was still open for business, it would've been weird if it wasn't—but this surpassed even her high expectations. She normally went to bed well after the market closed at ten, so she'd never seen it crowded. Now, though, at dinnertime on a Friday, there were so many shoppers she could barely push through.

The real shocker, though, was that most of the jam-packed crowd was human. Not Gilgamesh's humans, either. Iggs must've been right on the money about the shopping needs of Washington's non-Heaven-aligned magical population because there wasn't a single sorcerer or warlock in sight. These crowds were all native magic users—shamans, magicians, hedge-wizards, and witches. Tons and *tons* of witches.

Just seeing all the different sorts of people with familiars on their shoulders made Bex's eyes go wide. She'd known there were more covens than just the Blackwood that had survived the purges in tiny enclaves, but she hadn't realized there were so many in the Seattle area, or even the entire Western Seaboard. There were *so* many humans buying and selling that their tables spilled out of the entry hall into the lower levels of the normal Pike Place Market, resulting in a flood of confused scalies who had to be cajoled into turning around by the lust-demon door guards before they got someone kicked.

Bex was surprised she hadn't heard more complaints about that, but no one seemed to be in a complaining mood. Everywhere she looked, humans and demons alike were having a grand time haggling and gossiping and ordering magical food from the dozens of steaming vendor carts.

For someone who'd lived her whole life in hiding, it was a beautiful sight. If Bex hadn't already been running late, she would have stopped to enjoy it. But her second alarm had already gone off, so she forced herself to pick up the pace again, jogging past the hastily bowing demon guards into the brick tunnel that led to the main Market.

This, too, looked very much the same as the night they'd taken it. As soon as she got out of the tunnel, the endless green hills of the illusionary Paradise rose to greet her. The golden statue of Gilgamesh was still there as well since, even with sorcery, it was impossible to move something that huge and tacky. The brightly decorated vendor tents surrounding the statue's base were much less fancy-looking now, though, and the merchandise they sold was much, *much* stranger.

Instead of lobsters and overpriced wine, the tables at the demons' Free Market sold curses, spell components, and illegal copies of Gilgamesh's sorcerous poetry. As Iggs had predicted, there were a lot of weapons and other contraband that never would've been permitted in an official Anchor Market, but there were also plenty of normal vendors selling magically-enhanced pastries that didn't go stale, cockatrice eggs for spell use or omelets, illusion-infused makeup, and scented candles that turned your apartment into a forest for magical purposes. Every table had something different, which was refreshing after years of seeing multiple rows of the same designer clothes, fancy chocolates, and monthly trend items over and over and *over*, but the biggest change was definitely the tree.

Towering even taller than the now heavily-graffitied statue of Gilgamesh, Adrian's oak tree had become the heart of the new market. Not only did its branches literally hold up the sky, which was still sagging slightly if you knew where to look, it provided much-needed shade in what would otherwise be a baking sunny field. Birds nested in its branches and pecked up the crumbs the shoppers dropped, while squirrels dug in the grass and held chittering duels across the tops of the vendor tents. There was also a healthy population of crows who stole shiny objects and pastries right out of shoppers' hands.

The animals were definitely less appreciated than the shade, but Bex had already told Iggs they weren't getting rid of them. She didn't know if the crows and squirrels had sneaked in or if they were simply part of the tiny Blackwood Adrian had built here, but she loved how they made Gilgamesh's sterile illusion feel more alive. She loved the rustling leaves and the smell of loam that reminded her of Adrian's forest. Loved it *so* much, actually, that she'd gotten Lys to open the Anchor's loading doors so she could drive their RV straight into the Market and park it directly on top of the oak tree's roots.

She'd only done it because she wanted to sleep beneath leaves rather than in a parking deck, but where the queen was, the government was. By positioning her RV under Adrian's tree, Bex had accidentally turned the entire area around the trunk into the rebellion's operational headquarters.

She was mostly fine with that. The constant parade of important people meant more security for her sister's hand, which was still hidden in its spiderweb ball way up in the oak tree's branches. Unfortunately, all that important infrastructure also meant that, in order to get to her bedroom, Bex had to run a gauntlet of responsibilities.

Normally, Lys would be the one waiting to pounce on her with a fresh pile of problems only the queen could solve. Tonight, though, the demon standing in front of the RV's screen door was a lot uglier, a lot shinier, and a *lot* bigger.

"Great Queen," he said, folding one pair of bulging bronze arms behind his back while the other pair spread out for his courtly bow.

"General Kirok," Bex replied, trying her best not to spit the name like a curse.

It still could've been one. Never in a million years would Bex have voluntarily chosen a war demon to lead her army. She'd tried to put her own anger aside for the sake of being a good queen to all Ishtar's children, but wrath demons weren't the only ones who saw the four-armed soldiers as traitors. Even five thousand years after their queen had sided with Gilgamesh, war demons continued to enjoy privileged status in Heaven, which meant all the *non*-privileged slaves hated their guts.

That wasn't a good look for someone who was supposed to lead a mixed force of demons into battle, but Kirokaltos wasn't just any war demon. Before Bex had freed him from his Heavenly master the night of the slave auction, he'd been a famous trainer who'd worked in the Hells, whipping war demons into shape as bodyguards and foot soldiers for centuries. He was literally the perfect candidate to transform their motley collection of runaways and refugees into an army capable of surviving a conflict with Heaven. He was also the only war demon big enough, old enough, and salty enough to make all the other war demons obey his orders without a fight.

Put it all together and Bex couldn't *not* make Kirok her general, but that didn't mean she had to like it. Eons of prejudice aside, the war demon's attitude got under her skin. He couldn't even lower his horns without making it feel like he was talking down to her, and tonight of all nights, Bex had no patience for it.

"Is this important?" she demanded, pulling herself to her full height, which fell slightly shorter than the general's second row of armpits. "I already read and responded to your troop report this morning, and I have a pressing engagement that I can't—"

"I wouldn't have wasted my time coming up from the training yard if it wasn't important," Kirok interrupted, which was another strike against him. Bex didn't usually stand on ceremony, but interrupting a queen was *not* a sign of respect.

"I've just received information that could change the balance of the war," the general continued in a low voice. "I need you to come with me to the command tent immediately, if it would please Your Majesty."

It would *not* please Her Majesty. Especially not when the bronze bastard said it in that condescending tone of voice. Bex was tempted to tell him off just for that, but for all that she loathed every aspect of his personality, Kirok was an astute commander. If he said something was important, it was *really damn important*. She still had twenty minutes before she was supposed to meet Adrian, and the command tent *was* just on the other side of the tree. She had time to listen to Kirok's information and still squeeze in a shower if she hurried, so Bex set a timer on her phone and motioned for the war demon to lead the way.

Chapter 2

"**O**kay," Adrian said as he placed three vine cuttings on the bed of soil he'd made in front of the giant golden doors deep below the Seattle Anchor. "Let's try this again."

"It's not going to work," Boston warned over the speaker of Adrian's phone, which was lying on the stone floor behind him. "It didn't work the last three times, and you've made minimal changes, so why should it—"

"Just note the timestamp, please," Adrian said irritably, rubbing his work-roughened hands together to get them to the right temperature. "Here we go."

He bent over and dug his warmed fingers into the dirt. Closing his eyes, he began to move, tracing curving, spiral lines through the rich soil. He cleared his mind as he worked, focusing only on the feel of the earth beneath his hands and the heat of the sunlamp he'd plugged into the tunnel's power grid shining on his back. He felt the dampness of the water he'd sprinkled over his growing area and the cold, slimy touch of the worms he'd brought in from his Blackwood. When he was connected to all of it, Adrian reached out with the living magic of his forest and gave things a push.

The little cuttings surged in response. Within seconds, the sin iron wall that filled Gilgamesh's golden doors was covered in a verdant mass of twisting vines. The plants were *so* aggressive, *so* vigorous, Adrian just knew it was going to work this time. Then, all at once, the riot of green turned black and brittle as the newborn plants shriveled before his eyes and dropped to the ground.

"Damn," he muttered as he pushed back to his feet. "Damn, damn, *damn*."

"I *told* you!" Boston's tinny voice cried over the phone's speaker. "You're never going to get different results if all you're doing is making minor tweaks to the same flawed premise!"

"They weren't minor tweaks," Adrian argued, picking up the dead plants in dismay. "Those were kudzu, wisteria, and English ivy. They're the most tenacious, destructive vines on the planet!"

"But they're still plants," his familiar reminded him. "That's what I keep trying to tell you. You can't use living things to break through sin iron. It's death made solid."

"You're exaggerating."

"I am *not*," Boston said in a voice so sharp, Adrian could see the cat's tail lashing in his mind. "The whole reason we're doing this over the phone is because that tunnel is so filled with toxic sin iron dust that I can't stay conscious for more than ten minutes. I honestly don't know how you're still alive, but you can't blame the plants for croaking."

Adrian crumbled the dead leaves in his fist as he glared at the seemingly unconquerable wall in front of him.

The giant cuneiform-and-lion-covered doors were still stuck in the open position, exactly as he'd left them the first time he and Bex had sneaked down here.

Between the two doors stood the black wall he'd stuck his head through to witness the prince and princess in the desert full of chains. He *knew* it was a portal because he'd used it, but after twelve hours of attempting to re-create the magic that had allowed him to phase through the sin iron, Adrian still hadn't managed to get so much as a fingernail inside.

"You could try taking quintessence again," Boston suggested. "That's what opened the doors initially, right?"

"I'm not taking any more of that garbage," Adrian snapped. "It's too expensive, it hurts my head, and more importantly, it doesn't work."

That was the most frustrating part of all of this. Adrian had *seen* the doors open and his body pass through the metal inside like a shadow. He knew what this place did, but he had absolutely no idea how or why. He'd come down here to answer those questions, but the more he learned about Gilgamesh's outposts on Earth, the less sense everything made.

Take the wall in front of him, for example. It *looked* like a door. It even still had an Adrian-shaped hole in it where Bex had melted the sin iron to drag him out after the prince had tried to kill him. When he stuck his hand into the crevice where his body had been now, though, all he felt was more sin iron.

It was *all* sin iron because the "wall" in front of him wasn't a wall at all. It was the tip of an iceberg, the tiny visible portion of what was actually a building-sized brick buried deep in the bedrock beneath Seattle. It was the weight at the end of the chain Bex had cut when she'd severed the Seattle Market from Heaven, the *literal* Anchor.

Adrian knew that last bit for a fact because he'd read the sorcerer's documentation about how the Anchors were weighed down. The old sorcery office had been full of technical diagrams detailing chain stress and weight distribution that he'd saved before Lys had remodeled the whole place into apartments, but none of them had said anything about a portal or a chain desert.

If he hadn't stuck his head through it, Adrian would've said it was impossible to make a portal out of a block of solid metal. But while he knew the doorway had worked at least once, it clearly wasn't working anymore. He didn't know if the break had happened when Bex melted the sin iron to save him or when she'd cut the chain, but after a full day of beating his head against it, Adrian was dangerously close to admitting defeat. No matter what he tried, it really looked like the sin iron wall actually was just a wall now, which meant this whole endeavor was yet another dead end.

"Don't let it get you down," his familiar said when he sighed. "We always knew this was a long shot. The whole point of cutting the chain was to separate the Anchor from Heaven. It makes sense that any sort of magical travel system would've been cut off as well. The same thing would happen if you ripped the roots out of a Blackwood. Even your aunt Lydia can't travel between groves that aren't connected."

"I know," Adrian groaned, pulling off his witch hat to rake his hands through his tangled hair. "It's just... Everything else here still works! There's a control room that lets demons manipulate sorcerously stretched space, for the Forest's sake. All of that magic is still functional, so why not this?"

"I don't know," Boston said irritably. "Sorcery makes no sense to me. What does a bunch of self-important poetry have to do with magic? It's ridiculous."

It was pretty absurd. Witchcraft was all about building connections and working within the cycles of the natural world. Adrian had learned more about sorcery than he'd ever wanted to over the last month, and as far as he could tell, the whole practice boiled down to popping a pill of quintessence and saying some magic words.

The poems didn't even make sense when he read the translations. Take the writing on the doors in front of him, for example. When he'd come down here this morning, Adrian had been certain that the yards of cuneiform carved into the towering golden slabs were the words to the spell that operated the portal inside. But when he'd brought a demon who read ancient Sumerian in to translate—or, rather, when he'd sent the demon pictures from his phone, since no one but him seemed able to tolerate the tunnel's toxicity—the man had insisted that the writing wasn't sorcery. It was a history.

After reading the entire translation, Adrian suspected he was looking at an early version of what would eventually become *The Epic of Gilgamesh*. The famous poem hadn't been written until long after the real Gilgamesh had conquered Paradise and was therefore wildly embellished. There must have been some truth to it, though, because the writing that covered every inch of the golden doors told the same basic story of the beautiful kingdom of Uruk, located in modern-day Iraq, and its noble king, Gilgamesh, who befriended a wild man named Enkidu.

According to the writing on the doors, the two men had shared a bromance for the ages. They'd roved all over the ancient world killing monsters and having adventures together. Everything had been going great until Ishtar, goddess of love and fertility, tried to seduce Gilgamesh. Since she was also the goddess of war and destruction—two things no king wanted in his kingdom—Gilgamesh rejected her, and, in classic mythological fashion, the goddess didn't take that well. She'd flown into a rage and sent a giant bull to destroy the kingdom of Uruk. The bull was supposed to kill Gilgamesh as well, but Enkidu fought it and died in his best friend's stead.

In the historical *Epic of Gilgamesh*, Enkidu's death was what spurred Gilgamesh to seek immortality by invading the lands of the dead, but the story carved into the doors never got to that part. This text was all about Enkidu: his wildness, his bravery, his loyalty, and all the adventures he and Gilgamesh had shared. It was practically the man's obituary, but for all the fantastical locations the text described, there was nothing remotely close to the black desert full of conveniently clumped, easily cuttable chains that Adrian was looking for. He didn't know why Gilgamesh had decided to record his dead friend's life on a pair of doors, but it was all *highly* unuseful.

"It's just so frustrating!" he yelled, his voice echoing down the tunnel as he kicked his boot through the pile of dead vines. "My plan worked! We *won*! Heaven should be crumbling under the wrath of the reborn gods right now, but we can't *do* anything because everything we need is locked behind a bunch of stupid walls!"

"That doesn't mean it wasn't a victory," Boston replied sagely. "The fact that Gilgamesh was forced to lock his Anchors and retreat proves that you were right. The chains *are* critical to his control."

"That doesn't matter if we can't reach them," Adrian argued. "This whole mess was my idea. I'm the one who said we should attack the chains, but I've spent the last four weeks checking every Anchor in the western half of the Americas, and I couldn't find a way into any of them! All the doors that were *supposed* to open into Anchor Markets just go to empty shops and closets now. I don't know if Gilgamesh removed the entrances or deleted the markets entirely, but there's no way in from this side anymore."

He threw his hand out at the melted slab of sin iron in front of him. "This portal was my last good angle. I already knew it didn't work, but I still thought maybe I could find a clue or a location or *something*. Even knowing the name of the place it went to would've been useful, but I haven't found a Hells-damned thing! Everyone else is doing their part. Bex built an entire city and freed thousands of kick demons from Limbo, but they're all sitting ducks for Gilgamesh if I can't do what I promised and get her to another chain!"

"You don't know that," Boston insisted. "Gilgamesh has ruled uncontested for five thousand years. Closing the Anchors *could* be part of some massive strategy to stall his enemies while he builds a counterattack, or he could simply be another cowardly dictator locking himself in his palace at the first whiff of rebellion. Personally, I'm leaning toward the latter. Successful as his strategy has been at keeping Bex off his chains, locking the Anchors seems to have hurt Heaven far more than it's hurt us. Have you been on any of the sorcerer forums recently? They're in absolute panic. Their entire infrastructure is built on the assumption that quintessence would always be available. Now that Gilgamesh has turned off the spigot, sorcerers are losing their empires left and right. It's the same story with the warlocks. They can't afford the magic that controls their slaves anymore, so they're just letting demons go."

The cat began talking more quickly as his excitement rose. "Everywhere you look, Gilgamesh's earthly forces are collapsing. By focusing so hard on keeping the Queen of Wrath away from his infrastructure, he's shot himself in the foot on every other front. If he doesn't reopen those Anchors and resume the flow of quintessence soon, he'll lose control over the living world entirely! I don't know how much the King of Heaven cares about that, but it's an absolute win for us. Can you imagine how much the Blackwood could expand if there were no more warlocks in our way?"

Adrian had imagined it plenty, but he didn't share his familiar's optimism. His mother and aunts had warned him over and over that the movements of Heaven were never what they seemed. He also didn't believe that the mortal king who'd been good enough to defeat the gods would cripple his own troops like this unless he was getting something vastly more valuable in return. This wasn't a panicked commander sacrificing his soldiers to save himself. This was a strategy. One Adrian didn't understand, which was the most dangerous part of all. He'd already wasted a month chasing dead ends. If he didn't figure out what Gilgamesh was actually doing soon, they could still lose everything. *Bex* could lose everything. The demons she'd freed, the haven she'd made, the hope she'd brought, it could all go up in flames if he couldn't solve this problem.

That was the thought that scared Adrian the most. He'd never feared failure because there was always a way to try again in witchcraft. Even if he died, his soul would go to the Great Forest to join all the witches who'd come before, but the demons didn't have that luxury. Bex had bet everything on this, including her own last life. If Adrian couldn't step up and be the miracle-working witch she thought he was, Gilgamesh was going to crush them, and it'd be all his fault.

"There has to be a way in," he muttered. "There's no such thing as a completely closed system. Somewhere, somehow, there *has* to be a chink in Heaven's walls. I just have to find it."

"Well," Boston said, "if you want to keep pushing tonight, you'll have to do it on your own. I'm late enough as it is."

Adrian's head jerked up in surprise. "Late for what?"

"My party!" his familiar replied excitedly. "I told you about it this morning, remember?"

Adrian vaguely recalled something about a party, but he'd been too busy trying to prevent the destruction of everyone he loved and everything they'd worked for to pay attention. Fortunately, Boston was happy to fill him in.

"I got invited to a meet-and-greet for local familiars," the cat explained. "Their witches are all self-taught independents, but it's still a fascinating opportunity to explore alternate approaches to the craft. I might even pick up some new tricks!"

Adrian didn't see how his Blackwood-bred familiar was going to learn anything from a bunch of hedge-witch cats, but that was a snobbish, closed-minded way to think. Boston's approach was much healthier, but Adrian was still glad he hadn't been invited. He could barely tolerate being in a room full of catty, posturing familiars on a good day. In his current mood, he was more likely to offer mortal offense than constructive conversation.

"Have fun," he said, turning back to the sin iron wall. "I'm going to keep working on this."

"Really?" Boston asked, surprised. "Aren't you supposed to meet Bex for dinner in ten minutes?"

That was precisely why Adrian needed to keep going. Tonight would be the first time he'd seen Bex in four weeks. He was desperate to have good news for her, something that would prove his reckless plan hadn't gotten them all trapped in a dead end. It wasn't looking like that was going to happen, but Adrian was determined to keep trying right up until the last second. He'd even brought a fresh change of clothes and a shower charm in his coat so he wouldn't have to waste time going home to get ready.

"Have it your way," Boston said when his witch didn't reply. "I'm off, and just so you know, the party's scheduled to run quite late, so I'll be spending the night here at the Anchor."

"Are you sure?" Adrian asked. "I don't mind coming back to pick you up."

"Yes, I'm sure," his cat insisted. "First, I'm perfectly capable of taking care of myself, and second, Lys made me promise I'd make certain Bex got you all to herself tonight. They even bought me a cat bed so I could sleep in the RV."

That sounded suspiciously like a setup, but if Lys wanted to make sure Bex was alone with him, Adrian wasn't about to complain. He'd been looking forward to this for days now, and while his excitement was dampened by the fact that he was most likely going to have to look Bex in her lovely glowing eyes and tell her that he'd failed, nothing changed the fact that he'd missed her terribly. They'd both been so busy this month, he hadn't even gotten to kiss her again, which was a tragedy. One Adrian fully intended to remedy as soon as he tried one last experiment.

"It's your time to waste," Boston said when it was clear that Adrian wasn't changing his mind. "Just make sure you don't get so caught up in fears for the future that you miss the present. You're not such a great and powerful witch that I won't report you to the Old Wife of the Flesh for forgetting your training."

"There's no need to bring my mother into this," Adrian said irritably as he dug the next batch of vine cuttings out of his coat's enchanted pockets. "And I'm not missing anything. I'm just being efficient with my time."

His familiar's answer to that was a loud harrumph, but Boston didn't say anything more except to wish him good luck as he hung up the phone and left Adrian to his witchcraft.

Back in the Anchor Market, Bex was beginning to worry that her "quick" detour to hear General Kirok's emergency was going to be anything but. Her first clue came when she stepped into the command tent and discovered a whole delegation of war demons already waiting for them. That wasn't too unusual since war demons, being *war* demons, tended to follow their general, but it was a bigger showing than she'd expected. They all lowered their horns when she stepped inside, but Kirok was right in front of her, so they could have been bowing to him.

Really, though, Bex didn't care if they were paying her respect or not. She just wanted to know what so many war demons were doing in one place and why there was a goblin sitting behind the operations desk that usually belonged to Iggs.

"*Bexxy!*" Prince Felix cried, popping out of his chair like a spring the moment she stepped through the tent flap. "Angel, darling, horned light of my life, it's been too long!"

He finished with a sharp-toothed smile, but Bex had already turned to growl at Kirok.

"What is *he* doing here?"

"Don't be like that," the goblin prince chided before the general could say a word. "When you needed guns for your little militia, which handsome goblin stepped up and delivered? I'm risking Heaven's ire to help you, sweetheart. That entitles me to a little royal access, don't you think?"

"It entitles you to payment, which we've already made in full," Bex said, crossing her arms over her chest. "You've already price gouged us once, Felix. You don't get to come back and squeeze for more."

"You wound me," he said, clutching the front of his hideous gold lamé suit. "I gave you a more than fair price considering the great personal risk I'm taking by tying my name to yours. My fellow goblin princes are going over-under on whether Gilgamesh crushes your rebellion immediately or waits until the end of the year. But betting on the underdog has always been my winning ticket, and you, my violent lovely, have always been my winningest dog of all."

"Thanks," Bex replied in a flat voice. "Is there a point to this?"

"Always," Felix promised with a sparkling smile. "As I was just explaining to your new bronze statue collection"—he waved a green hand at Kirok and his officers, who glowered—"I recently made a rather... *unique* purchase that I think you'll find highly relevant to your current situation."

He paused dramatically for several seconds until Bex motioned for him to get to the point.

"After your unprecedented military success convinced the Eternal King to take his ball and go home, quintessence prices have shot through the roof," the goblin explained. "Naturally, we at the Council of Goblin Princes have been leveraging this opportunity to the hilt. We've been selling off our quintessence reserves for an absolutely disgusting profit. *So* disgusting, in fact, that many of Gilgamesh's faithful find themselves too cash poor to afford our prices and have thus been forced to barter things they'd normally never part with."

Bex could see where this was going. "You bought a demon."

"I've bought a lot of demons," Felix said with a smile. "All of which I'm prepared to make available to you at a *very* reasonable price, but there's one specimen in particular I think you'll be interested in." He leaned forward. "Have you ever heard of a war demon named Havok?"

The "no" was already on Bex's tongue when Drox's ring jerked on her finger.

He speaks of the Dog of War! her sword cried excitedly.

Bex arched an eyebrow at the quick response. "Is he famous?"

"He's a legend," General Kirok replied reverently, not realizing Bex had been talking to her sword. "Havok was the Queen of War's champion before the fall of Paradise. It was assumed he'd perished during Gilgamesh's conquest, but the goblin claims to have found him alive."

"Got him for a song at the Mesopotamian cabal's liquidation sale," Felix confirmed. "The warlocks made a huuuuuuge deal about how ancient and historical he was. I thought they were just spinning a tale to jack the price on me, but the old quintessence addicts turned out to be legit. Now I've got a bona fide piece of Heavenly history chained up in my vault, and since we've always been such close friends, I'm giving you first dibs at taking him off my hands."

It took everything Bex had not to roll her eyes at the blatant huckstering, but the war demons were hanging on Felix's every word.

"This is an unprecedented opportunity, Your Majesty," General Kirok whispered in Bex's ear. "The legends of Havok are still told to young war demons to this day. His power was said to be surpassed only by that of the Queen of War herself. If those stories are even close to true, this could be our chance to shift the balance of conflict to our favor."

"Was it that far out of our favor?" Bex asked. "Your report this morning said we were up to five thousand soldiers."

"Five thousand runaway demons armed with black-market equipment and less than a month of training," Kirok corrected with a scathing look. "I've done my best with what Your Majesty has given me, but I can't work miracles. If it were five thousand war demons, we might stand a chance, but even the best-armed, best-trained lust demon is still a bird-boned weakling."

Bex was sure Lys would have something to say about that, but Lys had stopped talking to General Kirok within five minutes of meeting him, so maybe not.

"We can't face Heaven with what we've got," the general went on. "Even if your witch's plan to bring back the gods succeeds, Gilgamesh already beat them once, and his army is much larger now than it was back then. We're in for a fight no matter how things play out, and I think our chances of success will be much higher if we can get history's greatest war demon on our side."

Bex didn't see how one demon, no matter how great, could change the tide of an entire war. To her enormous surprise, though, Drox seemed to agree with Kirok.

Havok is no ordinary war demon, her sword insisted. *We faced him once at the Battle of Ox Bend two hundred years before Gilgamesh came to Heaven.*

"Wait," Bex said, ignoring the odd looks everyone else was giving her, "why were we fighting the Queen of War before Gilgamesh?"

Because war demons like to war, Drox replied crossly. *They especially liked to war on us. Wrath was the only tribe that equaled them in size and ferocity. We mostly won, but not always, and the defeats we did suffer were usually due to Havok. General Kirokaltos does not exaggerate his prowess. Havok is not equal to a queen, but he isn't far below. If we could add him to our ranks, we'd have another fighter capable of taking on a prince.*

That got Bex's attention. One of their rebellion's biggest issues—and her own greatest fear—was that the

Queen of Wrath was the only one strong enough to toe-to-toe it with Gilgamesh's sons. But while Bex was pretty confident in her prince-slaying abilities these days, she could still only fight them one at a time. That was bad math when there were at least five still-active princes and only one Rebexa.

Not true, her sword said. *The witch can kill them too.*

I'm not making Adrian cut off any more fingers, Bex thought back angrily.

Then take the goblin up on his offer, Drox snapped. *I'm no more keen to welcome an ancient enemy of Wrath than you are, but the old grievances are nothing compared to the threat of Gilgamesh.*

Bex didn't care about old battles she didn't even remember, but she was eager to add another fighter to their ranks, especially after what Kirok had said about the state of their army.

"Okay," she said, turning back to Felix, who'd been watching the silent exchange with keen interest. "We'll take Havok and every other demon you've got. How much do you want?"

The goblin shook his head. "For you, my angel, it's on the house."

Bex gave him a look of blatant disbelief, and Felix chuckled.

"This might surprise you to hear," he said, "but uncooperative demons are *extremely* expensive to contain. I normally avoid buying living merchandise for exactly that reason, but the deal was so good this time that I couldn't say no. Turns out, the joke's on me, 'cause this Havok guy is on a whole different level."

"I get it now," Bex said as a smirk spread over her face. "You're not here to make a sale. You need me to take Havok off your hands before he bankrupts you."

Felix shrugged. "I prefer to think of it as turning a liability into an asset. Currently, Havok's a wolverine tearing up my balance sheet, but if I give Mr. Ancient Menace to you, maybe Gilgamesh won't instantly crush your rebellion, which means I get to keep selling you weapons at a lucrative wartime markup. That's a win for both of us, but there is a catch."

"There's always a catch with you," Bex grumbled. "What is it?"

The goblin flashed her a charming smile that didn't touch his black eyes. "If you want your demons, you have to come get Havok tonight. As in right now."

"*Now?*" Bex cried in dismay, then she shook her head. "No, I can't. I have other plans."

"So cancel 'em," the goblin said, not even bothering to fake-smile this time. "This is a limited time offer, pretty horns. Every minute I keep that monster chained is costing me an arm and a leg. I've already lost a fortune waiting in this tent for you to show. If you make me sit on this until tomorrow, I'll have no choice but to cut my losses by dropping your vintage war demon down one of my bottomless pits."

"You wouldn't," Bex said.

Felix's green face split back into a grin. "Sweetheart, when it comes to protecting profit margins, there's *nothing* a goblin won't do. I'll even throw in all my other demons for free. Market's dead anyway now that the warlocks don't have enough quintessence left to control the slaves they've got. I'm offering you the deal of the century here! And all you've gotta do is come over and pick it up."

"I get that," Bex said with a wince. "But are you *sure* I can't convince you to wait until tomorrow?"

"Not on your life," Felix snapped, crossing his long arms over his chest. "This is money we're talking about. I know that doesn't mean much to you now that you're a queen or whatever, but it's my lifeblood. Running in the red is extremely dangerous for a prince of my stature, and I've got subjects of my own to think about. Now, are you in, or am I dumping these junk investments down a hole?"

Do it, Drox said. *I know you had other hopes for tonight, but Havok is a strategic weapon that could change the course of the entire war. Your witch will understand.*

Of course he would. Adrian was the most understanding man on the planet. Bex was the one who was pissed. She'd been looking forward to this dinner all week. What was the point of telling Adrian how she felt if she never got to see him again?

The whole situation made her want to scream, but Bex already knew she'd do it. Even if Drox hadn't agreed with General Kirok that this was a fate-of-the-war-level issue, Havok was a demon. She couldn't let Felix throw one of her own down a pit to save costs, even if his timing was the worst.

"Fine," she said bleakly. "I'm in. Just let me make a call first."

"Can you do it while we walk?" Felix asked, tapping a curving claw against one of the four golden

Rolexes strapped to his green wrist. "We're on a schedule here."

Bex heaved a long sigh and motioned for him to lead the way.

You should bring your demons with you, Drox suggested as she followed Felix out of the command tent. *Not that I think this goblin is capable of giving you trouble, but he's sold you out before.*

That was a good point. When Bex looked over her shoulder to ask Kirok about a security detail, though, Nemini was already standing behind her.

Bex jumped a foot in the air, stopping her sword a split second before Drox shot out to slice off Nemini's snake-covered head.

"When did you get here?" she gasped when she could speak again. "I thought you were still downstairs."

"Nothing is everywhere," the void demon replied calmly.

As usual, the cryptic nonanswer made Bex grind her teeth. Heart attacks aside, though, she was grateful that Nemini had been stalking her. Bex trusted the void demon to watch her back a lot more than she did Kirok, and unlike the general and his officers, taking Nemini with her wouldn't jeopardize their new camp's operations.

"You're with me, then," she said, motioning for Nemini to fall in behind Felix as she pulled out her phone to tell Adrian the bad news.

Chapter 3

Five minutes and three more sets of dead plants after Boston hung up the phone, Adrian was forced to admit defeat. If there were answers buried in that hunk of sin iron, he couldn't find them. He was out of vine clippings anyway, so he forced himself to step away from the golden doors, grabbed his broom off the floor, and headed for the elevator to face his fate.

Not that there'd be any actual fate to face. Bex would never yell at him for failing. She'd just sigh that little disappointed sigh of hers and tell him they'd figure something out, which was a billion times worse. Adrian hated making her worry or work harder. She did both of those things to an unhealthy degree already, which was a huge part of why he was doing this. It wasn't just about saving his family, his magic, and the entire world from Gilgamesh's tyranny. He wanted to save Bex, to give her a life where she wasn't constantly killing herself—figuratively and literally— fighting a never-ending war. It was the same promise he'd been making to himself since he'd found her dying on the ferry, and he was *messing it up*.

He rubbed his hands over his face as he stepped into the Anchor's creepy white elevator, which still had a giant hole in the bottom from where Bex had ripped it open getting them out. It was also missing its doors for the same reason. Both of these factors made the ride back up to the main Anchor hairy, but Adrian wasn't about to add a maintenance ticket on top of everything else. The demons were already spending a fortune in quintessence to keep this place functional. If Adrian was going to be the failure in the basement, he'd at least try not to be an expensive one.

But those were gloomy thoughts for later. He might not be going in with the good news he'd hoped, but this was still his first chance to see Bex in a month. If he wasted such a precious moment moping over past failures, he really would be a terrible Witch of the Present. So, before he hit the golden button to send the broken elevator back to the surface, Adrian dug into his coat pockets for the date kit he'd put together when he'd left his forest before dawn.

He'd brought his favorite shirt for the occasion, still freshly pressed thanks to Boston's masterful preservation charm. His own shower spell was a bit more slapdash, but this was hardly Adrian's first time pushing a deadline to its absolute limit. He had himself doused and scrubbed in under three minutes, a timeline that was greatly helped by the fact that he'd already shaved the normal way this morning. Adrian considered himself a steady-handed witch, but shaving charms were only ever one slip away from a slit throat. He'd grown a bit of stubble over the day, but nothing worth that risk, so he skipped the whole thing and just focused on getting his hair dry.

When he was as clean as magic could get him and dressed in fresh, sharp, witchy-black clothes, Adrian shoved his dirt-covered shirt and work pants into the spelled laundry pocket he kept for just such occasions and hit the button to take him upstairs. The magical elevator flew up so fast he was nearly knocked through the hole in the floor. He'd just finished his recovery when the doorless elevator rolled to a stop at a place that looked very, *very* different from the first time he'd come here.

Technically, this was still the same stretched space that had formed the old Sorcery Office. But while the dimensions of the sorcerous construct had merely been unfolded, not expanded, everything else had been renovated from the ground up. All the old constructions—the ugly beige carpet, the green-tinted fluorescents, the endless cubicles, the M.C. Escher architecture—were gone, replaced by a charming cobblestone street that looked like what would happen if someone held an infinity mirror up to a Mediterranean port town.

When Adrian stepped out of the elevator now, he was met with rows of brightly painted buildings that stretched as far as he could see in all directions. Everything was drenched in warm summer sunlight that actually followed Seattle's local day-night cycle, and the breeze that kept the air circulating smelled like the sea. The new aesthetic was as different from the old office hellscape as it was possible to get, but what really shocked Adrian no matter how many times he saw it were the people.

Even down here on the Anchor's lowest level, the endless streets were crammed with demons. They sat on every charming plant-strewn balcony of the new buildings, chatting through the open windows with their neighbors. Horned and sometimes winged children chased each other down the narrow streets while stooped old demons sat at the sunny intersections, playing card games and reminiscing.

That last part was a bit strange to Adrian since he was used to old demons being the strongest, like Lys or Nemini. But the life of a slave was hard, and warlocks were famous for underfeeding their demons to keep them biddable. This malnourishment resulted in entire generations who lived less than a tenth of what they should have, and those who did make it to old age were brittle and frail.

That was why there were so many demons sitting around down here rather than at the war demons' army training field four levels up. But despite technically being a refugee camp, the crowded streets didn't feel desperate. If anything, the mood here was more like a block party. Now that they were no longer living in isolation with their warlocks or being worked to death in the Hells, the demons were visiting with each other like they'd never had company in their lives.

Part of Adrian was sad that this tiny bit of freedom was all it took to make them so deliriously happy, but the rest of him was delighted that something good was *finally* happening. The fact that this many free demons could live together in one place without the warlocks descending on them like a plague of locusts was proof of how much their victory had already changed things. Now he just had to find a way to keep it up.

Feeling both elated and more depressed than ever, Adrian clutched his broom to his chest and began the long process of weaving through the crowded streets. All the chatting demons went quiet when they spotted him, but even though Adrian hadn't been back here in weeks, rumors of the queen's witch were widespread. The moment the demons spotted his hat and broom, the crowd parted to let him pass, giving Adrian a straight shot down the narrow streets to the Anchor's new back door.

Like all the remnants of Gilgamesh's rule, the old back door with its creepy golden eye was long gone. In its place was a stone structure that looked like an extremely tall medieval city wall. It even had a gatehouse and guards, most of whom were war demons. They gave Adrian a considerably harder time than the crowds in the street, but once he showed them the letter of passage Bex had written especially for him, they grudgingly let him into the gatehouse.

The stone building looked like part of the wall from the Anchor side, but as soon as Adrian stepped over the threshold, he found himself in a modern cement pedestrian pass-through. It was the same pass-through with the elevators and the unmarked gray door that he'd watched Yearling use the first time they'd come looking for the Anchor's back end, and on the other side was the park with the brewery where he and Bex had had their first maybe-date.

The familiar sight made him grin. It was still early for dinner, but the days had gotten so short now that the sun had already dipped below the islands on the other side of the bay, turning the whole sky a rich purple. It was an absolutely beautiful start to the evening, but when Adrian looked around for Bex, he didn't see her anywhere.

That was unusual. Thanks to the new crowds and the longer walk out of the Anchor, he was two minutes late for their meeting, but Bex was never late for anything unless she was dying. Adrian had expected to find her leaning against the railing with her phone in her hands, texting to ask where he was, but the only people enjoying the view on this chilly October evening were the brewery customers huddled under the heating lamps. He was pulling out his phone to make sure he hadn't gotten the meeting location wrong when the slim device buzzed in his hands, and Bex's name popped up on the screen.

Adrian picked up the call as fast as he could flick his finger. "Hey," he said the moment he got the speaker to his ear. "I'm here. Where are you?"

"Still inside," came the irritated answer followed by the familiar sound of Bex's sigh. "I'm sorry, Adrian. An emergency came up, and I have to cancel tonight."

"What kind of emergency?" he asked at once. "Do you need help?"

"It's not the sort of thing you can help with," Bex said in a frustrated voice. "Again, I'm really, *really* sorry. I swear I'll make it up to you."

"You don't have to do that," Adrian said, trying desperately not to sound as disappointed as he felt. "I just want to see you." He thought a moment then asked, "What about tomorrow? Could we do a raincheck?"

"I'd love to," she answered with a speed that made his sinking heart lift. "What time?"

"How about brunch?" he suggested hopefully. "I know you're busy in the mornings, but I'd rather see you sooner than later."

He was worrying that sounded a little desperate when Bex jumped on it.

"I'd *love* to eat brunch with you."

The naked enthusiasm in her voice made Adrian grin. "It's a date, then," he said. "See you tomorrow, and be careful on your emergency."

"I will be," she promised with a smile he could hear through the phone. "I'll see you soon, and sorry again."

He was opening his mouth to say she didn't need to apologize when he heard a loud *thump* over the speaker followed by what sounded like Bex getting into a car. The call dropped after that, leaving Adrian standing alone on the empty observation deck in his best clothes with nothing to do.

He looked over his shoulder at the closed gray door he'd just come out of with a frown. Leaving the Anchor was easy, but getting back in meant going all the way around to the front entrance, and he just didn't see the point. The sin iron wall was clearly a wash, and even if Bex was no longer coming with him, he still needed to get back to his Blackwood. He'd been neglecting his forest horribly during his search for a way into Gilgamesh's locked Anchors. If he wanted to keep calling himself a witch, he needed to get home, so with a final sigh for his lost evening, Adrian found himself a dark corner where the streetlights didn't overlap, hopped onto his broom, and rose into the sky.

Since it was so dark already, Bran's illusion kicked in at once, making him look like a flock of crows to the scalies walking on the pier below. It was a truly lovely evening to be flying over Puget Sound: the leaves were changing, the moon was nearing full, and the boats were all out, looking like floating jewels on the dark water. From this angle, the Space Needle even lined up perfectly next to Mount Rainier, making it look like he was flying through a postcard. Bex would've loved every second of it, but she wasn't here, so Adrian barely noticed. He was too busy racking his brain over the problem that had been eating him alive for the last thirty days.

How was he going to fix this?

He hated that Bex had canceled on him, but in a way, it was a stroke of luck, because now he had one more night to find a solution. Today's work had been a dead end, but as Boston had reminded him earlier, the sin iron door had always been a long shot. What he *really* needed was a new angle. Some diabolically clever, out-of-the-box scheme that would get Bex onto a chain—preferably multiple chains—without Heaven noticing.

That had been the gold standard from the start, but how? How, how, *how*? He'd already tried all his good ideas and no small number of his bad ones, and he was still just as locked out as he'd been at the start. He supposed Gilgamesh would have to reopen the Anchors eventually, but did the demons have enough quintessence to make it that long? No one had shown him any specific numbers, but Adrian knew how much magic-stretched spaces guzzled. If they had to wait for

Gilgamesh to crack, their new base might run out of gas and collapse without Heaven having to do a thing.

Now that he thought about it, Adrian had to wonder if that hadn't been the plan from the start. Without access to quintessence, it was only a matter of time before the demon-captured Anchor became unable to support itself. If it came down, Bex and her demons would be forced out into the open again for the Eternal King to crush at his leisure. It was exactly the sort of cheap, patient strategy Gilgamesh was famous for, and it was going to work if Adrian couldn't find a way around, which brought him right back to the question that had started all of this.

How?

By the time he'd flown across the water to Bainbridge and set his broom down in the clearing outside his cabin, Adrian's mood was as dark as his forest. If Boston had been there, he would have laid into his witch for getting distracted by future problems when his Blackwood needed him right now. It would've been fair criticism, too, but in a rare stroke of good luck, there wasn't actually as much work waiting for him as he'd feared.

Autumn was a time of shutting down for forests. Since this was his grove's first big seasonal transition, Adrian figured he'd need to ease the new Blackwood into it, but all the deciduous plants seemed to be making the switch to dormancy just fine. His back garden was a disaster, and his house was covered in so many fallen leaves that he had to shovel them off the porch, but the forest itself appeared to have weathered his absence with minimal impact.

Since he didn't have Bex with him like he'd expected, Adrian went ahead and walked a full circuit, but he only found two trees that actually needed his help. One was a maple that had gotten too close to the inlet's beach erosion and fallen over, and the other was a fir tree that had been blocked from sunlight and was growing sideways into his neighbor's property. Both were easy fixes involving a little root moving and some stakes, leaving Adrian with plenty of evening on his hands.

He briefly considered going inside to finish the hasty cleaning he'd started this morning in anticipation of Bex's arrival, but housework no longer felt worth the effort now that it was just him. He didn't even feel like cooking dinner. It all just seemed like too much work, so he settled for grabbing a bowl of nuts and dried fruit from his pantry and walked out to the ridge overlooking the moonlit inlet to keep working on the problem that had consumed his entire life.

How to get Bex onto another chain?

There *had* to be a way. Even if Gilgamesh had disconnected the doors to the Markets, the Anchors themselves had to still be there. Even the Eternal King couldn't move building-sized sin iron weights on a whim, and if other Anchors had golden doors underneath them like the one in Seattle, then his plan to get back into the chain desert might not be dead after all. He was making a mental list of all the ways he might be able to tunnel down to a sin iron portal that *hadn't* been cut off—insubstantiation potions, hordes of moles, stone-to-sand transmutations—when Adrian heard the flap of large wings very close above his head.

He almost didn't look up. Witchwoods were the favorite habitat of several nighttime fliers, none of whom liked being gawked at. Adrian tried to be a polite neighbor whenever possible, but something about these wings sounded off. They were too loud for an owl, too large for a nighthawk, and too elegant to be a lost goose. His forest didn't seem to know what to make of them either, which was the main reason Adrian looked. When he finally craned his neck back, though, what he saw nearly made him tip off the branch he'd been sitting on.

A gigantic bird was perched in the tree directly above him. From the size, hooked beak, and distinctive black-and-tan plumage, it looked like an eastern imperial eagle. That couldn't be right, though, because there were no imperial eagles of any sort living in North America. He was wondering if this one had escaped from a zoo when the bird flapped down to the ground in front of him, and Adrian realized he'd been half correct. It *was* an eastern imperial eagle, but it wasn't alive. It was a taxidermy. A masterfully-done one crafted with expert skill and animated by magic he didn't recognize, and though it hadn't done anything except look at him, Adrian began to back away.

"Who do you belong to?" he asked, putting his hand on the tree behind him in case he needed his forest's help. "What are you doing way out here?"

The eagle tilted its head, its beautifully painted glass eyes blinking just like a living bird's. Adrian was about to ask his questions again when the raptor stuck out its foot to show him the neatly rolled piece of paper tied to its leg with a piece of scarlet ribbon.

Not sure if he was being brave or stupid, Adrian stepped forward and untied the knot. The eagle stood still as a statue the entire time, its knife-sharp beak hovering inches above Adrian's bare hand. He nodded his thanks for the lack of goring and backed away to unfurl the note, which was written on a piece of incredibly thin onionskin paper, probably to save on weight.

Mr. Blackwood, read the elegant but efficient handwriting. *Please forgive the unorthodox nature of this letter. You are a difficult man to contact, but I trust you will find the effort worth your while. I understand you are looking for ways to circumvent the defenses of the Eternal King. Such efforts have long been of interest to me, and I have information I believe you will find beneficial. Should you wish to discuss such matters, it would please me to receive you this evening. Sharif will show you the way, and, fate willing, I look forward to the pleasure of your acquaintance soon. Yours et cetera, M.*

Adrian read the letter two more times before looking back at the eagle. "Are you Sharif?"

The taxidermy raptor ducked its head, which Adrian interpreted as a yes. He looked back at the note with a frown, holding the thin paper up to the moonlight to see if he could spot any hidden spells or symbols, but there was nothing. It looked like perfectly normal paper. If it hadn't been tied to the leg of a magically animated bird of prey from the other side of the planet, he wouldn't even have questioned it.

Tucking the letter carefully into his pocket, Adrian leaned back against his tree so his mind could churn without having to worry about keeping his body upright. On the one hand, mysteriously appearing invitations to talk about the exact problem he was most desperate to solve were absolutely not to be trusted. On the other, this could be the break he'd been looking for. Following a mystery note from a magical eagle was no crazier than trying to dig hundreds of feet under a major city in the hopes of hitting a tunnel with a golden door.

Frowning, Adrian flicked his eyes back to Sharif, who was still waiting patiently on the leaf-littered ground. Given the too-perfect timing, Adrian suspected the bird worked for Aunt Muriel. That would explain the *M* at the end, except the Old Wife of the Future never signed her letters, and that wasn't her handwriting. She also didn't talk like that. If it hadn't come attached to the foot of a giant eagle, Adrian would've assumed the flowery note was from a Victorian gentleman inviting him to a weekend at his country estate.

The whole thing was just so... so *weird*, and that wasn't a word Adrian used lightly. What kind of magic could animate a dead eagle so perfectly? Why use it to send invitations, and why send them to *him*? If this M person was an enemy of Gilgamesh, surely Bex would've been the better choice, but the wording made it clear that the sender specifically wanted to talk to Adrian. The question was *why*?

He leaned harder against his tree, drumming his fingers against the bark and wishing that Boston was here. Of course, if his familiar had been present, he would've been yowling *TRAP!* at the top of his lungs. Adrian was thinking the same thing, but taking the safe route hadn't gotten him anywhere so far, and it wasn't as if he had anything better to do tonight. Also, he was curious. Boston liked to joke that Adrian was the real cat in their partnership, and maybe that was true, because even though he knew taking this bait was a colossally terrible idea, there was no way Adrian wasn't going to do it.

"Let me get my broom," he told the eagle.

Sharif replied with a soft screech as Adrian hurried back to his porch to grab Bran. He briefly considered sending a message to Boston, but he *really* didn't want to risk being talked out of this, so he pulled a fresh hair off his head and left it in the usual spot instead. When he was sure his familiar had enough for a tracking spell should one become necessary, Adrian returned his witch hat to his head and walked back into the clearing, where the eagle was waiting.

"After you," he said, climbing onto his broom.

Sharif gave another little screech and hopped into the air, beating his huge wings as he lifted into the night. Adrian followed more quietly on Bran, rising like a shadow to chase the giant eagle north.

Chapter 4

Following an eagle through a clear, moonlit night should have been no challenge for a witch on a broom. There must've been more going on inside Sharif than just taxidermy, though, because the eagle flew faster than any living bird Adrian had ever seen. He cut over the countless islands and inlets of the Puget Sound like a fighter jet, forcing Adrian to push Bran to his top speed just to keep their guide in sight. If Sharif hadn't been flying due north in a perfectly straight line, they would have lost him entirely.

By the time they reached the open water of the Salish Sea near the Canadian border, Adrian was starting to wonder if Sharif was taking them all the way to the Arctic. He was digging through his pockets for a warming charm strong enough to keep his broom from icing over when the tiny dot of the eagle far ahead stopped racing forward and started diving straight down toward the water.

Adrian signaled Bran to follow with a wince. The eagle was getting dangerously close to the choppy ocean with no sign of pulling up. He was frantically hoping this wasn't about to turn into a diving adventure when his broom suddenly broke through the hazy field of a Nevermind spell, and a beautiful island came into view.

It glowed like a golden lantern floating on the dark sea. The island was very small, only half a mile across at its widest point, but what land it did have was dramatically vertical and, oddly, covered in palm trees. Its smooth, sandy shore also looked nothing like the typical rocky Pacific Northwest coastline, but the strangest sight of all was the ring of buildings that sat atop the island's rocky center like a crown.

It looked like an ancient Arab fortress crossed with a Roman villa. There was a fire-lit outer wall for defense, but that didn't matter to a witch on a broom. Adrian was easily able to look over the fortifications into the elegant complex of sandstone buildings, lantern-lit gardens, and fountain-filled courtyards.

Just like the palm forest outside, it was all enormously out of place. The light-colored buildings with their gauzy silk curtains fluttering from every open window were completely inappropriate for an island this far north. Given the size of the Nevermind hiding the place, Adrian assumed there must be some kind of weather-management spell at play, but the sandy beach Sharif led him to felt as cold and windy as the rest of the night when they finally touched down.

Adrian pulled his coat closer around his body as he stared in disbelief at the wall of date palms waving in the moonlight just up the sand in front of them. Even he'd be hard-pressed to keep a palm tree alive in the Pacific Northwest, let alone a whole forest of them. Other than being a little wilted from the current cold, though, the trees didn't appear overly stressed. He was moving up the beach to get a closer look when Sharif snapped at him so fast, he nearly lost another finger.

"Okay, okay," Adrian said, holding up his hands in surrender. "I get it, you're still guiding. Lead on."

The eagle nodded and flapped back into the air, soaring between the palm trees as it led Adrian down a wide path made from crushed seashells to the sandstone fortress's front door.

"Front gate" would've been a better description. The defensive wall surrounding the island's inner complex looked much taller from the ground than it had from the air, and its entrance was sized to match. The two enormous wooden doors carved in a motif of crashing waves weren't as big as the golden ones below the Anchor, but they were still three times Adrian's height and lit with a pair of bonfires burning in brass braziers. That plus the palm trees made Adrian feel like he was on a movie set. The urge to run around and look at everything was overwhelming, but Sharif snapped at him every time he set so much as a toe out of line, so Adrian forced himself to be patient and stay with his guide. He was wondering how an eagle operated a castle gate when the huge doors started to open all by themselves, swinging out soundlessly to reveal a large, white-paved, tree-lined courtyard with a beautiful copper fountain burbling in the middle.

He'd already noted the basic layout from the sky, but—like everything else tonight—seeing it up close was a surprise. The fountain was *much* bigger and more ornate than he'd expected, with intricate swirls of hammered bronze that glowed like fire thanks to carefully-placed accent lights in the fountain's base. Adrian hadn't thought this place had electricity, but the bonfires on the walls must have been just for show. Now that he was inside, all the lighting was modern, and there was a ton of it.

In addition to the fountain, every tree along the courtyard's edge—a mix of ancient apples, pomegranates, and olives—was tastefully spotlit. All this ambient illumination plus the moon overhead made the courtyard nearly as bright as day, giving Adrian a perfect view of the old-fashioned teak lounge chair set up next to the fountain, where a handsome middle-aged man in plain but well-cut clothes was reading a book while an elderly dog snored on a pillow at his feet.

Adrian froze in the giant doorway. Sharif continued on without him, swooping over to land on the fountain's hammered bronze lip with a proud screech. The man looked up from his book with an indulgent smile and pulled something out of his pocket to toss at the bird.

"Very good, Sharif," he said as the eagle snatched whatever-it-was out of the air and gobbled it up. "You may return to the library."

The eagle screeched again and took off, rising high into the night before folding its wings to dive through an open window on the third story of the complex's largest building. When it was gone, the man carefully set down his book and rose from his chair to face Adrian at last.

"Mr. Blackwood," he said, his olive-skinned face lighting up with a radiant smile. "What a pleasure it is to finally meet you. I am Malik al-Fatheen, but you may address me as Malik. Thank you for accepting my invitation."

"My pleasure," Adrian said, staring hard at the man as he tried to spot the trap.

75

There had to be one. Anyone who could put up a Nevermind big enough to hide an entire island was not to be underestimated, but there was nothing overtly mystical-looking about the man standing in front of him. His dark hair was curly and peppered with natural gray, not the shocking white of those who dedicated themselves to the bones, which had been Adrian's first guess after the taxidermy eagle. His face bore all the normal wrinkles of someone who'd spent his life smiling in the sun with none of the unsettling smoothness some high-ranking sorcerers developed after years of abusing quintessence, and his eyes were a perfectly normal shade of bluish gray with no glow or other signs of unnatural power. Honestly, he looked more like a wealthy Arab businessman relaxing at his vacation home than a magical threat, which meant Adrian was now very confused.

"I'm sorry," he said, leaning on his broom like a walking stick. "I don't mean to be rude, but... what are you?"

"A fair question," Malik replied, stepping over his dog, a golden retriever with an entire muzzle full of gray who was still snoring on the ground. "And a complicated one. More complicated than I would prefer to answer out here in the cold."

He gestured at the large building behind him that the eagle had disappeared into. "Would you be so kind as to join me inside? I don't often bring my island this far north, and I'm afraid my garden is unsuited for entertaining in such weather."

The wind *was* bitingly cold, but Adrian was too caught up in the rest of what he'd said to notice.

"You can move your island?"

"Among other things," Malik replied, reaching down to wake the snoring dog.

She opened her eyes at his touch but seemed to have trouble standing up. Malik helped her gently to her feet, keeping his hand on her back and whispering encouragement as she very, *very* slowly began to walk across the courtyard.

"Thank you for your patience," he told Adrian as he steered the elderly dog around a potted fig. "Maya is approaching her end, I'm afraid. Her sight and hearing are long gone, but until she is ready to take her leave of this world, I will not abandon her."

"I don't mind," said Adrian, who was using the slow pace to gawk at everything. "Will you make a taxidermy out of her as well when she passes?"

"Absolutely not," Malik replied, his voice affronted. "The life beyond death is cruel, and Maya is a gentle creature. She deserves better for all her years of faithful companionship than to be put back to work. When her time comes, I shall bury her under her favorite spot in the garden. She would like that best, I think."

"I'm sorry," Adrian said. "I didn't mean to be rude."

Malik waved the words away. "Think nothing of it. I am long inured to Blackwood bluntness."

"You know my coven?" Adrian asked, surprised.

"Not a bit," the man replied. "But I know your mother very well." He flashed Adrian a shockingly white-toothed smile. "She also asked what I do with my dogs."

"How can you know my mother but not our coven?" Adrian pressed, refusing to be distracted. "She never leaves the Blackwood."

"Is that so?" Malik said, his eyes—which Adrian still couldn't decide were blue or gray—twinkling with laughter. "How remarkable to be in the company of the only child in the world who knows everything his mother does."

Adrian snapped his mouth shut as Malik began to laugh. "Forgive my teasing," he said. "I receive few guests these days, and the absence has left me a poor host. Come, come, let us go inside, and I will answer all your questions."

Adrian nodded and allowed himself to be led through a pair of elegantly carved sandalwood doors into a delightful sitting room.

Like everything else on the island, the space had clearly been designed for hotter weather with arched ceilings and enormous windows to allow for maximum cross-breeze. The sandstone walls were hung with paintings from a variety of cultures and time periods, and the lighting was tasteful and low, leaving the whole place dim and cozy, like a firelit lodge.

"Would you care for a drink?" Malik asked as he escorted his elderly dog to a cushion beneath the grand piano that took up most of the room's center. "I have tea, coffee, or wine if you'd prefer."

"Tea is fine," Adrian said, moving to the wall to get a better look at one of the oil paintings, a beautiful swirl of impressionist colors he would've sworn was a Van Gogh. The decoration next to it—a golden Egyptian scarab set with green-and-blue enamel—was definitely museum-quality, and the piano was an antique Bösendorfer with actual ivory keys. Clearly, whatever Malik was doing out here, he had money to burn.

"Here you are," his host said when he returned, handing Adrian a glass teacup filled with a beautiful, red-tinted liquid that smelled like summer. "Rose hips and jasmine from my own garden. I know it's nothing compared to what a witchwood can produce, but I hope you'll find it acceptable."

Adrian took the cup with a nod of thanks, but when he moved to sit on one of the room's colorfully upholstered sofas, Malik shook his head.

"I'd prefer if we continued our conversation in the library," he said, glancing pointedly at the dog snoozing on her bed. "Maya might be deaf, but she is a fitful sleeper and sensitive to movement. I do not wish to disturb her unnecessarily."

Adrian nodded and motioned for him to lead the way, marveling that a man who lived in a place this grand would put so much thought into an old dog's comfort. He was also eager to see the rest of the house, which was looking more and more like a treasure trove with every step they took.

Sure enough, the next room was a music studio featuring a world tour of stringed instruments. There was a sitar, a lyre, violins, a cello, dozens of guitars, a hammer dulcimer the size of a table, and a full upright harp in the corner. After that was a hallway packed with paintings that Adrian *knew* were from famous artists, followed by a breezeway lined with blown-glass sculptures displayed on hooks. Then came a gigantic room full of books that—Malik informed him—was *not* the library but a legal collection containing tablets, scrolls, and law books from dozens of different cultures and time periods. It was only after this that they finally reached the library itself, which did not in any way disappoint.

"You certainly have a wide variety of interests," Adrian said, tilting his head back to take in the enormous, circular room that looked more like a museum's main hall than a private home.

"I enjoy celebrating mankind's accomplishments," Malik replied proudly as he led them across the stone floor, which had been cushioned into soundlessness by dozens of overlapping Persian rugs. "Any beast can fight for survival, but *this* is what makes us human."

He waved his hand at the dazzling collections all around them, and while Adrian normally preferred forests to buildings, he found it hard to disagree.

Malik's library wasn't the biggest he'd ever seen, but it was hands down the most interesting. The circular room was three stories tall and capped with a dome of colored glass that turned even the moonlight into a pale rainbow. The curving walls were stacked to the ceiling with books in dozens of different languages. Narrow balconies and ladders provided access to all the various collections, and—just like every other part of Malik's house that Adrian had seen so far—there was art crammed everywhere it would fit.

Displays of cut crystal dangled from every light fixture, and the rolling library ladders were each unique works of wrought iron sculpture. The reading chairs scattered across the library's ground level were draped in an impressive collection of Navajo blankets. Even the fireplace that heated the room was decorated with an Islamic glass mosaic. And, of course, there was the taxidermy.

Adrian had already spotted Sharif perched on a piece of driftwood between the library's first and second tiers, but there were animals everywhere. The open area below the glass dome was full of stuffed birds suspended on wires so that they appeared to be in flight, while the bookshelves were overrun with small mammals, their furry bodies forever frozen in time. On the ground level, a full-size caribou guarded yet another dog bed, and some kind of leopard— Adrian wasn't familiar enough with the species to guess which—was posed ready to pounce by the ladder that led to the library's upper stories. Even if the eagle was the only one that came to life, it was still an incredible display, and Adrian didn't bother keeping the wonder off his face as Malik led him to a pair of high-backed leather chairs positioned in front of the fireplace.

"It's amazing," he said as they sat down. "Did you make all of this yourself, or are you a collector?"

"A bit of both," Malik replied as he placed his teacup on the end table, which was itself a masterpiece of mahogany woodworking carved to look like a badger standing on its hind legs. "I enjoy working with my hands, but I also enjoy supporting artists. The result is a rather full house, I'm afraid. What you see here are just my current favorites. I've got three times as much packed away in a warehouse on the mainland." He smiled sheepishly. "It's a bit of a problem."

"You should open a museum," Adrian suggested as he placed his broom on the carpet beside his chair.

"I donate to several," Malik assured him. "But enough about my hobbies. I promised you answers, and now that we are comfortable, answers you shall have."

Adrian scooted forward in his chair, teacup clutched in anticipation.

"You asked me what I was," Malik said slowly, folding his hands—which Adrian could now see were surprisingly scarred for a scholar's—in his lap. "As with all men who've lived a full life, there are many answers to that question, but the simplest is that I am a sorcerer."

Adrian stiffened instantly, and Malik held up his hand.

"It is not what you are thinking," he promised. "Despite the tales spread by his sycophants, Gilgamesh did not invent sorcery. It was the common magic in the kingdom of Uruk for centuries before his birth. After his successful conquest of the afterlife, King Gilgamesh did his best to stamp out all knowledge of the original forms, but, as you can see, he was never entirely successful."

Malik finished with a proud smile, but Adrian couldn't believe what he was hearing.

"You're saying you're an *original* Uruk sorcerer?" he demanded. "As in from five thousand years ago?"

"Among other things," Malik said, picking up his teacup again. "And don't make me sound so old. I've kept up with modern times far better than the Old Wives of the Blackwood, I think."

That wouldn't be difficult, but Adrian refused to be distracted. If Malik really was what he claimed, then the promises in his letter might not be so far-fetched after all.

"You said you had information about circumventing Gilgamesh's defenses," he said, scooting even farther forward in his chair. "What do you know?"

"That depends on what manner of attack you're planning," Malik replied, sipping his tea. "There are many ways to bring down a king."

"Then tell me the one with the highest chance of success," Adrian pressed. "This isn't a philosophical debate. Gilgamesh is a slaver and a tyrant who's done his best to eradicate every other magical tradition, including yours. People are suffering right now because of his rule, and—"

"Really?" Malik asked, his graying eyebrows lifting in surprise. "Who?"

Adrian blinked. "Who what?"

"Who is suffering?" Malik repeated. "Obviously, someone is. There is always suffering, but I've been observing humanity for thousands of years, and I think we're having a remarkably good run at the moment."

"How can you say that when all of demonkind is enslaved?" Adrian demanded.

"Ah," Malik said, shooting him a smile. "There is the confusion. You said 'people' were suffering, but demons are not people. They are tools created by

Ishtar to do her grunt labor. They mimic humanity because the gods had limited imaginations, but they are not us. Simple mistake to make."

"It's not a *mistake*," Adrian said angrily. "Demons might have been made by Ishtar, but they're not tools. They're people who love, mourn, and yearn to be free just like everybody else. Even if you were right, which you're *not*, demons aren't the only ones Gilgamesh has hurt. You just said he stamped out all the original sorcerers except for you, and he's been trying to do the same to witches for eons. If the Old Wives of the Blackwood hadn't spent their lives building our defenses so high that even Gilgamesh doesn't dare to cross us, my magic wouldn't exist."

"You're not wrong," Malik admitted. "But you're not entirely right, either. It's true that Gilgamesh has behaved as a tyrant, but his cruelty was born of necessity. He does not hate the other forms of magic. He simply cannot allow what magic brings."

"You mean usefulness?" Adrian challenged. "Beauty? Knowledge? Ease of living?"

"Chaos," Malik said quietly, his eyes pinned on Adrian's like daggers. "You are a child of peace. You do not know what it was like five or even two thousand years ago, when monsters roamed the earth freely and wild witches stole children to fatten like piglets."

Adrian scoffed. "That never happened."

"It *did* happen," Malik insisted. "I know. I lived through those dark times. The power of the cycles can be gleaned from many sources, and not every coven was as conscientious as the Blackwood. Witchcraft's dark reputation is well earned, as is sorcery's. I myself

84

was once part of the great army of Uruk. I used my magic countless times to rain down fire upon my kingdom's enemies. I thought I was doing what was right, that my sins were necessary to make my people safe, but war is never finished. Even if you kill every man, woman, and child among the enemy, your own people will fracture and fight amongst themselves. That is humanity's tragedy, and magic only makes it worse. Its wonders are nothing compared to the damage such power can do in the wrong hands, and since everyone's hands are wrong at some point, Gilgamesh decided that magic must be taken away for the good of all."

"That wasn't his decision to make!" Adrian yelled.

"You are right," Malik agreed. "But he made it all the same, and who's to say the world did not turn out better because of it? Even without their magic, humanity has accomplished miracles. They have cured plagues, built farms capable of feeding thousands off the work of a few, and gone to the stars. They even figured out how to destroy each other by the millions with the push of a button, and all without magic."

He sighed. "I suppose that proves nothing can keep humans from killing each other, but it was *different* this time. Unlike the destruction of Sodom and Gomorrah, the world had grown up enough by the Atomic Age to be horrified by what such weapons could do, and humanity's endless wars began to cease."

"You can't give Gilgamesh credit for that one," Adrian said.

"Perhaps not," the sorcerer admitted. "But it could be argued that humanity only survived long enough to reach that necessary inflection point because he removed the sword from the toddler's hands."

Adrian's fingers tightened around his teacup. "If you were on Gilgamesh's side this whole time, why did you send me that letter?"

"Because I'm *not* on his side," Malik said sharply. "I am on humanity's side. I am on the side of what is best for *everyone*, which is often much more complicated than the simplistic battle lines of war. There is no 'us' or 'them' in the greater good. There are only wretched problems and imperfect solutions, but sometimes, *sometimes*, we get the opportunity to do better."

Malik leaned forward in his chair, his eyes— which Adrian still couldn't decide were blue or gray— shining with excitement.

"I believe you are such an opportunity. I invited you here because, in all my years of watching, you are the only one I've seen who has learned the purpose of Gilgamesh's Anchors and still decided to destroy one."

"I didn't destroy it," Adrian said quickly. "Bex did. She's the demon Queen of Wrath, and—"

"I know who she is."

Adrian arched an eyebrow, and the sorcerer chuckled. "I am over five thousand years old, Mr. Blackwood. If I did not know the destructive power of Ishtar's Sword by now, I would truly be a hermit. That said, I've never seen her do anything like this.

Something—or some*one*—changed her usual script, and I believe that someone was you."

"I was in the right place at the right time," Adrian hedged, though he couldn't keep the proud look off his face. "And please, call me Adrian."

Malik smiled wide, his eyes crinkling. "Your intimacy is a great gift. One I shall treasure, for I believe it is you, Adrian, who is the key to breaking Gilgamesh's stalemate."

"What stalemate?" Adrian asked. "Gilgamesh won. He controls the entire world."

"Not all of it," Malik said, raising a finger. "Not yet. We still have a chance to make this world a better place for all people, and I am now certain that chance is you."

His insistence was enough to make Adrian blush.

"You keep saying that," he muttered, taking off his pointed hat to run a hand through his dark hair. "But why me? I'm just a witch. A damn good witch, but there are plenty of those in the Blackwood."

"The Blackwood has many charms," Malik agreed, "but audacity is not among them. They are preservers, gardeners. They can put up a tremendous fight when threatened, but their vision ends at the borders of their witchwood. You know this perfectly well, which is why you came to Seattle."

He spoke as if all of this was obvious, but Adrian was gaping by the end.

"How do you know so much about me?"

"I've kept tabs on your progress for many years," Malik informed him proudly. "Since you were a baby, in fact. As I mentioned when you first arrived, I am well acquainted with your mother. Well enough to know how very much she loves you, and that her plans for you did not match my own."

Something clicked inside Adrian as Malik spoke. His eyes darted to the older man's hair, which was the same thick, curling black as his own beneath the gray. He looked at Malik's olive skin, so different from his mother Agatha's paleness but, again, so much like Adrian's. Even the way the sorcerer's eyes refused to pick if they were gray or blue fit, and suddenly, Adrian felt so full he might burst.

"You're my father," he blurted out.

"I am," Malik admitted with a grin, "and a very proud one at that."

Adrian flopped back in his chair. "I don't believe it," he said, which wasn't true at all. He *absolutely* believed his mother would be all over the handsome, charming, cultured Malik like a familiar in the catnip. What he didn't understand was, "Why didn't you contact me sooner?"

Malik's face grew sad. "That was your mother's wish. She wanted you raised in the coven, as most Blackwood witches do."

"But they gave me to the warlocks," Adrian said angrily. "If you were watching, why didn't you show up then?"

"That was *my* wish," Malik said firmly. "A boy must make his own choices, and you'd made your desire to study witchcraft very clear. I didn't want to complicate matters by interfering, or to earn your mother's formidable wrath." His lips quirked. "I am still quite enamored with her, you see. If I'd prevented her favorite from returning, she might have never spoken to me again."

Adrian sank deeper into his chair, shell-shocked. No one had ever called him his mother's favorite before, not even his mother. He knew she'd fought tooth and nail for his right to become a witch because his aunts reminded him of it every time he did something they didn't approve of, but Adrian had always assumed that was because Agatha was too kindhearted to force a child to return to a place he hated. It had never occurred to him that he might be special beyond his ability to escape the warlocks and run home.

"I understand why you didn't show up back then," he said at last. "But why invite me here now? What changed?"

"You did," Malik replied, finishing his tea. "When you insisted on going back to the Blackwood, I assumed you would grow up to be like they were, but I was wrong. You think very differently from the other witches. *Act* differently. You make others act differently as well. Take the Queen of Wrath. She's been beating herself to pieces against the same unbreakable wall for eons, but within one month of meeting you, her tactics changed completely, and she started *winning*."

Adrian blushed. "That wasn't all me."

"It never is," Malik agreed as he set down his empty teacup. "But I've seen enough wars to know the common patterns, and to know how *un*common it is when something breaks those patterns. It was your idea to attack the Anchor, yes?"

Adrian nodded, and Malik spread his scarred hands.

"There you have it. The ability to see beyond the walls of the established system and exploit the flaws hidden in plain sight is a rare and precious talent, but it is far from your only one. You are indeed, as you say, a 'damn good witch,' but the Blackwood lays claim to only half your bloodline. The other half comes from me, which is why I sought you out in particular."

He moved his chair closer, leaning forward until his face was just a few inches from Adrian's own.

"I believe you have the right combination of audacity, creativity, and persistence to learn my sort of magic. The ancient sorcery of Sumer." He lowered his voice to a whisper. "*Gilgamesh's* magic."

"I thought Gilgamesh used quintessence sorcery," Adrian whispered back.

Malik scoffed. "And where do you think he got it from? He stole the entire system from us, though he had to dumb it down for his followers. The recitation-verse poetry method used by today's sorcerers is a crutch, a simplistic mnemonic designed to let closed-minded fools manipulate powers that would normally be beyond their comprehension. That is why modern sorcerers can write two hundred pages quibbling over pronunciation but can't make a new spell unless they're cribbing lines from other verses. They can only use the tools that Gilgamesh has given them, but you and I both know that popping some quintessence and reciting words written by someone else isn't *magic*. It's parroting, brainless theft, but my power—*true sorcery*—is all about what's up here."

He tapped his finger against Adrian's temple.

"Real magic requires a creative mind," he said. "It demands risk, daring, and tenacity in the face of loss. It is completely unsuitable for building a stable empire, which is why Gilgamesh stamped it out. He cannot let that knowledge escape because a true sorcerer would know all of Heaven's weaknesses and how to exploit them. That is why Gilgamesh killed his own teachers, but it is also why you can succeed, *if* you're willing to learn."

"Of course I'm willing," Adrian said. "If there's a back door to Heaven's magic, I *absolutely* want to learn how to open it. But if sorcery is the key to bringing down Heaven, why haven't you done it already?"

"Because I am old," Malik replied, sitting back in his chair with a sigh. "Five thousand years is four thousand nine hundred more than any mortal was meant to live. I have the knowledge to sustain my physical body indefinitely, but my mind is tired. I am not so audacious as I used to be, and, like all old men, I have fallen into my ruts. I reached my limits long ago, but your epic is just beginning."

"Is that what you want from me?" Adrian asked. "To do what you no longer can?"

"I want what every father wants for his son," Malik replied. "I want you to surpass me, to achieve what I was unable to." His smile grew cocky. "I'm afraid I'll be a tough act to follow. I've done much with my life."

"I don't know," Adrian said with a cocky smile of his own. "I'm a pretty quick learner."

"Then let us begin!" Malik proclaimed, shooting to his feet. "You'll need this."

He reached into the pocket of his linen trousers and pulled out a small velvet bag. It felt like a coin purse when he placed it in Adrian's hand, but when Malik opened the drawstring, the pale light that poured out made Adrian jump.

"That's quintessence!"

"An unfortunate concession to these modern times," the sorcerer said brusquely, taking Adrian by the arm and steering him toward the open space in the middle of the library floor with surprising strength.

"In the old days, magic belonged solely to the gods. That's why witches have always been heretics. Your ancestors learned to make their own power by harnessing the great cycles of the world itself, which the gods did not appreciate. Impressive as that is, however, witchcraft's origins mean it has always been limited by the laws of nature. Sorcery, on the other hand, is a wish granted to the caster by the gods. It works instantaneously and has no limits save for those imposed by the gods. Fortunately for us, they're dead, which means the only barriers to sorcery nowadays are the ones we place on ourselves. We do still have to make up the power, though, which is why we must resort to this."

He took a coin of quintessence from Adrian's bag and held it up between his fingers.

"Quintessence was Gilgamesh's greatest discovery. Before he figured it out, it was impossible for a sorcerer to rebel against the gods who were the source of his power. With quintessence, though, control over magic fell into the hands of men, and the gods became unnecessary. That is how an army of mortals was able to conquer Paradise, and it's still the only way sorcery can be used today."

"All right," Adrian said nervously, "but I still don't understand why *I* have to use it. I've already got my own magic through the Blackwood."

"And that is not to be underestimated," Malik agreed. "But, as I mentioned earlier, witchcraft's strength is also its limitation. A witch is nearly unstoppable inside their witchwood, but their power drops dramatically when they leave their forest. Take yourself, for example. What magic could you cast right now that doesn't rely on the premade charms in your pockets?"

"Not much," Adrian admitted. "But just because witchcraft requires setup doesn't make it inferior."

"I never said it was inferior," Malik insisted. "I said it was *limited*, which is not a criticism. Sorcery also has limitations. Without the blessing of the gods or the quintessence that replaces it, all the magic of Heaven is nothing but imaginings and pretty words. The key is choosing the magic whose limitations do not limit your goals. For example, it's entirely possible to cast sorcery using the magic of the Blackwood, but the resulting spell would move at the speed of a growing tree, which isn't very practical."

Adrian didn't know about that. His forest on Bainbridge was proof that trees could grow very quickly when a witch was involved. But he could also admit that waiting a month every time you wanted to cast a spell would be inconvenient for the sort of fast, flashy magic sorcerers seemed to prefer.

"All right," he said, setting his witch hat on the floor next to his broom. "Say I take the quintessence. What happens next?"

"Magic," Malik replied at once.

"But *how*?" Adrian demanded. "I've eaten quintessence before, and all it did was give me a headache."

"Because you did not give it an outlet," his father said authoritatively. "Quintessence is merely power. To be useful, that power must be *used*. Historically, this was done through the gods. A sorcerer would pray for an outcome—the destruction of his enemies, say—and the gods would grant or deny his wish depending on their whims. With quintessence, however, the burden of command falls upon the sorcerer. To cast a spell with quintessence, a sorcerer must have a divine level of understanding. He must know *exactly* what he is trying to accomplish, and he must be able to understand it *quickly*. Move too slow, and the quintessence will burn through the body and damage it."

Adrian was pretty sure he'd already experienced that. He wanted to ask his father if taking quintessence incorrectly had any long-term health effects, but Malik was still talking.

"This is why Gilgamesh taught his sorcerers poetry," he went on. "To wield the power of the gods without destroying oneself, a sorcerer's mind must be lightning-quick, his will adamant. That's an impossible burden for many people, so the Eternal King gave his sorcerers a crutch. He wrote thousands of poems, each line of which represented a specific magical effect. By tying the magic to predetermined trigger phrases, he made it so that his sorcerers didn't have to think. They could simply take the quintessence, recite the right words, and *poof*, the spell would be cast exactly—and *only*—as their king intended."

He finished with a flourish, but Adrian just stared at him.

"That's horrible," he said at last.

"It was the only way," Malik replied with a shrug. "If Gilgamesh didn't teach his sorcerers to be brainless, half of them would blow themselves up within the first year, and the other half would quickly grow to become a threat to Heaven. Neither of those outcomes were desirable, which is why Gilgamesh's sorcery focuses solely on rote memorization. The most powerful sorcerers know the verse system so well, they're able to cast enormously complicated spells using only a handful of key reference phrases. This speed is crucial because the faster you cast, the more quintessence goes into the spell rather than into you."

"Again, that's *horrible*," Adrian insisted. "You make it sound like sorcerers are playing chicken with their lives!"

"An accurate observation," Malik acknowledged. "But every power comes with risk, and you're actually in a privileged position for this one. As a child of the Blackwood, you have a naturally high tolerance to toxins, and as the son of a sorcerer who's been using quintessence for a *very* long time, you've been inoculated from my side as well. That's two paths of resistance working in your favor, which gives you the ability to take enormous amounts of quintessence without ill effect."

Adrian wasn't surprised to hear that. His ability to stomach quintessence was the entire reason the Spider had tried to kidnap him, but he didn't like hearing the same argument from his father.

"Is that the reason you want to teach me?" he asked bitterly. "Because my body can handle a lot of quintessence?"

"It's the reason I think you'll survive," Malik said. "I want to teach you because you've proven yourself to be a clever, audacious, creative person who is capable of finding and exploiting Heaven's weaknesses. That is someone with the potential to be a *great* sorcerer, which is the only sort I'm interested in training. The fact that you are also my son is merely the gilding on the lily."

Adrian was horrified to find himself blushing by the end. He knew he was being buttered up, but that didn't stop it from working. The witches of the Blackwood weren't exactly free with their praise. Even when his mother told him he'd done well, there was always room for improvement. Compared to that, Malik's unreserved encouragement was a rush, which was why the next words out of Adrian's mouth came far too quickly.

"How do I do it?"

Malik's smile spread even wider. "The core concepts are very simple," he said as he placed the quintessence back in his son's palm. "Since it originated as the will of the gods, the most important element of sorcery is a strong vision. It's not enough to merely want something to happen. You must *know* it will happen. Sorcery is a magic of belief. Formerly belief in the gods, but now belief in one's own self. A sorcerer must be able to answer his own prayers, and we do so with this."

He tapped the coin of quintessence.

"When you place that in your mouth, the power of the gods will course through your veins like lightning. A sorcerer's magic relies on directing that lightning before it strikes him. Again, this is extremely difficult for most people, but you have yet another advantage in that you are already a trained witch. Thanks to your years spent witnessing the miracles of the Blackwood, there is very little you innately assume to be impossible, which lowers the unconscious mental friction for envisioning a spell."

"Growing up in the Blackwood does foster an open mind," Adrian agreed, frowning at the glowing coin in his hand. "But what kind of spell do I envision? Do I just imagine lightning shooting from my fingers?"

"You can if you wish," his father said. "Though I thought we'd start with something a little more practical. It's a much more advanced technique than I'd usually try with a beginner, but you're already so accomplished, I'm sure you'll have no difficulty."

Once again, Adrian's cheeks heated at the shameless flattery, but that didn't stop him from asking, "What technique?"

Malik's grin turned smug. "I believe the modern term would be 'teleportation.'"

Adrian nearly dropped the bag of quintessence. "You know how to move instantaneously?"

"Don't make it sound so impossible," his father chided. "I just told you that sorcery is a magic of belief. If your first thought is that something can't happen, all you're doing is ensuring that it won't. You need to understand to the core of your being that there is *nothing* a sorcerer can't do provided he can wrap his head around the problem. This includes instantaneous movement. It's not even that difficult, once you have the right mental model. Now, let's try this again. Do you believe that I can teleport?"

Adrian nodded, and the smile returned to his father's face.

"Would you like to learn how to do it yourself?"

Adrian nodded again even more rapidly, and Malik chuckled as he dug into the bag of quintessence.

"Two coins ought to be enough," he said, pulling out another white, glowing, quarter-sized disk, which he placed next to the first coin of quintessence Adrian was already holding in his hand. "I want you to picture being back in the room where Maya is sleeping. It's fine if you can't remember every detail. Just hold whatever you do have in your mind. Squeeze that memory until it becomes as real as the ground you're standing on. Can you feel it?"

"I'm trying," Adrian said, struggling to remember exactly what the first room in Malik's house had looked like. He'd only walked through it once, and a lot had happened since then. He'd been extremely interested in everything, though, and soon enough, a picture appeared.

"I think I've got it."

"Good," Malik said. "Now that you've got your destination, you need to envision how you're going to get there. As a Blackwood witch, a nature metaphor is probably easiest, so I want you to imagine all the rooms between this one and your target like leaves on a branch. They appear as separate entities, but they're all part of the same tree, just as all the trees in a witchwood are part of the same forest. To get from one tree to another might require miles of walking, but you do not need to walk, for you are a sorcerer. You understand that these two things are, in fact, one and the same. Combine the forest in your head. *Know* that it is actually all one place."

"But it's not one place," Adrian argued. "A forest is a tapestry of thousands—"

"Ah, ah, ah," Malik interrupted. "Even if you know separation exists, you must not let it intrude upon your understanding of what you are doing. When you return home after a long day, you do not think 'I am going to my bedroom.' You think, 'I am going home.' Even if you live in a palace of a hundred rooms, 'home' is a singular place: the place you must go. This is how the teleportation spell is able to function. Practice this method of thinking long enough, and you'll eventually be able to see the entire world as one entity, for that is what it is: one planet, one home. The greatest illusion is the illusion of separation. Free yourself from this falsehood, and you will find that any destination in the universe is no more separated from you than the ground beneath your feet."

That was a pretty big mental leap, but Adrian did his best. As his father instructed, he imagined all the rooms of Malik's sprawling house as leaves on a branch. A fern frond specifically, because fern leaves were small and close together. Once he had the image in his head, he imagined himself picking up the branch. They'd passed through five rooms on their way here with a real-world distance of several hundred feet. If he imagined them as five leaves on a fern frond, though, the distance was only about as long as his wooden pinky finger. Easily crossable, in other words, but when Adrian instinctively reached for the Blackwood that lived in his heart, Malik grabbed his hand.

"Not that," he said when Adrian's eyes popped open. "I keep telling you, it will not work. Even if the Blackwood agreed to grant you power for this, forests are not known for traveling quickly. If you use witchcraft to power this spell, you will move at the speed of a growing tree, which is not what we want. To make this work, you *must* use power that does not suffer nature's limitations."

"So you keep saying," Adrian grumbled. "But I don't *like* taking quintessence. It feels wrong."

"You're ingesting power meant only for the gods," Malik reminded him. "Of course it's going to feel unpleasant, but it is necessary for this and far more sustainable than chopping off a finger, which is the only other way to get instant power."

He tapped the articulated piece of oak that had replaced Adrian's left pinky.

"You'll get used to it," he promised as he closed Adrian's fist around the glowing coins. "Go ahead. Give it a try."

Adrian grimaced at the tingling feeling of the quintessence against his bare skin. He didn't want to look like a coward in front of his father, though, so he popped the two coins into his mouth and bit down.

As always, power filled him in a rush. It was every bit as scary and uncomfortable as he remembered, but Adrian forced himself to get over it and concentrate on the spell. He envisioned the room, envisioned the fern, envisioned himself moving the tiny distance between the leaves. He did everything his father had told him, and then he pushed the overwhelming surge of quintessence toward his goal.

The moment he moved the magic, Adrian's body swung like a clapper in a bell. The resulting ringing knocked all the thoughts out of his head. For a horrible moment, he was certain he'd broken something. Then the ringing vanished as swiftly as it had come, replaced by a soft snore coming from the ground at his feet.

When Adrian opened his eyes again, he was standing beside the grand piano above the sleeping dog, *exactly* where he'd pictured in his head. The quintessence burn was already fading out of his system, leaving only a feeling of jubilation. He'd done it! He'd teleported! He was still celebrating his success when Malik appeared beside him, popping out of the air with the same ringing sound Adrian had just heard inside his head.

"Well done!" his father cried, handing Adrian his broom and hat, which he'd left behind on the library floor. "That was perfect!"

Adrian took his things by habit, but the triumphant smile was already slipping off his face.

"That sound," he said in a shaky voice. "That's the same ringing I hear when a prince shows up."

"Naturally," Malik replied. "You think Heaven's sons invented popping all over the world? Gilgamesh stole the technique from sorcery same as he did everything else. That's why I'm teaching you this."

"I know," Adrian said, "but..." His voice trailed off as he looked down at the bag of quintessence he was still clutching in his hand. "I didn't realize it would sound the same."

"The ringing is from the shock wave generated by passing so quickly through the magic of the universe," his father explained. "Even sorcerers cannot travel without moving. The farther you go or the larger the object you're attempting to move, the bigger the ring, but it's just sound and a bit of shaking, nothing to be afraid of."

"I wasn't afraid," Adrian said, blowing out a breath. "It's just..." He put his witch hat back on his head as he tried to think of the best way to put this. "It looks very bad," he said at last. "Bex won't like it."

"Then don't show her," Malik advised with a conspiratorial wink. "This is *your* power, Adrian. Your inheritance. Now that you know the method, you can teleport anywhere that you can imagine, provided there's no other magic preventing your arrival, of course. I wouldn't recommend attempting to teleport into the main Blackwood, for example. Gilgamesh burned that particular bridge eons ago, and running into a barrier at the speed teleportation requires can be *quite* distressing. That said, the Eternal King doesn't tend to erect such walls within his own lands."

"He doesn't?" Adrian asked, shocked.

"Of course not," Malik said. "The only ones Gilgamesh trusts enough to teach real magic to are his princes, and why would he wish to bar his sons from any part of his domain? They are his faithful servants. Walls are for enemies, so if you can travel like a prince..."

"I can go anywhere," Adrian finished.

Malik's grin grew even wider. "I did promise to help you get around Gilgamesh's defenses," he said, clapping his son on the shoulder. "Do you think this might solve your problem?"

It could solve *all* of Adrian's problems if applied creatively enough. "Thank you," he said, shaking his father's hand. "This helps more than you know. I have to go now, but can I see you again? Tomorrow night, perhaps?"

"There's nothing that would please me more," Malik said, using Adrian's hand to pull his son into a hug. "I have waited a long, *long* time for this, Adrian. I can't say how happy it makes me to see my son using magic like a true sorcerer."

The way Adrian had imagined the spell in his head had been closer to witchcraft than sorcery, but he wasn't about to undermine the first fatherly approval he'd ever received.

"I promise I'll make good use of this," he said, hugging the older man hard.

"And I look forward to hearing all about it," Malik replied, pulling another bag of quintessence out of his pocket and pressing it into Adrian's hands.

"For all the practicing I know you're about to do," he said with a wink. "Don't get caught."

Adrian grinned and fished out two more coins. A second later, he added a third before sliding both bags of quintessence into the deepest of his coat's enchanted pockets. When everything was safely stowed away, he tucked his broom under his arm and nodded to his father one last time.

"Thank you again."

"It was my greatest pleasure," Malik said, pressing a hand to his forehead and then to his lips before waving it at Adrian. "Safe travels."

Adrian grinned and popped the quintessence into his mouth, breaking all three coins in one bite. He didn't take nearly as long envisioning his destination this time. Thanks to the roots wrapped around his heart, his Blackwood was the one place he always knew how to get back to. Sure enough, Malik and his lovely house vanished the moment the magic hit. He was traveling much farther this time, and as predicted, the ringing was much louder, but nothing unmanageable. Adrian was feeling quite pleased with himself until he crashed into something that did not move.

It felt like he'd run headfirst into a tree. His whole body went reeling, falling out of the spell like a broken doll. When he opened his eyes again, he was gasping on his back on the road outside of his forest.

Adrian rubbed his hands over his face with a groan. Great Blackwood, he was an idiot. He'd been so excited about teleporting home, he'd completely forgotten the week of work he'd put into prince-proofing his forest. If it hadn't hurt so damn much, he'd have been enormously proud that he'd managed to build an effective barrier against magic he hadn't even understood at the time. Unfortunately, it was hard to feel anything through the waves of nausea. He was still fighting not to throw up when he felt his phone buzz against his chest.

Too sick to even push off the pavement, Adrian fumbled a hand into his coat. Fortunately, he always kept his phone in the one pocket that was actually just a pocket. His head was spinning so badly he didn't think he could've called up one of his enchanted pockets if his life depended on it, but he did manage to get his phone near enough to his face to swipe his nose over the green Accept Call button.

"Hello?"

"Are you all right?" Boston's frightened voice demanded over the speaker. "I just felt something hit our Blackwood!"

"I'm fine," Adrian lied, rubbing his throbbing temples. "Just an experiment gone wrong."

"An experiment with what?" his familiar snapped. "Blowing yourself up?"

"Something like that," he muttered. "Is everything okay over there?"

"As okay as it ever gets," Boston reported. "My party ended a while ago, but Iggs was still up, so we're in the wrath demon village working on my Riverlander. It's a fascinating language."

"I'm glad you're enjoying yourself," Adrian said. "But why is Iggs still awake? I thought he taught defense classes in the morning."

"He does, but he's staying up until Bex gets back."

Adrian went still. "She's still not back from her emergency?"

"I don't know what's going on," Boston said before he could ask. "Iggs has been annoyingly tight-lipped about the whole thing."

Adrian heard Iggs say something indignant in the background, and Boston harrumphed. "He says it's not a problem, just some business with the goblins. I think that sounds like a *huge* problem, but Iggs insists it's fine, though he does say he'll call you first if they decide to mount a rescue."

"Good to know," Adrian said, closing his eyes. "I'm going to bed now. Keep an eye on things there for me, would you?"

"If I didn't always keep an eye on everything, I wouldn't be much of a cat," Boston informed him scornfully. "I have to give Iggs his phone back now. See you tomorrow."

Adrian cut the call and dropped the hand he'd been using to hold up his phone, letting his aching body sprawl onto the pavement. When the rolling nausea finally subsided, he set himself to the task of getting up. It took a while, but eventually, Adrian made it to his feet, brushed the leaves off his clothes, and set his witch hat back on his head. His broom was the only thing missing, but when Adrian leaned over to grab Bran off the asphalt, the wooden broomstick rolled out of his reach.

"What's your problem?"

The broom's raven handle turned sharply away from him, and an impression of deep insult stabbed into Adrian's mind. Bran didn't like this new teleporting. It was unnatural. Also, flying was *his* job.

"Don't be jealous," Adrian said, crouching back down to pet the raven's carved wings. "Sorcery will never hold a candle to you. *You* never left me sprawled on a street about to barf."

The broom rolled another inch farther down the road, and Adrian sighed.

"Come on," he cajoled. "I'm never going to stop being a witch, and what's a witch without the world's best broom?"

The carved eyes turned to glare at him, and Adrian gave the broom his most charming smile. "Surely you're not going to make me walk all the way up the hill in the dark? Don't you want to get back to your nook by the fire in my nice, dry house?"

As usual, bribery did the trick. Bran pecked him several times to make sure his displeasure was known, but he let Adrian climb on in the end, lifting them through the dark, windy forest toward the cabin on the hilltop.

Chapter 5

The trip to Felix's vault took forever.

When he'd said he had Havok locked up, Bex had assumed he meant under his operation on the pier. Instead, the goblin prince shuffled her and Nemini straight into his limo, which was double-parked on the cobblestone street in front of the Pike Place Market main entrance.

They'd been driving ever since. Two damn hours stuck in a limo with a seven-foot-tall goblin who liked to sprawl over every available surface. Nemini didn't seem to care about the drive or the invasion of her personal space any more than she cared about anything, but Bex was supremely uncomfortable and bored out of her skull. Unlike Felix's gold-plated phone, her cheap internet had stopped working the moment they left Seattle, leaving her with nothing to do but stare out the window as the goblin chauffeur drove them east down the endless highway.

She wouldn't have minded so much if there'd been something to look at. The mountains of central Washington were beautiful in the autumn, but the sun had set before they'd left, and between the limo's intense window tinting and the quickly fading twilight, she couldn't see a thing. Finally, after what felt like an eternity, they turned off the highway onto a small state road that T-ed into an even smaller road, which eventually ran through the middle of a mountain town with a Bavarian theme surrounded by a ring of tourist-friendly chain motels.

"Leavenworth?" Bex read as the limo rolled past the lit-up sign. "Your vault's in *Leavenworth*? The place from the billboards where they stuck fake-German fronts on all the buildings so they could sell Christmas crap all year long?"

Felix nodded without looking up from his phone, and Bex's jaw dropped.

"Do you do business anywhere that *isn't* a tourist trap?"

"Why would I?" the prince replied, putting down his phone at last. "Goblin magic is all about money, and who's freer with their money than tourists? My stuff's actually pretty low-key since tourist exploitation is only a small portion of my portfolio. You wanna see a real machine in action, you should check out my cousin's operation down in Florida. Lucky bastard's got all of Disney funneling into his pockets. Now, *that's* some quality profiteering!"

Bex rolled her eyes. "That still doesn't explain why we had to drive so far. If tourists are your only requirement, there's plenty of money-sponges closer to Seattle. How do you even get to your vault if it's way out here?"

"Oh, I never come this way myself," Felix said, squinting through the limo's tinted windows at the line of Christmas-light-covered motels dressed up as chalets. "If I need to check on my assets, I just transfer myself over. Very convenient, but non-goblins don't tolerate the rounding well. Visitors who come in via accounting tend to arrive plus or minus a few organs.

109

Great for a laugh, not so much for survival rates, so, seeing as you're such a valued client, I took it upon myself to escort you personally. You're welcome."

Bex shook her head and grabbed the door handle as the limo came to a stop. "Let's just get this over with."

"After you, Your Majesty," Felix replied with a bow.

Fighting the urge to sigh, Bex opened the door to see where blindly trusting a goblin had landed her.

Shocker to no one, it was a gift shop. Felix's limo was parked in front of a two-story building so covered in faux-German kitsch it looked like a cuckoo clock. The front porch was packed with factory-carved wooden figurines of gnomes, bears, moose, and other animals that were too cheaply made to identify. Once you got past the wooden army, the shop's windows— every one of which was bracketed with cutesy red shutters that were far too small to actually close—were stacked even higher with mountains of fake nonsense. There were aluminum beer steins being sold as pewter, overpriced acrylic sweaters being passed off as wool, and cheap plastic toys at handmade prices. There was also the usual assortment of CBD products you saw for sale everywhere in Washington, but the main business here was clearly rip-off fakery. Classic goblin establishment, in other words.

Bex didn't know how that was working out for them. It was almost ten at night, so the store itself was closed. Felix must've called ahead, though, because there was a goblin dressed in lederhosen waiting to open the door the moment the prince's shiny shoe hit the welcome mat. He did so with a groveling bow, practically prostrating himself before his prince as Felix swept inside.

"The vault's downstairs," Felix announced once he was in, walking through the shop in a crouch so he wouldn't bump his seven-foot-high head against the faux-wood rafters someone had glued to the drop ceiling. "Don't touch anything."

Any other time, Bex would've been insulted by the implication that she couldn't keep her hands off the racks of "I got high in the Cascade Mountains!" T-shirts. In a goblin shop, though, that warning was legit. She was barely two steps inside the door, but Bex could already feel the sticky hum of the greed magic running over her skin.

Demons were usually pretty resistant to tricks like that, but the Leavenworth goblins must have been using some industrial-strength mojo because Bex could feel the little stabs of covetousness coming at her from every direction. By the time they reached the rear of the shop, she was seriously considering buying Adrian a souvenir potholder. She'd actually started reaching out for the display case when Nemini poked her in the back, giving Bex the shot of emptiness she needed to rip herself free of the literal tourist trap and follow Felix down a tiny stair into a basement storage room with a huge, natural stone wall at the back.

"Here we are," the goblin prince said, walking up to the rock face. "I haven't used this door in a while, so just give me a second to find the... *ah ha!*"

He scraped away a layer of dust to reveal something that looked exactly like—but couldn't possibly be—a credit card reader. It was one of the older models where you had to actually swipe the card instead of just tapping or inserting the chip, but still absolutely not something that should be sticking out of a granite rock face like a fossil. The whole thing made no sense even by Bex's low standards, but Felix reached into his front coat pocket and pulled out a perfectly normal-looking credit card, which he promptly slid through the card reader.

"Ye*ouch*, that's high!" he cried when the reader beeped green, shaking the hand holding the credit card as if he'd just been stung. "I knew a queen would be an expensive date, but that's some straight-up gouging."

"What are you talking about?" Bex asked, moving closer to Nemini, who was watching the goblin prince with her usual passive interest. "I thought we were going to your vault. Why do you have to pay?"

Felix shot a scathing glare over his shoulder.

"Don't be a mark, sweetheart. We're crossing into goblin country. Of *course* there's an entry fee. I had my maintenance team put in the card reader since plastic's a lot easier to haul around than bags of gold, but it's always cost money to get around down here. Normally, travel expenses would be your responsibility, but I'm the one who insisted on an express pickup, so the door fee is on the house tonight." He winked at her. "Only the best concierge service for my favorite royal beauty."

Normally, Bex would have glowered at that, but she was far too interested in the stone wall, which was swinging open like a door now that Felix had bought their way in. On the other side was a large, natural cave filled with moss and lichen. The stone was a completely different color than the rock face outside— black instead of granite gray—but the biggest shock was at the end of the cave, where a small goblin was sitting at a wooden reception desk playing solitaire under the light of a green-shaded banker's lamp.

"Heya, Fisnistle," said Felix as he closed the door behind Bex and Nemini. "Long time no see."

"My prince," the little goblin squealed, scrambling out from behind his desk to throw himself on the floor.

"Excellent groveling," Felix observed as the goblin prostrated himself. "But save it for later. We need to use the elevator."

The goblin hopped back to his feet and ran over to the wall behind his desk, which had looked like just another part of the cave. The moment he touched the rock, however, the whole cliff slid away like a curtain, revealing a large stone shaft with an old-fashioned hand-operated cage elevator.

Felix walked up to it at once, shoving the folding lattice doors open with one hand while he waved for Bex and Nemini to get inside with the other. Bex did so slowly, partially because she resented taking orders from a goblin, but mostly because the bottom of the elevator was made from the same open metal lattice as the doors. The crisscrossed steel didn't flex when she stepped on it, but the gaps were big enough to stick her boot through, and she didn't like how she could see straight down into the darkness below. She was threading her fingers through the diamonds that formed the elevator walls for extra support when Felix tapped her wrist.

"You don't want to stick your hands out on this ride, darlin'," he warned.

Bex pulled her fingers back at once. Felix nodded in satisfaction and turned back to his employee, who was still climbing onto the stool that allowed him to reach the elevator's control panel.

"Take us to the secure vault."

"Which one, Your Wealthiness?" Fisnistle asked in the politest voice Bex had ever heard from a goblin. "Gold, secrets, firstborns, souls—"

"Alternate compensation," Felix interrupted, taking out a monogrammed handkerchief to wipe his green brow. "And make it snappy. She's running the meter hard."

Both of the goblins turned to glance at Bex, but neither said another word as Fisnistle punched an unlabeled button toward the top of his panel. The cage shuddered as something in the gearbox opened with a *clunk*, and then the lattice floor dropped out from under Bex's feet as the elevator fell straight down.

She almost grabbed the cage wall on instinct before she remembered Felix's warning. Curling her hands into protective fists, Bex forced herself to be still, letting her body float off the open-mesh floor as the shaft they'd been hurtling down vanished, leaving their elevator in free fall over the most enormous cavern Bex had ever seen.

It looked like Felix's goblin had dropped them straight into the center of the earth. The hole was *so* big, Bex couldn't even see where they'd be crashing to their deaths. She glanced at Felix to see what he was planning to do about that, but the prince didn't look ruffled in the slightest. Neither did Nemini. They both just stood there, casually floating in free fall as if being dropped into a fathomless pit was a perfectly normal part of their day. Bex was striving to match their calm and be a queen, dammit, when something snatched their plummeting elevator out of the air.

Bex slammed into the cage floor with a gasp. She yanked her head up next, her burning eyes going huge when she saw that their falling elevator had been caught by a bus-sized, furry-legged, black-carapaced, dozen-eyed *spider.* For one long second, Bex could only stare at the glistening mandibles sticking through the metal cage above her head. Then the spider made a clicking noise and began to descend, clutching the elevator like a prize as it scurried down a strand of webbing so fine and thin, it was practically invisible in the dark.

"Now do you see why I told you not to stick your hands out?"

Bex whirled around to find Felix grinning at her, which was better than laughing. Barely.

"Beauty, isn't she?" the prince said, reaching up to pet the tips of the spider's dripping fangs. "I wanted a dragon after I watched that movie about the wizard kids and the goblin bank. Stupid director made us look like stumpy idiots, but the vault design?" He pressed his green fingers to his lips in a chef's kiss. "Inspired! Alas, pretty much every dragon left in the world is locked up inside the Blackwood, and those witches won't sell for love or money."

His gleaming eyes flicked back to Bex with new interest. "Say, haven't you gotten cozy with one of those tree huggers recently? I don't suppose you could—"

"No," Bex said, crossing her arms over her chest to keep them farther away from the spider.

"Your loss, baby," Felix said with a shrug. "Then again, maybe I dodged a bullet. Spiders aren't as flashy as dragons, but they're smart, diligent, and they work for peanuts. Well, human sacrifices, but you get the idea."

Bex really hoped she didn't, but there was no point arguing ethics with a goblin. At least being carried by a giant spider gave Bex time to see all the details she'd missed while falling to her death. For example, the pit below them *wasn't* an endless, empty abyss as she'd originally assumed. It was actually quite crowded with giant spiderwebs and hordes of goblins.

The crowds were all moving along the non-sticky support strands that crisscrossed the chasm like suspension bridges. On the sides of the pit where the webbing connected, hundreds of holes had been carved into the cliff face, leading to caverns of all sizes. It almost looked like a circular city, except none of the caves seemed to be homes or shops. The goblins didn't look like citizens, either. They scurried across the web-bridges like worker ants with their arms full of clothing, sports equipment, computers, and Ishtar knew what else. It was all so strange and unexpected, Bex actually forgot about the mortal peril facing her no-longer-reincarnating body and pressed her face against the elevator cage to get a better look.

116

"What's all that stuff they're carrying?"

"Treasure," Felix said proudly. "What that means varies from goblin to goblin, but we all live for it, and my people have good pickings. American consumer culture's been great for us. Just look at those premium finds!"

It looked like a lot of junk to Bex, but the goblins did seem happy. The figures below were even smaller than the goblins who worked at Felix's tourist trap on the pier, but they were all grinning just like their prince did when he landed a juicy contract. Bex had the sinking feeling that made him the better monarch, but there was no time for being jealous. In the minute she'd been gawking, the giant spider had already carried their elevator across the giant pit to the cave-riddled cliff on the opposite side.

The hole the spider shuffled them into was medium-sized—bigger than some but definitely not the biggest. Inside were even more tunnels that branched off into open warehouses full of objects being sorted into bins by an army of goblins with clipboards. The spider didn't stop at any of these, though. It kept going all the way to the end of the cave, which was sealed off from the rest by an enormous metal door.

There was just enough room at the lip where the door met the stone for the spider to set down their elevator. It did so with surprising delicacy, placing the cage on a cushion of webbing so gently, Bex barely felt the landing.

"Here we are," Felix said as the elevator goblin scrambled off his stool to open the lattice door. "After you, ladies."

Bex squared her shoulders and stepped out of the elevator into a white cushion of spiderwebs she *really* hoped weren't sticky. They were a little, but she was able to yank her feet free without losing one of her combat boots. Nemini, of course, had no such trouble. She moved through the webbing with her typical grace, her yellow eyes focused on Felix as the prince used his long legs to step over the webs entirely and land on the clear strip of stone in front of the giant door.

"Let's make this quick-like," he said as he pulled a large ring of old-fashioned skeleton keys out of his suit pocket. "I told Fisnistle to hold the elevator, but baby girl up there isn't the patient sort."

The giant spider clicked her mandibles as if to underscore his point. Now that they were actually here, though, Bex wasn't worried.

"You brought me in to free a demon, right?" she said as she shook the last of the webbing off her feet and joined him in front of the door. "That won't take long."

"Love the confidence," Felix said as he located the correct key and fit it into the tiny keyhole at the center of the giant vault door. "But I'll warn ya, this guy's a weird one. So far as I can tell, his old warlock never let him out of his bindings for any reason, not even to fight. Kinda defeats the purpose of buying a war demon, in my opinion, but what do I know about the divine thinking of Heaven's chosen?"

His warlock likely couldn't overpower him, Drox whispered in Bex's mind. *Just like you, humans need to be stronger than the demon they're naming if they want their commands to stick. As one of Ishtar's queens, you are naturally superior, but a warlock must fake his authority with quintessence. If this truly is the same Havok we fought in Paradise, then he's well over five thousand years old. You don't last that long without real power behind you.* The sword's voice grew smug. *I bet his old master couldn't survive the amount of quintessence necessary to make him kneel.*

"Good," Bex said quietly as Felix finished unlocking the vault door. "Any demon who refuses to submit to Gilgamesh's lackeys is one we want on our side."

Don't get overconfident, Drox cautioned. *You're much stronger than you used to be, but you already freed a hundred demons from Limbo today. Even drawing on your people's anger to lessen the burden, speaking that many names takes a toll, and there's no extra wrath to burn down here if you need a boost.*

That was true. As horrifying as Limbo could be, at least the rage of her trapped people gave Bex's bonfire an endless supply of fuel. The hardest part was not taking too much power and burning out of control, but all that free fire also meant she wasn't feeling nearly as drained as she should've been. She was physically tired because it was late and she'd been working since dawn, but Bex was sure she was good to handle one demon. That said, Drox didn't deliver warnings for no reason, so she went ahead and started heating up, sending wisps of smoke curling under the collar of her leather jacket as Felix finally got the vault open.

"There we go," he said, his voice straining with effort as he pushed the giant metal door inward. "I'm sure I don't have to warn you to keep your hands to yourself. Goblin vaults are as greedy as their masters, and this one hasn't eaten in a while."

He flashed Bex a sharp-toothed smile, but she wasn't intimidated. She was burning with righteous fury that this goblin had locked one of her people in his bank vault like an object. Even if Havok had been her enemy once, he was still a demon. Since she was the only free queen left, that made him Bex's responsibility. One she was happy to uphold as she followed Felix through the door into a large, gloomy stone room with a bank of security monitors glowing in the middle.

"This is where I keep my trouble cases," the prince explained as he walked toward the team of bowing goblins who'd been watching the monitors. "As you know from personal experience, individuals are my treasure of preference, which means I get a lot of cageable sorts. I can usually bring them around—the right motivation can turn anyone into a productive asset—but this guy..." Felix shook his head. "Let's just say I'm happy to let you take him off my hands. He's the worst white elephant I've ever gotten stuck with, which is going to be a really funny joke when you see him."

"Where is he?" Bex asked, looking around the vault, which didn't seem to have anything in it other than the monitoring station and a bunch of smaller metal doors set into the walls like plugs.

"Last cell on the left," Felix said, taking a seat in the office chair one of his goblins had just rolled over. "I'll do this by remote, if you don't mind. Wouldn't want to interfere with your royal business."

Didn't want to risk his green skin, more like. But this was what Bex had come here to do, so she motioned for Nemini to follow her across the barren stone to the door the goblin had indicated.

The metal slab was set flush into the vault's black wall. The only opening was a finger-sized hole near the bottom for air. There was no handle or knob that Bex could see, but the door unlocked with a *clunk* when she touched it. This was followed by another *clunk* behind her, and Bex looked over her shoulder to see that Felix was raising a steel security cage out of the floor to protect himself and his people. That made her a little nervous, but she knew better than to show it. She kept her face hard and confident as she placed her hand on the metal door's smooth surface and gave it a push, swinging the slab open to reveal the cell inside.

Given how close the doors were to each other, she'd expected a cubby just big enough to fit a prison bunk. As with everything involving goblin magic, though, what you saw wasn't what you got. This usually meant getting cheated, but for once Bex actually got more than she'd bargained for because the inside of the cell was enormous. There were no lights or windows, but her excellent night vision was still able to make out a stone room large enough to serve as a hangar for a midsized airplane. She was wondering what sort of monsters Felix normally traded in that he needed a cell this big when she caught sight of the demon chained to the vault's far wall.

The only reason Bex recognized him was because of his four arms. Every war demon she'd ever met had been bronze-skinned and dark-haired. They never wore armor because their metal skin *was* their armor, but for some reason, this one was covered from horns to feet in bone-white plates. Even his face was covered in a white mask carved to look like humanity's worst caricature of a demon. Bex had no idea how he saw anything through those tiny eye slits, but at least she understood Felix's white-elephant joke now. The war demon looked more like a carved-bone idol than a living creature. If one of his plated fingers hadn't been slowly tapping against the others like he was keeping time, Bex wouldn't have believed he was alive at all.

"Is that him?" she whispered.

I think so, Drox whispered back. *He feels like the Havok we faced in the past.*

That was hardly a definitive answer.

"How do you not know?" she demanded. "You always know every demon."

Normally, yes, but I can't see this one's true name.

Bex wrinkled her nose. "Don't you know it from when we fought him before?"

No, Drox said, frustrated. *The Queen of War hid her champions' names when you battled to keep you from wresting control of her demons. You obscured your own troops for the same reason. I thought I'd finally be able to see it now that you're the only queen left, but his truth is still hidden from my sight.*

"Is that going to be a problem?"

122

Only one way to find out, Drox said, transforming into a sword.

Bex sent him back into his ring at once. Former enemy or not, Bex didn't want to start this conversation with weapons drawn. Five thousand years was a long time, and they had a shared enemy now. Even a war demon wouldn't be prickly enough to keep infighting while Gilgamesh was stomping his boot on their entire race. All the other war demons she'd freed had come around, so Bex clenched her fist around Drox's buzzing ring and stepped forward.

"Havok."

The chained demon raised his head, and Bex went still. From the doorway, his armor had just looked like armor. Excessively full-coverage armor, but still nothing too strange for a former champion of the Queen of War. Now that she was closer, though, Bex could see that the bone-white plates weren't just colored that way. They *were* bone, huge external protrusions that moved with him like the scales on an armadillo.

The sight almost made Bex step back. She'd heard war demons got more armored as they got older, but this was insane. It looked like his horns—which usually only covered the top of a war demon's head—had grown down to engulf his entire body. She was wondering how heavy all that bone must be when the chained demon began to speak.

"Well, well, well," he said in a voice so deep, Bex felt the rumble inside her chest. "Look who's still kicking around. Haven't seen you in a while, Bonfire. Here for a rematch?"

123

"The opposite, actually," Bex replied, fisting her hand tighter around Drox to keep him from answering the challenge. "I've come to set you free."

That announcement was usually met with joy, or at least surprise, but while Bex couldn't see anything through Havok's carved mask, his voice sounded deeply unimpressed.

"And what makes you think I'd accept?"

"Because you're chained to a wall," Bex snapped, pointing at the giant iron ship chains that crisscrossed his armored body like stitches. "In my experience, people in prisons generally want to get out."

"Only if there's somewhere better to flee to," the demon replied with a shrug, leaning his armored plates against the stone like he was just resting there and not locked in place. "But why would I want to go with you? You're the loser queen. Even I know you've spent the last five thousand years getting killed over and over. Why would I want to escape into that?"

"Because that's not how it is anymore," Bex said with a proud lift of her chin. "It's true I've been fighting and dying for our people for a long time, but look at this."

She held out her hand and called her flames, filling the dark prison with blazing light.

"I've got my fire back," she said as she pushed the flames higher. "By the grace of Ishtar and the help of a witch, everything I lost has been restored, and I've been using that power to turn the war in our favor. I've already taken over one of the Anchors that enables the Eternal King's power, and we're working on conquering more. Once we rip out the underpinnings,

Gilgamesh's whole bloated empire will fall." Her fire leaped higher as her voice rose. "I will tear down his false Heaven, break open the Hells, bring back the gods, and return all of Ishtar's children to their rightful Paradise!"

Bex's flames were flaring up to the cell's high ceiling by the time she finished. She didn't know if Havok could see the light through his bone mask, but there was no way he could miss the heat, and that was enough to make her grin. She'd yet to meet a demon who wasn't awed by her bonfire. She was about to ask again if Havok would like her to set him free when the demon's armored shoulders began to shake. Her first thought was that she'd gone too hard and driven him to tears, but then he raised his carved face, and Bex realized Havok was *laughing*.

"You think that's all it takes?" he cackled, looking straight at her with his mask's carved eyes. "A little fire and a single victory? *That's* all you think you need to bring down the conqueror of the gods?"

"It's more than anyone else has done," Bex snapped, but the idiot was still laughing at her, making her fire burn hotter with rage. "What do you know, old man? You've been locked up in warlock chains since the fall of Paradise. You don't know anything about the war we're fighting now!"

Havok's laughter cut off like a dropped knife. "I know you can't win," he said in a scornful voice. "I realize strategy has never been a wrath demon strength, but even you must see that nothing has actually changed. What does it matter if you got your flames back? You had your fire the first time Gilgamesh invaded. You were also two feet taller, with the full support of Ishtar, and you *still* got swatted out of the sky like a bug. Do you really think things are going to be different now?"

"Yes," Bex growled.

The war demon stiffened against his wall.

"Delusion is a dangerous trait in a queen," he warned. "You can't just will a weaker army to victory over a stronger. Defeating an opponent as entrenched as Gilgamesh will require brilliant tactics, superior numbers, and overwhelming strength of arms, but I don't even need to leave this cell to know that you have none of those. All you've got is the same idiot bravado that got you killed the first time, and you want me to go along? To throw myself in with your bad lot just because I'm chained to a wall?"

"I can leave you there if you want," Bex snarled, stomping forward until she was burning right in front of him. "You think I don't know how strong the enemy is? I've died fighting Gilgamesh a hundred and ninety-eight times. I know better than anyone how high Heaven's walls are, but the only other option is to leave our people in slavery forever!"

"And you think that makes you a good queen?" Havok demanded, leaning forward until his chains were groaning. "You brag about your tenacity like it has accomplished something, but all that dying you're so proud of hasn't changed a Hells-damned thing. All of Ishtar's creations are still slaves, and Gilgamesh still rules every inch of the Heavens, Hells, and Earth. Even if I took your offered freedom, you couldn't help me keep it. You might've captured an Anchor, but the moment Gilgamesh decides he wants it back, the fire of Heaven will fall from the sky, and your new rebellion will be just as dead as all your previous ones."

He leaned back against the wall with a shrug. "Face it, Coward Queen, you're a lost cause. If you couldn't beat the Eternal King back when you were truly Ishtar's Sword, there's no possible way you can do it now. I've no interest in wasting my time with losers, so I respectfully decline your offer of a jailbreak."

He settled against his chains as if that was the end of it, but Bex wasn't close to finished.

"I'm not leaving you here," she snapped. "Believe in me or don't, I don't care, but you're so expensive to keep around that Felix is planning to throw you down a pit. As the only queen left, it's my responsibility to safeguard all of Ishtar's children, which, unfortunately, includes you. I'm not failing my sacred duty for the sake of one rude war demon, so you're just going to have to put up with me saving your life."

"Oh, I am, am I?" Havok replied in a dangerous voice. "And what if I don't want to be your responsibility? What will you do then, Wrath of Ishtar? Force me?"

"Why do war demons have to make everything into a fight?" Bex asked in an exasperated voice. "I get it: you don't like me. You've made that very clear, but we're still on the same side."

"I never put myself on your side," the war demon reminded her, rising back to his full height, "and I've had enough of your arrogance. You want me to acknowledge you as queen? Prove your worth. Face me in combat. If you win, I'll bow to your strength and join your cause, but if *I* win, I'll send you back to Ishtar and save all the fools who follow you the pain of yet another Coward Queen defeat."

Don't do it, Drox warned before Bex could say a word. *Fighting amongst ourselves is pointless, and Havok is no idle threat. I've been searching since we came in, but I still can't find his name. Either he's become strong enough to hide it on his own, or something else is interfering. Either way, it's not worth the risk. Just leave him to his fate.*

"No," Bex snarled. "You're the one who's always telling me to be a queen. Well, a queen of Ishtar protects her demons, which is why I'm going to thrash this idiot until he agrees to let me save his worthless life."

That is not wise.

Bex didn't care. She didn't even want Havok on her side anymore, but getting him out of here was Felix's price for saving all the other demons he'd bought on fire sale, and she *did* care about them. Mostly, though, Bex was tired of being told she couldn't do it. She'd been called a failure so many times that she'd started to believe it. She'd honestly started to think that a martyr's death was all she could give to her people, but Adrian had changed that. He'd brought her back to life, given her another chance, and Bex would be damned to all the Hells combined before she let this bone-faced bastard tell her they couldn't win.

That sort of logic is why you and War were forever fighting, Drox scolded as Bex stripped off her leather jacket and tossed it to Nemini, who was still waiting by the door. *Your sister's demons always knew how to get under your skin, and you* always *let them.*

"Least I still have skin," Bex grumbled, glaring pointedly at Havok's plate-covered body as she rolled her own bare shoulders under her tank top. "Get out here, and let's do this."

Drox dutifully transformed from a ring to a sword, but when Bex raised him to cut Havok's restraints so they could have a proper duel, the war demon stepped forward on his own.

He lifted his four arms as he went, popping the giant chains that Bex only now realized had never actually held him. He ripped his cloven feet out of the iron manacles on the floor next, casually kicking the metal away as he stepped forward to take position in front of Bex.

"When you're ready, Executioner of the Gods."

Bex had never heard that nickname before, but she was too angry to think about it. Her wrath was burning hot and fierce, honing her bonfire to a cutting torch as she lunged forward to slide Drox's narrow black blade between the joints of the war demon's enormous armor.

She aimed her first strike at his knee, her favorite target when fighting war demons. A good slice there would drop the armored bastard on his back and give Bex her choice of openings, but just as she was about to drive Drox's point into the sweet spot, the war demon vanished.

Bex blinked in surprise. There'd been no warning, no telegraphed movement. He'd simply stepped away faster than her eyes could track, leaving her stabbing at nothing. He stepped back in again just as quickly, smashing her now overextended sword to the ground with his bottom right fist while the top one flew up to land in the hollow of her jaw. There was a flash of crunching pain, and then Bex was on her back across the room with no idea how she'd gotten there.

Rebexa!

Bex sat up with a wince, rubbing the shattered jaw her regeneration was still putting back together. What the Hells was that? The punch had come out of nowhere, which should've been impossible. War demons' greatest weakness—some would say their *only* weakness—was that their armor made them slow. All the ones she'd fought before had moved like snails, but Havok seemed as fast as she was.

He's faster, Drox warned, his disembodied voice closer to panic than Bex had ever heard it. *Behind you.*

Bex rolled out of the way just in time to save her skull as both of Havok's upper fists flew through the space where she'd just been. She hadn't even heard him coming, but he was suddenly everywhere, and while he had no weapon, he didn't need one. His armored fists were the size of cannonballs, and they were flying at her like shots, forcing Bex to leap out of his reach as he drove her backward.

You can't let him control the fight, Drox said as they retreated across the cavernous cell. *We have to slow him down. Feint left. We'll try his other knee.*

Bex had a better idea. Havok's legs were a fortress of overlapping armored plates and his footwork was immaculate. A very hard target, in other

130

words, but fighting unarmed meant he needed his fists for both attacking and defending. He was already coming at her with all four, so Bex waited until he unleashed another barrage before dropping low and stabbing up for a precision strike at the inside of Havok's forearm.

The move should have skewered his arm. Drox wasn't meant to be a stabbing weapon, but fifty centuries of constant fighting had worn his once-thick black blade down to a spike, and Bex had a good angle with plenty of force from the ground. Even Havok's overgrown armor should've been no match for the two of them, but when Drox's point hit the war demon's bone plates, Bex's stab stopped cold.

The shock was enough to leave her frozen. Even back when she'd been a pile of ash, her sword had never failed to cut. She'd stabbed Drox through steel girders and golden princes without a whisper of resistance. He should have gone through Havok like a spear through a fish, but his black tip hadn't even scratched the war demon's armor. Bex was still pushing in a desperate effort to get *something* out of the first hit she'd managed to land when Havok's lower left fist shot down to wrap around her right arm.

Bex dropped her sword with a scream. The demon's armored hand was so huge, he was able to grab all the way from the base of her wrist to the bend of her elbow. Her fire flared in response, scorching his white plating, but Havok didn't even seem to notice. He just squeezed harder, crushing Bex's sword arm until she felt her bones crumble inside her muscles.

It was the worst pain she'd ever felt, or at least the worst she could remember. But while Bex was writhing in Havok's grip, her dropped sword had already jumped back into her left hand.

Strike now! Drox yelled as his hilt slammed into her palm. *Before he rips your arm off!*

Bex normally hated when Drox gave her obvious advice, but with the pain of her pulverized bones making a haze in her mind, she'd never been more grateful for his guidance. She latched onto the order like a lifeline, abandoning the sinking ship that was her right arm to throw all her strength into her left.

If Havok had been a cocky prince, he would have been too busy enjoying her suffering to notice the shift, but he was a war demon. A soldier through and through, which meant he wasn't even looking at the arm he'd destroyed. That threat was neutralized, so he'd already moved on to the next, catching Bex's counter before she could swing Drox past her shoulder.

She kept pushing the attack anyway. Havok had caught her sword with his hand, which meant Drox's cutting edge was pressed against his palm. The giant war demon was just as armored there as he was everywhere else, but unlike forearms, palms had to bend. Flexible armor was usually easier to cut than rigid, but no matter how hard she pushed, Drox's blade couldn't get through.

Now, Bex started to panic. She only remembered the tiniest fraction of their five-thousand-plus years together, but she was certain she'd never encountered anything that Drox couldn't cut. Even when she was

132

grinding him against what should've been Havok's softest part, though, pushing her sword through the war demon felt like trying to push a stick through a metal pole. Bex had no idea what Havok had done to make his armor so strong, but they clearly weren't getting through this way, so she pulled Drox back into his ring, leaving the huge demon grabbing at nothing.

That was finally enough to throw Havok off his guard. Bex couldn't take advantage of the lapse, though, because he was still crushing her right arm. That would've been a serious problem if she was still the burned-out queen she used to be, but Havok wasn't the only ancient demon in this fight. If he wanted to keep holding on to the Bonfire of Wrath, Bex was going to make him pay for it.

With that, she threw all of her anger and frustration into her fire. The flames rushed over her like a purifying tide, sweeping away her pain and fear until there was only righteous fury. Grab her, would he? Call *her* weak? Bex would show him. She didn't even need Drox to beat this fool. He'd gotten too close already, so she stepped closer still, using his hold on her broken arm to lever herself right up against Havok's armored chest as her flames turned into an inferno.

It was the hottest fire she'd ever managed on her own. Not quite as intense as the heights she'd reached when she'd drawn off her demons to melt the Anchor chain, but Bex's fury was still enough to engulf them both in the white-hot flames she'd used to boil the prince during the Blackwood battle.

That was almost certainly going too far, but she was just so *angry*. Angry at Havok for being a stubborn, ungrateful ass. Angry at herself for messing up and getting hurt. Mostly, though, Bex was angry that this—*this*—was what she'd missed her date with Adrian for. They could've been cozied up in front of his fireplace right now, but *no*. She was here, dealing with this *bullshit*, because a Hells-damned war demon was too prideful to take freedom when it was handed to him on a platter.

That last thought fanned her flames hot enough to crack the stone under their feet. As satisfying as it would've been to turn Havok to ash, though, Bex had never killed a fellow demon, and she didn't intend to start now. She wasn't above scorching him within an inch of his life, however, so she let her fire rage. But when she looked to see if the war demon had had enough, Havok's demonic mask was grinning down at her through the flames.

"You think this is impressive?" he taunted over the roar of her fire. "Arrogant girl, I am the Dog of War! No pain or suffering can halt my march. The eons have only made me stronger, but you haven't changed a bit. Five thousand years of dying, and you're still just an angry child playing with fire. No wonder Ishtar named you her champion. You're just as spoiled as she was."

"Don't you dare slander my mother!" Bex snarled as her flames shot to the ceiling. "Ishtar was our creator and protector! Even after Gilgamesh murdered her, she used what little power she had left to send me back so I could help her people. She's the only reason our hope still exists! You don't deserve to speak her name, you traitorous—"

Her tirade cut off with a gasp as Havok released her broken arm to slam all four of his fists into her stomach. Just like before, the punches sent her flying, except this time, Havok followed. He was on her before she hit the ground, pinning her down so she couldn't move. Bex responded by dumping her fire into him, burning so hot that even her skin started to blister, but it didn't do any good. Whatever his stupid armor was made of, her fire couldn't get through it any more than Drox could. Havok didn't even seem to feel the heat as he settled his crushing weight on top of her stomach and began methodically pummeling her to death.

It would absolutely be her death, too. She hadn't even considered the possibility when she'd accepted his challenge, but unlike the war demon, Bex's body *wasn't* armored. Her regeneration had kept up with the damage so far, but between the scorching fire and the constant healing, her powers were rapidly reaching their limit.

She had to get out of Havok's hold before he sent her to a place she couldn't come back from, but the stupid old demon was impossibly strong, and she didn't have any leverage down here on the floor. If she didn't break out in the next few seconds, though, it was going to be a moot point, so Bex played the only card she had left, focusing all her raging fire into the space between them.

It didn't burn him. *Nothing* burned this bastard, but that wasn't her goal this time. Bex was focused on the pocket of air between their bodies, superheating the gas until even Havok's weight wasn't enough to hold back its expansion.

The resulting explosion threw them both across the room. Bex landed hard enough to crater the stone. Her flames guttered from the shock, but it still hurt less than Havok's endless punching, and Bex was so mad right now that nothing could've put her out.

"You... selfish... *asshole*," she gasped, coughing mouthfuls of boiling black blood onto the broken floor as her regeneration raced to repair her crushed lungs. "You're this strong, and you still refuse to help us? You could've been eating Gilgamesh's princes for breakfast, but I've never even heard of you! What've you been doing all this time? Sitting around in prison, feeling sorry for yourself?"

"It's none of your business what I did," Havok replied as he stepped casually out of his own crater. "But I promise I spent my years better than you spent yours. At least I never led the people who worshiped me to pointless deaths because I was too stubborn to admit there was a fight I couldn't win." He tilted his armored head. "Are you sure you're not actually the dead Queen of Pride come back to life?"

Bex was spitting the blood out of her mouth to insult him back when Havok charged her.

Now that she was no longer constantly getting caught by surprise, Bex could see that the war demon wasn't actually as fast as she'd originally assumed. He was simply very efficient, sprinting across the cell without a single newton of wasted force. His movements were so perfect they were almost mesmerizing, but Bex had his number now. Her bonfire had already flared back with a roar, lighting up the prison like the sun to show her exactly how and where he'd hit.

She'd already learned she couldn't block him, so Bex played it smart, pretending to brace until the very last second. When Havok's gigantic body was hanging over her like an anvil, she shifted her fire to blast herself to the right, leaving him charging straight into the cratered wall she'd just pushed out of.

Bex grinned as she flew out of the way. Havok might be the most technically-skilled opponent she'd ever faced, but even he couldn't fight momentum, and war demons were *heavy*. There was no way he could stop himself before he slammed face-first into the wall, by which point Bex would already be behind him. She wasn't sure what she'd do when she got there, since this fool seemed to be one hundred percent armor, but there had to be something. No one was strong everywhere. She just had to keep pushing until she found his weak point, and then she'd win.

That felt like a solid plan, but before Bex could fire the blast of flame that would reverse her flight and shoot her into Havok's blind spot, something grabbed her foot. The sudden stop came hard enough to snap her neck. When Bex looked back to see what had snagged her, her burning eyes flew wide.

She hadn't been wrong earlier. Havok *had* hit the wall; he'd just been ready for it. The two arms she'd thought were flying out to punch her had actually been moving up to catch himself against the stone, turning his crash into a controlled landing while his other two arms shot out to catch her. She'd still almost made it, but almost didn't save you when the enemy was this strong. Havok had only three fingers locked around the toe of her combat boot, but that still gave him enough leverage to slam her body to the ground.

Once again, Bex hit the stone hard enough to leave a crater. This time, though, Havok didn't let her crawl out of it. He just whipped her body back up and slammed her into the floor again, crashing her head against the stone until her vision went dark.

If she'd been her old self, that would've been the end, but Bex wasn't a burned-out husk anymore. The bonfire Adrian's magic had rebuilt inside her was too strong to be scattered by a few bone-crunching hits. It burned through her like phosphorus, and for the first time since the beginning, Bex let it go, incinerating her clothes below the knee, including the boot Havok was using as his handle.

The black leather turned to ash in an instant, allowing Bex to slide her foot out of the war demon's fist. She pushed down with her free leg at the same time, kicking herself up and around to stab her smoking sword into the demon's arm.

Just like before, Drox's point couldn't get through, but that wasn't Bex's goal this time. She was sliding Drox along the demon's armored plates, searching for weakness. For several terrifying seconds, nothing happened, but then Drox's worn blade slipped between the joints of the bone plates that covered the demon's elbow and punched into Havok's arm like an awl.

Bex roared in triumph when she felt her sword go in. It was the first real hit she'd landed since the fight began. But when she started moving her blade back and forth to cut the tendons beneath the demon's hardened exterior, Havok yanked his arm back. Since her sword was still buried inside, Bex got jerked off her feet as well, sending her flying into the fists of the three other arms she hadn't injured.

The punches weren't as strong as usual since he'd pulled her into his fists rather than swinging at her, but they still hurt. The first landed square in Bex's nose. The second cracked her collarbone, while the third landed in her stomach. By the time she pulled Drox back into his ring so they could escape, black blood was pouring down Bex's face. She was struggling to see when a fourth punch landed on her left ear, ringing her head like a bell.

The fight became a blur after that. Since she was the one with the sword, Bex should've had the advantage on reach for once, but the skill and efficiency she'd noticed during Havok's charge were out in full effect now. No matter which way she dodged, Havok's fists were already there to batter her back into place. It took every bit of her attention just to keep him from landing another bone-breaking hit, which was why Bex didn't notice the war demon was driving her into a corner until her shoulders hit the stone.

Her fire was guttering by this point. She was still furious at the whole situation, but her wrath was rapidly being smothered by fear. She'd thrown everything she had at Havok, and it hadn't even slowed him down. Now he had her pinned against two walls with nowhere to run and no room to dodge his horrifically destructive punches. Even the arm she'd managed to skewer was back in action, forcing her to go completely on the defensive as Havok pummeled her.

You have to break out, Drox said as she fended off a double punch that came from above and below at the same time. *If you let him keep you trapped like this, he will kill you.*

If you've got suggestions, I'm open, Bex thought back, swinging Drox so fast that his blade was a black blur in front of her.

She'd already tried kicking out Havok's knees, but she didn't have boots anymore now that she'd burned them off, and hitting the armored demon with her bare feet hurt her far more than it did him. She didn't have enough fire left to cook him, though she suspected it wouldn't have worked even if she did. Bex didn't know if it was his armor or his age or what, but Havok seemed impervious to everything. He didn't burn, couldn't be cut, he didn't even seem tired. His stance was just as steady now as it'd been at the fight's start. Bex, on the other hand, was panting like a forge bellows.

Since fire was useless, Bex was tempted to snuff her flames and just go at him with her sword. But while extinguishing herself would conserve energy, dying more slowly was still dying. What she really needed was a way out of this corner. Bex was still trying to come up with the miracle that could accomplish that when one of Havok's full-strength punches finally got through.

She'd just lowered her sword to fend off a strike to her throat when both of his top fists suddenly crashed into her shoulders. She managed to spoil the left punch by tilting sideways, but the right one landed straight on the joint, dislocating her sword arm with a sickening *pop*.

The combination of force and pain sent her to the floor. It wasn't a stone-cratering crash like the others, but this fall was a lot scarier because Bex wasn't sure how she was getting back up this time. Havok was already on top of her, pinning her to the ground yet again with his lower pair of arms while the upper ones wrapped their hands around her throat.

She'd dropped Drox when her shoulder snapped, but though her loyal sword had jumped right back into her hand, Bex couldn't get enough leverage to swing him. She couldn't do *anything* except lie there and struggle as Havok's armored fingers dug harder and harder into her windpipe. She was wondering whether he intended to choke her out or just keep squeezing until her head popped off when the huge demon suddenly went still.

Bex sucked in a breath the second he stopped squeezing. His hands were still locked around her throat, but she could get air if she wiggled. Her fire had gone out completely at some point during the tussle, and her regeneration was lagging dangerously behind, but though Havok was still on top of her, he didn't seem interested in hitting her again. He was just sitting there, staring into the distance like someone had flipped his off switch, and standing behind him with her bare hand pressed against the demon's armored shoulder was Nemini.

"Stop."

Bex felt the giant demon shiver at the quiet word, and then Havok turned his huge head as if he wasn't sure where the voice was coming from.

"What are you?"

"What remains," Nemini replied, pressing her fingers harder into his armor.

Bex went still on the ground, waiting for Havok to keel over from the shock of Nemini's emptiness like all her victims did. But though the void demon had been in contact with him for several seconds at this point, Havok didn't go down. He did, however, stand up, leaving Bex coughing on the floor as he released his choke hold and stepped back.

"I wasn't going to kill her," he said calmly as Nemini moved to Bex's side. "I merely intended to convey a lesson, and since pain has long been the only teacher the Queen of Wrath will listen to, I judged this the best way."

His expressionless white mask turned back to Bex. "Give up," he told her. "It doesn't matter how hard you try or how much you hope. You cannot win this war. You couldn't do it five thousand years ago, and you certainly can't do it now."

"You don't know that," Bex wheezed as Nemini helped her off the bloody ground.

"I absolutely know it," Havok said with a glare she could feel through his mask. "I'm not even a queen. If you can't beat me, you have no chance against Gilgamesh, which is the only fight that matters. Princes can be reborn and armies rebuilt, but so long as the Eternal King sits on his throne, Heaven will never fall. You're not strong enough to rip him off it, which means your rebellion is doomed."

He turned and walked back to his chains on the wall. "That is the lesson I wished to teach. Take it along with the life I have so graciously spared and leave me be."

He started putting his manacles back on after that, bending the warped metal around his wrists and ankles like clay. He didn't glance in Bex's direction again, but she pushed away from Nemini and staggered over anyway, her bare feet leaving bloody footprints in the ash that covered the prison floor as she walked across the cell to kneel at Havok's feet.

The giant war demon froze when her knees hit the ground. "What are you doing?"

What are you doing? Drox demanded at the same time.

"What I have to," Bex whispered as she stared up at Havok.

"You're right," she said, forcing herself to speak the truth even though it burned like bile in her throat. "I can't win this war alone, but what you don't know yet is I don't have to. My rebellion has made an alliance with a witch of the Blackwood to bring back our dead gods."

"What difference do you think that will make?" Havok demanded. "The gods were alive the first time, and Gilgamesh still won."

"Through treachery," Bex insisted, fisting her bloody hands on the ground. "But a war demon like yourself should know that a surprise attack only works once. Gilgamesh's true nature is known by all now, and when Holy Ishtar, Wise Anu, and Clever Enki are returned to us, we will rise up like never before to take back what he stole."

Havok sighed inside the shell of his armor. "If that's what you think, then you have learned nothing."

"That's not true," Bex said. "I've learned that even if the gods return, I'm not strong enough to be their sword. You were absolutely right before. I *can't* beat Gilgamesh as I am, which means I'm the weakest link. A weak queen has no right to ask others to follow her, and so I'm begging you to share your knowledge and make me better."

Rebexa, no! Drox cried in her head. *You can't accept teaching from the Dog of War! He's been our enemy longer than Gilgamesh!*

"Doesn't matter," Bex insisted, keeping her eyes on Havok. "I don't have time for that kind of thinking anymore. I *have* to get good enough to win because this is my very last life."

Don't tell him that! Drox roared, but Bex wasn't paying attention because for the first time since she'd walked in, Havok seemed interested.

"You've lost your reincarnations?"

Bex nodded. "They weren't getting me anywhere, so I traded all my futures for one final present at full power. That's how I got my fire back, and it's why I'm kneeling before you now."

She lowered her burning eyes. "I can't lose again. If I fail this time, it's forever, but I've seen with my eyes and felt with my bones how strong you are. I don't know if that's good enough to defeat Gilgamesh, but it's better than where I am now, so if you can bring me up to your level, I'll do whatever you say. I'll bow down and call you master in front of everyone if that's what it takes, but I will not give up until my duty is fulfilled."

By the time she finished, Drox was so furious he was chewing into her finger. Bex was pretty angry herself. She'd always hated being on her knees, but this was more important than her feelings. A fact Havok must've realized, because the next sound Bex heard was his chains hitting the ground.

"I never thought I'd see the day when Ishtar's haughty favorite would swallow her pride," he said, crossing all four arms over his chest as he looked down at her. "The years have changed you, Bonfire. It's too soon to say if it's for the better or the worse, but the fact that you're willing to bend your stiff neck at all shows there might be hope for you yet."

That was the sort of backhanded compliment Bex had come to expect from war demons, so she had no trouble keeping the irritation off her face.

"Then you'll train me?"

Havok held up three armored fingers. "Three days," he said. "I'll give you three days to prove that you're not the same idiot who got smacked out of Paradise. If you improve enough to impress me within that time, I'll join your army as requested. If you don't, I'll kill you and save your people the shame of yet another failed rebellion."

"Challenge accepted," Bex said, ignoring Drox's growl as she got back to her feet and held out her hand. "Thank you for giving me a chance."

Havok's carved mask tilted down toward her offered hand. He stared at it for a solid fifteen seconds, then he turned without a word and marched toward the prison's open door. Bex dropped her hand with a sigh and turned to follow, but she'd barely taken a step before something heavy, soft, and warm landed on her shoulders.

"Your coat," Nemini said quietly as she laid the worn leather bomber jacket over Bex's bloody shoulders. "I thought you'd want it."

"Thank you," Bex whispered, clutching the familiar leather around her. "For saving my jacket and for saving me. He said he intended to stop, but I'm pretty sure I'd be dead right now if not for you."

The void demon shrugged. "Death comes for us all."

That was a typical Nemini response, so Bex didn't read too much into it. She was about to follow Havok to the door when the void demon continued.

"I'm glad yours didn't come tonight, though."

"Me too," Bex said, reaching back to squeeze Nemini's hand. "Me too."

The void demon squeezed her back, sending emptiness flooding through Bex's mind. It felt particularly awful after coming so close to death, but Nemini looked as happy as she got, so Bex bore it for her sake, walking hand in hand with her demon back into the main vault, where Felix was throwing a fit over the damage to his prison cell.

Chapter 6

Adrian woke to the sound of rain on his windows. It wasn't technically Seattle's winter downpour season yet, but fall had still seen its share of cold, rainy mornings. Or afternoons, Adrian realized when he glanced at the clock.

He leaped out of bed with a curse. He'd slept until one. That was unheard-of for him, not to mention incredibly rude since he'd promised Bex they'd get brunch. It wasn't technically too late yet. Seattle was a modern city, which meant there were places here that did brunch all day. But when Adrian grabbed his phone to see just how crazy a brunch he'd need to put together to apologize, there were no messages waiting on his lock screen.

He lowered his phone with a frown. Even when she got super busy, it wasn't like Bex not to text him when they had plans. It could be that she was also sleeping in after her late-night emergency, or maybe she hadn't gotten home yet.

Adrian *really* hoped it was the sleeping-in one. He still didn't know why she'd canceled their date, but any emergency that took all night *and* all morning was a bad one. Whatever it was, he needed to get back to the Anchor as soon as possible. Even if Bex wasn't there, Boston was, and if Adrian forgot to pick up his familiar, he'd never hear the end of it.

That was enough to make him scramble. He was starving after his distracted pantry dinner last night, so he grabbed the entire bag of fancy artisan dinner rolls he'd bought for his canceled dinner date with Bex. Since he'd gotten them the day before yesterday, the little rounds were stone stale. He didn't want to waste the time firing up the woodburning stove to toast them, though, so Adrian made it work with pure jaw strength, gnawing at the rock-hard bread while he put on his clothes. When he was dressed and more or less fed, he went outside to assess the weather, which was still a steady, drenching rain. Great for his forest, terrible for flying.

Bran's raven illusion didn't work in daylight, but cloudy weather usually meant Adrian could get away with a quick zip across the bay, *if* it was dry. Like most things made from wood and dried grass, his broom despised water. No matter how many moisture-repelling charms Adrian promised, there were some weather situations Bran just didn't do. Steady, cold rain was at the top of that list, and the moment Adrian touched his broom's handle, he knew it was going to be a no-go.

As his witch, Adrian technically could have made Bran do it, but he didn't like bullying his broom. He also didn't particularly relish the thought of flying through freezing rain, especially not on a grumpy broom crafted by a famously grudge-holding witch. He wouldn't put it past Bran to "accidentally" drop him in the bay every day for the rest of the month if Adrian forced him to fly in this weather. If his broom was on strike today, though, that meant a six-mile walk to the ferry dock.

The thought made him grimace. Adrian wasn't one to shy away from a little hiking, especially on a lovely island like Bainbridge, but that was pushing it. He also saw no reason to go for a wet slog when there was a better option on the table.

Moving casually so as not to raise suspicion, Adrian lifted Bran off his hook by the fire and stuck him in the pantry. He told his broom this was to keep his bristles safe from the damp, but his real motive was witness removal. Bran wasn't usually a sharer, but Boston could ferret secrets out of a rock, and while Adrian wasn't ashamed of what he was doing, he also didn't want to have to face his familiar's inquisition if he could help it. He'd explain everything to Boston once he understood the process better himself. For now, he went back into his bedroom, shut the door, and drew the curtains so no one could possibly see him digging into his coat pockets for Malik's bag of quintessence.

He judged two coins sufficient for teleporting into the city. Far trickier was picking a landing spot that wouldn't get him kicked into Limbo by a frightened scaly or mistaken for a prince. Fortunately, he already had an excellent candidate in mind: a place guaranteed to have no scale-eyed humans, no demons, *and* where he wouldn't draw suspicion when he suddenly appeared out of nowhere. It was the only choice, really, so Adrian closed his eyes and started working on building a metal image of the stone tunnel with the golden doors at the very bottom of the Anchor.

He'd been extremely reckless with his teleportation home last night, so he made sure to do it properly this time. Just like in Malik's library, he went through every step of visualizing where exactly he wanted to go and how the magic would take him there. The fern analogy didn't work as well without rooms, so Adrian imagined the winds instead, how they blew across the bay in great rivers of air. How they could carry a molecule of oxygen anywhere that wasn't completely sealed off, even down into a tunnel hundreds of feet below the ground.

When he could see the whole journey in his head like a movie, Adrian popped the two coins of quintessence into his mouth and crushed them between his teeth. As always, the deadly magic shot through him like lightning. This time, though, he knew how to direct it, sending the pulse of power into the image he'd crafted like a wish in his mind. Just like on his father's island, the result was instantaneous. By the time the thought crossed his mind that maybe he shouldn't be doing this in the heart of his forest surrounded by all his teleportation-canceling safeguards, he was standing in front of the same impenetrable black wall he'd beaten his head against all yesterday.

The *clang* of the ringing bell was still echoing down the stone tunnel when Adrian pumped his fist in silent triumph. He'd done it! He'd been worried since he didn't know the tunnel a fraction as well as he knew his forest, but the trip had been astonishingly easy. He didn't even feel tired. Maybe he really *was* a quintessence natural!

Twenty-four hours ago, that thought would have made him cringe. Now, though, all Adrian could think about were the possibilities this new magic put on the table. He could go anywhere—*literally* anywhere he could imagine! That was an intoxicating thought for a witch who'd been running into nothing but dead ends for four weeks. But before Adrian could throw himself into any of the marvelous new plans that were filling his head, he had to find his cat.

Thanking the Forest he'd forgotten to turn the lights off last night—an oversight that had just saved him from teleporting into a pitch-black tunnel—Adrian hurried toward the open elevator shaft. Since he was the only one who could come down here without choking on toxic sin iron dust, the elevator itself was still up at the demons' residence floor where he'd left it last night. While Adrian waited impatiently for it to come back down, he pulled out his phone to make double sure he hadn't missed any calls, but his log really was blank. Even Boston hadn't messaged, which was the most alarming part of all, now that Adrian thought about it.

Iggs and Bex had plenty to keep them busy, but his familiar was stranded here until Adrian picked him up, and Boston wasn't normally one to suffer in silence. Even with no phone of his own, he always found a way to let his witch know whenever he felt he was being ignored. There should have been a mountain of missed texts waiting, but the only record Adrian saw was the call from last night when he'd run into his own ward.

Feeling more nervous than ever, Adrian hopped onto the elevator the moment it arrived and began mashing the up button. By the time the broken box made it back to the top, he was ready for anything, but the demons' new city looked the same as it always did. The narrow streets were slightly less crowded, since all the kids were at the new school Lys had set up, but there was no sign of disaster. Some of the demons even waved at him, a nicety Adrian attributed to his witch hat. He was sprinting up the grand stone staircase that led to the Market—and hopefully some answers—when a familiar voice called his name.

"Adrian?"

He looked up to see Boston peering over the railing one story above him.

"Boston?" he called back, shocked. "What are you doing up there?"

"Killing time waiting for you," his familiar replied, galloping down the crowded stairs until he was close enough to leap onto Adrian's shoulder. "Where have you *been*?"

"I overslept," Adrian said, reaching up to pet his cat. "I'm very sorry. I didn't mean to strand you here, but why didn't you call me?"

"Because the line I usually use was busy, and I didn't want to bother Iggs again," Boston replied with a flick of his tail. "I knew you'd show up eventually, so I thought I'd use the opportunity to go exploring. The recursive magic used to create this place is absolutely fascinating. If it wasn't all done with Gilgamesh's filthy sorcery, I'd be almost jealous."

Adrian's face gave a guilty twitch before he hid it. "Do you know where Bex is?"

Now it was Boston's turn to wince. "I do," he said slowly, looking at his paws. "But she's a little... busy at the moment."

"Why are you saying it that way?" Adrian asked suspiciously.

"Because you're not going to like it," his cat replied, hopping off his shoulder. "Follow me."

Easier said than done. Since it was the only way up or down the new Anchor, the central staircase was always packed, and sliding through a crowd of busy demons was a lot less work for a slinky black cat than a full-grown man. Eventually, though, Adrian made it to the level just below the Market. It was the same floor Bex had built her wrath demon village on, but Boston didn't go down that tunnel. He went the other way instead, leading them through a pair of big metal fire doors that Adrian swore hadn't been there yesterday.

"That's because they weren't," Boston explained when he mentioned it, trotting ahead down a long cement tunnel. "This whole area is new as of this morning. I happened to be lurking around the control room when Bex came back and ordered them to put it in."

"But why?" Adrian asked, struggling to keep up with his familiar's quick pace. "And where did she come back *from*?"

"Not sure," Boston confessed. "But she arrived in the wee hours with a whole tour bus full of new demons. I think Goblin Prince Felix rented it to her after she finished some job for him in the mountains, but I don't know the whole story."

Adrian couldn't imagine what sort of job Bex would've been doing for goblins in the mountains, but he was dying to find out. Fortunately, the hallway they were jogging down had only one destination: a pair of press-bar aluminum doors that looked like they'd been lifted straight out of a high school gym. They even had little safety glass windows cross-hatched with black lines, which was how Adrian was able to see the light of Bex's fire from halfway down the hall.

"What in the Great Forest—"

He ran up to the doors, not even bothering to look through the window before he hit the bar and burst into what appeared to be a giant, fireproofed arena. There was a cement ring around the top where people could watch and a metal staircase leading down into the pit, where Bex was standing at full burn, fighting...

Adrian wasn't sure, exactly. The thing moved faster than his eyes could track. Every few seconds, he got a glimpse of what appeared to be a suit of white armor, but it never stopped moving long enough for him to say for certain.

Whatever it was, it was giving Bex the fight of her life. Adrian was used to seeing her dominate, but even with her bonfire flaming all the way to the arena's extremely well-ventilated ceiling, she couldn't seem to get the upper hand. The white armor was simply too fast, darting around her sword strikes to plow its fists—all four of them—into her flame-covered back.

The blow sent her flying, but Bex was still Bex. She righted herself as he watched, flipping over in mid-arc to kick off the arena's blackened wall as she launched herself back at her opponent, whom Adrian was pretty sure was a war demon at this point, given the number of arms.

That wasn't too unusual. Bex had gotten into a lot of dominance scuffles with war demons since she'd become an official rebel queen, but Adrian had never seen her struggle like this against another demon. He'd expected her to flatten her enemy with that flying charge, but the armored demon stepped out of the way as if she was moving in slow motion and kicked her out of the air instead.

The sudden change in momentum sent Bex plowing into the ground, and Adrian's heart missed several beats as her fire flickered. That was all he could stand to watch, but when he ran for the metal stair to go to her, a huge hand caught him by the arm.

"Don't."

Adrian looked over his shoulder in surprise to see Iggs leaning against the wall just inside the doors. The wrath demon's face was set in the angriest scowl Adrian had ever seen, but his back was planted against the concrete like he'd been bolted to it, and from the hold he had on Adrian's elbow, the witch wasn't going anywhere either.

"What's going on?" Adrian demanded, turning back to Bex, who was still hauling herself out of the crater. "Who is that demon, and why are you letting Bex fight him alone?"

"Because it's not my place to 'let' my queen do anything," Iggs said in a furious, frustrated voice. "And because she ordered all of us not to interfere, which means you, too."

It was on the tip of Adrian's tongue to say that Bex didn't give him orders, but undermining her authority was a sorry way to treat someone who meant so much to him. He also didn't want to interfere with whatever plan she had going, because there *had* to be one. Adrian couldn't think of any other reason Bex would be letting herself get beat up by another demon in the heart of her own fortress.

But knowing there had to be a method to this madness didn't stop him from flinching when she reached up to snap her broken shoulder back into place. That *had* to hurt, but Bex didn't make a sound. She just wiped the boiling blood off her flaming temple and got back to it, launching a series of lightning-fast sword strikes that the other demon blocked with his bare hands.

"How long has this been going on?" Adrian whispered over the din of battle.

"Too long," Iggs whispered back, his jaw clenched tight. "Bex came home around three this morning with a charter bus full of demons Felix had apparently been keeping in the mountains. They were all pretty normal warlock rescues, except for that guy."

He nodded sourly at the armored demon, who'd just punched Bex into the wall again.

"Apparently, his name is Havok, and he's some kind of big deal from Paradise way back when. *I* don't remember ever hearing anything about him, but our village was far from the war demons' part of the Riverlands. Anyway, they've been going at it since the command room finished building this place, so about seven hours now."

Adrian winced. Even for a legitimately divine warrior like Bex, seven hours was a long fight, especially since she didn't seem to be winning.

"Do you know *why* they're fighting?"

"Nope," Iggs said as his lips peeled back from his large fangs, "and believe me, I'm pissed about it. Nemini was there when it happened, but you know how she is. I'd have better luck getting information out of a rock. All I know is that Bex and Havok made some kind of deal where she has to beat him."

Adrian looked at the arena's scorched walls and the black-stained floor with new trepidation. "*Can* she beat him?"

"My queen always triumphs," Iggs said stubbornly, but his face was grim. "Until it happens, though, there's nothing we can do. Lys already tried to make Bex take a rest and nearly got their horns bitten off."

"Good thing I don't have horns, then," Adrian said, but before he could take a single step toward the stairs, Iggs grabbed his arm again.

"Please don't," the demon begged. "I know you care. We all care, but I've never seen Bex in this state before. Whatever happened last night put her on the warpath, and she won't thank you for getting in the way."

Adrian realized that, but... "She's killing herself."

"It's not as bad as it looks," Iggs promised as his red eyes flicked back to the pillar of fire darting all over the arena. "And it won't last much longer. Even the Bonfire of Wrath can't keep raging like that forever. She'll burn out eventually, and then maybe she'll be ready to talk. I'll call you when it happens, but in the meantime, you should probably get out of here. Bex's control over her fire has been slipping for hours, and she'd never forgive me if I let you get incinerated by accident."

Given that there were fresh scorch marks on the floor directly under their feet, that seemed like a reasonable concern, but Adrian didn't want to leave. At the very least, he wanted Bex to know that he was here, but her attention was laser-focused on her opponent. The last thing Adrian wanted was for her to take another of those horrible quad-punches because he'd been a distraction. So, after making Iggs swear up and down to call him the moment Bex was free, Adrian quietly slipped back out into the hall.

And immediately began marching down it at full speed.

"Where are you going now?" Boston demanded as he galloped after his witch.

"To do something," Adrian snapped. "I don't know what kind of deal Bex made that involves her getting beaten to a pulp for seven hours straight, but it doesn't take a Witch of the Future to guess it has something to do with the war against Heaven. *Everything* horrible Bex does to herself is because of that stupid war, so I'm going to make sure she gets a chance to *stop*."

"And how do you mean to do that?" his familiar asked, leaping onto Adrian's long coat to clamber up his back. "We've already tried every plan we could think of to get into the Anchors, and they all fell flat. I'm not flying to Portland on a broom again so you can spend another week poking around Pioneer Square for doorways that don't go anywhere."

"We're not going back to Portland," Adrian promised as he plucked his cat off his shoulder. "But I do need to go check on something, and I want you to stay here."

"*What?*" Boston yowled, struggling in Adrian's hands. "No! I'm not letting you abandon me again!"

"I'm not abandoning you," Adrian said as he set his familiar on the ground. "I'm trusting you to be my insurance. Bex is taking a beating in there, but none of her demons know anything about medicine or healing magic. You do. That's why I need you here. Someone has to be close enough to save Bex's life if things go wrong."

"Shouldn't that be your job?" Boston asked sourly. "She's your cross-species romance."

"That's why I'm doing this," Adrian insisted, clenching his fists. "This has to stop, Boston. So long as this war continues, Bex is going to keep putting herself in more and more danger. Every one of those risks is a gamble, which means sooner or later, she's going to lose. I can't let that happen, so I'm going to go see if I can't find a way to break us out of this stalemate, and I need you to stay here in case today is the day Bex fails."

His familiar heaved a long sigh. "All right," he grumbled. "I'll do it for you, but what insanity are you running off to try? We used up all our good ideas ages ago."

"I'll tell you when it works," Adrian promised, turning away to keep running toward the stairs. "Don't let her die!"

Boston yelled something back, but Adrian didn't hear him. He was already charging down the crowded stairwell, taking the ornate steps two at a time until he was back on the lowest level. The demons didn't even look at him this time as he ran back into the busted elevator and hit the button for the tunnel. The moment he was safely alone again at the very bottom of the Anchor, Adrian dug the bag of quintessence out of his pocket and got to work.

His goal this time was a lot trickier than his previous teleportations. Not only would he be traveling farther than he'd ever gone before, his target was a place he hadn't been to in years. He had no recent mental images or roots in his heart to guide him on this journey, but if Adrian had understood his father's explanation correctly, that didn't matter. Sorcery was a magic of understanding, not knowledge. Malik had described it as a wish you granted to yourself, and while Adrian didn't know what it looked like anymore, he understood *exactly* where he wanted to go.

If sorcery worked the way he thought it did, that should've been enough, but Adrian still took a full ten minutes writing a list on his pocket notepad of every detail he could recall. He also took time to remember as much as he could about the black desert he'd seen on the other side of the sin iron wall. Not because he wanted to go there—as eager as Adrian was to get his hands on a chain, he wasn't cocky enough to teleport under the nose of the prince who'd already tried to kill him—but because the desert's existence proved that all of Gilgamesh's Anchors were connected.

As his father had told him last night, that connection was the key. The Anchors of Heaven weren't just random outposts scattered over the globe. They were all weights holding down the same wheel. Since there was only one wheel and hundreds of weights, this meant there had to be a point where all those chains came together, and if they were all together, then he should be able to jump between them like a spider hopping between strands of web.

That made sense to him. Adrian could envision exactly what he wanted the magic to do. So before he could lose his nerve, he grabbed four coins of quintessence from his pouch and shoved them into his mouth.

Just like the three times he'd done this before, the spell happened instantaneously. He felt his body swinging, heard the *clang* of the golden bell ringing through his head. The whole thing was over in less time than it took to sneeze, and when Adrian opened his eyes again, he was standing behind the black-draped vendor tables in the Blackwood's section of the Boston Anchor Market.

It was all he could do not to shout for joy. He'd done it! He'd teleported across the country into a locked Anchor and landed *exactly* where he'd pictured!

Not bad for someone who'd started doing sorcery less than twenty-four hours ago. Adrian's only regret was that his father hadn't been here to see it. No one was here, actually, which meant the other part of his plan had also worked. Cutting the second chain would've been an even bigger fight than the first if the Anchor Markets had been doing business as usual, but the nice part about Gilgamesh locking his doors against the demons was that he'd locked everyone else out as well. There were no nosy sorcerers or warlocks or golden Anchor Guards to worry about, just empty tables and silence. Beautiful, beautiful silence stretching all the way to the giant golden statue with Adrian's target glittering like a thread in its upstretched hand.

He'd never been so happy to see Gilgamesh in his life. As Adrian had noticed the first time he'd gone to the one in Seattle, all Anchor Markets seemed to have the same basic layout. He hadn't been to the one in Boston since he was a kid, but other than being in a bigger grassy field, it looked pretty much the same as the Seattle Market. If Adrian looked down the gap between the tents, he could even see the slave-auction stage with its statue of the Coward Queen running away.

He was tempted to go over and smash it, but he didn't want to push his luck. Even with no one around, this was still enemy territory. He'd taken this risk for a singular purpose, so Adrian stayed on target, creeping between the colorful, empty vendor stalls toward the Market's center.

This was the part of his plan he was least sure about. Getting inside the locked Anchors was just the first hurdle. They still had to actually cut the chain, which wasn't possible without Bex. Adrian would have to think of a way to bring her in here that wouldn't freak her out. For now, though, he focused on doing reconnaissance, sneaking along the grass paths until he was just one line of tents away from the base of Gilgamesh's giant statue.

As he'd noted earlier, Boston's Anchor Market was bigger than Seattle's, but it still had the open ring of grass that separated the lowly mortal vendors from the place where Heaven's chosen denizens arrived. Adrian had never laid eyes on the actual doors when he'd come here with his sisters, but he knew roughly where they were. Even when the Market was empty, though, he didn't feel comfortable just walking up, so he decided to take a look from cover first, slipping into an elegant blue-and-gold tent that normally sold designer jewelry.

Once he was hidden from the clear blue sky, Adrian dropped to his knees on the Anchor's ever-present carpet of perfect green grass and pulled out his gardening knife. He hadn't heard so much as a breeze since he'd arrived, but he still held his breath as he wiggled the sharp tip into the weave of the velvet tent. When he saw the light that meant he'd poked through to the other side, he slid the knife down as quietly as possible, cutting a slit just large enough to peek through. When he put his eye up to the hole, however, what he saw almost made him yelp.

This whole time, he'd been operating on the assumption that the Anchor was empty. He'd crept around because that was what you did when you were behind enemy lines and because he didn't know if Gilgamesh had cameras on this place. Teleporting in had gotten him past the main security, so he wasn't expecting anything too heinous, but it seemed he'd vastly underestimated the Eternal King's paranoia because sitting in front of the doors to the chain bridge that led to Heaven was an enormous golden lion.

It was the size of a school bus: a gigantic predator with a regal mane and a swooping, deadly-looking metal body made from the same butter-yellow gold as the doors beneath the Anchor. There was even cuneiform carved into its haunches, and its roving, watchful eyes were made from the same interlocking golden rings as the princesses'. It was lying in the grass with its head resting on its paws at the moment, but Adrian had no doubt that if he'd just walked up to the doors instead of hiding in a tent, the lion would have pounced on him before he could run. As unwelcome as that complication was, though, the lion was nothing compared to what was shimmering behind it.

The fake sunlight in the Anchor was so bright, he hadn't been able to see it at first. As his eyes adjusted, though, Adrian realized the entire statue of Gilgamesh was surrounded in a barrier. It looked like a haze of golden light, but it covered the monument from tip to base. Possibly even lower, given the way the cuneiform symbols that floated in the glow like dust motes were bobbing in and out of the grass. Adrian couldn't read cuneiform, so he didn't know what all that floating notation did, but it couldn't be anything good. He was still dealing with the crushing disappointment of finding yet another wall when a peal of golden bells shattered the Anchor's silence.

He hit the grass the second he heard it, curling his body into a ball behind the velvet tent flaps just in time as the princes appeared out of thin air on the grassy path directly to his left. There were two of them, one of which Adrian was shocked to discover he recognized. It was the filthy prince from the chain desert, the one who'd tried to kill him, or at least the Yearling-dressed version of him.

Adrian was sure the prince would be even less hesitant to kill the real him. That fear made him hold his breath, crouching in perfect stillness behind the velvet tent flap, which wasn't actually wide enough to hide him at this angle. Fortunately, his witchy attire made up the difference. Between the tent's deep shadows and his insistence on always wearing head-to-toe black, the princes' creepy mirrored eyes slid right over him to lock on the towering, magic-wrapped gold statue at the Market's center.

"There," said the prince Adrian didn't recognize, a stocky man with an ornately-embroidered eyepatch and a grim expression that was already sliding into a look of relief. "What did I tell you? Everything is fine."

"It is *not* fine," the desert prince insisted, his black-stained gauntlets curling into fists. "I know what teleportation sounds like. Someone rang themselves into this Anchor, and it wasn't one of us."

"There is no one but us," the one-eyed prince said, which only seemed to make the dirty prince angrier.

"With respect, *brother*," he replied through clenched teeth, "I've been tending the chains for five hundred years. They're incredibly sensitive to magical disturbance, and the chain for this place was ringing like a gong. Sorcerous movement is the only thing that causes a reaction like that!"

"And *I'm* telling you it's not possible," the one-eyed prince argued. "With the exception of your eternal post, all the Celestial Princes are currently confined to Heaven or the Hells. How could there have been a bell if none of us were around to ring it?"

"Because it wasn't one of us!" the dirty prince cried. "That's why I summoned you! I think we've had a breach."

From the sneer on his haughty face, the one-eyed prince clearly thought that was rubbish, but he didn't keep fighting about it. He clapped his golden gauntlets together instead, filling the air with a smaller ring of authority as he called out, "You there, lion! Has anyone entered the Eternal King's Anchors today?"

Adrian could no longer see the golden lion from his new spot on the ground, but he heard the metal beast rise to its feet. Its voice rumbled through the ground a second later: a cold, deep sound that never could have come from a living creature.

"None but the sacred sons of Heaven."

The one-eyed prince turned back to his brother with a *There, you see?* smirk. The prince from the chain desert glowered in reply, but he didn't push the issue any further. He just grumbled something under his breath and vanished, leaving the Anchor as suddenly as he'd popped into it. When his brother did the same a moment later, Adrian took his chance to bolt, timing his own exit to make sure his teleport bell was hidden inside the prince's peal as he frantically wished himself back to his safe spot in the tunnel beneath the Seattle Anchor.

He collapsed on the stone floor the moment he arrived, gasping in relief. That had been way too close. He was so, so, *soooo* lucky the lion hadn't spotted him, or he would have died just now. But while Adrian was elated to still be alive, the last of his hopes for the chain plan were going up in smoke.

If the prince in the chain desert could hear every time Adrian teleported into an Anchor, that was the end. Even if he could figure out how to teleport Bex directly onto the chain, it still took time to cut through so much sin iron. Add in the lion and the weird golden barrier, and even Adrian's optimism couldn't come up with a way to pull this off. If they couldn't get to the chains to cut them, though, what else was there? All of his plans—even the terrible ones—had revolved around bringing back the gods. They certainly couldn't beat the endless armies of Heaven without divine intervention, but if Gilgamesh already had counters in place for all the possible moves, what was he going to do?

For once, Adrian's too-busy, know-it-all brain didn't have an answer. He didn't even know where to start. Logically, he knew there had to still be a way to win. No defense was perfect, but damned if he could find a clever workaround this time. He couldn't even turn to Boston for help because then he'd have to confess that he'd been dabbling in sorcery. His mother and aunts were out for the same reason. Bex would have understood—she was always ready to do whatever was necessary to win—but she was also the last person Adrian wanted to discuss his failures with.

That canceled out all his usuals, but there was still one person Adrian could bring this problem to who wouldn't judge him. He hadn't wanted to bother him again so soon, but if there was ever a time he needed a father's advice, it was now. He didn't see how Malik could possibly make the situation any worse, so Adrian fished another handful of quintessence out of his pocket and filled his thoughts with the picture of the hidden island across the sea.

The moment the connection was clear in his mind, he shoved the magic into his mouth and vanished again, leaving nothing but an empty tunnel echoing with the peals of golden bells.

Chapter 7

Adrian was *very* glad sorcery functioned on the understanding of a place rather than specific knowledge, because his father's island looked nothing like what he'd pictured.

It was still afternoon in Seattle, but the beach he was standing on was bathed in bright-blue moonlight. There were no lights on the horizon from land or other ships, making him feel like he was far out at sea, though not the Salish or even the northern Pacific. The breeze here was warm and tropical, and the few stars he could see through the glaring moonlight weren't the ones he was used to, which would only be possible if he were in a different hemisphere.

Clearly, Malik had moved his island. Even now that Adrian was popping all over the world himself, realizing that felt a little surreal. Also terrifying, because he'd only taken enough quintessence to power a trip up the Western Seaboard, not across the planet. He had no idea what would happen if the quintessence ran out mid-teleport—if the sorcery would just drop him in the ocean or take the remaining balance out of his soul—but he must have squeaked by this time, because he didn't feel any different. Just confused and slightly lost. He'd intended to teleport to the front door of Malik's mansion, not the beach. He was starting to wonder if he *had* actually messed up and teleported himself to a completely different island when a large shadow padded out of the trees.

Even with the moon shining bright as daylight, it took Adrian several seconds to recognize the stuffed leopard from the floor of Malik's library. The big cat trotted right up and sat down on the sand, looking at him with patient glass eyes that glittered in the moonlight, and Adrian smiled.

"Did Malik send you to find me?"

The leopard bobbed its head, and Adrian let out a relieved sigh. "Thank the Forest," he muttered, glancing over his shoulder at the huge, dark, unknown ocean surrounding them. "Can you take me to where he is?"

The leopard nodded again and started trotting back the way it had come. Adrian followed as close as he dared, sticking to the big cat's pawprints as the leopard led him down a narrow path through the palms. He couldn't even see the house from where he'd landed, so Adrian was expecting a hike, but they barely walked twenty feet before they reached the sandstone wall of Malik's fortress.

It was clearly a different section than Adrian had seen on his first visit. This area was much more overgrown, and there was no grand gate topped with bonfires, just a simple wooden door barely large enough for a wheelbarrow to squeeze through. It looked like the ancient-fortress version of a garden gate, so Adrian wasn't surprised at all when the leopard pawed the door open to reveal a sandy lot full of building materials.

There were piles of rough-cut stone, heaps of scrap metal, and a handsome stack of fresh-hewn timber that still had the paper barcodes from the lumberyard stapled to the ends. Adrian was wondering if Malik got the wood shipped in or if he just teleported everything over when the scalies weren't looking when he realized the leopard was no longer with him.

After a panicked search, he spotted the big cat on the other side of the supply yard, waiting beside what appeared to be a large barn. An extremely *nice* barn with stone walls and a roof made from thatched palm leaves. The building was nestled up against the base of a cliff to shelter it from the weather, which was how Adrian realized they must be on the opposite side of the island from where he'd arrived last night. That cliff was most likely the back of the big hill that the main house was perched on.

Or, at least, that was his assumption. The cliff was too steep for him to see any buildings, but there was a sandstone staircase zigzagging down its face that matched the mansion's style, so Adrian was pretty sure of his location. The stone barn certainly looked like the Malik-version of a backyard shed. It might have been constructed from rustic materials, but the precise way the huge sandstone blocks fit together without a trace of mortar matched everything else he'd seen of his father's dedication to quality craftsmanship. Even the barn door the leopard was patiently waiting beside appeared perfectly fitted when Adrian finally reached it, swinging open silently to reveal the most spectacular workshop he'd ever laid eyes on.

The barn was even bigger than he'd initially realized. It was *much* longer than it was wide, with a towering ceiling lined with warm yellow shop lights and huge fans for ventilation. It was easily big enough to hold a private jet, and yet not an inch of space had been wasted.

The stone floor was covered in workstations for every sort of artisan craft Adrian could imagine. There was a woodworking bench with power and hand tools along with a vacuum system to keep down the sawdust, a smithy with multiple forges and an auto hammer, a taxidermy shop filled with tanks of chemicals and tanning supplies, a pottery wheel and kiln, *two* metalworking stations—a big one with welding torches for ironwork and a smaller one with casting molds, electric grinders, and etching tanks for fine metals—and those were just the ones that Adrian recognized. There were tons of other tools and stations that he had no idea about. There was also a magical crafting area full of paints and cuneiform clay tablets, as well as a drafting board and telescope by a side door for making star charts.

The longer he looked, the more he saw. Between the rows of meticulously labeled storage lockers and the tool racks hanging on the walls, there seemed to be equipment here for every craft humanity had ever invented. The combined effect was so overwhelming, Adrian didn't even notice his host standing in the sculpting area beside a giant block of white stone until the leopard trotted over to him.

"Ah," Malik said, putting down his chisel and hammer to scratch the big cat behind the ears. "Thank you, Najwa. You may return to your stand now."

The taxidermy leopard bowed its head and padded off, not even looking at Adrian when he stepped aside to let it slip past him into the night.

"Welcome back," Malik said, turning his smile on his son. "Forgive me for receiving you in such a state"—he waved down at his plain cotton work clothes and leather apron, both of which were covered in white dust from the block he'd been carving—"but I was not expecting to see you again so soon."

"Please don't apologize," Adrian said, stepping all the way inside so he could close the door behind him. "I'm the one who came early, though I'm glad I did. This place is incredible! Do you actually know how to use all this stuff?"

"I've always enjoyed working with my hands," Malik replied with a shrug. "And a man must keep up with the times or relegate himself to the shadows of obsolescence." He picked up his chisel and hammer again and turned back to the white block in front of him. "If you'd be so kind as to let me finish this last part, I'll be right with you."

"Don't stop on my account," Adrian said, coming over for a better look. "What are you carving?"

"A woman, hopefully," Malik said as he set his chisel carefully against the white block. "But one can't be certain of anything at this early stage. Even the best-laid plans can still find ways to go awry, so I've learned to keep my expectations flexible." He tapped his hammer against the chisel's end with a smile. "Perhaps she will be a pile of rubble."

That seemed overly pessimistic to Adrian, but he had to admit the block didn't look like much at the moment. It didn't even look like stone, now that he was standing next to it. The white surface was smooth and faintly lined, making it look more like a giant hunk of bone than rock.

"What is that?"

"A spinal fragment from an ancient leviathan," Malik replied without missing a tap of his hammer. "You may touch it if you wish."

Adrian did very much wish. He slapped his hands against the giant white block at once, shivering when he felt the magic that still hummed inside.

"How did you find a piece this big?" he asked excitedly. "Leviathan bones are incredibly rare components. I know Bone Witches who'd give up both arms for a chunk like this."

"It was not so difficult," Malik said, his eyes focused on the tip of his chisel. "Leviathans were common before Gilgamesh rose to power. Like all monsters of the ancient world, they were created by the gods to scare humanity into prayer and obedience. And sacrifice." His face grew dark. "I saw many innocents thrown into the sea in my younger days. It was one of the acts that drove Gilgamesh to declare war on the gods. After his victory, he hunted down and killed every remaining leviathan and sank their corpses to the bottom of the ocean so that they would never again terrorize the world."

Malik fell silent, turning his hand to run his scarred knuckles against the ancient bone. For a chilling moment, his face looked like it belonged to a completely different person, and then his smile snapped back as if it had never left.

"I've salvaged many of their skeletons over the years," he continued, giving his chisel one final tap before setting his tools down on the dusty bench beside him. "Their bones have the same beauty and flexibility as ivory, but without the tragedy of killing elephants. Fantastic carving medium, and quite plentiful if you know where to look. But you didn't come over to talk about sculpture. I can see from your face that you've encountered a problem. How can I help?"

"I really appreciate it," Adrian said earnestly as Malik led him to a pair of wooden Adirondack chairs placed in the sand just outside one of the workshop's many side doors, which were kept open for ventilation. "Though, before I start, would you mind telling me where we are?"

"The Indian Ocean, about five hundred miles off the northern coast of Madagascar," Malik replied as he settled into his chair. "I prefer to keep my island in equatorial seas whenever I can. It's better for the plants and better for me. I was born in a warm land and have never adjusted well to the dark and cold of the more extreme latitudes."

The palm forest definitely seemed perkier now that it was no longer being forced to endure a Pacific Northwest autumn, but the thought of moving an entire island to the other side of the world still boggled Adrian's brain.

"How did you do it?" he asked as he sank into his own seat. "Teleporting yourself I get, but an island is the top of a mountain in the ocean. How can you move something that big?"

"Big and small are meaningless descriptors," Malik replied with a dismissive wave. "It takes a bit more quintessence, but transporting the land under your feet is no different than moving the clothes on your body. The key is to keep an open mind."

"Your mind must be turned inside out, then," Adrian said as he dug the toe of his black boot into the sandy—but very stationary-feeling—ground. "Even if you can move mountains, how do you account for the differences in ocean depth between locations? Do you raise and lower the sea floor to keep yourself above water?"

Malik laughed. "Now you're just being ridiculous. Not everything has to be solved with magic, you know. I've traveled the world for thousands of years, so what makes more sense? That I expend enormous amounts of quintessence rearranging the geography of the ocean floor or that I've mapped out all the places with the right depth to keep my home above water?"

Adrian scowled, and his father reached out to pat him on the hand.

"This is what I mean when I say sorcery is a magic of understanding. It is tempting to focus only on the power that forces the impossible to be possible, but even the gods worked within what was already available whenever they could."

The way he said that made Adrian smile. "You sound like my mother."

"Agatha is a wise and practical witch," Malik said. "It was those qualities that drew me to her, even more than her beauty."

"Making the most out of what you have is a core tenet of witchcraft," Adrian agreed, then he frowned. "But sometimes, what you need just isn't available, which is why I've come." He turned around in his chair to look his father in the eyes. "I've hit a problem I don't know how to solve, and I'm hoping you can help."

"I'd be delighted to try," Malik said, turning around in his chair as well so that they were face-to-face. "What is it you need?"

Adrian let out a long breath. He'd known his father would help him because that was how their relationship had started, but it was still a huge relief to ask for assistance and just get a yes, no questions or equivocations or lectures attached. But while he was feeling extraordinarily grateful, now that the moment was actually here, Adrian realized he wasn't sure what to say.

The easiest thing would've been to tell the truth. The night they met, Malik had mentioned choosing Adrian because he was the first one who'd learned the truth about Gilgamesh's chains and still decided to cut one. The Morrigan had also mentioned speaking to him, which was proof positive that Adrian's dad was already in the know. But knowing about a plan wasn't the same as supporting it, and while Malik had kicked this whole thing off by offering to help Adrian get around the Eternal King's defenses, he still clearly agreed with Gilgamesh on several points, including the destruction of the gods.

That seemed to be a common theme among non-demons. Even the Morrigan had questioned whether the gods deserved to be brought back, and it made Adrian nervous about telling his father his real intentions now. If he told Malik he wanted to resurrect Ishtar and his dad objected, he might stop helping. It could also torpedo their whole relationship less than a day after it'd begun.

The second possibility scared Adrian a lot more than the first. A week ago, he would have laughed at the idea of caring what a sorcerer thought, but he *did* care. He cared enormously, and not just because Malik was his father. He was the only person other than Bex and her demons who treated Adrian as an expert. Not an apprentice or a foolish child, but someone capable and respectable who knew what he was talking about. He was desperate not to undermine that good opinion. If he didn't tell his dad, though, then he'd come all the way out here for nothing.

That decided it. All this ego-stroking didn't amount to a hill of dirt if Adrian couldn't actually pull off the job. He'd already tried and failed every option he could think of, and Malik *had* offered to help. He wouldn't have done that if he wasn't at least willing to try, and he already knew whom his son spent his time with, so Adrian decided to trust in his father.

"I can't get to the rest of the chains," he said. "They're the strings that hold up Gilgamesh's entire empire. I know Bex can cut them if I can just get her to one, but every path I try is blocked."

He held his breath as he finished, but his father just nodded. "I thought that might be your problem."

Adrian blinked in surprise. "You're not mad?"

"Of course not," Malik said with a smile. "In case I wasn't clear last night, I invited you here because of your audacity. I myself would never dream of doing what you're attempting, but that's why I'm an old man collecting trinkets on an island while you're out there fighting to change the world. That's why I'm so eager to help you. Not because you're my son, but because something *has* to change, and unlike me with my staid old comforts, you're still desperate enough to do it."

Adrian chuckled. "That's hardly a ringing endorsement."

"Really?" his father said, lifting his eyebrows. "I thought it was great praise. Change has always come from the young and hungry. That's why I taught you teleportation first. I wanted to throw you straight at the enemy and see what you'd knock loose. Seeing as you're back here already, though, I assume it didn't work."

"Oh no, it worked amazingly," Adrian insisted. "I was able to teleport straight into the Boston Anchor. I thought Gilgamesh wouldn't bother defending the inside of a locked door, but he was ready for me. Not only was there a giant golden lion sitting directly in front of the door to Heaven, Gilgamesh's entire statue was wrapped in a glowing ward that I can only presume is a hard stop against anyone who doesn't have the king's personal seal of approval."

"Those are problems indeed," his father said, drumming his fingers thoughtfully on the wooden arm of his chair.

"I haven't even gotten to the worst part yet," Adrian warned. "I'm pretty sure Bex and I could still make it work if our only obstacles were a lion and a ward. It's the princes we can't deal with."

Malik looked alarmed. "Princes?"

"Two of them," Adrian said with a nod. "They appeared practically on top of my head just a few minutes after I started my reconnaissance. From what I overheard of their conversation, they heard the ring of my teleport through the chains themselves, which means a surprise attack is off the table. Even if I teleported our entire army in, the princes would just hear us coming and bring their own army to slaughter us."

His hands were squeezed to bloodless fists by the end. Adrian didn't normally indulge in fits of rage, but it was just so *frustrating*. Every time he thought he'd found a solution, Gilgamesh threw something else in his way. He felt like a rat trapped in a maze that was constantly being rearranged, but he wasn't giving up. He'd find a way to get Bex to those chains if it killed him.

But while Adrian was working himself into a righteous fury, his father rose from his chair to grab a wooden dowel from the pile next to his carving table.

"That is quite the list of obstacles," he said as he carried the long wooden rod back to his seat. "But I'm not surprised to hear them. Gilgamesh is a famously cautious and forethoughtful king. There's a reason he's never faced a serious threat to his power in five thousand years. As well constructed as his defenses are, however, even the Eternal King is still subject to the world around him."

"What does that mean?" Adrian asked.

Malik smiled. "It means that just as I can only move my island between locations with terrain suitable for keeping my beach above water, Gilgamesh can only protect that which he controls. No matter how many guards he stations or walls he builds, he cannot change the fundamental nature of Heaven and Earth. Here, I'll show you."

Holding the long dowel between his fingers like a pencil, Malik bent over and began sketching in the sand in front of their chairs. As expected from someone who'd been making art for five millennia, his drawing skills were top-notch, and soon, Adrian found himself looking at a precise diagram of two perfect but separate spheres that were connected by a series of flowing lines.

"Imagine these two circles are the lands of the living and the dead," Malik said, pointing the tip of his dowel at each sphere in turn. "They appear separate now, but during the reign of the gods, their edges overlapped. That is why there are so many myths of heroes entering the underworld. Long ago, the two spheres used to be locked tight together, but Gilgamesh used the power he stole from the gods to separate them, and now, there is a great gap of empty darkness in the middle."

"Bex mentioned things going dark after she cut the chain," said Adrian, who was now sitting on the edge of his seat. "But why did Gilgamesh pull the worlds apart?"

"Because dead gods are very difficult to keep that way," Malik explained, giving him a wry look. "I'm sure I don't need to say this to a witch, but the great cycles of life are incredibly powerful. *So* powerful that just being near them is enough to give slaughtered gods the strength to push out of their graves. Gilgamesh couldn't allow that, so he moved all of Paradise as far from the living world as possible. That's why what used to be a short ferry ride through the mists now requires enormous bridges to cross safely. Heaven is very literally farther away than it used to be."

That made sense given what Bex had told him about what she'd seen on the chain, but Adrian still couldn't believe it. He knew Gilgamesh was strong, but he couldn't wrap his brain around the sheer amount of magic it must have taken to push two things as interlocked as life and death apart.

"It was nearly impossible," his father agreed when he mentioned this. "Even with the stolen power of the gods at his command, Gilgamesh failed his first several attempts. But the Eternal King is nothing if not persistent, and he got there in the end."

He smiled as if that was a joke, but Adrian was scowling.

"How do you know all this?"

"Because I watched it happen," Malik said, looking up at the starry night sky. "Uruk was my homeland, which made Gilgamesh my king. Countries were not so big in those days, and it was not unusual for a ruler to lead his armies himself. I fought many wars under Gilgamesh's banner, and even after he left his country to rule Paradise, I kept a close eye on his progress. Partially because to do otherwise with the most powerful man in creation would have been suicide. Mostly, though, I was curious to see what he'd use all that power for."

"And?" Adrian prompted.

Malik looked down at the ground again. "And I am disappointed. I'd hoped he would make the world a better place, and he did, to some extent, but the majority of Gilgamesh's strength has always been spent keeping the gods in their graves, which is an enormous waste of his potential. He could have changed the destiny of all mankind! Instead, he took magic away and killed everyone who knew how to bring it back."

Adrian was happy to finally hear his father disparage Gilgamesh, but, "I thought you said the removal of magic was a good thing. Didn't you compare it to taking away a sword from a toddler?"

"Just because there were positive externalities doesn't mean it wasn't a waste," Malik snapped, looking angrier than Adrian had ever seen him. "Humanity's wars did become less brutal without magic, and I am grateful for any preservation of life, but Gilgamesh was—*is*—a sorcerer, the same as me. He was famous for his love of magic, yet he still took it away, and not because it saved lives. He stole our power out of *fear* because all that casting and creation made his grasp on the gods too unstable to maintain. He systematically destroyed humanity's greatest achievement to solve a mechanical technicality. How is that the act of a great king?"

Considering all of witchcraft had nearly been stomped out for that "mechanical technicality," Adrian wasn't about to disagree. Raging over Gilgamesh's sins wasn't helping them win, though, so he decided to nudge things back in a more productive direction.

"What are those lines?" he asked, pointing at the gently waving squiggles Malik had drawn between the two circles.

"Ah," his father said, calming down a little. "That's what I made this diagram to show you. Those are the Rivers of Death that carry souls to the afterlife. They used to be wide and slow moving, but now that Gilgamesh has pulled the worlds apart, their course has been stretched thin and narrow, causing them to flow very quickly. This makes them extremely dangerous and difficult to control, but Gilgamesh can't do anything about it because the rivers are not part of his kingdom. Even Ishtar, who claimed the Rivers of Death as part of her divinity, couldn't do more than snake them through her Riverlands. No one has ever controlled them because the Rivers of Death are older than the gods. They do not exist to bring souls into Paradise. Paradise was built around *them*, and nothing—not the Eternal King or his Hells or all the walls of Heaven—can impede their flow for long."

Adrian's pulse beat faster with every word. He'd been so focused on the chains, he'd entirely forgotten about the rivers, which was *stupid,* because they still had one flowing right outside the door that used to open onto the chain in Seattle. He'd never given it much thought because the water in their river was dark, not blue and glowy like the deathly water he was used to, but Bex was still able to feed her people with it. If wrath demons could eat sins out of its water, then it was still a River of Death, which meant it still flowed directly up to Heaven without any lions, barriers, or princes in the way.

"I think you just gave me a great idea," Adrian said, rising from his seat. "Thank you for your help."

"I'm not sure what I did, but I'm happy to have been of service," his father said, standing up as well. "It's not often an old sorcerer gets to employ his esoteric knowledge toward a useful end."

"It was *marvelously* useful," Adrian assured him. "You just gave me an entirely new angle. I still have to actually make it work and run it by Bex, but I think this might be exactly what I was looking for."

He flashed Malik an excited smile, but his father was scowling.

"Do you take everything you do to the Queen of Wrath for approval?"

"Everything that involves her," Adrian said. "She *is* the queen, and she's been fighting this war for a lot longer than I have. You don't have to worry about Bex, though. I know she's called the Bonfire of Wrath, but she's the kindest, most caring, most dependable person I've ever met. I trust her with my life."

"That is good," Malik said, patting his son's arm. "It is good to trust. I had someone I felt that way about once."

"Really?" Adrian said. "What happened to them?"

His father turned back into his workshop with a sad smile. "The gods killed him."

There was a world of pain in those words, and Adrian winced. "I'm sorry."

"There's nothing for you to be sorry about," Malik said as he returned to the bench where he'd set down his sculpting tools. "It happened a long time ago.

You have your own life to live, and I'm actually quite keen to hear what the Queen of Wrath thinks about your plan. Please let me know what you come up with. I'd love to hear your ideas."

"I'll tell you as soon as I've got something," Adrian promised.

"Wonderful," his father said as he picked up the chisel to resume his carving. "I'm not always on my island, but I'll leave Sharif on watch. Just tell him you wish to see me, and I'll drop everything to come running."

"It's not that important," Adrian said, brushing a curl behind his ear self-consciously. "I mean, it *is* important, but you don't have to drop everything."

"I must and I will," Malik said, pausing his hammer to give Adrian a serious look. "I neglected you for twenty-five years and almost missed my chance to teach a great new sorcerer and a wonderful son. I will not be so stupid twice. Promise you'll come to me if you have a breakthrough. Even if it seems trivial, I want to hear it. You are my highest priority right now, Adrian. Don't be afraid to act as such."

By the time he finished, Adrian was grinning so wide his face hurt. He'd never thought much about what it'd be like to have a father, but so far, he was enjoying the experience enormously. His mother had always given him attention, but he'd still had to wait his turn. He'd never resented her for that—he'd been Agatha's apprentice as well as her son, which meant he knew exactly how many directions an Old Wife of the Blackwood got pulled in—but to have someone as obviously knowledgeable and powerful as Malik say so clearly that Adrian ranked first... well, that was a new feeling. One he liked very, very much.

"I'll let you know the moment I have anything," he promised. "And thank you again."

"Thank *you*," Malik said, placing his chisel against the white bone to resume his sculpting. "It is a great pleasure to have a brilliant son. I'm very much looking forward to seeing what you'll do next."

Twenty-four hours ago, that much flattery would've made Adrian suspicious. Now it just made him giddy as he waved a fond farewell to his father and stepped back outside, digging into his pockets for the dose of magic that would take him back to the Blackwood to give his latest theory a try.

Chapter 8

Bex slammed into the wall of the arena hard enough to crack the stretched space. For a terrifying second, the black void was visible through the crumbling cement. A blink later, the hole was gone, instantly repaired by the sorcery they'd paid all that quintessence to maintain. Bex's own damage, however, took a lot longer to heal.

There certainly was enough of it. Crashing into the wall had pulverized her spine, pelvis, and both legs. The regeneration she'd inherited from her divine mother normally took care of things like that in seconds, but while her limbs did straighten out eventually, Bex didn't stand back up.

She didn't burn, either. It'd been nineteen hours since she'd driven the bus full of terrified demons she'd freed from Felix back to Seattle, which meant she'd been fighting Havok for eighteen. Eighteen straight hours of nonstop combat with no sleep and no food. Eighteen hours of being broken over and over.

That was enough to crush even a queen's will, but Bex still hadn't quit. Even when her fire flickered out for the last time two hours ago, she'd kept pushing out of the craters and going for Havok, much to the dismay of the three demons watching from the cement balcony above.

"He's going to kill her," Iggs said in a small voice.

"She's going to kill herself," Lys snarled through the clenched teeth of the angry male body they'd been making bigger and bigger over the past three hours.

"Everyone dies," Nemini said, though even she sounded less stoic than usual.

"Should we call Adrian?" Iggs asked for the fiftieth time. "He's not a demon, so she can't order him out like she does us. Maybe he can use a spell to—"

"We don't need a damn spell," Lys snapped, casting off their human illusion so they could spread their wings. "I'm ending this."

"*Lys!*" Iggs shouted, but it was too late. The lust demon had already flown into the blackened arena to land between the armored war machine and their queen.

"Stand down," they snarled, stretching their dusky pink wings out like a wall in front of Bex, who was still struggling to pull her blood-soaked body out of the rubble.

Havok crossed two of his four arms over his bone-armored chest, which wasn't even charred despite the rivers of fire Bex had been pouring into him.

"Or what?"

"You don't want to know the answer to that," Lys warned, lifting their chin. "I might be no match for you in strength, but there are worse things than getting punched, and I am *very* creative at those." They peeled back their lovely lips to show their small, sharp fangs. "This fight is over. Now stand *down*."

By the time Lys finished, Iggs had scrambled down the ladder to back them up. It couldn't have been a very intimidating display for a demon who'd just been kicking a queen around like she was nothing, but Havok must have seen something he didn't want to mess with, or perhaps he was secretly tired as well. Whatever the reason, after twenty seconds of staring Lys down, he nodded his armored head and turned away, walking to the other side of the damaged arena while Lys and Iggs rushed to their queen.

"*Bex!*" Lys cried, waving frantically at Iggs to move the rubble Bex still hadn't managed to crawl out of. "Hang on, baby girl, we've got you!"

Iggs's head snapped up in surprise at the endearment, which was to be expected. He'd joined the team after the Bex of this life was already a teenager, which meant he'd never heard any of her old names. Lys was normally careful not to use them once Bex made it out of childhood, but the strain of seeing the queen they'd built their entire world around being beaten over and over must have snapped the lust demon back into their old habits. As soon as Iggs lifted the chunk of wall holding Bex down, the lust demon snatched the Queen of Wrath into their arms like an infant and fled. Iggs didn't have wings like Lys, but you wouldn't have known it from how fast he sprinted up the ladder and out the door after them, leaving Havok alone in the blasted arena.

Or almost.

Nemini perched on the railing by the exit, watching the armored demon with calm, yellow eyes to see if he would give chase. Watching to see what he would do period, because in the twenty-four hours she'd been aware of his existence, she hadn't seen

Havok do anything but sit around, talk down to Bex, and fight. Nemini's life might be a void of nothingness, but even she still read books. Havok didn't even sit down. He just stood in the corner he'd walked to with his four arms crossed, staring at the door Lys had fled through with Bex like he meant to stay in that exact position until they got back.

Nemini frowned. She'd seen a lot of strange behavior over her long, long life, but this was odd even by her standards. Odd enough to merit a closer look.

With that, she released her grip on the railing and fell, dropping thirty feet to land soundlessly on the arena's scorched floor. Even after five thousand years, the lack of noise was a novelty. She never used to do anything that didn't demand attention, but her need to be noticed had been shattered along with everything else when the Queen of Pride had died. Now, she was nothing, and nothing made no sound as Nemini walked across the arena to stand directly in front of Havok.

As she'd noticed last night when she'd followed Bex into Felix's cell, the war demon didn't seem to see her. Even when she waved her hand in front of his face, his head didn't move. No part of him did. There was no shifting of weight, no rise and fall of breath. If he hadn't just been talking and moving, Nemini would have said he was a bone statue.

Frowning slightly, she reached out to lay her bare fingers as gently as falling petals on the war demon's armored chest. Just like back in Felix's cell, that got his attention, but while his body jerked at her touch, the slits of his mask passed right over her head like he didn't see her at all.

Interesting.

Nemini pulled back her hand and crossed her arms thoughtfully. She was too old not to suspect what that blindness meant but too empty to do anything about it. She knew better than anyone the pointlessness of trying to stop the inevitable. Even the vaunted Queen of Pride had fallen before it, leaving her demons plummeting into the abyss.

Nemini had been plummeting for five thousand years. She knew perfectly well that she was a powerless shadow. Nothing she'd done had ever changed their peoples' tragic fate. It was meaningless to even try, and yet...

And yet.

Silent as the air she still breathed, Nemini hopped back up to the observation balcony and positioned herself in front of the exit Lys had carried Bex through. It was a pointless gesture—if the Queen of Wrath couldn't beat Havok, an empty husk of a void demon had no chance of keeping him from going anywhere he wanted—but Nemini had been doing pointless things for Rebexa's sake for a long, long, *long* time. It was the only comfort she had anymore, so she stayed right where she was, standing in front of the doors like a pillar as she waited for Havok to make his inevitable move.

Bex woke up to pain.

It wasn't the *worst* she'd ever felt, but her whole body was throbbing in time with her pulse. She had aches in places she hadn't known she could get aches in, and she was cold. Really cold, actually, which felt nice on her sore muscles but was starting to make her shiver. She was trying to curl into a ball when something soft rubbed across her face, which Bex just now realized was wet.

"Shh," Lys's voice said from somewhere above her. "It's okay. You're safe. I've got you."

The soft thing—a towel, Bex realized belatedly—scrubbed across her face one more time before moving up to her horns, and Bex cracked her aching eyes open to see that she was lying in a bathtub. That had become pretty normal these days, but this wasn't the beautifully carved stone bowl in Adrian's greenhouse. It was the tiny plastic RV tub for the en-suite bathroom in what used to be their client bedroom. The one they'd turned into an office.

She'd always thought that was a waste. Other than her master suite upstairs, the front bedroom with its big window was the biggest in the Winnebago and the only one with an actual bathtub. Not that any of them ever took baths. Even back when they'd had clients to put in here, the tub was mostly used for washing off blood since it was a lot easier to wrangle an unconscious person into a bathtub than a shower.

Bex presumed that was why she was in it now, though she'd never seen the tub used like this before.

She was submerged in glowing water up to her shoulders. The soft blue light turned the yellowed plastic greenish and made Bex's pale skin look translucent. Lys was kneeling in their true form on the linoleum floor beside her, using their leathery wings to shield Bex from the bathroom's glaring overhead light. Through the door behind them, dozens of empty glass bottles lay scattered across the former guest room's shag carpet, making Bex's eyes go wide.

"Lys," she whispered, grabbing the edge of the plastic tub with her dripping hand. "*Please* tell me you didn't just use a million dollars' worth of deathly water to heal a few bruises."

"It was more than 'a few bruises,' and you know it," Lys snapped, throwing the damp towel onto the bathroom's yellow floor with an angry *slap*. "That armored asshole beat you unconscious! I couldn't wake you up and didn't know how bad your internal injuries were, so I took a page from Adrian's book and dunked you."

Bex sank into the water with a sigh. Considering the last thing she remembered was breaking a cement wall with her back, she couldn't blame Lys for freaking out, especially since it seemed to be working. Thanks to her mother's glowing water, Bex's injuries were healing before her eyes. Even the tiredness from being awake for over thirty-six hours was gone, leaving her body feeling light and energized. Her mind, however, was a different story.

"You shouldn't have wasted so much," she grumbled, glaring at the glowing water where it lapped against her naked legs. "I would've been fine. This isn't like when I was burned out. I can heal from almost anything now, and we don't have deathly water to waste on—"

"It wasn't a waste," Lys said in a voice that made Bex jump. She hadn't heard her lust demon sound this scared since their first prince, but when Bex looked at them now, Lys's wings were shaking.

"He beat you for hours," they whispered, reaching into the water to grab Bex's hand, "and you wouldn't let it *stop*. I know you're back to being the Bonfire now, but that doesn't mean you can take damage forever. You just kept throwing yourself at him, and your fire was getting lower and lower." They squeezed her fingers hard. "I thought he was going to kill you, and I couldn't do anything except watch."

"He wouldn't have killed me," Bex said gently, wrapping Lys's clawed hand in both of hers. "Havok was training me."

Lys's amber eyes grew murderous. "That wasn't *training*. I can't eat a demon's emotions like I can a human's, but I know what pleasure looks like. He was beating you for his own amusement. He was *enjoying* your defeat. If you learned anything from that nightmare, it's because you're smart enough to adapt, not because of anything he did." Their face fell into a deadly scowl. "You should have let Felix throw him down a pit."

"You know I couldn't do that," Bex said practically. "I don't leave demons to die, no matter how

jerky they act. Even if he was having fun at my
expense, it doesn't matter." She glanced down at the
still-healing bruises on her stomach with a grimace.
"It's pretty obvious that Havok's the best fighter we've
got right now. Whatever the cost, we need him."

"No, we don't," Lys snarled. "I don't care how
good he is. I'd rather storm Heaven with Adrian's cat
than trust our backs to a masochist traitor."

Bex's lips quirked. "That's not saying much.
Boston's no slouch, but I get your point. I don't trust
Havok either. I just don't see how we're doing this
without him."

"We'll do it the same way we did before he
showed up," Lys said with an exasperated scowl. "This
is war, Bex, not a martial arts competition. No one
expects you to duel Gilgamesh for the fate of all
demonkind. The man killed the gods, for Ishtar's
sake!"

"Why do you think I'm pushing so hard?" Bex
snapped. "Even if Adrian's plan works, Gilgamesh has
been fortifying his position for thousands of years. He
has armies and princes and my own sisters locked
under his spell! That might be too much to fight even if
we do bring the gods back, but you've seen how
powerful Havok is. If we're going to have a prayer of
pulling this off, we need him on our team. *I* need him,
because I can't fight all those princes by myself."

"I know that," Lys said, finally letting go of Bex's
hand. "But there has to be a way that doesn't involve
you being that asshole's punching bag. He nearly
killed you today. How can you be the queen who leads
us back to Paradise if you die at the hands of some

197

puffed-up war demon because you're too stubborn to realize when a jerk is toying with you?"

"This isn't about being stubborn," Bex insisted. "I have to do this *because* everyone's depending on me. Our Anchor's packed to the rafters with runaway demons who're counting on the queen to take them to freedom. Adrian's been working himself around the clock to get us an opening, and you and Iggs have been doing the jobs of seven demons to keep this place from falling apart. I'm so amazingly proud of what we've accomplished, but all that work and sacrifice won't mean squat if Gilgamesh is waiting for us at the gates of Heaven and *I can't beat him!*"

"If Gilgamesh is waiting for us, we're lost no matter what," Lys said, finally giving her a smile. "That's why every plan we've made starts with bringing back the gods. Fighting the Eternal King yourself was never on the agenda. I thought you understood that, but Havok clearly punched you in the head one too many times."

Bex sank back into the tub with a sigh. "That's not—"

"If killing Gilgamesh ourselves was possible, we would've done it eons ago," Lys argued over her. "Before they locked the Anchors, there were giant bridges leading straight to the Holy City all over the world! We could've sent a strike team up any of them, but we've never even considered a plan like that because fighting Gilgamesh head-on is a stupid pipe dream of an idea. Once again, this is the man who *defeated the gods*, and he's only gotten stronger since. He's so bloated on quintessence that he can't even leave Heaven anymore! That's not an enemy you can beat, so *please* stop wrecking yourself and giving me heart attacks preparing for a fight that's *never going to happen!*"

Bex closed her eyes. It wasn't that Lys was wrong—see "The Ballad of Lys the Always Right"—but it wasn't that simple. She knew she didn't have a chance if she ever ended up fighting Gilgamesh one-on-one, but the Eternal King wasn't the only danger. Even if all their plans worked and the gods came roaring back, it was still going to be a hell of a fight against a deeply entrenched enemy, and Bex was terrified she wasn't up to the task.

She'd fought three princes since she'd gotten her fire back, but she'd only ever won by the skin of her teeth, and she hadn't really beaten the crazy prince at all. She'd only pulled it off by going nuclear in Limbo and nearly burning herself out again because of it. Even after all that, Adrian had still had to sacrifice a finger to finish the bastard for good.

They couldn't keep doing it. They'd made it this far because Heaven kept underestimating them, but that wouldn't be the case anymore now that they were a full rebellion. Whatever Gilgamesh was planning to hit them with next, he was going to do it with all the strength at his disposal.

That was why Bex was pushing so hard on this Havok thing. The war demon wasn't just another fighter who could take a prince. He was the wall. Beating him was the hurdle Bex had to clear at any cost because when Gilgamesh finally decided to stop messing around and crush them for real, all the fights were going to be this hard.

If she couldn't beat Havok in an arena where there was nothing else to worry about, she'd never be good enough to take more than one prince at a time. If Bex couldn't at least reach that level, then it didn't matter whether they brought the gods back or not. If Ishtar's Sword couldn't kill Ishtar's enemies, the second war for Heaven would be over before it started, and she'd be the one who'd lost it.

That isn't true.

Drox's voice was quiet and weak, making her flinch. Bex's sword was normally as inexhaustible as the metal he was made from. Now, though, he sounded like a tired old man, which upset Bex far more than Lys's yelling.

"Would you mind getting me something to eat?" she asked the lust demon, who was still hovering over the tub. "I'm starving."

"Of course," Lys said, rising to their feet at once. "Sorry. I'm still not used to you needing food. What do you want?"

"A sandwich from the banh mi shop on the corner would be nice," Bex said, which was absolutely true. The deathly water had removed her tiredness, but she hadn't eaten anything since yesterday afternoon, and her stomach felt like it was about to cave in. Asking for that sandwich in particular, though, meant Lys would have to leave the Anchor and walk two blocks, buying Bex some much-needed alone time with her sword.

Thankfully, her lust demon didn't seem to notice the ruse. Lys was already putting the order in on their phone. They'd go pick it up with their own hands as well since Bex's new mortal appetite meant she was now vulnerable to poisoning. Lys had taken it as their personal mission to make sure the queen's food was safe, and after telling Bex a dozen times to call Iggs if she needed anything, they stepped out of the bathroom and left her alone.

Bex didn't move until she heard Lys leaving the RV. Only when she was absolutely certain that she was alone did she lift her hand out of the glowing water to address the real problem.

"What's wrong?" she asked, positioning her fingers so that Drox's black ring was dripping right in front of her nose. "What were you talking about earlier, and why do you sound like you're dying?"

I'm not dying, Drox said irritably. *It's just been a humbling day.*

That was the gods damned truth. For some reason, though, hearing Drox complain about it got Bex's back up.

"We're not doing that badly," she argued. "Sure, Havok's kicking our ass, but that's what I asked him to do, and it's not like we're rolling over. He's the most skilled opponent I've ever faced in this life, and I still managed to hold my own for eighteen hours. That's really good! I know I'm not where I need to be yet, but I was getting in some solid hits before I started getting too tired. If I can keep that momentum up, it's only a matter of time before—"

You're missing the point, her sword interrupted. *It doesn't matter how long you fight Havok or how hard you try. We'll never beat him like this.*

"How can you say that?" Bex demanded, sitting up so fast, she sloshed glowing water all over the floor. "I know I'm not as good as the original Rebexa, but she had centuries of practice being Ishtar's Sword. There's no way I can match that at only twenty-four, but I'm learning fast. I almost got Havok several times today! If I can just push a bit harder, I think I can finally figure out how to stab through his—"

You can't, Drox said sharply, making her jump. *You can't beat Havok by trying harder because the problem isn't with you. You're not as good as the old Rebexa, you're better. Gilgamesh was the first real challenge your original incarnation faced. You underestimated him as badly as his princes have underestimated your current self, which is why he was able to beat you so quickly. But the queen you are now is a sword forged in fire. You are tougher, stronger, more disciplined, and more determined than the original Queen of Wrath ever was. Your footwork today was flawless, your swordplay without fault. I have been your weapon for all of my existence, and I can say without hesitation that our failure today was in no way related to your skill. That's why it's impossible for you to defeat Havok by improving, because you're already at the top.*

Bex's jaw was hanging open by the time he finished. That was the most unequivocal praise Drox had ever given her, but it still felt like a slap in the face.

"Then what's the problem?" she asked when she could speak again. "If I'm that good, why can't I beat him?"

202

Her sword heaved a long, tired sigh through her head.

Because I'm not that good.

"That's ridiculous," Bex said at once. "You're the divine Blade of Wrath forged by Enki himself. There's nothing you can't cut."

There didn't used to be, Drox said bitterly. *There was a time when I could have sliced the sun from the sky, but that is no longer the case. You were right when you said you landed good hits on Havok. You should have beaten him back at Felix's. The only reason you didn't was because you couldn't pierce his armor. That was my failing, not yours.*

"It's not your failing," Bex assured him. "Havok's just tough, but there's no nut that can't be cracked with the right leverage. We just need to figure out how to—"

There's nothing to "figure out," Drox snarled, his ring rattling angrily on her finger. *I was made to be the Queen of Wrath's sword. It is my life's purpose to assess and correct any flaws that might lead to your defeat, and after fighting Havok for eighteen hours, there can be no doubt that your greatest weakness is me.*

"You're not," Bex insisted.

I am, her sword insisted right back. *I know you're trying to make me feel better because we share a mind, but I have no need for such coddling. I am a divine weapon forged by the gods! I'm not burdened with petty insecurities. The only thing I care about is effectiveness, and a sword that cannot cut is useless.*

Bex flopped back into her bath with a sigh. "Well, what do you want to do about it? I agree it sucks that we can't cut Havok, but you're my sword. It doesn't matter if you rust down to the hilt. I'm not getting another weapon."

Your loyalty is appreciated, Drox said. *But I wasn't suggesting you replace me. As you just stated, such a thing would be impossible. We were created to be a pair. You cannot get another sword any more than I can get another queen. We have always been and will always be together, which is, unfortunately, our entire problem.*

Bex heaved another sigh. "What does that mean?"

It means that I've been through the same hardships as you have. All the tough battles and the long years, the wounds and the grinds and the dents.

His ring twisted on Bex's finger, moving in a slow circle to show her how worn and scraped the black band had become.

You're not the only one who's been ground down by time, Drox said grimly. *We are both old swords, but while the fire of the Blackwood was able to restore you to your full glory, I remained unchanged.*

"That doesn't matter," Bex insisted. "Ground down or not, you still slay princes."

I thought the same thing at first, he said as his ring grew heavy. *That's the sinister trap of age. It sneaks up on you so slowly, you don't realize what the years have stolen until you try to do something you've always done and suddenly discover that you can't. As you said, we were still killing princes, so I was able to ignore how thin my blade had become. I thought so long as I was sharp and you were strong, there would always be nothing we couldn't cut, but Havok proved me wrong. You are stronger than ever. I was the one who could not get through.*

Bex folded her fingers over her ring's scraped surface. She hated every part of this, but she couldn't deny the truth when it was spoken straight into her head. She'd been there, too, after all. Havok was damn good and damn fast, but she'd seen her sword land. She should have been carving Havok's arms off left and right, but her hits never did any damage, and while she was desperately trying to make a dent, Havok was painting the ground black with her blood.

That was no way to win a fight. Bex had assumed it was her fault because everything was always her fault. It had never occurred to her that her sword might be the one who wasn't up to the challenge. She still didn't want to believe it, but Drox was never wrong about stuff like this. If he said he was the problem, then he was the problem, and that was a problem.

"What are we going to do?" she whispered, sinking lower into the tub until the glowing water was up to her chin. "You're a divine blade crafted by the god of creation, but Enki's been dead for five thousand years. I don't even know if the forge where you were made still exists now that Gilgamesh has paved Paradise and turned it into his ugly city."

It doesn't, Drox said. *I felt it fall during the war.*

"We could ask Adrian to have a look at you," Bex suggested, determined to banish the ancient sadness from her normally stoic sword's voice. "The first bonfire didn't do anything, but that's probably because he asked the Great Blackwood to heal me, not you. If we did it again—"

It wouldn't work, Drox said. *Your witch is unquestionably powerful, but his magic comes from the great cycles. Even the fire he used to refill you came from the flames of life, which is why you can no longer reincarnate and have to eat physical food. To restore what the eons had taken, he had to change the nature of your divine essence and make you mortal like him. The fact that he was able to do so is the greatest miracle I have ever witnessed, but such a feat was only possible because you are a daughter of Ishtar, who is goddess of both life and death. You have always straddled two worlds, but I am a tool made by Enki. I was never alive to begin with, which makes me incompatible with the magic of the Great Forest.*

"That doesn't mean Adrian can't help you," she said stubbornly. "His witchcraft can do anything."

I'm sure he'd be flattered to hear you say so, but an eternal sword forged in the lands of death is as far from the living magic of a witch's forest as it gets. I'm afraid our natures are simply too different, but that's fine, because I don't need his witchcraft. I already know how to restore myself.

"You do?" Bex cried, sloshing an investment portfolio's worth of magical water onto the bathroom floor as she surged to her feet. "Why didn't you say so earlier?!"

Because I'm not certain it will work, Drox replied in a voice so grim that she sat right back down again. *You're not the only one who was born with a god inside you. Just as Ishtar's river flows forever through your veins, the spark of Enki's creation still burns within my core. That is what makes me a sacred blade rather than just another lump of sharpened metal, but, as you just said, the gods are*

206

gone. Ishtar has always been a special case because life and death were both her domain, but my creator has no connection to the sacred rivers of reincarnation. So far as I know, Enki is actually dead, which makes asking him for repairs a challenge.

"A challenge?" Bex repeated incredulously. "I'm surprised it's an option at all."

Death doesn't mean the same thing for gods as it does for mortals, her sword assured her. *They were true eternal beings before Gilgamesh found a way to kill them. Even at the height of his betrayal, though, the Eternal King could never completely finish the job because the gods are not part of the great cycles. Time does not touch them. They do not change, do not age, do not diminish. They have no beginning and thus can never end. The best Gilgamesh could do was beat them down so low that they no longer had enough power to affect the world around them. A god who can't do anything is as good as dead, but they're not actually gone. The spark of Enki has always been and will always be forever within me. I don't know if it's strong enough to do anything, but if I can survive what it will take to reach him, there's still a chance that he can help.*

"If there's a chance, we'll take it," Bex promised, climbing out of the tub at last. "But what precisely do we need to do, and what did you mean by 'surviving what it takes to reach him'?"

Exactly what it sounds like, Drox replied. *You could only speak to Ishtar in the gaps between your lives. My path to Enki is no different. To reach the gods who dwell in death, I will have to die.*

Bex froze in place, glittering water dripping down her naked body as she stared in horror at the black ring on her finger.

Don't look at me like that, Drox said scornfully. *Even before Gilgamesh killed them, the gods resided in the afterlife. Death has always been the only guaranteed way to reach them.*

"That doesn't mean you should do it!" Bex cried, her bare feet slipping on the wet linoleum as she grabbed Drox's ring. "Is it even possible for a sword to die?"

No, he said. *Which is why I've never suggested this course of action before. Unlike a daughter of Ishtar, I don't have life and death built into me. I was made to endure forever, which made sense back when the gods thought they'd always be around to repair any damage my blade might take. Now that that is no longer the way of things, my only hope is to do whatever it takes to get to Enki and pray he has enough power left to restore me without the aid of his divine forge.*

"Sounds like a pile of impossibilities to me," Bex said as she grabbed a fresh towel off the rack.

Nonsense, her sword scoffed. *Just because I'll never die on my own doesn't mean death is unreachable. If I have no natural end, I'll just have to meet it unnaturally, and the most efficient way to achieve that is for you to shatter me.*

"What?" Bex shrieked, dropping her towel on the soaked floor as she grabbed her ring again with both hands. "Absolutely not! There is no way I am shattering you!"

It's the only practical solution, Drox argued in the same exacting voice he used when he was correcting her form. *To get to Enki, I must die. For a sword, that means breaking. If I shattered against an enemy, you'd be left undefended and likely follow me to my demise. If you break me yourself, however, we keep control over the situation. Or rather,* you'll *keep control. I'll be dead, so it will be up to you to make sure I get put back together.*

"I'm not doing it," Bex said fiercely, shaking her head until the water flew from her long hair. "I don't care what you say. I won't break my own sword. I admit you're worn down, but Havok's armor is the first thing we've ever found that you can't cut. You're still able to slice chains and princes just fine, so why should we take the risk?"

Because I wasn't slicing them "just fine," Drox argued. *It took us fifteen hits to cut through the sin iron chain to the Seattle Anchor, and that was after you'd softened it with your fire. If I'd been my old self fresh from the forges, I could've cut that entire bridge in one strike.*

Bex crossed her arms stubbornly over her chest. "We still did it."

That doesn't mean it wasn't disgraceful, her sword insisted. *You're the one who decided to risk everything on one final life, but we can't win that gamble if I'm dragging us down. I was made to be Rebexa the Bonfire's sword. My entire purpose is to bring you victory. If I've become too dull to achieve that, then I'd rather be shattered. Better I was gone entirely than to stay and become the reason my queen—the* last *queen—fails.*

Bex covered her face with her dripping hands. She didn't want to listen to this, but she couldn't shut it out because Drox was saying the same things she had. She'd also stood before Ishtar and chosen one last chance at success over an eternity of failure.

She couldn't deny her sword the same wish, but this all felt so wrong. Drox was so much more than just her weapon. He was her partner, *part* of her, the only one who'd been there through it all. Breaking him felt like killing a piece of herself, especially since there was no guarantee she'd be able to get him back. If she shattered Drox and couldn't get to Enki, or if she *did* get to Enki and he wasn't able to do anything, then she'd have broken her sword for nothing. The whole thing felt like a terrible idea, but Drox's ring was as heavy as a brick on her finger.

It is the only way, his deep voice rumbled. *A queen must do whatever is necessary to achieve victory. The standards are no lower for a queen's sword. This is my duty and my right, Rebexa. I will not be kept from it.*

Bex sank to her knees on the bathroom's cold floor, but she couldn't get away. Drox was already speaking through her, filling her thoughts with his calm assessment of how to break a queen's unbreakable blade. She hated every single word, but Bex still forced herself to listen. When she was sure she understood, she pushed herself off the floor and wrapped her dripping body in a towel to go do what must be done.

Chapter 9

"So he's just standing there?" Lys asked over the phone. "Are you sure?"

Nemini's answer was too quiet for even Bex's sensitive hearing to pick up through someone else's speakers. The void demon must not have said anything alarming, though, because the shoulders of the no-nonsense androgynous body Lys had put on to deal with tonight's crises relaxed.

"Just keep an eye on him, then, I guess," they said, scrubbing a hand over their short horns. "And if he *does* start moving, call me immediately."

Nemini must have said she would because Lys hung up a second later, shaking their head at their phone with a look of bewilderment.

"It seems Havok's gone catatonic," they reported, glancing over at Bex, who was sitting at the RV's dining table, dressed in a fresh T-shirt and her comfiest leggings, unwrapping a banh mi sandwich the size of a football. "I don't know if you broke something or if he just doesn't care about life when a fight's not happening, but Nemini says he's been impersonating a statue since we left."

"Better than causing a problem," Bex said, turning the sandwich around as she looked for the angle that would let her fit it into her mouth.

This always happened when she sent Lys for food. Despite feeding Bex like a human for months now, her lust demon still hadn't grasped the basic mechanics of physical eating. It felt wrong to complain about having too much of a good thing, but Bex legitimately had no idea how she was going to get the stuffed log of French bread past her teeth without dislocating her jaw. She was making a play for the smallest corner when Iggs stuck his head through the RV's side door.

"We found all the stuff you wanted."

Bex forgot about dainty eating after that. She crammed the sandwich into her mouth, devouring it in fast, efficient bites as she charged down the RV steps, nearly tripping over Boston in the process.

"Sorry!" she said when she'd swallowed enough sandwich to speak again.

"It's fine," Boston replied in a crisp, sharp voice that didn't sound fine at all. "I'm used to being forgotten at this point."

"Adrian didn't forget you," Iggs assured him. "Everything's just crazy right now."

"Crazy times are when a witch needs his familiar the most," Boston argued with a lash of his tail. "I am not a pet to be left behind while he does other things! Not that he's even shown me that much consideration." The cat's green eyes narrowed to furious slits. "At least pet cats get left with a food bowl."

"I'll feed you," Iggs said eagerly, pulling out the bag of cat treats he'd started carrying everywhere now that the Anchor Market was full of familiars.

Boston turned up his nose at the processed tidbits and trotted over to the pile Iggs had set down on the roots of Adrian's giant oak tree. The collection included a warded plastic cooler, multiple metal clamps, and two giant pieces of granite that Iggs had broken off the base of Gilgamesh's statue, one of which still had a carving of a kneeling queen on it. Bex found that grimly fitting, but Drox was the one who got the final say. This was his show, so Bex pulled her sword out of his ring and started waving his blade back and forth over the pile of materials with one hand while she finished her sandwich with the other.

"Looks like we're set," she said three minutes later, when Drox had finally given the assortment his seal of approval. "Thanks for all your help. It means a lot."

"Happy to be of assistance," Boston replied from his perch on the oak tree's branches directly below where the Queen of Greed's hand was still hanging inside its spiderweb orb like a macabre Christmas ornament. "I'm just glad that *someone* still values my skills and that Iggs and I were able to find everything so quickly. Some of your requirements were extremely difficult to meet."

He looked pointedly at the warded cooler. Bex couldn't read the cuneiform on the seals as well as Lys, but she already knew that the box contained small meteorites that had been magically reverted to the temperature they would have been before they fell out of space, approximately -420°F. The rocks had originally been made to sell to Heavenly denizens as party tricks for instantly freezing drinks, but they also served as an excellent source of extreme cold beyond the naturally-occurring limits of Earth. A fact that

Boston had had to tip Bex off to since Adrian wasn't there.

"Where is he, anyway?" Bex grumbled, glancing at her phone for the millionth time. She *really* wanted to talk to Adrian before she went through with breaking Drox, but he seemed to have dropped off the face of the planet. He hadn't even been by to check on his familiar, a lapse that Boston was taking very, *very* personally.

"He'll show up when he shows up," the cat said, clearly trying to sound like he didn't care even though his ears were pressed flat against the top of his head.

"I'm sure there's a good explanation," Iggs insisted in his friend's defense. "Adrian never ignores people on purpose. The only time he gets like this is when his work's going super well. Maybe he's on the verge of a breakthrough!"

"We could use some good luck," Bex said, but her heart wasn't in it. She was about to destroy the sword that was the other half of her soul. Considering they'd only kissed once, calling Adrian her boyfriend was probably a stretch, but Bex would've given anything for him to hug her and tell her it'd be okay right now. Alas, it looked like she was on her own tonight. Adrian's phone wasn't even going to voicemail anymore.

"You don't have to do this right now, you know," Lys whispered as Bex handed them her phone for safekeeping. "Havok's not causing a crisis anymore, and you haven't gotten any real sleep in two days. It might not be a bad idea to wait."

"If I wait, I'll chicken out," Bex said firmly, bending over to tighten the laces of the white running shoes she'd borrowed from Nemini to replace her burned combat boots. "I don't have the courage to make this decision twice. If I'm doing this, it's gotta be now."

Lys didn't reply to that, but Bex had been with them all her life. She could tell from the tone of their silence that they hated every part of this. Bex felt the same way, but Drox would not be reasoned with. He was already pushing against her mind with all his strength, his ring yanking her hand toward the two giant lumps of granite Iggs had rolled into position on either side of the warded cooler.

With a final deep breath and a nervous look at Lys, Bex let herself be dragged over. Pulling her sword out of his ring, she laid Drox's long, thin blade across the tops of the two waist-high granite boulders like a bridge. The next step was locking him into place, but she was shaking so much that she kept dropping the clamps. It got so bad that Iggs had to step in and help, holding the metal vises steady so Bex could screw them down.

When Drox was clamped into position across the stones, she grabbed the warded cooler and shoved it into the gap beneath him, positioning the sealed box of freezing cold directly below her blade's weakest, most damaged point. She took several minutes getting the alignment exactly right, but even when Drox declared everything perfect, Bex didn't move on to the next step.

"Are you *sure* you can't reach Adrian?" she asked, looking up into the branches where Boston had disappeared. "You're connected to the forest, too, right? Can't you ask the trees to give him a poke or something?"

"I'm sorry, I don't control my witch," the cat's voice floated from somewhere inside the canopy of oak leaves. "But I *am* a member of the Blackwood coven, and I assure you that my skills are quite sufficient. The whole reason I asked you to do this here is because I'm using the oak's branches to facilitate the barrier I just put up to shield the rest of the Anchor from whatever happens when a divine sword of Ishtar breaks."

The air around them did smell strongly of forest now, but that only made Bex's anxiety worse. She knew why this had to be done, but it had all happened so quickly. She didn't know if she could—

Rebexa.

Her eyes closed as Drox's voice went through her like a knife.

Now is not the time to be a coward, her sword growled, rattling against the stone she'd clamped him to. *The witch cannot do this for you.*

"I don't want him to do it for me," Bex said. "I just want..."

Comfort. Support. Even a lie would do in a pinch. She just needed *something*, because she couldn't do this alone. Drox was like her father and her brother and her mentor all rolled into one. Now she was just supposed to break him without hesitation, but her hands were shaking so badly. Lys would've happily held them, or Iggs or Nemini or any of her demons, but Bex couldn't be weak in front of them. Adrian was the only one she didn't have to be a queen for, but he wasn't here. There was no comfort coming, so Bex squeezed her shaking hands into fists and called her fire.

It took longer than it should've to get it going. Fanning her flames was always harder when she was sad or scared, but Bex had had a lot of practice being the Bonfire of Wrath these days, and soon, her hands were burning bright.

She cupped them in front of her face to breathe the fire even hotter, digging deep into the memory of what had been done to her people. She thought about all her people who were still trapped in Limbo. She thought about the generations of demons damned to the Hells and the Paradise that had been stolen from them. Most of all, though, Bex thought about Gilgamesh and how if he hadn't been such a backstabbing, power-hungry traitor, none of this would've happened. If he'd just been content to stay a human king, Paradise would still exist, and Bex wouldn't be standing here, about to kill her other half. All of her suffering, all of Drox's suffering, all of *everyone's* suffering was Gilgamesh's fault, and for all their sakes, Bex was going to make him pay.

With that final furious promise, the Bonfire of Wrath flashed hot as a welding torch. Bex kicked her foot out at the same time, knocking open the cuneiform-covered cooler to release the unnatural cold inside. The frozen draft shot up like a spear, sending a wave of frost across Drox's metal face as his black blade instantly cooled to subzero temperatures.

When her sword was so cold she could feel it in her own head, Bex dropped her burning fist like a hammer, hitting him with the full fury of the flames of wrath. That normally wouldn't have been a problem for Drox since he'd been crafted specifically to endure her heat. Even with extreme thermal shock weakening his metal, she'd thought the stones would crack before he did. That would be a very Drox way to go out, but the years must have worn her sword even thinner than she'd realized, because his black blade shattered on the very first punch, filling Bex's mind with a sound she'd never heard before.

It was a crack, like breaking glass but deeper, and it wasn't in her ears. The noise came from inside her, splintering behind her eyes like her mind was flying apart. Bex tried to pull back her fist to stop it, but it was too late. Her sword—her precious sword, the extension of herself—was falling to pieces before her eyes. The broken shards dropped like jagged spears, leaving only a worn hilt.

Bex's burning hand was still reaching out to grab it when something new flashed behind her eyes. It was like a fire, but not her fire. This was a terrifying explosion of white, a searing, blinding brilliance that spoke in a voice like a thunderclap.

COME.

Bex had no choice. She went, falling forward through the empty space where her sword had been like she was falling down a well.

Adrian was bouncing on his broom as he touched down on the dark, flat roof of Pike Place Market's main building.

He'd had to fly over because he'd used up all the quintessence Malik had given him on experiments, but the rain had moved off, and Bran needed the exercise, so he didn't mind. He'd been teleporting too much anyway. Taking quintessence was much less awful now that he knew how to use it, but Adrian had been hitting it hard all day. His insides actually felt a little gooey from all the ultraprocessed magic he'd shoved through himself. He had zero regrets, though, because his new plan had *worked*. He'd finally figured out how to get around Gilgamesh's security! All he needed to do now was show his findings to Bex, get all the demons on board, and Heaven was as good as toppled!

Just thinking about it made him giddy. He'd already used the very last of his quintessence teleporting to Malik's island to tell him the good news, but his father hadn't been home. Sharif was there, though, so Adrian had left instructions for Malik to join him as soon as possible. Really, though, Bex was the person he was most excited to tell about his breakthrough. So much so that he almost fell off the fire escape he was using to climb off the roof into a dirty brick alley covered with multicolored globs of chewed gum.

It was a disgusting entry point, but the door by Seattle's infamous Gum Wall was the only way into the Anchor Market that didn't require running a vendor gauntlet. The door itself was also covered in chewed gum, but at least there was a sanitary lever now that let him open the door with his foot. Adrian did so with a flourish, tucking his broom under his arm as he marched into the large brick depot where the sellers still unloaded their goods before carrying them into the Market.

Unlike the rest of the Anchor, this place looked exactly the same as it had the first time Bex had brought him here. The only real difference was that the tunnel into the Market was now guarded by demons instead of golden-armored Anchor Guards. Two war demons, to be precise.

Adrian's soaring spirits dipped slightly when he saw them. He did his best to match Bex's "all Children of Ishtar are equal" attitude, but war demons were a stretch. He didn't know if it was the culture or the fact that they fed off conflict or what, but he'd never met a war demon who could let anything, no matter how inconsequential, pass without a fight. This included Adrian, who, despite already having the letter of passage Bex had written for him out and ready in his hands, was immediately detained.

"Do we have to go through this every time?" he groaned as the shorter war demon started patting him down with all four arms. "I'm the queen's witch. I grew the tree that's holding up the sky!"

He pointed down the brick tunnel, where the Anchor's false blue dome was sagging like a canvas tent against the branches of his oak, but the bigger of the two war demons just snorted.

"Queen's witch, eh?" he said, plucking off Adrian's hat so he could leer down at his face. "You don't look like any witch I've seen."

Adrian was dressed all in black with a witch hat and a broom in his hands. He'd even worn his boots with the curled-up toes. The only thing he was missing to complete the witchy stereotype was Boston on his shoulder, but that wasn't the war demons' problem.

"Male witches *do* exist, you know," he told them with a glare. "You want me to curse you to prove it?"

"No need to get feisty," the taller demon said, smirking at the other guard, who was still patting Adrian down. Not that he was going to find anything. Adrian's coat was enchanted to feel empty no matter how much he'd crammed inside its hundreds of pockets, and eventually, the guards were forced to let him go.

"*Thank* you," Adrian said angrily, cramming his hat back on his head. He was plotting the fastest course to the arena where he'd last seen her when he reached the end of the tunnel and ran face-first into the crowd.

"What the—"

The Anchor Market was *packed,* but not with the usual magical humans and merchants. This crowd was entirely made up of demons, and they didn't look happy. No one was rioting or anything like that, but all the faces around Adrian were pinched and scared. It was extremely odd, but when Adrian tapped the shoulder of the person in front of him—a male sorrow

221

demon with deep-blue wings and a well-tailored vest that could have been a legitimate antique or just a hipster accessory—the man told him there'd been a commotion with the queen.

"What kind of commotion?" Adrian asked.

"Nothing that's destroyed us yet," the man replied with the Eeyore-like glumness that seemed to be an inborn trait of sorrow demons. "We all felt the break, though."

"Felt what break?" Adrian demanded, his voice getting more panicked with every word.

The sorrow demon gave him a flat look. "If I knew that, you think I'd be standing around waiting for someone to explain?" He shook his head and pointed over the crowd at the green leaves of Adrian's tree. "Whatever it was happened over there, but you can't get in. The queen's servants are keeping everyone away from—*hey*!"

The sorrow demon's shout was lost as Adrian hopped back onto his broom and rose into the air. He flew over the crowd like a shot, making a beeline for the RV he could see parked beneath the oak tree's branches. He landed just a few seconds later, touching down inside the ring of grass that a well-ordered squad of war demons was keeping clear through sheer intimidation.

"What do you think you're doing?" the biggest one demanded before Adrian's feet could hit the ground. "Market's closed, human! This is demon business, so get back outside the—"

"*Adrian!*"

Adrian was still turning around when Iggs pulled him into a bear hug.

"I'm so glad you're here!" he cried, squeezing Adrian so hard the witch's ribs ached. "It's okay, General Kirok. This is Adrian Blackwood. He's with us."

The war demon was still scowling when Iggs finally let Adrian go, but he didn't do anything to stop them as Iggs pulled Adrian away from the crowds.

"Sorry about him," Iggs said. "Kirok's a pompous ass, but he's an effective pompous ass. I thought we were going to have a panic, but he got the whole Market on lockdown and kept it that way. I have no idea how, but miracles like that are why Bex puts up with having a war demon as her general."

Adrian hadn't known Bex had a general, much less a war demon general, but that seemed like the lesser issue at the moment.

"What's going on?" he asked frantically as they walked around the demons' faded white Winnebago. "Why is everyone panicked? And where's Bex?"

Iggs's eyebrows shot up in surprise. "Don't you already know? She left you a billion messages."

The blood left Adrian's face as he scrambled to get his phone out of his pocket. When he hit the button to turn on the screen, though, nothing happened.

"It's out of power," he said, cursing himself for an idiot. "I'm so sorry. There's been so much going on, I forgot to charge it."

He was terrified Iggs would be furious at him for that. *He* was furious with himself, but the wrath demon actually looked relieved.

"I'm glad to hear it was an honest mistake," Iggs said, clapping Adrian on the shoulder. "I knew it had to be something like that. Bex'll be happy to hear it, too, when she gets back."

"Back?" Adrian repeated as he shoved his useless brick of a phone back into his pocket. "Back from where? Where did she go?"

"That's the problem," Iggs said, his tanned face falling into a worried scowl that made him look ten years older. "We don't know. She was supposed to be breaking her sword, but then there was this giant *crack,* and everything went crazy. By the time we recovered, she was gone."

Adrian stopped dead in his tracks. "Gone?" he repeated when Iggs looked back. "How was she gone? And why in the world would she break Drox?"

"Because he asked her to," Iggs said, motioning for the witch to keep following him around the RV.

Adrian did so at maximum speed, racing around the Winnebago's blunt nose at slightly less than a panicked run. When he finally came around the corner, though, what he saw stopped him cold yet again.

It looked like a bomb had gone off at the base of his tree. The oak itself was fine, as was the spiderweb-wrapped hand dangling from its branches, but everything else was blasted to pieces, including what appeared to be the remains of a red plastic cooler and the rubble left behind by what must have once been two very large pieces of granite. Adrian had no idea why any of it was here, but Boston and Lys were standing over the wreckage like sentinels, talking together in hushed voices that stopped when Adrian came into view.

"Well, well, well," said Boston, swishing his tail with a level of scorn that only cats could achieve. "Look who finally decided to grace us with his presence."

"I didn't know I was needed," Adrian said, striding across the blackened grass to join them. "My phone ran out of power, and I didn't notice. I'm so sorry. I swear I wasn't ignoring you on purpose!"

"Oh yes, that makes me feel *so* much better about being abandoned for hours," his familiar replied in a voice dripping with disdain. "I'm sure everyone here is delighted to know you meant no offense. We simply weren't important enough to merit a thought in your mind."

"It's not like that," Adrian groaned, rubbing an exasperated hand over his face as he turned to Lys, who he hoped would be more reasonable. "What happened?"

"That's none of your business," the lust demon replied in a voice so sharp, Adrian swore he could feel it stabbing him in the ears. "You had your chance to be part of this, but you weren't there when she needed you, so shove off."

"*Lys!*" Iggs cried, running to Adrian's side. "He wasn't trying to hurt Bex. His phone ran out of power. Cut him some slack! He already said he was sorry."

"I'm not accepting any apologies on my queen's behalf," Lys said, turning their back on the witch as they crouched back over what appeared to be the epicenter of the blast that had destroyed everything.

"Bex will decide if he deserves forgiveness when she gets back. Until then, he's not getting a thing from me."

Adrian winced at the naked hostility, but Lys had always been a ball of spikes when it came to Bex, and these were hardly ideal circumstances. Lys's words had been harsh, but the way they'd wrapped their arms around their androgynous body looked more terrified than angry to Adrian. Iggs looked epically freaked as well, whispering frantically to Lys while the lust demon just kept shaking their head.

It was clear he wouldn't be getting anything useful out of them anytime soon, so Adrian stepped away from the whispering demons and walked over to Boston, who was sitting on the bottom step of the demons' Winnebago, cleaning the ash out of his fur.

"What in the world happened here?" Adrian whispered, crouching in the blackened grass beside his familiar. "Why would Bex break her own sword? And how did everything get blown up?"

"Oh, I'm sorry, are you talking to me now?" Boston replied, looking up from his grooming with an expression so scornful, Adrian would almost rather he'd clawed him in the face. "I didn't realize you still valued my opinion after you *abandoned me.*"

"I am very, very sorry," Adrian said, mentally preparing himself to repeat those words multiple times a day for the next several months. "I didn't mean to ignore you or Bex or anyone. I just got caught up in my work and didn't notice my phone was dead. That was my stupid mistake, but I swear it wasn't malicious."

"I know," Boston said as his angry glare softened into a sad one. "But mistake or not, you really dropped the ball this time, Adrian. Bex did everything she could to contact you short of taking the ferry over to Bainbridge herself. She dragged her heels until the very last second, but you never called her back, and eventually, she ran out of time and had to shatter Drox by herself."

That was what everyone kept saying, but Adrian still couldn't believe it. "Why in the Hells would she shatter her own sword?"

"Because it was the only way," Boston replied, finally getting over his ire now that he was doing his favorite thing—being the one in the know.

"Remember that big war demon Bex was fighting when you left? Well, it turned out she *couldn't* beat him, and apparently, that failure was the straw that broke the camel's back. I'm not entirely sure of the logic since I'm neither a demon nor a divine creation, but Drox became convinced that he was the weakest link and demanded that Bex break him in an attempt to activate the spark of Enki, the god of creation who forged all the queens' swords."

His green eyes flicked to the tree above them. "I was brought in to install safeguards for the Anchor, since no one knew what would happen when a Blade of Ishtar was destroyed. It should've been your job, but I was all the Blackwood they had, so I did my best."

"You did amazingly," Adrian assured him, placing his hand on the healthy roots he could feel beneath the burned grass. "The tree's not even touched."

"I endeavor to uphold the standards of our coven in all things," his cat replied, puffing out his chest for a moment before the worried look came back. "But it still almost wasn't enough. None of us were prepared for the shock wave that happened when the Blade of Wrath snapped. It hit the demons hardest, but I was still blown out of the tree. By the time I made it back to my feet, Bex was nowhere to be found."

"That explains why the whole Anchor's in a five-alarm panic," Adrian said, glancing back at Iggs and Lys, who'd stopped talking and were now just staring at the epicenter of the blast as if they could bring Bex back through sheer will. "Any idea where she went?"

"To Enki, presumably," Boston replied. "That *was* the point of all this. But you know how Bex's demons get whenever they don't know her whereabouts, and that explosion wasn't exactly comforting. Iggs swears she's still alive, and he's the one who would know, but there's nothing we can do at this point except wait for her to come back."

Adrian breathed a sigh of relief. Missing was still bad, but at least he was no longer terrified that Bex had died while he'd been distracted. But while he was feeling much better, Boston reached out to smack the brim of his hat.

"Don't think this not being a total disaster means you're off the hook," the cat scolded. "I don't know Bex half as well as you do, but even I could see that she was terrified tonight. The demons didn't give me all the details, but from what I overheard, it wasn't guaranteed that Drox would survive this process. Bex might have just killed the sword that was practically her familiar with her own hands. I know she's a hardened warrior, but that's too much for anyone to go through, and you left her to do it alone." He shook his head. "I'm no expert on human relationships, but I'm pretty sure that makes you a terrible boyfriend."

"I'm pretty sure you're right," Adrian agreed glumly as he straightened his hat. "But I know how to make it up to her."

Boston snorted. "Does it involve groveling?"

"Bex hates groveling," Adrian reminded him. "And this is *so* much better." He leaned closer, breaking into a grin as he whispered excitedly to his familiar. "I did it."

"Did what?" Boston whispered back, then his green eyes went huge. "Don't tell me you finally got into an Anchor!"

"I did a lot more than that," Adrian promised as he held out his arm. "Come back to the Blackwood with me, and I'll show you everything."

That would normally have been Boston's signal to leap onto his shoulder while asking a billion questions, but his familiar's ears snapped flat back into the fur on his head.

"You can't *leave*!" he hissed. "Have you learned *nothing* from this?"

"There's no point in me staying," Adrian argued, glancing at the demons, who were still keeping watch over the place where Bex had vanished. "You said yourself there's nothing we can do until Bex gets back from wherever she's gone. We have no way of knowing how long that's going to take, so I mean to spend my time making sure she's got something good to come back to. That's always been my part in this fight, and I'm not going to fail her. I've already got everything I need. All that's left is to make the final jump from theory to practice, and that'll be a lot easier with the world's best familiar at my side."

"Flattery will get you nowhere," Boston warned, though Adrian didn't miss the little smile on his face. "But all right. Let's see the breakthrough that was so big, it made you forget how to use a phone."

"That's my curious cat," Adrian said, rubbing his hand over Boston's back.

"Yes, yes," his familiar said, tolerating the petting with the utmost dignity. "Now, let's get out of here. The atmosphere is growing unpleasant."

It was getting pretty tense. Now that Adrian was no longer terrified or trying to convince Boston not to hate him, it was hard to miss the heavy aura of fear as the crowd of nervous demons began to push in on the war demons' circle. Iggs had already moved to help General Kirok keep the nervous mob back. No one was doing anything yet, but it wasn't a good situation. If Adrian offered his assistance, though, he might end up having to use curses on Bex's subjects, which would make things even worse. The safest course was to remove himself entirely from the situation, which also suited Adrian's needs since he hadn't thought this would be a long trip and had left several magical projects cooking in his forest as a result.

"You left in-progress spells unattended?" Boston yowled when Adrian mentioned this. "I can't believe it. I let you out of my sight for one day, and you forget every bit of proper procedure!"

"Relax," Adrian said as he hopped onto Bran. "They're not witchcraft."

The cat gaped at him in horror. "Then what are they?"

"The solution we've been looking for," Adrian promised, scooping Boston into his arms right before he hopped back on his broom and launched them into the air.

Boston dug his claws into his witch's sleeve with a yowl as Adrian shot them over the angry crowd and down the tunnel. He threaded his broom between the guards who'd given him a hard time earlier and flew straight for the exit, ignoring the war demons' shouts as he leaped off his broom and walked out into the alley. The moment he was sure no scalies were looking, he hopped back on Bran and flew straight up between the buildings. The sudden lift kept Boston distracted as he clung to Adrian for dear life, but the second they leveled out in the cloudy night sky, his familiar shot to the front of the broomstick.

"Adrian Arthur Llewelyn Blackwood!" he cried, arching his back like the black cat on a Halloween decoration. "Why does your coat reek of quintessence? What in the Great Forest's name have you been doing in my absence?!"

"Thinking outside the box," Adrian replied as they shot over the water. "You've been working with me on this all month. You know exactly how many dead ends we've hit. Well, last night, I was contacted by someone who helped me get around all that."

Boston's eyes narrowed to suspicious green slits. "Contacted by whom?"

"You'll find out in a minute," the witch promised. "Because I already invited him to join us."

His familiar almost fell off the broom. "You invited a *stranger* to the *Blackwood*?"

"He invited me to his house first," Adrian said defensively. "And he's an ally, not a stranger. His help is the only reason I've made any headway against Gilgamesh's defenses."

"Being Heaven's enemy doesn't make someone our friend!" Boston hissed, arching his back even higher. "Just who is this mystery person you've been ignoring your *actual* allies to conspire with?"

That was too complicated to explain to a mad cat on the back of a broom. Boston was about to see for himself anyway, so Adrian let the issue hang and just focused on flying as they sailed over the dark bay toward Bainbridge.

Chapter 10

When they reached the forest, Adrian directed them down, weaving Bran between the dark trees like a nighthawk to land them on the road that ran along the Blackwood's inland border. His broom had just touched down when the man who was already waiting by the tree line stepped away from the hemlock he'd been inspecting to give them a dazzling smile.

Boston responded by dropping into a hissing crouch and digging his claws into Bran, who protested by dumping the cat onto the pavement. The familiar recovered at once, clawing his way up Adrian's coat to perch furiously on his shoulder instead.

"*Adrian!*" he cried, every black hair standing on end. "That's a *sorcerer*! Why is there a *sorcerer* waiting for us?!"

"Because I asked him to," Adrian said. "This is the ally I was telling you about, the one who's been helping me figure out how to circumvent Gilgamesh's defenses." He paused, taking a deep breath in preparation for the words he'd been rehearsing since he'd left for the Anchor.

"Boston," he said proudly, "this is Malik al-Fatheen, my father."

His familiar's hackles dropped a fraction. "Your father?" he repeated skeptically, looking back and forth between Adrian and Malik, who was still crossing the empty road to join them.

Despite never having seen him anywhere but his island, Adrian wasn't surprised that Malik looked more at home on Bainbridge than he did. The forest was still damp from this afternoon's rain shower, but his father was dressed for the weather in an elegant camel trench coat, olive-green Wellington boots, and perfectly stitched buckskin gloves. He looked like a country gentleman out for a stroll on his estate, but his smile was as warm as a kitchen hearth when he walked up to shake Adrian's hand.

"Sharif informed me of your message just a few minutes ago," he said. "Thank you so much for inviting me to see your work. I'm impressed you found something so quickly."

Adrian shook his father's hand with a grin. "Thank *you* for coming all the way out here on such short notice."

"An invitation to the Blackwood is a rare and precious gift," Malik said humbly before turning his smile on the puffed-up black cat who was still growling at him from Adrian's shoulder. "But before we go any further, you must introduce me properly to your companion. Is it possible that I have the honor of being in the presence of *the* Boston of the Blackwood, world-renowned expert on modern magical materials?"

The lavish compliment was enough to make Boston stop growling, but the cat's voice was still suspicious when he asked, "How do you know about that?"

"Because I am a great fan of your book."

The cat's green eyes went huge. "You've read my book?"

"I never go anywhere without it," Malik said, pulling a well-thumbed paperback out of the pocket of his trench coat. "Your *Field Guide to Magical Reagents* is an essential reference."

By the time he finished, Boston's jaw was resting on Adrian's coat collar. "But..." he said at last, "the printer told me we only sold a hundred copies."

"Of which I own three," Malik said proudly. "One for daily use, one to keep as a backup, and one as part of my library's reference collection." He opened the copy from his pocket to show Boston the note-covered front page. "I'd be honored if you'd sign it for me."

Boston sat in stunned silence for a moment, then he leaped off Adrian's shoulder so fast that his witch was sent stumbling.

"Let me get my stamp pad!"

Adrian recovered just in time to see his familiar tear up the hill into the forest, and then he turned back to his father with a grin.

"Nice going. You just made his year."

"He wrote a good reference," the ancient sorcerer replied as he slid the book back into his jacket. "Not one I have much personal use for, admittedly, but I still found it interesting to familiarize myself with the thinking of the creature Agatha chose to be my son's companion."

Adrian wasn't sure if that was sweet or stalkery, but it'd made Boston ecstatic, so he kept his comments to himself and motioned for his father to follow him into the woods.

Malik did so with great enthusiasm, striding up the muddy hill without hesitation and asking his son about every plant they passed. The interrogation made Adrian feel like he was walking with his mother, but unlike the Witch of the Present, Malik's questions weren't tests. He seemed legitimately excited to be here, and since Adrian could think of nothing more worthy of excitement than his forest, he was happy to answer every question that came out of his father's mouth.

By the time they made it up the hill and into his cabin, Boston had his stamp kit ready on the table. Adrian had plenty of time to get a fire going and put the kettle on while the cat pressed his ink-covered paw onto the front page of Malik's book with great ceremony. When the signing was finally over and Malik had answered all of Boston's questions about which parts of the book were his favorites, Adrian had tea ready for everyone, distributing the mugs across the table while Boston went to the sink to wash the ink off his toe beans.

"I'm sorry I can't offer you a seat," he said as his father accepted the steaming tea with a polite nod. "I do most of my work standing, so I never bothered making chairs."

"I'm not so decrepit that I can't manage a few hours on my feet," Malik assured him, removing his coat and hanging it on a peg beside the now-roaring fire. "I'm far too excited to sit down in any case. You would not believe how long I've wanted to see inside a Blackwood."

That seemed odd given his relationship with Adrian's mother, but Boston was already trotting back to the table on his clean paws and took it upon himself to explain.

"That's because you're a sorcerer," the cat announced with the confident authority of someone whose entire writing career had just been validated. "No minion of Gilgamesh has ever been permitted within the Great Blackwood. As Adrian's familiar, I should be demanding that he remove you from his grove at once, but you're obviously a man of excellent good taste, and I'm very curious to hear how Adrian ended up with a sorcerer for a father."

"That was my good fortune," Malik said humbly, "and I am not the sort of sorcerer you are thinking of. I've sworn no allegiance to the Eternal King, nor do I abide by the laws of Heaven. I am an original sorcerer from the ancient kingdom of Uruk and the only survivor of Gilgamesh's first purge."

By the time he finished, Boston's eyes were the size of hickory nuts. "That must be why Lady Agatha chose you!" he cried, leaping onto the table. "You're like us, an enemy of Heaven."

"I prefer to think of myself as an ally of humanity," Malik said. "My warrior days are long behind me, but I have been training my son in the magic of his heritage. It is my greatest hope that he will surpass me and succeed in my vision of making the world a better place."

"He's been teaching me his magic so I can use it against Gilgamesh," Adrian translated. "All of Heaven was built on sorcery. The real, ancient Sumerian kind, not the cribbed lines modern sorcerers throw around. If I can learn how to use Heaven's own magic—"

"You'll be able to unravel the Eternal King's control," Boston finished, looking pleased with his witch for the first time since they'd been reunited. "Well, at least now I understand why you've been so preoccupied."

"Adrian is a natural talent," Malik insisted. "Even I've been astonished by the swiftness of his progress, and my hopes were already very high. I'm dying to hear about the breakthrough that drove him to invite me over in the middle of the night." He turned back to Adrian expectantly. "Go on. Don't keep us in suspense."

He motioned impatiently with his tea mug, but Adrian was too flustered to obey. He still wasn't sure if the effusive praise was sincere or if his father was simply trying to win him over faster. Either way, it was absolutely working. After a lifetime of struggling for even a sliver of his aunts' approval, Malik's open admiration made Adrian feel invincible, which was the only reason he had the guts for the plan he laid out next.

"I've already established that teleporting into the Anchors is a no-go," he said. "The princes' reaction to the bells is—"

"Wait, wait, wait, wait, *wait*," Boston interrupted, holding up his paw. "Teleportation? Princes? What in the Hells have you been doing?"

"The first sorcery I taught him was how to move as Gilgamesh's sons do," Malik explained.

"And the first thing I did with it was teleport into the Boston Anchor," Adrian followed up. "But the spell makes a bell noise that the princes can hear, which means they all came teleporting after me."

Boston blinked several times while he processed all of that.

"I'm happy you're still alive, then," he said in a shaky voice. "But if teleporting into an Anchor triggers the alarm, how do you intend to reach the chains?"

"By *not* going in at all," Adrian said, grabbing the diagram he'd made earlier and spreading it out on the table between the three of them.

"These two circles represent Heaven and Earth," he said, tapping the two rings he'd copied from the image his father had drawn in the dirt earlier that afternoon. "As you see, they're totally separate, zero overlap, which means the Rivers of Death"—he slid his finger to the thick black lines he'd drawn between the two circles—"have to pass through the emptiness between them."

"So what?" Boston asked. "We're trying to cut chains, not rivers."

"But the chains *follow* the rivers," Adrian said excitedly. "That's why Gilgamesh always builds his Anchors in cities! He needs to build in population centers because the Rivers of Death have always been the connectors between our world and the afterlife. *That's* how Gilgamesh is able to string giant chains across what should otherwise be a howling empty void. He's just following what's already there."

He turned back to his father. "It's exactly what you said before. Gilgamesh has a lockdown on the chains, but no one controls the rivers. We've still got one flowing right under the Seattle Anchor. The chain's connection is long gone, but the river can't be stopped because, unlike the Wheel of Reincarnation that puts souls back in, the full cycle of life and death is too big for Gilgamesh to control!"

"It's too big for anyone to control," Malik said. "Even at the height of their power, the gods never could figure out how to stop humanity from dying. But while your assessments are correct, I still don't see what you intend to do. The rivers you speak of aren't like the gentle, glittering waters of Paradise. These are the raw headwaters of death, icy and dark. Not even the daughters of Ishtar can survive in them for long."

"Ah," Adrian said with a grin. "But I don't have to survive them. I just have to take a page from Gilgamesh's book and follow them."

"How?" Boston asked. "Are you going to build your own ferry to the lands of the dead?"

"I thought about that, actually," the witch said. "But I don't know anything about boat building, and even if I did, shipping an army down a fast, narrow, deadly river seems like a recipe for disaster. No, I think Gilgamesh already found the best solution, which is why I'm also going to build a bridge."

Now Boston looked really confused. "Out of what?"

"My trees!" Adrian cried, throwing his hands out with a flourish before dropping them right back down to his diagram.

"All this time, we've been killing ourselves trying to get Bex onto a chain so she can cut it.

Gilgamesh, likewise, has been focusing all of his efforts on keeping us away from the chains. That's why we've been running into so many walls. We've always been striking at Heaven's most protected spots. But if we go *around* those walls, hit where Gilgamesh *isn't* watching, we can cut all the chains we want!"

Adrian thought that was pretty straightforward, but Boston still looked baffled. Malik, however, was staring at him in wonder.

"Where is Gilgamesh not watching?"

"Here," Adrian said, slapping his hand down on the gap between the circles. "Every chain in the world runs through the empty space between life and death. All this time, we've been trying to reach the chains through the Anchors, but that's only one end of the line. To actually reach Heaven, the rest of the chain has to go allllll"—he slid his hands up and down the diagram's empty space—"through here. And since a cut anywhere on a line breaks it, any part we can reach will do the job. If we can get Bex onto a chain *after* it leaves Earth but *before* it reaches reach Heaven, Gilgamesh won't even see us coming!"

"Not to keep belaboring the issue, but how do you intend to do that?" Malik asked. "The reason Gilgamesh does not guard the middle portions of his chains is because they hang in nothing. You're talking about a journey into the space between life and death. How will you reach that without dying yourself if you don't use an Anchor?"

"By going through the Anchor we already control," Adrian explained, his voice shaking with excitement. "Like I said before, there's a deathly river flowing right under our noses. I already decided not to use a boat, but there's something much older that also follows water, and unlike building a ferry, it's something I know all about."

"Roots," Boston said at once, his head snapping up.

"Bingo," Adrian replied with a grin, grabbing a pencil out of his enchanted pocket to draw a new line between the circles.

"Bridges aren't the only things that cross rivers. Trees have always instinctively followed water, and I've already got a well-established oak inside the Seattle Anchor. If I keep growing it using the river as a guide, I should be able to build us a new, living bridge straight to here."

He tapped his pencil point on the spot where all the snaking rivers came together to enter the circle representing Heaven.

"Paradise is much smaller than Earth," he explained. "Gilgamesh's Anchors are scattered all over the planet, but they were all made to hold down one wheel, which means all the chains must eventually come together at a single point. The Rivers of Death follow the same logic—millions of souls from all over the world flowing into a single afterlife. Now, since the chains follow the rivers *and* the place they're all going to is smaller than the place they came from, there should be a stretch where all those chains and rivers converge."

Adrian looked at his audience with a determined grin. "That's our target. Right before the rivers and chains enter Paradise, there should be a sweet spot where everything clumps together. If I grow my tree along the river to that point, Bex should be able to walk right out on the roots and attack multiple chains at once. Even better, she'll be doing it from inside Gilgamesh's blind spot. By the time he realizes he's under attack, the chains will be cut, the Wheel of Rebirth will spin free, and the gods will be reborn!"

He finished with a flourish, chest heaving from the exhilaration of revealing his grand plan, but his father and familiar were staring at him with matching expressions of disbelief.

"*Can* you grow a tree into the void between life and death?" Malik asked at last.

"A good witch can grow a tree anywhere," Boston said, "but no good witch *would*." He turned back to Adrian with a scowl. "I understand what you're proposing, but the Blackwood is a living thing. Forcing it to go beyond the boundaries of life would take all the magic in your forest and possibly kill the entire wood. Even if you are willing to sacrifice your grove for this, it'd take a whole season to grow any part of a tree across the distances you're describing."

"Not if I cheat," Adrian said, taking the last coin of quintessence out of his pocket and placing it on the table.

Boston recoiled when he saw it, but Malik looked more intrigued than ever.

"What are you going to do with that?"

"Answer my own prayers," Adrian said, keeping his eyes on his father. "Boston's absolutely right about the costs of growing the tree I just described. He only knows half the story, though, and so do you, because

I'm not just a witch or a sorcerer's son. I'm both. That's why this is going to work, because sorcery is a magic of understanding, and there's nothing I understand better than witchcraft. You told me the first time we met that I couldn't power sorcery with forest magic because it was too slow, but you never said anything about going the other direction."

"You mean using quintessence to power witchcraft?" Boston asked.

"*Exactly!*" Adrian cried, grinning at his cat. "All my life, people have made a giant deal about my high quintessence tolerance. I always saw that as a bad thing because it made me a target for the warlocks, but I was looking at it all wrong. Thanks to my father, I now know that quintessence can be used against Heaven as well, so that's exactly what I'm going to do."

He slapped a hand against the place on his chest where his heart would have been. "I can use myself as the bridge. Now that I know how to handle it properly, I can swallow enormous amounts of quintessence without harming my body. Since my heart is woven into the Blackwood's roots, that means my forest has access to all that power as well. I don't need to kill my grove or wait a season to make this happen. *I* can be the reservoir my trees drink from! And I can use the enemy's own power to do it."

He clenched his fists tight. "Don't you see?" he asked, looking back and forth between his familiar and his father. "This is *it*. This is how we're going to win!"

Just saying those words out loud made Adrian feel like he'd already done it. This wasn't just the solution to their current problem. It was the breakthrough he'd been waiting for his entire life. The fear that kept the Blackwood witches trapped in their forest, the power that forced demons to bow to their slavers, the endless war that had ground Bex into a shadow of herself, *this* was how they beat it. This was the power that would tear down Heaven!

But while he was absolutely convinced, Boston still looked skeptical.

"Are you *sure* you can use quintessence on trees?" he asked. "I always heard it was poisonous."

"Of course I'm sure," Adrian scoffed, pointing out his cabin's window at a line of straight, dark trunks that were still visible thanks to the light pollution bouncing off the underside of Seattle's low clouds. "I've been doing it all afternoon. I didn't want to waste your time with an unproven theory, so I experimented, and the results were even better than my hopes. I managed to grow ten acorns into hundred-foot trees using nothing but quintessence! Not even the Old Wives can grow a tree from seed to sky in less than twenty-four hours, but I did it in twenty minutes, *without* harming the interior cellular structure or the roots."

He moved his finger back to the new line he'd drawn on his diagram. "We've already established that nothing impedes the flow of the Rivers of Death toward Heaven. If I can replicate this evening's success on my oak in the Anchor, we'll have our very own living stairway to Heaven! And the *best* part is that everything I grow will be part of my forest, which means I'll have total control. If a prince or anything else tries to teleport in to stop us, I'll just have my tree dump him into the void. We'll have our very own defended assault path! One that's way better than Gilgamesh's gold-plated bridges, because unlike sin iron chains, plants can *move*. We'll be fast, mobile, and completely undetectable! Heaven won't even know what hit it."

That was the part he was *really* proud of. Sorcery was his father's skill and witchcraft was his mother's, but combining the two belonged to Adrian alone. He was the only person in the world who could possibly pull this off, and while there were still a few kinks to iron out before he was ready to grow an oak into the void between life and death, he was confident he'd figure it out. Right now, Adrian felt like he could do anything, and from the grin spreading over his father's face, Malik agreed.

"Quintessence-powered witchcraft," he said, shaking his head in wonder. "It's incredible."

"It's abomination," Boston snapped, staring at Adrian with a very different expression. "This is bad witchcraft, Adrian. Hasn't your mother always warned you about the danger of free power?"

"But it's *not* free," Adrian argued. "Quintessence is incredibly expensive. The only difference is that the enemy's footing the bill this time. I'm not abusing free power. I'm making Gilgamesh pay for his own destruction, which he absolutely should after everything he's cost us."

"I can't disagree there," his familiar said with a desperate look. "But this still feels wrong. We don't even know where quintessence comes from. For all we know, it's ground-up souls."

"So what?" Adrian demanded. "The forest eats dead things all the time. Even if quintessence is made from souls, it's not as if we're keeping them from Paradise. There is no more Paradise! So long as Gilgamesh has the cycle of rebirth chained up, none of us get to go anywhere when we die. That's why we need to do this, Boston! Gilgamesh's war threw the whole world out of balance. If we topple his regime, we'll restore that balance, which makes this the best witchcraft there is. The Blackwood benefits, Bex and her demons benefit, you and I and the whole world benefit if Heaven falls! Surely that's enough good to justify using an unorthodox power source. Aren't you the one who wrote that the greatest force in nature is adaptation?"

"That was my favorite quote from the foreward," his familiar muttered, staring down at the table. He stayed that way for a solid thirty seconds, and then he gave his whiskers a shake.

"All right," he said as he lifted his head. "I still think this is a bad idea, but we've been making bad ideas work since we came to Seattle. I actually like this plan better than the time you filled your forest with curses. At least this way, Gilgamesh will be the one who gets bitten."

"Yes, exactly," Adrian said, petting his cat. "*Thank* you."

"Well, I thought it was genius from the start," Malik declared, walking over to throw his arms around Adrian. "My brilliant, *brilliant* son! I should have sought you out ages ago."

Adrian blushed, unsure how to respond. He was just about to try hugging his father back when Malik suddenly let him go.

"I can't wait to see your new magic in action," he said, turning back to the table where the diagram was laid out. "Where are the problems?"

"Sorry?" Adrian said, unable to follow the sudden change in subject.

"The problems," his father repeated impatiently. "Combining sorcery and witchcraft is revolutionary, but you didn't call me out to your forest in the middle of the night just to brag. There are still parts of this plan you haven't worked out, yes? So, let's solve them."

That *was* why he'd asked Malik to come over, but the sudden switch caught Adrian by surprise. Fortunately, Blackwood witches learned early to be quick on their feet, and after a few seconds of bewilderment, Adrian leaped back into the fray.

"There are still a few sticking points," he admitted, grabbing the diagram from his father and flipping the paper over to reveal the math he'd done on the back. "Boston already spotted the biggest, which is volume. Whether it's coming from the forest or quintessence, growing any part of a tree to the size we're talking about requires a *lot* of power."

"I knew it," Boston said, walking right on top of Adrian's giant sheet of paper to check the numbers for himself. "What's the damage?"

Adrian took a deep breath. "Seven tons of quintessence."

"Seven *tons*?" Boston cried, nearly falling off the table. "I take it all back. This is a horrible plan! Where in the world are you getting seven tons of quintessence during a shortage? And how in the Great Forest are you going to use it? Even your big mouth can't chew that many coins at once."

"Ingestion is another problem," Adrian admitted, rubbing the back of his neck self-consciously. "I already tried grinding it up and chugging it like a potion, but the coins seem to lose potency the moment you break them."

"At least fifty percent," Malik confirmed. "But that's because coins of quintessence prioritize stability. They were made for safety and convenience, not volume."

"Then how do sorcerers cast big spells?" Adrian asked.

"By working in teams," his father replied. "Grand sorcery requires the efforts of hundreds, which is why Gilgamesh has so many sorcerers. He needs the numbers to spread out the load since most normal humans start to suffer significant brain damage after ten coins."

Boston's ears went flat against his skull. "Brain damage?"

"That won't be a problem for me," Adrian said confidently as he picked up his trembling cat. "Remember what the Spider was always going on about? I'm a quintessence machine."

Boston looked slightly mollified by that, but Malik was frowning.

"Even if toxicity isn't an issue, the sheer amount of quintessence required still presents a mechanical challenge." He frowned harder, tapping his scarred fingers on the paper where Adrian had shown his work. "There's nothing for it. We'll have to use liquid quintessence."

Adrian blinked. "It comes in a liquid?"

"That's how it begins," his father explained. "All quintessence is originally in a liquid state, but it's highly volatile, which is why it's usually pressed into coins. That's the only form safe enough for mass distribution. Raw liquid quintessence is far more powerful, but its inherent instability means you almost never see it outside the Holy City. Fortunately, I've been obsessively acquiring quintessence since Gilgamesh invented it. I've hoarded quite the stockpile over the years, including several barrels of liquid."

"Really?" Adrian said breathlessly. "Can we buy them off you?"

"Absolutely not," Malik replied sternly. "I will give you as much as you need. I insist upon it."

He looked absolutely serious, but Adrian couldn't believe what he was hearing.

"You can't do that," he said, clutching the table. "Gilgamesh stopped the flow of quintessence a month ago when he closed the Anchors. The global supply has gotten so tight that even single coins are selling for thousands. If the liquid stuff is as potent as you claim, we could be talking about millions of dollars' worth of quintessence. You can't just give that to me because I'm your son!"

"You being my son has nothing to do with it," Malik insisted. "I'm giving you my quintessence because you have done exactly what I hoped when I sent Sharif to fetch you. You have exceeded my expectations. You might have only come up with it to achieve a military advantage, but the magic you just described will change the world! I would give all that I own just to see you attempt it. Compared to that, a few barrels of liquid quintessence from my stockpile is very cheap, especially since I wasn't using it anyway."

"You're puffing up his head," Boston warned as Adrian's face burst into a beaming smile.

"Talent needs to be nurtured," Malik replied, never taking his eyes off his son. "How much liquid quintessence do you think you'll require?"

Adrian snapped out of his happy daze to think. "I don't know," he confessed after almost a minute. "You said it's more potent, but without knowing how much more potent, I can't do the calculations to—"

"I'll just bring everything I have," Malik said. "Be right back."

Before Adrian could say another word, his father vanished in a deafening crash of bells, leaving him and Boston rushing to cover their ears.

"I thought you moved the trees so that couldn't happen," Boston said when the noise died down.

"I did," Adrian replied, rubbing his temples in a desperate attempt to stop his head from ringing. "And it worked, by the way. The impact you felt last night was me trying to teleport into my forest and hitting my own ward like a bug on a windshield, but the sound-dampening matrix only seems to stop people from teleporting in, not out." The smile returned to his face. "A brilliant and convenient design element in hindsight."

"You are getting insufferable," Boston informed him as he hopped off the table. "Aren't fathers supposed to destroy your ego?"

"Only bad ones," Adrian said. "Good ones build you up, which makes Malik the father of the century. Without him, I'd still be killing plants in a tunnel. Now, we're on track to win it all!" He paused to dig his dead phone out of his pocket. "I should let Bex know."

"Not about the sorcerer," Boston warned as Adrian jogged to the back of his house. "Since you decided to neglect me so terribly, I've spent more time in the new Free Market than you have, and the sentiment there is highly sorcerer-unfriendly. They have bonfires on Fridays where they literally burn the servants of Gilgamesh in effigy. If Bex finds out your father's one, she's going to want Malik's head on a platter."

"No, she won't," Adrian said confidently as he hauled himself up the ladder to his office loft to plug his dead phone into his solar charger. Not that it did much good since it was still the middle of the night, but he hadn't had time to install real solar panels or batteries yet, which meant the little charging station was all the electricity he was going to get. He was wondering if quintessence could be converted into voltage when Boston called up from the floor below.

"What makes you so sure Bex won't kill him?"

"Because she's not judgmental, and Malik's a good guy," he called back, leaving his phone plugged into the charger in the hope that the morning sun would fill it up before Bex returned. "She's the queen of wrath, not prejudice. Also, Malik's the reason we're about to go from losing this war to winning it, which is what Bex cares about the most."

"If you say so," Boston replied as his witch hopped down the ladder. "What are we doing first? I wouldn't normally ask such an obvious question, but you planned all of this while I was abandoned in the Anchor, which makes it very difficult to do my job."

Adrian rolled his eyes at the editorializing, but he didn't say a word. Boston had every right to be angry, but while the cat could hold a grudge to rival Adrian's aunt Lydia, he was an impeccable familiar. He'd grouse about this for months, but he'd do his job perfectly. He was already at it, listening attentively while Adrian explained, with diagrams, exactly how they were going to do the impossible.

Chapter 11

Bex was standing in Paradise.

Not the one where she saw Ishtar during her reincarnations, with its beautiful green hills and glowing rivers. This was a war-torn waste of ash and dust without a single drop of water. The only reason Bex recognized it was because she could never not know the land of her birth, and because she'd seen the white fortress glistening in the distance before. That was Gilgamesh's Holy City, the one she'd seen at the end of the golden bridge when she'd gone out to cut the chain.

The sight of those towering, pure-white walls was enough to make Bex step back. Fortunately, the Holy City of the enemy was very far away. So far that the only reason Bex was able to see it was because she was standing on top of a mountain.

That was odd. Bex didn't remember ever hearing about a mountain in Paradise, but that was unquestionably where she was standing. The mountain was enormous, too, a great spike that rose like a thorn straight up from the charred remains of the Riverlands. And pinned at the top of that spike like a severed head was a beautiful, ash-covered temple with a single blown-out door.

Bex let out a breath that was half wonder, half dread. She recognized this place, but she couldn't remember why or what it was. Drox could have told her, but her precious sword lay broken on the mountain path beside her. His hilt was still in one piece, but the rest of him had been shattered like a mirror, the black pieces lying scattered in the mountain's ashy dust.

Moving in fits and jerks, Bex bent down and began collecting Drox's fragments into her shirt. The sword's jagged pieces were razor-sharp, but Bex had dressed for combat tonight, not fashion. Her black cotton T-shirt was as thick as a sail, giving her a safe place to cradle her shattered partner as she rose back to her feet and approached the temple's broken door.

Nostalgia grew with every step. She couldn't recall Drox ever mentioning a temple on a mountain, but just like when she'd recognized her sister's hand stuck on the end of the princess's arm, Bex knew to her bones that she'd walked down this exact road many, many times. She was also certain that it hadn't looked like this. The temple above her should have been gleaming with gold, not blackened with soot, and the elegant door at its base looked like it had been bashed in with a battering ram. There was even an old blood splatter on the stone path in front of it.

Bex bent over to press the fingers of her free hand against the large black stain. All the demons in Paradise had been damned to the Hells since the war, which meant whoever spilled this blood had been dead for at least five thousand years. She would've expected any blood marks to be long gone by now, but the stain on the ground was still as dark as fresh paint.

Bex didn't know if that was because it never rained here or if there'd simply been so *much* blood that the years hadn't been able to wear it all away. She couldn't even tell if the black blood had come from one demon or many, but its origin was clear. Long ago, someone had made their last stand at this position. The bloodstain ran up to the broken doors' threshold but not across it, proof that whoever had died here had done so before the temple had been opened. There was only one person in Paradise who could have committed such a heinous act, so the real question was: What was inside this place that Gilgamesh had wanted badly enough to smash his way in?

With a shallow, shaky breath, Bex lifted her foot over the line where the black blood ended and stepped into the great hall of what could only have been a palace meant for the gods. Even after being abandoned for eons, the whole place still shimmered with the endless glint of gold. Bex normally hated the color because it reminded her of Gilgamesh, but this was no tacky prince or gilded statue. This was true divine majesty.

All the parts low enough for humans to reach had been stripped and looted, but the upper half of the towering hall was an untouched relic from the time before the fall. The arched ceiling in particular was a work of wonders: an enormous, flawlessly-carved golden relief of the gods in all their glory. Bex spotted Ishtar at once, standing above the sundered main door with her wings outspread and her six horns held high. Holy Anu stood beside her wearing the Crown of Wisdom as befit the god of kings.

There were hundreds of other figures carved into the ceiling beside them, but those were the only two Bex recognized, which suddenly struck her as a problem. She hadn't thought finding Enki would be an issue, because how did anyone overlook a god? Now that she was actually here staring up at the roster of Heaven, though, Bex realized she had no idea which of the divinely perfect faces was her sword's maker.

Drox could have told her. Just as she'd instantly spotted Ishtar, her sword would've been able to point at Enki without her even having to swing him. For the first time in Bex's life, though, Drox wasn't around to give her advice. He'd entrusted her with everything he was, but he couldn't speak or help. She was completely on her own this time, which was a far more terrifying feeling than Bex had been prepared for.

Clamping her jaw against the dread that was growing in her stomach, she called her fire to her free hand and raised it in front of her like a torch. If breaking Drox had brought her to this place, then Enki must be somewhere nearby. Her plan was to follow the destruction left by Gilgamesh's ancient army since their king had probably been leading them toward whatever was most important, but there turned out to be no choices to make. The golden hall had no turns or side rooms. It simply continued forward, leading Bex under the carved faces of the long-dead gods until she reached another door at the temple's opposite end.

The first thing Bex thought when she saw it was that Gilgamesh was a copycat. The giant golden doors in front of her looked exactly like the ones she and Adrian had found beneath the Seattle Anchor, except these weren't decorated with cuneiform or lions. Their giant fronts were covered with two fifty-foot-tall bas-relief figures: Ishtar on the left and Anu on the right.

The images were so lifelike, Bex half expected them to look down and ask her what she was doing here, but of course they didn't. The king and queen of Paradise had been dead for five thousand years. These were just their shadows, two divine ghosts standing with their hands still raised to stop any who dared approach. An impotent gesture that was made even more pathetic by the giant hole that had been melted through the gold at their feet.

Stepping into that breach felt more blasphemous than anything else so far, but Bex hadn't shattered her sword to look at some art. The spark of Enki she'd unleashed when she'd broken Drox had brought her here for a purpose, and Bex bet it was in the place Gilgamesh had broken the gods' sacred doors to reach. She just prayed the thieving king left something for her as she ducked through the slagged hole and came out in a room that looked totally different from the rest.

There was no gold here. No war-damage mosaics or carved figures. Just white. Pure, blinding, unrelenting white. So much white that Bex couldn't actually make out the room's size or shape because the white was all she could see.

She dropped her head at once, focusing on her feet while she waited for her eyes to adjust. This left her staring at the running shoes she'd borrowed from Nemini to replace her beloved combat boots. The white sneakers looked gray compared to the snow-white floor beneath them, but at least the contrast gave Bex's eyes something to adjust against. Eventually, she was able to look into the room without blinding herself, but she still didn't see anything but white. It was the only place in the temple she hadn't been to, though, so Bex squinted her eyes as tight as she could get them and stepped into the room.

Thank Ishtar she'd let her eyes adjust. If she'd stumbled in blind, she never would've noticed the ripples running across the floor, making it look like she was walking on the surface of a white lake. She was tapping the ground with her toe to make sure it would hold her weight when the whole room shook, and a figure emerged from the white.

It was a man. A giant one with a body carved from what appeared to be black marble. His hair and beard were made from sculpted bronze, and he was wearing armor made from thousands of overlapping hammered-bronze scales. It looked like an early version of the golden armor the princes wore, but this was no son of Gilgamesh. Despite everything that had been done to them, the Celestial Princes were still human. This man looked like a temple statue that had come to life, right down to the ceremonial golden hammer clutched in his right hand.

The only part of him that looked remotely biological was the slit across his stone throat. *That* looked fresh as butchered meat. The wound was even still gushing, sending a waterfall of white down the stone man's neck into the collar of his breastplate.

The sight made Bex go still. Not because of the violence; she was used to that. Bex was frozen because, before this moment, if anyone had asked her what color the gods' blood was, she would have said black like her own. It had never even crossed her mind that the gods could bleed white, but the figure in front of her was most certainly a god, and his blood was as white as driven snow. As white as the muck that poured out of the princes when she slew them. Quintessence white.

That sight, more than any other, was what made Bex's black blood run cold. Fortunately for her, the god didn't seem to notice.

"This is a surprise," he said in the same thundering voice that had brought her here, despite the fact that his stone mouth never moved. "Never thought I'd see one of Ishtar's brood again."

Bex fell to her knees in an instant, clutching the shirt with Drox's pieces against her stomach as she bowed her horns to the floor.

"Holy Enki."

That was a total guess. Unlike her mother, whom she'd recognized instantly, Bex had no idea who this god was. He was holding a hammer, though, so Bex rolled with her gut and kept her horns low, trusting in the gods' famous love of worship to keep her from being struck by lightning or cursed or whatever it was this particular deity did when slighted.

She must have guessed correctly, because the god nodded at his name. He leaned forward next, his metal eyes—which were made from the same interlocking circles as Gilgamesh's princesses, just in bronze rather than gold—turning with a whirring *click* to focus on the sword shards in Bex's shirt.

"Finally broke, did he?" the deep voice rumbled. "It seems the years haven't been kind to any of us."

"Drox didn't break on his own," Bex said, lifting her head a fraction so she could look the god in the face. "He asked me to shatter him so that we could come here. I am Rebexa, Queen of Wrath, daughter of Ishtar, and in my mother's name, I beseech the Great Enki to reforge my sword so that I may slay Gilgamesh and reclaim our lost home."

The god tilted his stone head, reaching up to scratch the slit in his neck as he considered her words.

"A rash aim," he said at last. "But Ishtar's Wrath was always rash. Who else would break her own sword to find me? Who else's sword would suggest such madness? It must be as you say." The god's stone lips curved into the ghost of a smile. "Very well, Blade of Death. Show me what you have brought."

Bex bent over to lay Drox's pieces on the rippling white floor, taking great care to place each one gently rather than dump them. When all the shards were pieced back together in front of Enki's massive, bronze-sandaled feet, the god crouched down to run his stone hand over the wreckage.

"You certainly did a thorough job," he rumbled, picking up one of the crooked slivers that had been part of Drox's cutting edge. "Was this damage present before he was shattered?"

"Yes, Great Enki," Bex said, too happy that someone was actually doing something to worry about the grim tone of his voice. "He was a perfect sword for eons, but time wore both of us down. I was fortunate enough to be restored in the fires of life, but Drox's damage could not be repaired."

"Of course not," Enki said dismissively. "My swords were forged to serve the queens of death. The fires of life would have been completely incompatible."

"But you can fix him, right?" she asked eagerly.

The god's metal eyes narrowed. "You think to make demands of me?" he asked in a scornful voice. "Is five thousand years all it takes for the child of Ishtar to forget her place?"

Bex dropped her horns again at once. "Forgive me, Great Enki. I did not mean to offend."

He nodded, satisfied with her deference, but Bex was starting to sweat. She hadn't wanted to believe Drox when he'd said that Enki might not have enough strength to fix him. After all, Ishtar had also been killed by Gilgamesh, and she'd still brought Bex back to life a hundred and ninety-eight times. Surely, *surely,* the great Enki would have enough oomph left to fix one sword.

Even with her head down, though, Bex couldn't miss how sluggishly the god moved. He'd had to set his hammer on the ground and brace his weight against its handle just to reach down, and the wound on his neck *still* hadn't stopped bleeding.

Now that he was closer, Bex saw that the god was actually wounded in multiple places, including a stab to his chest that had punctured his immaculately crafted armor. None of the other injuries were gushing like the one in his throat, but they all contributed to the white essence that was leaking down Enki's stone legs to join the pool beneath Bex's feet.

A lake of the white blood of the gods.

"Figured it out, did you?"

Bex yanked her head up just in time to see the god slump to the ground in front of her.

"This is where it ended," his booming voice informed her miserably. "Anu and Ishtar were already dead, and the queens had failed to protect us. All of Paradise was on fire, and Gilgamesh's army was everywhere, so I sounded the horns and summoned everyone who was left to return here, to the Temple of Creation."

Enki nodded at the whiteness all around them.

"This is where the gods first set foot upon the world, the most sacred of all sacred places. If we were injured, this was where we healed. If we were lost, this was where we could be found." He looked down at black marble fingers he'd pressed against the rippling white lake to keep himself upright. "I built this temple with my own hands. I thought it would enshrine us forever, that the glory of the gods would endure until the end of time, but he broke down the doors and killed us with Ishtar's own sword. The sword *I* made."

Bex nodded gravely. "Gilgamesh destroys everything."

"Of course you would say that," the Great Enki muttered. "How obvious the ending must seem now to those who can look back, but we who lived through it were caught completely by surprise. I know that is difficult for you to understand. You are the Sword of Ishtar, a weapon made for destruction. It is not your nature to comprehend the joy of creation, so you will have to take me at my word when I tell you that the king of Uruk was our greatest success."

"Success?" Bex repeated in shock. "You're right, I *don't* understand. How can the man who destroyed everything possibly be called a success?"

"Because he was able to do it at all," the god said with a look that might have been proud if it hadn't been so bitter. "The entire purpose of the Paradise Project was to lift humanity out of its base animalistic nature. By cleansing mortal souls of their sin and giving gifts to the worthy, we sought to refine this rough wilderness into a better, more peaceable world. Our progress was slow and uneven, but in Gilgamesh, we found everything that we desired: a sorcerer king whose multiple reincarnations had granted him great power. Power he used to uplift his subjects and spread the divine light of civilization far and wide."

The bleeding god smiled. "He was everything we wished humanity to be, and we showered him with gifts because of it. Wise Anu himself tutored him in statecraft, but he was an energetic child who was skilled with his hands, so I taught him how to use the hammer, chisel, and forge. His battle skills were honed by Ishtar, who also taught him how to turn his kingdom into the most fertile land ever cultivated. He was as close to our divinity as any mortal could be. We were certain he would become the light that could lead humanity out of its darkness, until..."

"Until he betrayed and killed you," Bex finished.

The great Enki slumped lower with a bitter sigh. "Even gods can be deceived. We wanted so badly for Gilgamesh to be what we hoped, we allowed ourselves to become blind to what he was. By the time his true face was revealed, the strongest of us were already dead, and it was too late."

"But it doesn't have to stay that way," Bex said, lifting her head. "Gilgamesh's sins don't have to go unanswered. The other queens have fallen, but I'm still here, and I have my fire again. I'm even working with a witch to—"

"A witch?" Enki scoffed. "Don't waste your time. They're just human bumblers, barely more than animals. They're not *real* magic."

"They are absolutely real magic," Bex said hotly, too angry on Adrian's behalf to care that she was correcting a god. "It's because of his witchcraft that I got my fire back, and we *all* got a second chance. I can cut the chains Gilgamesh has used to bind the Wheel of Reincarnation and bring the gods back to life. All I need is for you to repair my sword, and we can *finally* turn this defeat around!"

She was grinning by the time she finished. Even grievously wounded, Enki was still a god. There had to be something he could do. It didn't even have to be a miracle. All she needed was for him to put Drox back together, and the two of them would take care of the rest. Surely, the god who'd built a temple as grand as this one could manage that much, but Enki had already turned away.

"No."

"No?" Bex repeated, dumbfounded. "What do you mean, 'no'?"

"Mind your tone," the god warned. "And 'no' means exactly what it says. I will not fix your sword."

Bex held her breath, waiting for him to continue, to say anything that would explain this madness. But the great Enki just sat there, bleeding his white blood onto the ground as if he had all the time in the world, and the longer he stayed silent, the angrier Bex got.

"I didn't come all this way to give up," she growled, rising to her feet. "Drox gave his life to get me here because he believed in you. I did, too. I've fought for the gods for over five thousand years! We're closer to destroying Gilgamesh's Heaven than we've ever been, but I can't fight your war without my sword. I'm not asking you to risk yourself. I just—"

"That is exactly what you are asking," Enki interrupted, glaring at her with his metal eyes. "Do you know how much it costs me to appear before you even in this meager state? Gilgamesh cut us as low as we would go. He cuts us still, bleeding and leeching what little remains of us so that the glorious gods will never rise again. I'm not even truly here. The visage speaking to you now is merely a memory, a phantom conjured by the blood Gilgamesh spilled ages ago. So much blood that not even the bloodthirsty king of Uruk could use it all."

He nodded at the white lake under their feet, and then he sighed.

"I know violence is a queen's answer to everything, but what you ask is impossible."

"There has to be a way," Bex insisted, grabbing Drox's broken hilt off the floor and clutching it to her chest. "I know your divine workshop is gone, but the tools of man have come far in the last five thousand years. I can find you new forges and metals, get you whatever you need to—"

"Arrogant creature," Enki snarled, his stone lips curling into a sneer. "You think to tell the God of Crafters how to do his craft?" He pointed at Drox's broken hilt. "You think the circumstances that permitted the forging of a divine blade can be duplicated with simple materials bought from the markets of men? Stupid girl! Your sword is a product of the gods the same as you are. Just as you can only be reborn through Ishtar, your sword can only be mended with my power, and all of that is gone."

"There has to be something left," Bex said desperately. "If the gods were truly as powerless as you say, Gilgamesh wouldn't need so many chains to keep them bound. Your spark was able to bring me here. That means there has to be something left that we can use." She pressed a hand against her own chest. "I was made from Ishtar's body. Use me if you have to. Just give me back my sword!"

The god lifted his chin with a dismissive sneer. "That's not how it works," he informed her. "You can't make a sword out of flesh. Even if I could somehow transmute your weak body into an appropriate substance, you are no longer pure." He narrowed his bronze eyes. "I can see the fire of life burning where your sacred immortality should be. You've become as death-bound as the common demons Ishtar made to muck out her rivers. I'm not sure you could swing one of my creations now."

"I can always swing my sword," Bex said hotly. "But fine. If I'm no good, tell me what you *can* work with, and I'll get it for you. I'll get you anything you need, just fix my—"

"*Enough!*" Enki roared, lurching back to his feet. "You're just like your mother, always demanding miracles and expecting others to make them happen. Ishtar never listened when I told her something wouldn't work, either, but you can't force what's not possible. Even if a suitable forge still existed, I couldn't use it because the creations of the gods come from *us*. Our divine essence is what fuels your magic and gives you your deathless nature. That wasn't an issue back when we were infinite, but if I was to honor your request and fix your Drox, there'd be nothing left of me! I'd be even further reduced, even more diminished. I wouldn't even be able to manifest the echo you speak to now! You're asking me to give up the last sliver of my divine power and become a ghost in truth, and I'm not doing that to fix a broken old sword."

"Why not?" Bex snarled. "You haven't done anything else with your power in five thousand years."

Enki's face grew furious. "That is not how you speak to a god."

"I'll speak to you like a god when you start acting like one!" Bex yelled, lifting her horns high as she glared at him. "I came to beseech the help of the Great Enki, but all I've found is a sad old man! You've spoken better of Gilgamesh than you have of my sacred mother. But while you cower in your grave, hoarding the few drops of power your betrayer deigned to leave you, Ishtar never stopped fighting. For five thousand years, she has waited in her rivers, throwing her sword back at the enemy whenever I fell into her hands. I've been her blade even when I could no longer burn, but now, for the first time in eons, we have an opportunity to change things."

She held up her fist, which was already burning like a torch in her fury. "The Bonfire of Wrath is alive again. We've taken Gilgamesh's lands and stand ready to attack the foundations of Heaven itself! You want to know why I'm filled with the fires of life? It's because I *am* mortal now. I gave up all of my rebirths, all my infinite futures, for the one chance *right now* to burn Gilgamesh to the ground! Not because I'm Ishtar's Sword, but because I am a queen. Every demon in creation is depending on me to free them from Gilgamesh's Hells, but I can't do that if you won't *help me*."

"Why should I care about demons?" Enki asked sullenly. "They're Ishtar's creations, not mine. What does their fate matter to me?"

"It matters because we're all on the same side!" Bex roared. "Because, unlike the *Great Enki*, we're still fighting to reclaim Paradise for *all of us*. If we're successful, all the gods will be reborn, including you! You don't have to sit here being a memory in a bloody room. You can leave this prison, rebuild your forges, and go back to how things were before!"

She shook Drox's broken hilt in his face. "Everything you want is right in front of you, but I can't drag you into that future by myself. I *need* my sword, which only you can repair, so please. *Please*."

She lowered her horns again, bowing her head lower than she ever had to anyone except Ishtar herself. She stayed that way for a solid minute, and then the bleeding god sighed.

"I see now why Ishtar chose you to be her executioner," he rumbled. "Even five thousand years after her death, you remain as blindly loyal as ever. You would even see me die to give your mother her victory, but you don't understand. There is no more victory. Even if the gods were reborn today, Gilgamesh has Anu's crown and Ishtar's sword. He even has my hammer. This one is just a memory."

He glanced at the golden hammer he'd set on the floor with a sad shake of his head.

"If you bring us back, he'll just kill us again, but for all the power he's stolen, Gilgamesh is still human. Death will come for him eventually as it does for all mortals, and then this whole problem will solve itself."

Enki smiled as if he'd spoken great wisdom, but Bex could only stare at him in horror.

"That's your solution?" she demanded at last. "Wait for Gilgamesh—the *Eternal King*—to die?"

"Don't sound so disbelieving," the god chided. "I know your mother has thrown you back many times, but surely, even you can grasp how little time matters to the deathless. Ishtar still rages at Gilgamesh because she is prideful, but the rest of us don't care anymore. I am, of course, still upset that my best student betrayed and killed me, but not enough to give up the final bit of power that keeps me minimally functional."

He pointed at Drox's shards on the rippling white floor. "Without my sacred forges, the only way to repair your sword would be to bathe him in my own divine blood. To honor your request, I'd have to stab

270

myself in the heart." He shook his head. "I don't enjoy being a ghost, but it's better than the alternative, which is to wallow in semiconscious nothingness until Gilgamesh dies and his chains degrade. I have little enough left as it is. I'm not giving up my only remaining comfort to satisfy the vengeful delusions of Ishtar's least successful child."

"I don't give a damn about your *comfort*," Bex snarled. "You might be willing to wait around until Gilgamesh croaks, but my people have been languishing in the Hells for five thousand years! They're still suffering right now and will be suffering forever if you *don't help*."

"That is not my concern," the god said, turning his gaze away. "Your answer has been given. Begone, Executioner of Ishtar, and do not disturb what little remains of my existence again."

With those final words, Enki reclaimed his hammer and began to sink back into the floor. The white lake had just made it over his bronze sandals when Bex's hand shot out to grab his arm.

"One final question."

Enki looked hideously offended, but Bex had her horns lowered again, so he acquiesced.

"Be quick."

"You said earlier that the only way to repair Drox without your forges was to plunge him into your own body," she said, keeping her head bowed. "Did I hear you correctly?"

"You did," the god said suspiciously. "But why do you—"

He hadn't even finished the question before Bex leaped straight up the god's black marble body to stab Drox's broken hilt into the slash wound across his throat.

"WHAT ARE YOU DOING?" Enki roared, swinging his golden hammer at Bex in a frantic effort to knock her away.

"What I was made for," Bex snarled back, dodging his blow easily as she wedged the broken hilt deeper. "I am the Sword of Ishtar, last queen of her people! There is *nothing* I will not do for their sake! I'm certainly not going to leave them in eternal suffering so a spoiled old goat can rot away in his crypt in comfort."

"You will not get away with this!" Enki cried as he dropped his hammer to grab at Bex with his marble hands. "This is betrayal! Blasphemy! *Treason!*"

The list went on, but Bex wasn't listening. The god truly was weak, she realized. His carved stone muscles looked impressive, but his body moved slower than a normal mortal's. Even when she stopped dodging and let him catch her, he wasn't strong enough to pry her off, leaving nothing in her way as Bex wedged what was left of Drox's sword into the hole Gilgamesh's betrayal had sliced through the god's neck.

It was a harder target than she'd expected. Drox's broken end didn't give her much to work with, and the wound was surprisingly shallow. In the end, she had to finish Gilgamesh's work and rip the god's throat open wider to get Drox inside. It was a macabre spectacle, but Bex was angry enough to make anything work. Her bonfire was roaring to the top of the god's tomb, boiling the white lake as she plunged her black sword deep into the body of his maker.

"You will suffer," Enki gurgled as he fell to his knees. "Even if you claim to do it for her sake, Ishtar will never forgive an attack on another god. You have made yourself as great a traitor as Gilgamesh! We'll all be reborn someday, and when we are, I swear, I'll see you destroyed by Ishtar's own hand, Rebexa the *Betrayer!*"

"Fine by me," Bex said through clenched teeth, bracing her white-blood-soaked sneaker on the god's shoulder to hold him still as she started feeding the rest of Drox's shattered pieces into the stab wounds in Enki's chest. "If I live to see the gods return, that means I've won and Ishtar's children are free. I don't care what happens to me after that, so threaten all you want. I'm still getting my sword back."

The dying god cursed her name, but Bex didn't care. She held him down, feeding Drox into his wounds piece by piece. Only when every one of the black shards was inside Enki did she finally let go, her chest heaving as she staggered back to watch the god's body...

Bex wasn't entirely sure, actually. Enki had said his form here was just a shadow made from memory, but it'd felt real enough to her. He actually looked even more like a corpse now that she'd put him on his back, but as Bex waited for whatever was supposed to happen to happen, she realized the floor was getting lower.

The white lake of gods' blood was draining into Enki's corpse. The liquid moved like a waterfall in reverse, flowing backward into the wounds she'd fed Drox's shards into. Drop by drop, the blinding white of the monochromatic tomb vanished, revealing a circular room filled with yet more golden carvings.

Bex watched the transformation with a mixture of terror and satisfaction. Now that all the white was gone, the space didn't even feel holy anymore, which meant she'd actually done it. She'd actually killed a god, or at least what was left of one. She was still trying to wrap her head around that when the last drop of white rolled into Enki's stone body. The god's corpse crumbled to ash a heartbeat later, leaving a new creation in its place. A long black sword with a wide chopping blade so shiny, it gleamed like an obsidian mirror in the light of her fire.

"Drox," Bex whispered, scrambling across the ash-covered gold floor to grab the enormous sword's freshly-wrapped hilt. "*Drox!*"

Her fingers fumbled over the unfamiliar ridges of the pristine new leather. For a long moment, she heard nothing. Then a voice—that familiar, blessedly grouchy voice—spoke in her head.

My queen.

She bent over her sword with a sob. She was clutching him to her chest in relief when Drox finished his sentence.

What have you done?

Bex froze in place. Her first thought was, *How did he know?* Drox shared her mind while she was touching him, but he'd never been able to read her memories. He should have no idea what had occurred while he was broken. But before Bex could think of how to ask without making it sound like she was keeping secrets, she saw it.

The bonfire burning merrily across her hands was streaked with black. The flickering shadows were barely visible against bright yellow and orange flames. Someone who didn't know her fire inside and out probably wouldn't even have noticed them. To Bex, though, the black mark was all she could see, a shadow not even the blazing light of her bonfire could banish.

You have been stained with irrevocable sin, Drox said, his deep voice shaking. *Rebexa, what have you done?*

"What I had to," Bex whispered, sitting back on the ashy ground. "He was going to leave you broken, leave us *all* to suffer so he wouldn't have to be bothered."

So you killed *him?*

When Bex didn't deny it, Drox's horror filled her head.

I can't believe it, he said. *You killed a god. Betrayed one of our divine creators!*

"He betrayed us first," Bex argued. "I lowered my horns, I *begged* him to save us, and he told me to swing. He chose himself over everything else!"

Of course, Drox said. *He's a god.*

"He's a coward!" she yelled. "He'd rather let our people rot in the Hells for eternity than give up his own comfort. But I didn't fight and *die* for five thousand years so he could have a pleasant afterlife.

My duty is to Ishtar and her children, not Enki's selfishness."

She clenched her fist around her sword's new hilt. "I did what I had to do. Enki can punish me all he wants for that after we've won, but *until that point,* nothing—not even a god—is going to stop me, because I made Lys a promise. I swore to all of them that I would take them back to Paradise, and that's exactly what I'm going to do. I don't care who stands in my way. I *will* tear down Gilgamesh's Heaven and set all of Ishtar's children free."

She finished with her head raised high, daring Drox to say she was wrong. He'd always been the more pious half of their duo, probably because he still remembered living with the gods before the fall. Bex only knew this life, but she knew what she'd die for. It was the same thing she'd always died for, and when she dared Drox to challenge her on it, his new hilt just settled even more solidly into her hand.

Spoken like a queen.

Bex blinked. "You're not mad at me?"

I'm furious at you, her sword said, *but also proud. Never forget that I was made to serve the Queen of Wrath. Enki crafted me with one purpose: to help you do your duty, and that was what you did. Even though it stained your own fire with unforgivable sin, you put your people first. That is the act of a queen, and I will never fault you for it.*

"So you don't blame me?" Bex asked in a small voice, which was stupid. He'd just said he didn't, but she couldn't help herself. Other than Lys, Drox was the closest thing she had to a parent. Even Ishtar had only talked to her once that she remembered. She had to know he didn't hate her, but her sword just sighed.

I mourn for my creator as all creations must, but Enki is immortal. He'll return to life along with the rest of the gods, and most likely punish us both.

Bex went still. She'd been more than happy to face Enki's wrath, but she hadn't thought about Drox. Before she could apologize for dragging her sword down with her, though, Drox cut her off.

Done is done, he said firmly. *You did not fail your duty, Rebexa. I shall not fail in mine. I was, am, and always shall be your sword. We will pay for what happened here together, but until that reckoning comes, we should leave this place and go make use of this new power before anything else gets in our way.*

The brusque order made Bex smile bigger than any compliment. "You must be feeling better if you're telling me to hurry up." she said, scrubbing the ashy tears out of her eyes.

I feel extraordinary, her sword replied as she rose to her feet. *I knew I'd grown weaker, but I never realized how much I'd lost until it came back.* His shiny blade gleamed like black lightning as he turned in her grip. *I feel like a new sword fresh from the forges! Like there is nothing I cannot cut!* Drox had no mouth to smile, but Bex swore she felt him do it anyway. *Let's go see how Havok fares against us now.*

With a grin of her own, Bex turned around and started jogging back toward the melted door. She was opening her mouth to ask Drox how they got out of here—because she certainly didn't remember—when her foot went through the floor.

Bex fell forward with a yelp. In the time she'd been talking to Drox, the bottom of the tomb had turned as brittle as a dead leaf. Her first thought was that the effects of Enki's death had spread to the whole temple, but while it was no longer white or rippling, the ground still looked solid. Only the parts she touched were breaking, the ash-covered gold cracking like eggshell wherever she put her feet. It was the same thing that happened when her five minutes ran out in Limbo, but Bex wasn't in Limbo. This was Paradise, her homeland. It shouldn't be breaking under her—

That's why it's happening, Drox explained as she leaped from foot to foot. *You don't remember because it's been a hundred incarnations since the last time you tried to invade Paradise personally, but Gilgamesh used the authority of Anu's crown to banish you from his Heaven. Enki's spark is what brought you here, and it was likely only through his power that you were able to remain. Now that you've killed the last vestige of life he managed to preserve, that protection is gone, and the banishment once again takes precedence.*

"What do I do?" Bex yelled, running across the crumbling floor to grab the doors only to have the gold break off in her hand like rotted wood.

You don't have to do anything, her sword assured her. *We're not ready to assault Heaven yet. Let go, Rebexa! Your people will catch you!*

It didn't feel like anything could catch her. Bex had fallen out of Limbo hundreds of times, but at least that had just felt like falling. This was like being shoved off a cliff with an anvil tied to her feet. It wouldn't have been so bad if she could've held on to something, but everything she touched fell apart like crumbling dirt. By the end, she was only holding herself up by blasting her fire down.

Just let go, Drox said again. *Trust me!*

Bex did trust him. She'd always trusted her sword with her life, so even though it went against every survival instinct she had, Bex did it again now, snuffing out her fire to let the banishment drag her into the dark.

She fell like a stone. The drop was much, *much* longer than the one out of Limbo. Bex didn't even know what she was falling through, only that she was doing it at incredible speed, because the horrible feeling of having a weight tied to her feet hadn't vanished. It felt like there was a hand wrapped around her ankles, pulling her down harder and harder, faster and faster. Then, just when Bex was certain she was going to fall forever, the nothing she'd been hurtling through exploded back into light and color as she landed sprawling on the roots of Adrian's tree.

"*Bex!*"

She barely had time to turn her head before Lys flung their arms around her. "I was so worried," they sobbed, burying their face in her hair. "You have to stop doing this to me! My heart can't take it!"

"I'm all right," Bex whispered because she knew saying "sorry" would only make Lys even more upset. "Everything's all right."

"Is it really?" Iggs asked nervously from where he'd crouched beside them.

Instead of answering directly, Bex just held out her hand, showing her loyal demons the now-perfect black band gleaming on her finger.

The look of wonder on their faces then was worth killing a god for.

"Ishtar be praised," Lys whispered, leaning over for a better look. "Is he really—"

"Fully restored," Bex finished.

And handsome to boot, Drox added with uncharacteristic ego. *May I?*

Bex lifted her arm with a grin. If anyone deserved a chance to show off, it was her loyal sword. He'd stuck by her side for five thousand years, doing his duty above and beyond. Even when Bex had dragged him with her into blasphemy, he'd never faltered. That made him her pride and joy, so Bex happily gave the order, transforming her shiny new ring into a shiny new sword in the blink of an eye.

"Blessed gods," Iggs said, smiling so wide that every one of his fangs was on display. "He's *huge!*"

He was. Drox's rebirth was more than just a mirror shine. His blade was twice as wide as it had been before and half again as thick. All the metal the years had worn away had been returned in full, leaving him as heavy an anvil and as sharp as a cleaver.

"He's back to what he should be," Bex said proudly as she pushed off the ground. "I've only used him as a fencing weapon, but—as Drox has told me many times—he was originally a hacking blade designed to be swung with the full fury of the Bonfire of Wrath."

I could cut through mountains, Drox confirmed, his pride ringing through her head as big and flashy as his new blade. *But these aren't the demons you need to convince.*

He was right. Sitting under Adrian's tree, surrounded by her loyal crew, Bex hadn't laid eyes on them yet, but that didn't matter. She could feel the crowd waiting just a few feet away, the silent mass of demons who'd felt Drox break same as she had. They were the ones she'd done this for, so Bex pushed out of Lys's arms and stood up.

She brought her sword up with her, holding Drox high above her head as she walked over the blackened grass past the RV. Even Kirok's war demons didn't dare get in her way as the Queen of Wrath strode out of the shelter of her witch's tree and into the masses of her people.

They parted before her like the sea, scrambling out of the way as they frantically bowed their horns. Bex normally hated that, but it was necessary right now, because she wasn't here as herself. Tonight, she stood before them as their queen, the champion they'd come to Seattle to follow, but Rebexa was done hiding. This was what she'd burned up all her lives for, what she'd broken her sword and killed a god for. This was what she'd been born to do, and with Ishtar as her witness, her people would no longer cower.

"*See me, Children of Ishtar!*" she cried, lifting her sword higher as the bonfire covered her body and roared to the sky. "I have returned! The Blade of Wrath has been restored, and with it, we shall cut Heaven *down!*"

She was screaming by the end, and the crowd screamed back. The roar came from thousands of throats, but no matter what kind of demon was doing the shouting, the sound that came out was wrath. Pure, burning, righteous fury loud enough to shake the Anchor to its foundations. It shook Bex as well, causing her bonfire to roar up until it filled the sky. It was almost like what happened in Limbo, but without the terrifying loss of control, because these demons were not hunger-maddened shadows. They were Ishtar's people, Bex's people. Their fury was what she'd been made to burn for, and she raged like an inferno with it now, filling the Anchor with blinding light until not even Heaven could've missed it.

When her message was delivered and her fire finally dropped back to a more reasonable height, she looked over her shoulder to see Lys waiting with Bex's phone in their hands.

"Nemini just called," they informed her. "Havok's moving again."

"Good," Bex said as she took her phone back. "We have unfinished business."

Lys smirked at that. "And I can't wait to watch you finish it. But before you go running off to beat the fear of the gods back into him, you should know that Adrian came to see you."

Bex's fire gave a jump that had nothing to do with wrath. "Really?!"

"His phone ran out of power," Lys explained with a smile. "Apparently, he got distracted by some big breakthrough. Not that that excuses him ignoring you, but I thought you'd want to know."

Bex did want to know. Now that her sword was out of danger, all she wanted was to run to Adrian and tell him everything. Also kiss him and eat his delicious food and sit under his beautiful trees while he talked to her in that happy, excited way of his. The list was as long as her arm once she started making it, but before Bex could run off to enjoy any of it, she had to finish what she'd started in Felix's vault.

"Let's do this, then," she said as she stuck her phone back into her pocket.

"Ready when you are," Lys said, stepping into position beside her.

I'm ready as well, Drox said with an eagerness that wasn't like him at all. The sword Bex knew was cautious and patient. This Drox sounded almost giddy.

The more Bex thought about that, the less Drox's reaction surprised her. Having experienced going from a worn-down body to a restored one herself, she knew exactly how heady the power rush could be. Drox had certainly paid for it, so Bex let him have his moment, holding her new sword proudly out in front of her as she marched through the now jubilantly-cheering crowd to go thrash a cocky old war demon.

Chapter 12

It took Bex almost thirty minutes to make her way through the crowds. Not because of the bowing, for once, but because everyone wanted to talk to her. Honestly, Bex found it a little baffling. Given how the demons in Anchor had been acting all month, she'd thought her flames-to-the-sky sword-waving display would've made them even more scared of her, but the reality was the exact opposite. All the demons who'd been too afraid to stand next to her on the stairs yesterday suddenly wanted to shake her hand.

It was like the party after they'd freed the Anchor, except these weren't slaves she'd just set free. Some of them had been here for weeks. Most had never even seen her sword, so they couldn't be excited by how much better Drox was looking. If that wasn't it, though, then Bex had no idea.

"It's the hope," Lys explained when she asked about it. "The slaves you freed when we first took the Anchor already know what you are, but all of these new demons have never seen you do the queen thing. You were always in Limbo or skulking around on the stairs like you don't want to be noticed, which means they only knew you through the rumors. They had nothing concrete to believe in, so when we all felt Drox break, a lot of people thought it was the end. But then you came back like a phoenix with your roaring flames and your shiny new sword and a big 'we're going to win!' speech, so of course people lost their gods damned minds. They finally had the queen from the legends standing right in front of them! Do you know how long some of us have been waiting to feel that hope?"

When they put it that way, Bex almost felt bad. "Sorry I didn't make a bigger deal earlier, then."

"Queens don't say they're sorry," Lys scolded, but it was just a reflexive jab. The lust demon didn't even have their wings out, but they still looked like they were about to float into the air.

"This is *it*," they said, clenching their fists as the three of them made their way down the stairs, which were still full of celebrating demons. "You're on fire, Drox is back to full, and Adrian's got something huge he's cooking up in the Blackwood. I don't know how it all fits together yet, but I just know we're about to hit Heaven *hard*. After five thousand years, it's finally going to happen! Once you beat Havok into submission, it is *on*."

That was just the excitement talking, but Bex didn't bother telling Lys to calm down or be reasonable. They'd stood by Bex's side through all of this every bit as much as Drox. They deserved some giddiness, even if Bex didn't know how much her new sword was going to change things yet. It definitely felt like a good direction, though. She was getting almost as excited as Lys when they finally turned into the hall that led to the arena.

Bex didn't want any civilians getting hurt, so she ordered Iggs to stand at the mouth of the hallway and keep people back. When she was sure none of her new adoring fans would follow her into danger, she started jogging toward the arena with Lys hot on her heels. They'd almost made it to the end when Nemini stepped through the double doors to meet them, her normally blank face set in a slightly worried frown.

That killed Bex's giddy new mood real quick. Slight frowning was the Nemini equivalent of panic. Even the normally graceful Lys missed a step, causing them to bump into Bex's back as the queen scrambled to a halt.

"What's wrong?"

Instead of answering, Nemini stepped aside to let Bex look through the black-crosshatched windows into the arena. She did so in a rush, scowling when she saw Havok slamming his fists into floor and walls, pulverizing the concrete like he was being paid by the inch.

"What in the Hells is he doing?"

"I don't know," Nemini replied in a quiet voice. "But he's been at it for the last thirty minutes. The control room's repairing the damage as fast as they can, but as you can see, they're starting to fall behind."

Bex frowned at the terrifying cracks running all the way to the arena's ventilated roof. "If they get any more behind, this whole place will collapse, but it's all right. We'll stop him."

She held up Drox's shiny new ring as she finished, hoping to make the void demon actually smile for once. Nemini wasn't even looking at the ink-black band on Bex's finger, though. She was staring at the queen's face, her yellow eyes going wider and wider with a very un-Nemini look of horror.

"Bexa," she whispered as her snakes pulled themselves flat against her skull. "What have you done?"

Bex stepped back. Nemini hadn't called her Bexa since she was little, and she'd *never* said it like that. It was the most emotion she'd ever heard from the void demon, and the fact that it was coming out now turned Bex's black blood to ice.

There was only one thing she could think of that would make Nemini look at her that way. Bex hadn't thought the black stain she'd glimpsed in her fire would be visible when she wasn't burning, but she knew to her core that Nemini knew, which meant Bex had to say something *now*, or she was going to lose—

Her panicked thoughts ground to a halt when the horrified look suddenly vanished off of Nemini's face. It happened between one breath and the next, like the void demon had just crumpled the fear up and thrown it away. Bex was still trying to think of something—*anything*—to say in response when Nemini beat her to it.

"It doesn't matter."

"Of course it matters," Bex whispered, clenching her fists. "If you know what I did, then you know how bad it is, but you have to understand that I had no choice. I—"

"Did what you had to do," Nemini finished for her, looking at Bex with the same infinitely patient expression she'd worn in the RV when she'd told her to stop avoiding Adrian. "That's what you've always done, and that's why it doesn't matter."

Bex blinked in confusion, not sure if that was comfort or condemnation. She was still trying to figure it out when Nemini's hand reached out to land on her shoulder.

"The nice part about losing everything is that you get to decide what you pick back up," the void demon said. "I've been empty for a long, long time, but sometimes, there are old ideas that still cling in the strangest places. That's why I got upset, but then I remembered that I don't have to care anymore. When everything is equally meaningless, I'm the one who gets to decide what matters, and I decided lifetimes ago that that was you."

The emptiness seeping through Nemini's fingers was getting uncomfortable, but Bex ignored the spreading numbness, reaching up to grab the void demon's hand instead.

"Why?"

The word came out as a sad little squeak, and the edges of Nemini's flat lips curved into the memory of a smile.

"Because you always chose us," she said, looking at Bex with yellow eyes that were no longer flat or emotionless. "I've watched you struggle through every incarnation. You've changed in many ways over the eons, but in one way, you've always been exactly the same. No matter how awful things got or what it cost you, when the knife was at your throat, you always put your people first."

Her cold, dark-skinned hand turned over to squeeze Bex's fire-warmed fingers. "Every single time," she whispered. "Every crossroads, every trap, every impossible situation; whenever there was a choice to be made, we were the ones you chose. That's why I don't need an explanation, because whatever you did, I know you did it for us. That's what you've always done, and I'm sorry if I made you feel bad about it. My reaction came from an old and unexamined place. I hope that you'll forgive me."

"There's nothing to forgive," Bex said in a rush, lurching forward to hug Nemini tight. "Thank you."

Bex couldn't even say what she was thanking Nemini for—sticking by her, not hating her, understanding what she was trying to do even when she failed to do it. The truth was a little of everything, but there were no words for that, so Bex just held on harder, clinging to the demon who'd been there for her longer than any other until Nemini's void finally started pushing into her vision, and she was forced to let go.

"Sorry," she whispered.

"There's no need to apologize for the inevitable," Nemini replied. "Though you should probably go deal with Havok. Death comes for everyone eventually, but if he keeps hitting the walls like that, we're all going to meet our ends more rapidly than we would prefer."

Bex nodded, wiping the wetness out of her eyes before anyone saw. Drox had stayed respectfully silent the whole time, but his bloodlust was quick and sharp when Bex pulled him back into her hand.

Ready when you are.

Bex nodded again and placed her other hand on the press bar that opened the metal doors. "No one goes in except for me," she ordered, looking over her shoulder at Lys in particular, who'd already switched into their biggest fighter body. "Havok's acting erratically, and I'm not sure how my new sword's going to swing yet. I don't want to risk hitting one of you by accident."

Lys looked like they'd rather eat a bucket of nails than let Bex out of their sight again. Before they could say anything, though, Nemini put a hand on their arm.

"We'll stay here until you tell us otherwise," she promised. "Ishtar guide you to victory, assuming victory is possible."

"Would you stop it?" Lys snapped, ripping their arm away from Nemini to give Bex a salute. "Go thrash him good."

Bex promised she would and pushed open the door just wide enough to slip through. She shut it again the moment she was inside and leaned forward to see what she was in for.

Destruction seemed to be the answer. The whole arena the control room had built for her early this morning was wrecked. There wasn't an inch of cement that didn't have a crack or a chunk taken out of it. The metal railing that protected the observation balcony had been ripped out entirely, leaving Bex standing on a broken platform above Havok, who was currently punching a hole through the wall below her.

He stopped the moment she saw him, putting his armored fists down quietly, as if he hadn't just been throwing a building-wrecking tantrum.

"Good," he said, tilting his carved face up to look at her. "You're finally here."

"If you'd wanted me to come back, you could've just asked instead of destroying the place," Bex told him angrily. "Do you have any idea how expensive stretched spaces are to repair?"

"That is part of why I decided to destroy it," Havok replied, stepping back so he could glare at her properly. "Your time is up, Coward Queen."

"What are you talking about?" Bex demanded, ignoring the hated nickname in favor of getting answers. "You gave me three days."

"That was before you changed the stakes of our conflict," he said, lifting his top right hand to point at the shiny new sword clutched in Bex's fist.

Bex's face fell into a furious scowl. "Oh, I get it," she growled. "Now that I've a weapon that can actually cut you, you're chickening out on our deal." She rolled her eyes. "And you call me the Coward Quee—"

Her insult turned into a gasp as Havok launched straight up at her. It was a twenty-foot jump to the balcony from the arena floor, but he cleared it like he was hopping over a log to slam all four of his fists into the reinforced concrete under her feet. An explosion of broken cement followed, forcing Bex to leap out of the way. She landed a dozen feet behind him, coming up from a roll in the middle of the cracked arena with her sword ready in front of her.

Looks like he's decided not to join our rebellion after all, Drox remarked drolly as Havok came back down in front of them, his white armor dusty with pulverized cement.

"Let's not be hasty," Bex told her sword as she fell into a crouch. "Havok is still a valuable asset. He's

291

just pissed off right now, but if I can get him to calm down and listen, I—"

Bex never got to say what she was going to do. She hadn't even seen Havok move, but the war demon was suddenly right beside her, his two left fists already flying at her ribs.

If she hadn't just spent eighteen hours avoiding those exact punches, they would've caved her chest in. But Bex knew Havok's movements almost as well as her own by this point, and she managed to dodge at the last second. Unfortunately, this didn't stop Havok's fists, which continued straight through where she'd been, to put a fresh crack in the already beleaguered-looking floor.

Bex's patience evaporated after that. She had no idea what bee had gotten into Havok's armored bonnet, but like hell was she letting his hissy fit destroy their Anchor. She'd get her answers *after* she kicked his ass, so Bex lit up in an explosion, sending her flames flaring to the ceiling as she swung Drox's new sword straight at Havok's head.

He dodged, of course, but Bex knew he would. She'd been swinging at and missing Havok for the last twenty-four hours. She knew his dodges as well as she knew his hits, which was why this attack had been angled to make him step to the left.

The moment he did, Bex changed direction, slamming her foot into the cracked floor to brace as she swept Drox's cutting edge toward Havok's shoulder instead. The quick change put the war demon at a bad angle, forcing him to throw up his arm for the block. If Drox had still been a whittled-down shadow, he would have slid right off the war demon's thick armor, but this time wasn't like all the others. Swinging Drox's new, bigger blade took more strength than Bex was used to, but when her sword's gleaming black edge slammed into Havok's white armor now, the war demon was the one who broke.

The *crack* that filled the arena was the most beautiful sound Bex had ever heard. Drox must have agreed, because his satisfaction flooded her mind before the swing was even finished. Bex was giving him a mental high five when she realized her actual arms were still going.

Since Bex had never attacked with this new version of Drox before, she'd completely messed up both the power and trajectory. They'd gone straight through Havok's previously unstoppable armor like a bullet through glass, but her sword was still moving, pulling Bex with him as he slammed straight past Havok and into the floor behind him.

The *crack* that followed was even louder than Havok's break, and not nearly as enjoyable. Drox hit the arena floor like a battering ram, shattering the already-cracked cement and opening a hole into the residential floor below. For one long heartbeat, Bex could only stare in shock at the roofs of the high-density apartment buildings, then she pulled Drox back into his ring and threw both of her arms out in front of her, calling an enormous gout of fire to blast herself away from the hole.

She cursed as she flew. It hadn't even occurred to her that they could break through into other floors, which was *stupid* because that was exactly what she'd done to escape with Adrian back when this had been the Anchor's sorcery office. The control room didn't seem able to stop the collapse, either. The hole was actually getting bigger as more and more of the floor crumbled away. She was still trying to find somewhere solid to put her feet when she felt the wind off Havok's next punch coming in from the left.

Bex leaped out of the way at the last second, jumping all the way across the arena in the hopes of finding a safe place to land. She'd just found a corner that didn't seem to be collapsing when she whirled back around to face her opponent...

And came to a total stop.

A few feet away, Havok had landed in his typical guard position. He always kept his fists close in front of his body to attack or defend as needed, except this time, there were only three of them. His fourth fist— along with the entire lower half of his upper right arm—was missing.

That made sense given how Drox had gone right through his forearm into the floor, but Bex had cut the arms off war demons plenty of times. She was used to the bloody mess that followed, but Havok had none of that. *His* arm ended in an empty hole—no black blood, no gruesome stump, no mess of any sort. Now that she'd cut it open, Bex realized she could actually look into his armor, because there was nothing inside.

What in the name of Ishtar?

The question came from Drox, but Bex was thinking the same thing. All this time, she'd assumed Havok's armor was the result of a war demon's protective horns reaching their natural end state. He was super old, and the plates covering his body definitely looked like bone. Honestly, she'd expected to find a shriveled-up old man inside when she finally cracked him open, but this shell held nothing at all. Now that she thought about it, there hadn't been any blood the one other time she'd managed to slide Drox's blade between Havok's plates, either. She was still trying to figure it all out when Drox's voice shouted in her head.

Duck!

Bex barely heeded the warning in time as Havok's left fists—the ones she hadn't been staring at—swung through the air where her head had just been. The forearm she'd cut off must really have been empty, because losing it didn't slow him down at all. Havok came at her as fast as ever, pummeling Bex with his armored fists from above and below. She dodged the first few out of habit, then she got smart and threw up her sword, blocking on Drox's sharp new edge so that Havok would have to cut himself if he wanted to hit her.

It was a trick she'd pulled a few times, but Havok had always ignored her sword and kept punching before. Now, though, he gave Drox a wide berth, pulling his blows at the last second to avoid slicing his hands open. The uncharacteristic caution threw off his rhythm and allowed Bex to get ahead for once, hitting back with a series of quick strikes that shaved pieces off his armor until the floor was littered with scraps of white. She was about to try for something bigger when Havok caught her by surprise, sweeping his long leg up and behind her defense to kick her square in the side.

Bex stumbled with a gasp. She'd been doing so much better than usual, she'd forgotten how much it sucked to take a hit from him full-on. That kick had been lightning-fast, but it'd still landed hard enough to knock her breath out. She was still trying to get the air back into her lungs when Havok kicked her again in the same spot even harder, sending her skidding across the arena.

Right into the hole in the floor.

Bex saw the edge only after she'd gone over it. The next thing she knew, she was tumbling in free fall above a high-density housing complex full of terrified demons. She could already see their frightened faces through the windows of the charming residential building she was about to crash into like a meteor. She'd kill them all if she hit, so Bex pulled her sword back into his ring and called her fire, blasting herself backward to cancel her momentum in an uncontrolled frenzy.

That was sloppy, Drox scolded. *I thought we practiced this.*

"We didn't practice falling from the sky!" Bex shouted as she unleashed a second, much more controlled blast of superheated flame to right herself. She was about to launch back through the hole in the ceiling when she spotted Havok waiting at the edge like a wolf watching a rabbit den.

Bex's flight jerked as her fire faltered. There was only one way back into the arena, but taking it meant she'd also have to take whatever attack Havok was preparing. A punch that would send her flying right back into the building she'd just narrowly avoided was Bex's guess, but when she started scrambling to find a flight path that wouldn't get her socked, Drox's voice cut through her panic sharp as a razor.

Swing me at him.

"What good will that do?" Bex cried, staring at the war demon, who was standing a good fifteen feet above them. "There's no way you can reach!"

I can reach him, her sword replied with absolute certainty. *Trust me and swing.*

Bex didn't see how that was going to happen. Plunging him into Enki had doubled Drox's size, but all those gains were in width and heft, not length. Her new blade was infinitely smoother, sharper, and shinier than her old scratched-up one, but Drox's point extended no farther than it ever had. That should have made what he was suggesting impossible, but in all the years they'd been together, he'd never asked Bex for something she actually couldn't do. Every one of his absurd demands had always turned out to be achievable in the end, so Bex put her faith in her sword, grabbing Drox's hilt with both her flaming hands to swing him as hard as she could at Havok.

The first half of the attack looked exactly as useless as she'd expected. Her blade was miles too short for what they were attempting, but when Bex reached the point in the arc where Drox's tip came up level with Havok's foot, her sword did something he'd never done before. He reached *into* her bonfire, into the flames that were always burning at her core, and yanked some out for himself.

Bex was still reeling when all that stolen fire shot out of Drox like a whip, creating a searing line of flame that sliced Havok clean across the chest. The heat explosion that followed sent the war demon flying, clearing the way for Bex to launch herself back in. She did so with a fiery blast of her own, shooting up like a rocket through the hole in the floor and nearly all the way to the ceiling. She was searching for a safe landing spot when Drox's triumphant voice erupted in her head.

YES! he cried loud enough to make her ears ring. *BURN IN THE FIRES OF WRATH, YOU TRAITOROUS DOG!*

"Gods dammit, Drox!" Bex cried, windmilling her arms to regain her balance. "Don't distract me like..."

Her angry words trailed off as her sword directed her attention to the other side of the arena. When she'd seen Havok go flying, Bex assumed he'd only gone a few feet. Drox must have hit him a *lot* harder than she'd realized, though, because Havok's armored body was three-quarters of the way up the opposite wall. The explosion had lodged him in the cement like a bullet, and that wasn't even the craziest part. The *craziest* part was that not all of him was there. His white chest was singed black where Drox's fire whip had landed, but above that on the left where his shoulder and arms should have been, there was nothing. Havok's torso just ended like someone had snipped off his top corner.

"Holy Ishtar," Bex said as they finally landed back on the arena floor. "What in the Hells did you do?"

What I was made to do, her sword replied smugly. *This is the true power of a divine blade! I can't believe how far I let myself sink. I should've had you restore me ages ago. Just think how many princes we could have slain!*

Bex didn't think they could have slain any. Even with her restored bonfire roaring all around her, her arm still burned from the fire Drox had pulled through it. If he'd tried something like that before Adrian had healed her, he might have killed her.

From the way her entire right side was aching, Bex wasn't sure she'd escaped unscathed this time, but she couldn't argue with the results. Drox's surprise attack had split Havok's impenetrable armor from hip to neck. A few inches over and they would have cut him in half like a paper doll. As it was, the entire upper left portion of his body was missing, including his shoulder, a good chunk of his ribs, and both of his left arms. Since Bex had already chopped off his top right hand, this left Havok with only one fully functional arm to pry himself out of the wall.

The sight made Bex frown. She knew firsthand just how tough war demons could be, but to keep going after losing three arms and a third of your torso was pushing things even for them. Bex didn't expect a demon as old and salty as Havok to die from anything short of a beheading, but even he should've been surrendering by now.

If nothing else, the arena should have been covered in his black blood. Just like when she'd cut him before, though, there was nothing. He didn't even seem to be in pain as he heaved what was left of his body out of the wall and dropped back to the ground, turning his sundered torso to show Bex what she'd done. Or, more accurately, what she hadn't.

"What in the Hells?" she whispered under her breath.

Havok's sliced-open chest was as empty as his arm had been. All demons were black inside, so it'd been easy to mistake the shadows for flesh when he was stuck in the wall. Bex had certainly seen her own inky guts enough after dealing with a never-closing cut for seven years, but this wasn't a wound. It was a hole, a window into the hollow that was Havok's empty armor.

That's no war demon, Drox warned.

"No shit," Bex replied, keeping his new blade ready as she moved to put herself between whatever Havok actually was and the people she could still hear shouting through the hole in the floor behind her.

"What are you?" she demanded.

"What I have always been," the empty suit of armor replied. "The instrument of your destruction." He lifted his one remaining arm into position and beckoned her with his gloved gauntlet. "Let's finish this."

Bex thought it already *was* finished. Half of Havok's body was missing, but that didn't stop him from charging straight at her, swinging his one remaining fist wide for a haymaker.

The punch would've taken Bex's head off if she'd let it land, but while Havok's attacks were still whipcrack fast, it was a lot easier to dodge one fist than four. She ducked the blow with room to spare, but she didn't swing back. This was no longer about beating

Havok to make him join her army or even improving her own skills. Bex wanted answers, so when Havok flew past her, she pulled Drox back into his ring and shoved her bare hand into the armor's chopped-open torso.

It felt like reaching into a giant ceramic vase. Havok was moving too fast for Bex to get a look at his insides, but her fingers brushed against something that seemed to be dangling inside his neck. Havok spun away before she could catch it, dropping into a low crouch as his leg swept out to trip her.

It was a move he'd used countless times before in their fights. Jumping it was even easier now that Bex no longer had to worry about blocking his punches at the same time. She was already getting in position for another grab inside his chest when Drox reappeared in her hand and swung of his own accord, lopping off Havok's head from behind in a single, clean swipe.

"What was that?" Bex cried as she scrambled not to step on Havok's severed head, which was now rolling across the floor. "Don't hit things on your own!"

I am sorry, my queen, her sword replied, not sounding sorry in the slightest. *The opening I saw was too small to wait for permission, and it's not as if losing his head would kill him.*

Bex still wasn't happy, but Drox had a point. Even without its head, Havok's body was still throwing punches. Blind punches, but dangerous nonetheless. Now that she knew what was going on, Bex had no idea how Havok had seen anything to begin with. The helmet rolling past her foot looked just as empty as the rest of him, though Bex did finally get eyes on the thing she'd felt inside his neck. It was still dangling down the back of his helmet, seemingly untouched by Drox's decapitating strike.

His body was still swinging too wildly for her to get a closer look, so Bex finished the fight with two strikes to his legs, cutting each one off at the knee to finally drop the last of Havok to the ground. When the giant suit of empty armor finally stopped kicking, Bex walked over to his helmet and crouched low, sticking her arm up to the elbow inside the giant empty skull until she found what she was looking for.

When her hand came out again, she was holding a ring. A weighty, half-inch-wide black band that glistened the same way Drox's did under the arena's fluorescent lights.

"What the—"

It can't be what it looks like, her sword said at the same time, returning to his own ring for a closer look, which only made the similarities even more apparent.

"You sure about that?" Bex asked, turning the ring—which really did feel exactly like hers—over in her hand. "I mean, you'd recognize your fellow sword, right?"

Not necessarily, Drox admitted after a long pause. *Divine blades aren't like the queens we serve. We're Enki's tools, not his children. We don't all know each other by sight, and since our queens often fought amongst themselves, they took great pains to keep our powers secret from one another.*

Bex frowned. "So this could be another divine blade, then?"

It's possible, Drox said, *but utterly ridiculous. What kind of queen would leave her ring inside an empty suit of armor? Would* you *send me off to fight alone?*

Never. Other than when they'd disagreed over Adrian, Bex hadn't let Drox leave her person in living memory. But while his argument made sense, Bex's eyes still saw what they saw. She'd never held another queen's sword that she could remember, but even when it was stuck on her sister's severed hand, a divine blade wasn't the sort of thing you mistook.

There was only one way to be sure. Before her own sword could object, Bex grabbed the new ring and shoved it onto her finger right next to Drox's. She reached out with her mind at the same time, commanding the presence inside to step forward. She'd never used that move on Drox because Drox was dutiful, but Bex had to pry this voice out of its ring like a splinter. Even when she got it, the presence was resentful, tugging against her mind like a dog straining at the end of its leash.

I don't owe you obedience, Executioner.

"Don't call me that," Rebexa commanded in the hard, angry voice of a queen. "Whose weapon are you?"

You'll find out soon enough, the ring replied in Havok's voice. *Your years of running are over! You killed my creator and stained yourself in eternal sin for* nothing. *My glorious queen is already on her way. When she arrives, all that you have built will burn in the true fires of war!*

He bit into Bex's finger as he finished, drawing a stream of black blood before she managed to yank him off. She was still shaking the sting out when the room rocked beneath her feet.

Bex dropped into a crouch, looking over her shoulder at the hole in the floor. But while the damage she'd accidentally done to the arena was dire, the bottom of the arena didn't seem any closer to falling out than it'd been a minute ago. She was shifting her weight farther away from the cracks just to be safe when it happened again.

Her head popped up like a bobber as the arena's halogen lights started swinging wildly. It felt like the Anchor had just run into something. Bex was still trying to imagine what in the Hells that could be when Lys burst through the double doors.

"I know you told me not to come in, but—"

The lust demon stopped with a gasp when they nearly ran straight off the destroyed balcony. Bex expected them to jump back to safety, but Lys shed their human guise instead, flapping into the air on their leathery wings so they could fly down to Bex.

"We've got a serious problem," they said as they landed. "The Market..."

Their frantic explanation trailed off as they noticed the pieces of Havok's empty armor lying around Bex like scattered leaves.

"What happened to him?"

"He lost," Bex said, looking up at the shaking ceiling. "What's going on?"

"Not sure," Lys said, glaring at the phone that was still clutched in their clawed hand. "But I've got reports pouring in about explosions in the Market."

Guess he wasn't lying, Drox said as Bex glared at Havok's ring. Lys, however, nearly dropped their phone.

"*Please* tell me that's not what it looks like," they begged as they stared in horror at the black band pinched between Bex's fingers.

"I'm afraid it's exactly what it looks like," Bex growled, closing her fist around the heavy black ring. "Havok was never a war demon. He's another queen's sword."

Lys's amber eyes went even wider. "Was he sent to kill you?"

Bex snorted. "If that was his goal, he could've easily done it last night, or at any point today." She shook her head. "I'm more inclined to think this whole thing was a diversion. You know, stalling to buy time."

"Buy time for what?"

The Anchor rocked again as they finished, and Bex's scowl grew grim.

"Looks like we're about to find out," she said, clenching her fist tight around Havok's ring as she leaped back up to what was left of the balcony. "Get everyone evacuated! I'm going upstairs to find what's exploding."

Lys yelled back something affirmative sounding, but Bex was going too fast to hear the exact words, and they didn't matter anyway. Lys could always be trusted to do their job. Right now, Bex had to do hers, bursting through the double doors and nearly running over Iggs in the process.

"Call General Kirok and tell him to empty the armory," Bex ordered as she ran past.

"Why?" Iggs asked, running after her. "What's going on?"

"Don't know yet," Bex said as the cement hallway shook around them. "But Havok was a plant, which means we're in a trap. I want everyone and everything important moved out of the Anchor. Lys is already working on evacuations. I need you to tell Kirok to get our weapons out and then go save our village."

The Iggs of four months ago would have stumbled under that barrage, but her wrath demon had grown a lot since they'd become a real rebel army instead of just a squad. He obeyed at once, grabbing his phone out of the pocket of his jeans to make the call. Lys was already yelling into their phone for the floor leaders to start evacuating all the residential areas when they flapped through the doors out of the arena. That was all Bex had time to overhear before she left them both in the dust, charging down the hallway toward the stairs. She was almost there when she realized Nemini was running beside her.

"I don't think you want to be with me for this," Bex said.

"Wants are meaningless," Nemini replied as she matched Bex's breakneck pace. "You're going to need me."

That was probably true, but Bex had a better idea.

"Here," she said, tossing Havok's ring at her. "Take that as far away from here as you can."

Nemini didn't even look surprised as she snatched the heavy black band out of the air, but her voice was grim when she warned, "It won't work. Nothing can keep a sword from its queen."

"I know," Bex said, running faster. "But try anyway."

Nemini didn't look convinced, but she ducked her head and fell back. When Bex looked over her shoulder to see why, the void demon had already vanished.

If things hadn't been end-of-the-world-level dire, Bex would've done a double take. She'd always known Nemini had some kind of funky movement power, but she'd never seen the demon use it so blatantly before. Her eyes had literally been off of her for less than three seconds. She was still wondering about it when Drox bit into her hand.

Go faster.

Bex was already going as fast as she safely could, but Drox's instincts were always on the mark when it came to things like this. If he said "go faster," then they were going to lose if Bex didn't. The stairwell at the end of the hall was packed with panicking, fleeing demons anyway, so Bex stopped blindly charging forward and pulled her sword instead, swinging at the ceiling to cut herself another way through.

Just like when she'd accidentally swung him through the floor earlier, her new blade broke straight through the cement into the Market above them. Since it was a controlled shot rather than the continuation of a wild swing, they didn't smash the whole thing open this time. Drox sliced a perfect square, opening a hole just wide enough for Bex to jump through the ceiling and onto the grass of the Market above.

She landed next to what had been the slave auction stand before Lys turned it into a memorial. The stage Bex had cut in half was now covered in candles and flowers for all the friends and family who still suffered in the Hells. It was a very popular change, but the crowd of demons who normally prayed here was gone, chased off by the chaos that had engulfed the new Free Market.

It reminded Bex of the night they'd taken the Anchor, except this time, her people were the ones fleeing in panic. Another explosion went off while she was trying to get her bearings, forcing Bex to hit the dirt as a glowing ball of white fire the size of a car slammed into the merchant tents to her right. The explosion threw the screaming human vendors running for the exits off their feet, but Bex barely paid it any mind. She'd already shoved herself back up and leaped into the sky, lighting up like a comet as she streaked over the panicked crowd.

There was nothing strategically important to attack up here. The explosions were just a distraction, a terror tactic designed to disrupt their chain of command and stymie the demons' response. It was the same strategy Bex had used against Gilgamesh's forces, and damn if it wasn't working just as well the second time, but that fireball had come from inside the Market. That meant whoever shot it had to be close. Sure enough, the moment Bex flew past the vandalized statue of Gilgamesh, she spotted it.

There, standing in front of Adrian's towering oak tree, was a lion the size of a school bus. It looked like a golden statue come to life, but its eyes were made from the same interlocking metal rings as the princesses'. When it opened its mouth to roar, a ball of white fire came out instead of sound, blasting through the vendor tents like a runaway train car. It was an absolutely horrifying sight, but far, far worse was the woman beside it.

She was pure white, of course. From the path of destruction, it looked like the pair of them had walked right in through the Market's front door. But while the lion was clearly with her, the princess didn't seem to be giving it orders. Her attention was entirely on the oak tree as she used her towering height to reach up into its branches and pull down something the size and color of a silver basketball. Bex was too far away to see more details than that, but it didn't matter. She already knew it was an orb of spider silk with a woman's severed hand hanging like a talisman in the center.

The sight of one of Gilgamesh's doll princesses stealing her sister's hand—the same hand Adrian had given up a finger to win for her—sent Bex's fury into overdrive. She shot across the market with a roar, Drox's flaming blade already ready in her hands. She saw the golden lion's ears swivel toward the sound, but the construct's head didn't have time to turn before Bex's sword lopped it off.

The giant lion's glowing mouth went dark as its golden head tumbled to its feet. It must really have been more like a statue than a living thing, because the rest of its body didn't move at all. It just stood there like the headless lump of metal it resembled, blocking Bex's view of the alabaster thief standing behind it.

Snarling at yet another thing in her way, Bex leaped over the lion's headless body to land in the grass behind it. The area under the tree was still blackened from the explosive magic that had sent her to Paradise less than an hour earlier, making the white princess stand out like the moon against the night sky.

Bex bared her wrath demon fangs at the sight, swinging Drox at the intruder's head as she roared, *"Give me back my sister!"*

The princess dodged the attack easily, stepping to the side with a glare so cold, Bex felt it through her flaming rage. She'd already guessed which princess this was, but this was the first time—or at least the first in Bex's current memory—that she'd actually laid eyes on her. She was taller than Greed or Sorrow, taller even than Bex used to be back before the years had whittled her down. Her powder-white face was beautiful in the same doll-like way every princess's seemed to be, but the hate in her mismatched eyes—one golden, one mirror-silver like the princes'—made something deep inside Bex twitch like an old wound.

"You're her, aren't you?" she growled, tightening her grip on Drox's new hilt. "You're the traitor."

"And you're in way over your head," the Princess of War said as she tucked the orb with its stolen hand under her arm.

Bex kept her eyes on it as she crept closer. "Where's your prince?"

"I don't need him for a battle as insignificant as this," the princess informed her in a cold, musical voice, pointedly ignoring Bex's advance. "From what I've seen of your current skills, I alone should be

310

sufficient, but then"—her lips curled in a cruel smile—
"you were never a match for Heaven, were you?"

The haughty tone made Bex's jaw twitch. She
was raising Drox to shut her up when the princess
lifted her white-gloved hand, the one that wasn't
currently clutching the spiderweb orb with their
stolen sister.

For a moment, nothing happened, then Bex
heard a whistling sound from somewhere far to her
left. It sounded like a flying bullet. It hit the princess's
hand like one as well, slamming into her palm with an
echoing *thwack*. Bex winced when she heard it, but the
princess just smiled wider, her doll-like face splitting
into a cold, cruel grin as she opened her fingers to
show Bex a black ring.

"My sword did better than I expected," the
Princess of War said as she slid the black ring over her
white-gloved finger. "I knew you'd beat him eventually,
but I never dreamed it'd take you so long or that you'd
be willing to compromise yourself so thoroughly to
achieve victory." Her mismatched eyes flicked to the
faint, sin-black shadows dancing inside Bex's roaring
flames. "How far the Executioning Blade of Ishtar has
fallen."

"Don't call me that!" Bex roared, her fire flaring.
"You betrayed your own people and joined Gilgamesh
against us! You have no right to criticize me, you
traitorous piece of *garbage*!"

"Spoken like a foolish little girl who's forgotten
everything that was actually important," the Princess
of War replied, her cold voice dripping with scorn. "I
can't even count how many times we've had this exact

conversation, but that's only to be expected. If Mother let you keep your memories every time you got yourself killed, you might actually remember why I did it, and then you wouldn't be such a hard little worker."

Bex answered that insult with her sword. She was already burning full tilt, but she'd never felt her fire roaring like it was now. How dare this traitor pretend she wasn't at fault? How *dare* she belittle the lives Bex had sacrificed to save their demons—*all* their demons, War included—from the disaster she'd help create? The original Rebexa had died before the Queen of War's betrayal, but she'd heard the stories. Her sister had turned on all of them, plunging the beautiful lands of Paradise into so much chaos and destruction, Gilgamesh's army had barely needed to do a thing.

Just thinking about it was enough to send Bex's fire flaming higher than Adrian's tree. But while she'd swung Drox as hard and fast as she could at the princess's hateful face, he hadn't even gotten close. Her sword had barely made it a foot before it hit something with a *clang* and stopped. When Bex's eyes adjusted to her own wrath-fueled brightness, she saw it was a sword. A broad, heavy sword with a blade as shiny and black as Drox's own being held in an armored hand that looked exactly like Havok's, only this time, the gauntlet wasn't empty. The heavy, bone-white armor was wrapped around the princess's arm, covering her from fingers to shoulder in a shell of interlocking plates the same color as a war demon's horns.

Bex supposed that was appropriate for the Blade of War. A suit of armor was the only useful shape for the sword of a traitor who was constantly getting into fights. What she didn't understand was why the sword was still black. Every Blade of Gilgamesh she'd ever seen had been as white as its princess. Now that she thought about it, she'd never seen a princess holding her own blade, either. They normally turned into swords for their princes, but this white doll was standing cocky as a champion fighter with a black blade of Ishtar clutched in her undeserving hand. The same traitorous hand she'd offered to Gilgamesh when she'd sold out her own people.

That thought made Bex see red. She lunged forward with a roar, sliding Drox down Havok's blade to slam him through the guard and into the princess's gauntleted hand. That was the plan, anyway, but the Princess of War stepped out of the way with a smirk that just made Bex want to hit her even more. She was about to swing again when Drox grew heavy in his queen's hand.

Stop.

Bex didn't want to stop. She wanted to beat this traitor into white powder.

You're the one who said this whole thing was a ploy to waste your time, Drox reminded her. *Stop falling for it and figure out what they're wasting time* for.

Even in her burning rage, that logic was too good not to heed. It took monumental effort, but Bex was the master of the fire now, and she forced herself to pull back, settling her flaming feet in the grass as she glared at the smirking princess in front of her.

"What are you doing?"

"Putting on a show," the Princess of War replied with an innocent smile. "The Eternal King wants an example made of this place, and examples need to be showy."

"Examples can cut both ways," Bex growled, narrowing her burning eyes. "I've broken princesses before."

"Rampant, thoughtless violence *has* always been your strong suit," the princess agreed. "But even you can't burn your way out of this one."

Before Bex could ask what she was talking about, the Princess of War stomped her foot on the lion's severed head. A blinding flash followed as the beheaded lion roared its final bolt of white fire at the Anchor's false sky. The one Adrian's tree was still holding up like a tarp.

The explosion that followed was so bright, even Bex was forced to look away. By the time she blinked the spots out of her eyes and lifted her head again, the Anchor's blue dome had been blown to pieces. Little bits of burning sky were still raining down on her like ash, but Bex barely felt them. Her attention was entirely consumed by what the blast had revealed.

It was the same black nothing she remembered from after she'd cut the chain. There were no glowing rivers, no stars, nothing like the lovely landscape she'd seen while the golden bridge to Heaven was still intact. This was just blackness, a dark dome of endless void, with one glaring exception.

Directly above her head, shining like the moon about to crash into the Earth, was the Holy City of

Gilgamesh. It was *much* closer than Bex remembered seeing it when she'd stood on the chain, close enough to see the army of golden lions sitting on top of the fortress's white parapets. Absolutely massive ones that were much, much bigger than the bus-sized lion whose severed head was still crumbling under the Princess of War's carved foot. They were *so* big that Bex could see the gleam of their golden teeth from all the way down here as they opened their mouths in unison to reveal the white fire within.

"Beautiful, aren't they?" the Princess of War said, her mismatched eyes shining as she lifted her black sword to point at the horror she'd revealed. "Those are the Lions of Heaven. Their roars used to shatter entire kingdoms during the purges, but it's been so long since we had a real war, I'd almost forgotten how lovely they could be."

She lowered her blade and turned back to Bex. "I'm actually jealous that you get to witness their wonder again for the first time. Enjoy the spectacle of Heaven, Rebexa. Once the lions have made the futility of your situation clear, I'll be back."

Even with the literal might of Heaven hanging over her head like an axe, Bex laughed at that. "You can't possibly think I'll surrender."

That was what every other puppet of Gilgamesh was always telling her to do whenever they thought they had her cornered, but the Princess of War shook her head.

"It never even crossed my mind," she promised with a smile. "I've always told the Eternal King that bargaining with you was a waste of time. You're the

Bonfire of Wrath. You've never met a reasonable solution you couldn't burn to ash with your belligerence. That's why you're still just an angry child swinging a sword, while I've become the general of the greatest king who ever lived."

Bex growled in the back of her throat, and the princess's smile grew mocking.

"You're about to learn just how high the mountain you presume to climb really is," she said as she stepped back. "Even the famously delusional Coward Queen can't deny reality when it's blasting her in the face, and when the hard truth finally dawns, I'll be there to watch you break." She wiggled her gauntleted hand in a little wave. "See you soon, Bexa."

Bex swung Drox as hard as she could, handing him her flames before he could even reach. The resulting wave of fire melted what was left of the beheaded lion to slag, but the princess was already gone, vanishing in a peal of golden bells along with the spiderweb containing their sister's hand. Bex screamed after her, but the sound was lost in the roar of the lions as the cannons of Heaven began to fire.

The rain of white fire hit the exposed Anchor Market like a meteor shower. Even the Bonfire of Wrath was blown off her feet, her fire winking out in surprise as the blast slammed her into the trunk of Adrian's tree. The Blackwood was strong, so she didn't knock it over, but the oak was listing alarmingly to one side when Bex hauled herself back up to take a look at the damage.

It was even worse than she'd expected. The Market had already been wrecked by the princess's initial attack. Now, though, the burning tents and broken tables were gone entirely. With the exception of Adrian's tilting tree and Gilgamesh's golden statue, the entire Anchor Market was a blackened, cratered landscape. She was still trying to comprehend the magnitude of the destruction when her phone buzzed in her pocket.

Bex grabbed it at once, pinning the black device against her ear with her shoulder as she used both hands to push Adrian's oak back upright.

"*Please* tell me you're evacuating."

"Not a single person," came Lys's growling reply. "We've been betrayed. I don't know exactly when it happened, but General Kirok and his war demons took over the control room and removed all the exits."

Bex almost lost her grip on the tree. "*Removed* them?"

"Every gods-damned one," Lys confirmed. "All the doors that used to go outside lead to stone walls now. Iggs is working on it, but until he retakes the control room, we're locked in here like fish in a barrel."

Bex closed her eyes with a curse. Of course. Of *course* the war demons had betrayed them. Considering General Kirok was the one who'd encouraged her to go after Havok, they'd probably been planning this from the start, which meant the Princess of War was right. They *had* been completely outmatched, but they weren't dead yet.

"Keep moving people to lower levels," Bex ordered, raising her eyes to the light that was growing in the sky as the lions prepared to fire again. "I'll try to stop the cannons."

Anyone else would have asked "What cannons?" but Lys was a hardened soldier, and all they did was wish her good luck.

Bex shoved her phone back in her pocket and strode out across the smoking craters. She pulled Drox into her hand as she went, pointing his sharp tip at the white city floating above their heads.

"Can you hit that?"

Not from this range, Drox replied. *It's closer than it was but still not close enough. I don't think you can blast yourself up that high either.*

Not from the ground, maybe. Bex was leaning back to gauge whether or not she could make the jump if she climbed to the top of Adrian's tree when the sky flashed white again. The lions' roar thundered in her ears a split second later, shaking the ground as the next barrage of white fire poured down from Heaven like a purifying wave.

Straight into her.

Chapter 13

"**I** think that will be enough," Malik said as he set the repurposed, cuneiform-covered oil drum down next to all the others in the grass in front of Adrian's house.

"I should hope so," Boston muttered, giving the stacked barrels the evil eye from his perch in the branches of Adrian's heart tree. "How much damn quintessence does he think you need?"

"Don't be ungrateful, Boston," Adrian chided as he put the finishing touches on the grave-shaped hole he was digging between the tree's roots. "Malik is being very generous. We never could have gotten this much quintessence on our own, liquid or otherwise."

"That's exactly what I'm talking about," Boston hissed as he scampered down the fir tree's scaly trunk. "I know he said he's a hoarder, but there's a difference between stockpiling a few stolen barrels and keeping a whole warehouse full of the stuff! If liquid quintessence is so rare and volatile, why does he have so much of it lying around? And why is he so eager to give it to us?" The cat's green eyes narrowed. "He's up to something."

"Yes," Adrian said, crawling out of the pit he'd dug around his root-bound heart. "The same thing we are: overthrowing Gilgamesh. The Eternal King destroyed Malik's entire civilization and made a mockery of his magic. I don't find it suspicious in the slightest that he jumped in with both feet the moment we offered him a real opportunity to hit back."

"Well, *I* still think this whole thing has been far too convenient," Boston huffed, glaring at Malik through the dense branches. "He was too ready for this."

Adrian was dying to call that paranoid nonsense, but his familiar wasn't actually wrong. Officially, Adrian had invited Malik to his Blackwood to get an outside opinion on his grow-a-tree-to-Heaven plan, but if he was entirely honest, he'd mostly done it to show off. He was damn proud of his quintessence-fueled witchcraft, and he'd wanted his father (now that he had one) to be proud of him, too. He'd never dreamed that Malik would seize on his plan so fully, or that he'd do so much to help. The old sorcerer had already brought in more quintessence than Bex and her demons had seized during their entire raid on the Anchor, and all of it was liquid.

Even for a plan to defy the Eternal King and launch a direct attack on Heaven, that seemed like overkill, but Adrian couldn't complain. His father was doing precisely what he'd asked. Adrian just hoped he was good enough to handle it all. He hadn't hit his limit on quintessence yet, but Heaven's white magic was famously poisonous, and all poisons had a killing dose. Normally, he'd take a few weeks to test progressively higher concentrations until he figured out his toxicity limit, but Adrian didn't want to make Bex wait a minute longer than necessary.

His plan right now was to wing it until something forced him to stop. Not how he usually liked to work, but plans were famous for never surviving the first encounter with the enemy, so who was to say he wouldn't have ended up doing this anyway? He mostly wanted to make sure everything was ready before Bex got back. He'd still have to apologize for missing her calls, but Adrian was sure everything would be forgiven if he showed up with her very own private stairway to Heaven. He was imagining the way her beautiful face would light up at the news when something hit his forest hard enough to knock his breath out.

It hit Boston, too, startling the cat so badly he fell out of the tree. He landed on his feet a second later, shaking the needles out of his fur as he whirled toward his witch. "Where was that?!"

"Anchor," Adrian gasped, grabbing the tangle of roots that surrounded his heart. He didn't actually need to touch them, but they were right there, and he needed something to stabilize his shaking hands. He'd felt that hit like a gunshot, but that was impossible. His oak tree was in the middle of their Market. It shouldn't be getting hit by anything, unless—

The breath left his body again as he sank into his forest, racing through the roots that connected all Blackwoods to the tree he'd grown to hold up the Anchor's sky. It was difficult to wedge himself into a grove that consisted of only one tree, but Adrian was close to this particular oak. Even when it was in a panic, he was able to convince it to let him in.

And immediately started to panic himself.

The Anchor Market looked like a war zone. Trees didn't perceive things in the same way human eyes did, but Adrian could feel the vibrations of the explosions and the heat of the fire as clear as day. It felt like he was in the middle of a city that was being bombed, but Adrian didn't understand how that was possible until his tree pulled him toward its highest branches.

When Adrian's perception moved to the oak's crown, he understood. He didn't know how it had happened, but the fake sky he'd grown the oak to catch had been destroyed, revealing a blackness so dark and thick, he feared he'd be sucked into it. As scary as the void was, though, the thing floating inside it was worse.

Adrian had never seen Heaven's Holy City with his own eyes, but there was nothing else the giant white fortress raining down fire on the exposed Anchor could be. He'd known the Eternal King's capital must be on the border between life and death because Bex had been able to see it from the chain, but even though Malik had told him that Gilgamesh had moved the spheres apart, it had never even occurred to Adrian that the king would also be able to *move them back together.*

It still felt impossible, but there was no other explanation. That was the Holy City of Heaven with the base of its enormous white walls hanging less than a thousand feet above his tree's highest branches. He was still staring at them in horror when the golden lions on the city's battlements—which he'd assumed were just decorative statues—opened their mouths and unleashed a wave of white.

It happened like a camera flash. The light came in so fast, Adrian didn't realize it was an attack until the shock wave hit a split-second later, slamming into his tree so hard that Adrian was knocked right out of it.

He landed on his back in the hole he'd made around his pounding heart. He was still trying to get control of his adrenaline-flooded body when Boston jumped onto his chest.

"Well?" the familiar demanded. "What did you see?"

"Heaven," Adrian gasped, grabbing his cat as he struggled to sit up. "The Anchor is under attack!"

Just saying the words turned his stomach to ice. He'd taken too long, made one too many cocky promises he couldn't keep, and now everyone was going to—

"*Adrian*," Boston snapped, lashing his tail as he glared at his witch. "Panic doesn't help anything. The Anchor is a big place, and it's hardly undefended. It's not going to crumple at the first punch, which means we still have time to get over there."

They did, didn't they? Now that Adrian knew how to teleport, he could be at the Anchor in an instant, but to what end? As his father had so astutely pointed out the first night they'd met, a witch outside his forest was limited to the spells in his pockets. All of Adrian's powers and ability to help were here in Bainbridge, but he had one tree across the bay. So long as his oak didn't get incinerated, he had an in. He just needed to figure out how to use it.

With that thought, the plan came together in his mind like a whipcrack. Adrian leaped out of the hole he'd dug beneath his heart tree and started running for his house. He made it all the way to his front door before he remembered it was still the middle of the night, which meant his solar panel hadn't been able to charge his phone yet. Cursing his stupid past self for forgetting something as simple as plugging in a cable, he turned to run back to his tree and spotted Malik watching him from his perch atop the pile of quintessence barrels.

"Do you have a phone?" he demanded as he raced over to his father. "It's an emergency!"

"Of course," Malik said, pulling a brand-new, expensive-looking smartphone out of the inner pocket of his trench coat and unlocking the screen with his thumbprint. "But what sort of emergency are you having? The forest looks quiet to me."

"It's not here," Adrian explained as he grabbed the phone out of his father's hand. "Gilgamesh moved his city and is attacking the Anchor right now. I have to talk to someone to figure out what kind of help they need."

Malik arched a skeptical eyebrow. "If they are under Heaven's bombardment, I doubt they'll have time to take a phone call."

"I'm still going to try," Adrian said as he dialed Bex's number from memory. "Asking takes less time than guessing and getting it wrong."

He also had no idea how to help, but Adrian left that part out as he raised the phone to his ear.

Bex didn't pick up. That wasn't a surprise. No one was busier in an emergency than the queen, and that was assuming she was back from wherever she'd gone when her sword broke. Fortunately, after the debacle on the ferry, Adrian had made a point of memorizing all the demons' phone numbers, so he just moved on to his next target, which was Iggs.

That worked *much* better. The wrath demon must've already had his phone in his hand, because he answered before the first ring finished.

"Who is this?"

"It's me," Adrian said as he strode back toward his heart tree.

"Adrian?" Iggs confirmed as his voice flooded with relief. "Oh, thank Ishtar! I almost didn't pick up when I saw the weird number, but I'm super glad I did. We need help!"

"I know," Adrian said. "I felt the bombardment hit my tree. Is Bex back?"

"Yeah," Iggs said, his happiness evaporating. "But I almost wish she wasn't. We got set up hard. Turns out that Havok guy was working for Gilgamesh the whole time. All the war demons were. I thought it was suspicious when so many of them signed up to fight with us, and I was right. They're all filthy traitors! Unfortunately, they were damn well-organized traitors. General Kirok and his team took over the Anchor control room before we even knew what was up, and now we're screwed."

Adrian's mouth pulled into a grim line as he climbed into the ditch beneath his heart tree. "What can I do?"

"I don't know," Iggs confessed. "I'm working on a plan to take back the control room so we can open the exits and get everyone out of here before Heaven bombs us into oblivion. If you could help Bex buy us some more time, that'd be enough."

"I'll certainly try," Adrian said. "Call me back on this number if you need me."

"Will do," the wrath demon promised. "And thanks. I know Lys was mad at you earlier, but you always come through when it counts. Bex knows that, and we're grateful."

The heartfelt words made him feel ashamed. Adrian desperately wanted to tell Iggs that it wasn't true. The fact that he'd had to borrow his dad's phone just to make this call proved just how badly he'd failed at being a reliable partner, but there was no time to dump his baggage. Iggs had already hung up, leaving Adrian staring at his own reflection in his father's pristine phone screen. He was about to climb out of his hole to return the device when he spotted his father ducking under the fir tree's low branches to join him.

"Well?" Malik prompted when he saw his son looking. "What is the situation?"

"Not good," Adrian said as he handed the phone back. "I don't suppose you know how to stop a Heavenly bombardment."

"A bombardment?" the sorcerer repeated, his eyebrows lifting in surprise before dropping into a worried scowl as he slid his phone back into his pocket. "That is a difficult request. The Lions of Heaven are famous for scouring the world clean. Their roars are designed to take down even divine fortifications, which makes them nearly impossible to shield against."

"Then we need to stop them from firing in the first place," Adrian said as he lay down on the roots surrounding his heart. "Can you bring me a barrel of quintessence, please?"

His father's eyes lit up at the request, and he darted away, returning astonishingly quickly with two of the giant barrels clutched under his arms as if they weighed nothing.

"I'll get you as much as you need," he promised as he set the barrels down on the fir needles. "But what are you planning to do?"

"The same thing I was planning to do earlier," Adrian told him. "Just much faster and in a different direction." He dug his fingers into the loamy, root-filled soil under his back. "I've watched Bex cut through everything Heaven's ever thrown at her. I'm pretty sure she can wreck a giant lion, too. I just have to get her up to them."

Malik's face fell into a dire frown. "If you're intending to lift her using your tree, I'd advise against it. The Holy City sits upon the headwaters of death. That's how it's able to exist in both Heaven and the space between simultaneously, but the gap between life and death isn't something that can be traversed lightly. Without a chain or a river to guide you, reaching the Holy City is impossible."

"Not if I can see where I'm going," Adrian argued. "Gilgamesh's fortress is floating directly above my tree. I literally can't miss it."

Malik opened his mouth to keep arguing, but Adrian cut him off. "Bex is the most determined person I've ever met. If I give her an inch, she'll figure out how to turn it into a mile. We'll make this work. You just keep the quintessence coming."

"That, I can do," his father said, patting the barrels he'd brought over. "But please be careful. A battlefield is always dangerous even when you're not technically on it. I'd hate to lose my favorite son so soon after meeting him."

"I'll be fine," Adrian promised, determined to make that not a lie as he got a tighter grip on his roots. "Quintessence me."

Even as he said the words, Adrian was painfully aware that they hadn't actually discussed this part of the plan yet. His father acted like liquid quintessence was the answer to all problems, but it still had to be consumed. Even if it was super potent, Adrian would still have to drink it, and he couldn't do that while his mind was deep in the forest. He assumed his father would say something if what he'd asked was impossible, but Malik didn't say another word. He just picked up the quintessence, popped the plug, and upended the entire barrel over Adrian's head.

The liquid that came out was shockingly white. It lit up the nighttime forest like a floodlight, but the feeling when it hit his body was power. Adrian couldn't even say if the liquid was warm or cold. All he could feel was the magic inside it, a flood of pure potential that passed instantly through his skin.

If biting into a coin of quintessence was like chewing on lightning, this was like swimming in it.

There was so much power, Adrian would have been cooked instantly if he hadn't been holding onto his forest. The Blackwood gave him somewhere to put all that raging energy, removing his fear as he settled deeper into the pit beneath his tree.

"Are you good?" his father asked as he set the empty barrel down.

"I'm good," Adrian said, blowing out a shaky breath as the blindingly white liquid ran down his body to seep into the roots beneath him. "I'm good," he said again, his face breaking into a grin. "Keep it coming. I can take it."

Malik grinned back and grabbed the second barrel. When the next flood of quintessence came, Adrian was ready for it, drinking the thick, purified magic down like a drought-stricken tree. When he was so full of quintessence that he felt like a bolt of lightning himself, he let go of his body and sank into his forest, racing down the Blackwood's roots toward the lone oak across the bay that was already on fire.

Bex was in the worst fight of her life.

The barrages went off every twenty seconds. Each golden lion seemed to need a few minutes to recharge after it roared, but there were so many on the walls of Heaven that it didn't matter. They fired in rounds, bombarding the Anchor in a scatter pattern designed for maximum destruction. Bex learned early that she could hit the white shots away, but there were so many. For every one she caught, a dozen more got through, slamming into the cratered landscape like hammer blows on an anvil that was rapidly starting to crack.

Every new break in the floor ratcheted Bex's panic higher, but she couldn't stop it. No matter how fast she moved or how hard she swung, she couldn't be everywhere at once. She couldn't even stop a fraction of the destruction that was coming for her people huddled below. She hadn't felt this hopeless since she'd fought the Blade of Sorrow, except the despair wasn't an illusion this time. She was *actually* losing, and if she didn't figure out a way to make it stop, every free demon in the world was going to go down with her.

That thought sent her into a frenzy. She threw herself into the air, blasting as high as she could on her fire, but even though it looked like there was nothing between her and the white walls of Heaven's capital, she couldn't seem to get higher than the line where the sky used to be. The darkness the Holy City was floating in *looked* empty, but it pushed against her like a waterfall, slamming her out of the air and back into the dirt.

It was like that every time, but Bex didn't stop trying. She was the Queen of Wrath, dammit. Protecting her people from crap like this was the reason she existed, but she had no weapons that worked against this enemy. She couldn't reach the city, couldn't stop the lions. She hadn't even been able to protect Adrian's tree, which was lying behind her in a pile of splintered, smoking greenwood. The same blast had thrown their RV all the way back to the Market's sealed entrance. It was still technically in one piece, but the Winnebago's frame was wrecked. Everything was, except the golden statue of Gilgamesh. *That* stood tall and pristine, its hateful golden face smiling serenely as the white flash of Heaven's destruction went off again.

Bex met it with a roar of her own, smacking the cannon shot away from the remains of Adrian's tree. She couldn't do anything about the dozens of other fireballs, but she could still feel the oak's roots like a lattice under her feet. She'd learned from Adrian that the part of a tree you could see was only half of its body. The trunk was busted, but the roots were still alive, still strong. They were also the only thing left up here for her to protect, so that was where Bex made her stand, determined to defend Adrian's tree and everything beneath it to her last brea—

A noise knocked her out of her wild defense. It'd been so long since she'd heard anything except the roar of the lions, it took Bex several seconds to realize it was a voice calling her name.

The moment she realized what she was hearing, Bex's punch-drunk confusion exploded into panic. No one else should be here. She was the only one fast and tough enough to survive Heaven's attacks. If Iggs or Lys had come up to help, they were going to die. She had to get them back downstairs before the next barrage landed, but when Bex whirled around to see where the sound was coming from, Adrian's oak tree was looking back at her.

That was a surprise for a lot of reasons. The last time she'd seen the tree, it'd been a pile of exploded wood. Now, though, the oak was upright again, its thick trunk sending out a fresh crown of leafy green branches before her eyes. The gray bark wasn't even charred anymore, and molded into that bark was a face.

It looked like one of the Green Man sculptures she was always seeing in the windows of Seattle's New Age-ier stores, except this wasn't a carving. The face was formed by the natural wrinkles in the oak's bark, like one of those visions of the Virgin Mary religious humans were always finding in sidewalk cracks and pieces of burnt toast. The really shocking part for Bex, though, was that she recognized it.

"Adrian?" she said, scrubbing the dust and grit out of her eyes to make sure they weren't playing tricks on her. "Is that you?"

The face in the tree smiled at her with Adrian's smile, and Bex's poor, battered heart skipped several important-feeling beats.

"*Adrian!*" she cried, staggering across the blown-up dirt to grab the knobbly crags of the oak's new trunk. "What are you doing here? You have to get out! They're bombing—"

"I know," the tree said in Adrian's voice. "That's why I'm here. I've got a plan."

Hearing that almost gave her hope. For one beautiful second, Bex *almost* believed it was possible because Adrian always had a plan, and they almost always worked. Then the black sky brightened as the lions sucked in power for their next wave of destruction, and reality forced itself back in.

"I don't think even one of your plans can save us this time," she said, pressing her face against the tree as the horrible light got whiter and whiter. "Oh, Adrian, I messed up so bad. I'm the one who brought Havok here. I'm the one who put a war demon in charge of our defenses. I should've known better, should've been more careful, but I was stupid, and now everybody's going to die."

She didn't even realize what she was saying until the ashy tears started running down her cheeks. The cannons went off a second later, hammering the landscape all around them in destruction. None of the shots hit the tree this time, but Bex felt no relief. Just the crushing weight of the inevitable as she hid her face against the Blackwood's bark.

"I did it again," she whispered, squeezing her eyes tight. "I was so focused on the enemy in front of me, I didn't see the trap until it was too late. I just rushed ahead blindly, *again*, and now I'm going to die, *again*, except this time, there's no Ishtar waiting to throw me back."

Not that the goddess would bother after what she'd done. Even if Bex hadn't already thrown away her reincarnations, she was a godslayer now, a sinner just like Gilgamesh. Her mother would probably destroy her if they ever met again, and Bex had no one to blame but herself.

"It's all my fault," she sobbed, sliding down the tree to crumple on its roots. "I took the bait like an *idiot*, and now we're all trapped. I can't even surrender to save my people anymore since the Princess of War already said that's off the table. Gilgamesh is going to make an example out of all of us, and it's all my—"

She stopped when leaves brushed her face, and Bex looked up to find the tree bending down, its green boughs surrounding her like a miniature forest as Adrian pulled her closer.

"It's *not* your fault," he said firmly. "Gilgamesh is the one who did this. He's the one shooting cannons at innocents who just wanted to be free. That makes him the villain, not you. You've done nothing but try to save people since I met you, and that's exactly what we're going to do now. I know it looks bad, but we haven't lost yet. We can still turn this around."

"How can you say that?" Bex demanded. "What part of any of this"—she waved her hand wildly at the city of death floating above them—"makes you think we can win?"

"Because we always do," Adrian said, hugging her closer. "We've been facing impossible odds since we started, and we've *always* pulled it off. Gilgamesh defeats his enemies by making them feel how you're feeling now: like everything is hopeless, like there isn't a chance, but there *is*. He knows there is, and that's why he's coming down so hard. Heaven hasn't had to face a foe directly in eons, but Gilgamesh brought his dead city to the edge of the land of the living *because of you*. That's how scared he is. He's doing all of this because he knows that we can beat him. We can *do* this, Bex! I just need you to not give up on me."

His tree was hugging her hard by the end, pressing her face into the jagged bark as if he could squeeze her into believing. It was working, too, because Adrian was right. Bex had been fighting Heaven for thousands of years, but she'd never made progress until he showed up. All her lives and deaths, she'd just been treading water, but Adrian was going somewhere. His ideas always sounded crazy, but that was why they worked, because he attacked from angles no one expected. He'd gotten her with one just now, because when he appeared out of nowhere and said they could still win with that impossible confidence of his, Bex couldn't help but believe him.

"Okay," she whispered, leaning in to press a kiss against the oak's gnarled trunk. "What's your plan?"

"The first step is taking out those cannons," Adrian said, as if that were a simple thing. "I can get you up there with my tree, but I'll need you to keep us from getting blasted while I do it."

"I should be able to manage that," Bex said as she climbed up the trunk into his branches. "But how long a defense are we talking about? Not to complain about a miracle, but the last time you grew a tree here, it took half an hour. The whole Anchor will be pounded to dust by then."

"This will be much faster," Adrian promised, the image of his face moving up the tree trunk with her as she climbed. "Just make sure you hold on tight."

Bex barely had time to lock her hands around a limb before Adrian's tree started going up like a rocket. The momentum made the whole canopy sag, but the surprise was what almost made Bex lose her grip. She'd seen Adrian do a lot of witchcraft, but unless he was using something preprepared from his pockets, he never did it fast. Not that Bex was an expert or anything, but she'd been watching Adrian obsessively for months, and this blazing speed definitely wasn't his usual style.

Even his magic felt weird. Being inside one of Adrian's spells normally felt like stepping into a summer forest—warm, rich, and enveloping. This power felt more like a spear—a hard, sharp, destructive force stabbing them into the sky at a speed trees were never meant to go. Bex was no witch, but that struck her as wrong. Before she could say anything about it to Adrian, though, the sky above them flashed white again as the lions of Heaven fired.

She had no time for worrying about strange magic after that. She leaped up Adrian's rocketing tree like a monkey, locking her legs around the quaking branches so she could swing her sword at the incoming wave of destruction with both hands. She hit the ball of white fire square in the middle, slinging it back at the enemy like a home-run baseball. She didn't actually manage to hit the lion, but she did send the fireball over the wall, where it landed behind the battlements with an extremely satisfying explosion.

Bex whooped when she saw the flash go off. Now *that* she could get used to! She was angling herself to hit the next shot right back down the stupid lion's stupid golden throat when Adrian's rapidly rising tree crossed the arc where the fake sky used to be, and things suddenly became very different.

It was the same problem Bex had run into when she'd tried to blast herself up here. The moment Adrian's tree crossed the line where the sky used to be, the emptiness started pushing back. It reminded Bex of when she'd been dropped back into the river below the chain. She wasn't physically drowning, but the dark was as cold as ice water, and there was a strong force pushing against them like an invisible waterfall.

If Bex's legs hadn't been wrapped around the oak's branches, she would have been pushed right off. It was a good thing the lions had just fired. The pressure was so intense, she could barely lift her sword, and Adrian's tree wasn't doing much better.

The moment they crossed the pressure line, their rocketing pace had slowed to a crawl. They were still going up, but the tree was fighting for every inch, its branches wiggling like salmon swimming upstream. The slower pace made it much more likely they'd have to eat another barrage, but the lion cannons were no longer Bex's primary concern. She was far more worried about the cold she could feel creeping up her arms despite her raging bonfire. The freezing, final chill of death.

Having already died a hundred and ninety-eight times, Bex had more experience with the process than most. She didn't actually remember how any of her past selves had met their ends, but her body recognized the sensation with a dread bordering on panic. It didn't matter that she had no wounds or pain. The moment the cold began seeping into her skin, Bex's body became convinced that she was dying, and for someone who was actually mortal this time, that was a lot scarier than it used to be.

Calm down, Drox commanded as Bex began to hyperventilate. *You're not dying. That's just the river washing away your mortal life.*

That sounded a lot like dying to Bex. It also made no sense, because her mother's rivers had always been her lifeblood. Even after she'd been filled with the fire of life, deathly water healed her, so how—

This is not Ishtar's river, her sword replied in a grim voice. *This is the original form of death, the implacable flow of time that scours mortal lives away. See how it's flowing the wrong direction?*

He had a point. In Bex's experience, Rivers of Death—glowing or dark—always flowed toward Paradise. This pressure, however, was pushing them down into the void, which was entirely the wrong way.

Exactly, Drox said. *This is the problem Ishtar and the other gods sought to correct when they created Paradise. Only the gods and their creations can travel through this place safely, but you...*

He didn't have to finish. Bex felt the truth loud and clear through the numbness in her limbs. True death couldn't have touched the original Rebexa, but Bex wasn't her anymore. She wasn't even a creature of Paradise like her demons. She was something entirely new: a creation of the gods made mortal by the Blackwood's fire. A mortality that was rapidly being washed away by the freezing torrent pouring all around her.

All around *them.* Bex had been panicking too hard to notice earlier, but when her terrified fingers clenched around the oak's branches, the wood broke off in her grip. She let go immediately, but it didn't help. The branch hadn't broken because she'd squeezed too hard. It'd cracked because it was dead.

Bex lurched back to the trunk, knocking off a snowstorm of dead leaves in the process. The branch she'd just been standing on broke apart as soon as her foot left it, the hardwood crumbling to dust as it fell into the void below. Even the trunk was starting to feel hollow under her grasping fingers, causing Bex's fear to spike as the whole tree began to list to the left.

"*Adrian!*"

"I've got it," came the strained reply.

She couldn't see his face in the bark anymore, but his voice hummed through the crumbling wood like a plucked string. Everywhere it touched, life came back, sending out new green leaves to replace the dead ones and making the brittle wood solid again. It was like watching an entire growing season go by on fast-forward, but the effect was only temporary. The new green leaves had scarcely unfurled before they started withering before Bex's eyes, making her clutch the trunk even harder.

"We can make it," Adrian insisted before she could say a word. "It's only a few more feet."

Bex blinked in surprise. She hadn't noticed thanks to the whole dying thing, but while the strange downward pressure had slowed their progress, the tree had never stopped going up. They were almost within reach of Heaven's white walls now, so close to the Holy City's foundation that the lions on the battlements couldn't look down sharply enough to shoot them.

That clever bit of maneuvering snapped Bex out of her existential crisis. She still felt like she was dying, but she told her body to shove it and called her fire instead, fanning her flames as hot as she could to burn the cold away. It didn't work entirely, but it got her moving again as she climbed up the trunk to the highest branches at the tree's crown.

"Just get me onto the wall," she said, trusting the oak to hear her over the howling current of time. "I'll handle the rest."

Adrian didn't answer, but the tree kept going, so he must have understood. Bex crouched low as she rode the final distance. Then, the moment the ramparts of Heaven's city came into view, she leaped straight up with all she had, controlling her fire so the heat wouldn't touch Adrian's tree as she blasted herself over the crenellations and onto the paved white highway that was the top of the Holy City's wall.

Where she immediately started to fall again.

"What the—"

Bex windmilled her arms wildly, but it didn't do any good. She hadn't even landed that hard, but what looked like a huge slab of white stone to her eyes was cracking like an eggshell under her feet. She was still struggling not to fall through when Drox's voice exploded into her head.

It's the banishment! her sword cried. *The moment you set foot on the wall, we entered Paradise, the place Gilgamesh used Anu's crown to forbid us from being! This is what happened in the tomb of the gods! We're being kicked out!*

The moment Drox said it, Bex recognized the weight pulling at her feet. The ground wasn't actually breaking; she was being dragged through it. It was just like when her time ran out in Limbo, only this place didn't even give her the courtesy of five minutes. It started dropping her immediately.

That made sense considering Bex was Heaven's enemy number one, but while constantly-dissolving ground was better than getting kicked in the stomach, how in the Hells was she supposed to fight on a wall she couldn't even stand on? She hotfooted it for ten more seconds, but everywhere she placed her weight started crumbling immediately. In the end, it was either jump or be dropped, so Bex leaped backward, landing back in the tree with a curse.

"What's wrong?" Adrian's voice cried through the wood when she hit. "Why did you come back?"

"I can't stand," Bex explained frantically. "Gilgamesh banished me from Paradise, which means the ground here breaks everywhere I step. If I'd stayed on that wall, it would've dropped me straight back down to Earth."

There was a long pause, and then the whole tree began to shake. *"Why didn't you mention that earlier?!"*

"Because I didn't think of it!" Bex yelled, clinging to the thrashing branches. "I don't exactly get into Paradise much these days, and I've never been inside Gilgamesh's Holy City. I didn't know it was going to be a problem until it was!"

The tree rustled with a frustrated sigh. Then, in classic Adrian fashion, he moved on to the next plan.

"I'll be your ground, then," he offered as the thin branches of the tree's crown began to thicken and lengthen under her feet. "Do you think you can hit the cannons from here?"

Bex glanced at the line of house-sized lion statues, the closest of which was readying another blinding blast in its mouth not twenty feet away.

"I can hit them," she promised, pulling back her sword. "Just get me as close as you can."

The tree did its best, creeping sideways along the battlements like a vine. Bex could feel Adrian's magic straining to make it work, but he pulled it off in the end, moving her so close to the foot of the blasting lion that Bex had to stay low to avoid losing her head.

"Perfect," she said, lining up her sword. "Watch this."

Adrian didn't say anything, but Bex could feel his skepticism through the creaking branches. She completely understood why. They might've been right in front of it, but the base of the actual lion was still a good ten feet away. That was well outside of Drox's range no matter how far Bex stretched her arms, but just as she was no longer a pile of ash, her sword wasn't the shaved-down fire poker he'd been the last time Adrian had seen him. He was his true self again, a queen's divine blade. She needed only to swing him, so that was what Bex did, whipping Drox through the air to unleash a shining arc of fire just like the one he'd used on Havok.

The sight of Drox's glowing line slicing into the lion's hammered gold mane was the most beautiful thing Bex had ever seen. It cut through the construct like a red-hot garrote wire, dropping its giant head onto the white battlements with a *crash* that echoed throughout Heaven, and for one shining moment, Bex didn't feel like the lone holdout of a losing war anymore. She felt like a queen. A true divine fury that was going to tear down all of Heaven brick by brick! She was already turning to wing another whip of fire at the next lion in the line when the oak tree bobbed beneath her feet.

It felt like something heavy had landed on the branch behind her. She was so focused on hitting her target, though, Bex didn't actually look back to check. It was only when something grabbed the arm she'd pulled back for the swing that she looked over her shoulder to see the Princess of War was standing right behind her.

"That was a very stupid thing to do," the princess growled, her mismatched eyes gleaming in the Queen of Wrath's firelight. "What kind of suicidal idiot charges straight into the enemy's guns?"

"The kind who knows she can win," Bex growled back, ripping her arm free as she turned to face her new target. "Adrian, make me some room."

The tree rattled nervously in reply. As always, though, her witch came through, spreading his branches and tucking the oak's leaves under to form a wide, thatched platform. The tree had barely finished spreading when Bex whipped her sword up, throwing a blinding slash of Drox's new fire straight at her traitorous sister's face.

Chapter 14

The entire Anchor was shaking like a battleship under siege. They didn't have blaring alarms or flashing lights, but none were needed. Every demon and no small number of the humans who'd managed to escape the initial attack on the Market were already running for the lower floors as fast as they could go. The only one who wasn't fleeing into the basement was Iggs. He was standing under the blasting fake sun of the army training field on the Anchor's third floor. Soon to be its second floor if those damn cannons didn't stop.

"So they're all in there, then?" he asked, keeping his rage to a simmer as he glared across the magically-created grass at the brick warehouse that held all the weapons Bex had purchased from the goblins to arm her fledgling rebel army.

"Yes, sir," said the lust demon soldier who'd been waiting in front of the door when Iggs arrived. "Right before the shaking started, every war demon in our unit turned traitor. Half my squad shot the other half and retreated into the weapons depot. I was dragging the wounded into the hall when the whole Anchor went crazy. Everyone was shouting about an evacuation, so I handed my squadmates to one of the old safe-house leaders and came back here so I could report what happened to someone who wasn't traitorous war-demon scum."

"Good job," Iggs said, clapping the lust demon's bandaged shoulder so hard their currently male body almost tipped over. "I'll make sure the queen hears about your loyalty."

"Thank you, sir," the soldier said, but their amber eyes were full of fear. "I don't know if it'll matter, though. Half our army just killed the other in cold blood. I heard the screaming over my radio. I don't know how many they got, but the war demons outnumber us hard now, *and* they've taken over the building where we keep all the weapons that could've evened the fight. Unless the queen herself shows up, I don't see how we're going to survive this."

"If the queen could do everything herself, she wouldn't need an army or a warehouse full of guns," Iggs reminded them. "This is our war—all of us—so let's go win it."

The lust demon didn't look convinced, but they didn't drag their feet when Iggs motioned them to follow him through the double doors standing by themselves at the edge of the training field's fake tree line. These led straight out into the main stair, which was currently crammed with terrified demons running down to the lower levels. Flashes and booms echoed from the Market three floors up, along with Bex's scream of rage.

As a wrath demon, Iggs felt the sound to his bones, but he didn't run upstairs to help. His queen could handle whatever Heaven threw. It was his job to follow orders and keep her people safe. Iggs was the one who'd said they should turn this place into their fortress. He'd defend it to his dying breath, which wouldn't be too far away if the giant cracks in the stairway's stone mosaics were any indication. That was quitter thinking, though, so Iggs put it out of his head and started up the stairs, shoving people out of the way with one hand while the other grabbed his phone to call Lys.

They were leading the evacuation, so Iggs didn't actually expect to get through. To his astonishment, though, Lys picked up immediately.

"Tell me the bad news."

"It's not exactly news at this point," Iggs replied, looking over his shoulder to make sure the soldier he'd picked up was still with him. "All the war demons in the training camp shot their squadmates and forted up in the weapons depot. They're breaking their way through our stockpile as we speak."

"Hells damn them," Lys muttered. "There goes that plan."

Iggs could only nod. Those weapons were supposed to be their big play to turn the tables on the physically stronger war demons. Retaking the Anchor's control room was going to be a lot harder without guns, which was undoubtedly why General Kirok had ordered his toadies to break them, the four-armed backstabber.

Iggs clenched his fangs. He wasn't surprised the war demons had turned on them—their kind had always been traitors—but he hadn't expected them to be so coordinated or for *all* of them to jump. He'd worked with a lot of war demons over the last month. Every one of them had been a prickly bastard who'd pick a fight over anything, but they'd all still hated being slaves. Even when they'd refused to acknowledge Bex as their queen, they'd seemed legitimately excited about being set free, so why had this happened? What did they even think they were getting out of this double-cross? Especially since it looked like Gilgamesh intended to bring the roof down on their heads same as everybody else's.

"I'm going to keep working on the evacuation," Lys said when the silence had stretched too long. "But I can only cram so many people into the basement before they realize there's no way out. Do you think you can take the control room without guns, or do I need to give people shovels and tell them to start digging?"

"Definitely don't do that," Iggs said. "I saw what almost happened when Bex broke a hole in the Anchor's outer wall during her fight with Havok. If you do that on purpose, your whole evacuation center might fall into the void."

"Better that than to go back to the warlocks and the Hells," Lys said with a finality that chilled his blood.

"It won't come to that," Iggs promised. "Guns or no guns, I'm getting into that control room and getting you an exit. The queen entrusted this job to me. I won't let her down."

"You never do," the lust demon said before they switched to Riverlander. "Ishtar guide your sword."

As always, their pronunciation was horrendous, but the fact that they'd tried at all made Iggs grin from ear to ear. "May her blessed queens watch over us," he answered in kind before cutting off the call.

"How are you going to take the control room without guns?" asked the lust demon soldier, who was still behind him. "The war demons didn't stop to explain their evil plan before they shot us, so I don't know what they're up to, but if it's important, I'm pretty sure General Kirok will be guarding it himself. Other than the queen, there's no non-war demon that can take him without a weapon."

Iggs jerked his chin into the air. "War demons aren't the only warriors Ishtar made. We don't need guns to win this fight. We've just gotta get our backup."

"We?" the soldier said nervously, but Iggs was already plowing ahead, using his size to shove a path through the panicked demons up the stairs until he reached the Anchor's second floor.

The sounds of battle got louder with every step. Down in the army's training area, the bombardment had sounded like distant thunder. Up here where there was only one layer between them and the Market, the *boom* of the cannons was deafening. Everything was still holding for now, thank the gods, but the cracks were starting to get scary.

A piece actually fell out of the ceiling in front of them when they turned off the stairs into the long hallway opposite the one that led to the arena where Bex had fought Havok. Iggs jumped over the broken chunk of cement without pausing, dragging the lust demon soldier behind him as he charged down the hall to the security door at the end.

"Wait," the soldier said nervously when Iggs stopped to punch in the door code. "Isn't this the door to the wrath demon area? The one the queen ordered us to never ever enter?"

"Yep," Iggs said as he shoved the door open with his shoulder and barreled into a village that was already on high alert.

The towering trees and fake sky made the cracks in the walls harder to see here, but Heaven's bombardment was still shaking the ground like an earthquake. If they'd been any other sort of demon, the villagers would've been in a panic, but these were the people of Wrath. The war for Paradise had only just ended by their reckoning, and their fighting instincts were still honed to a razor's edge. By the time Iggs and his terrified soldier made it into the square where Bex brought her new rescues, all five thousand of the demons she'd freed from Limbo were ready and waiting.

"What are you doing here?" demanded an old demon with tall horns that Iggs immediately recognized as Zargrexa, the village chief Bex had brought in during her last trip into Limbo. The old lady must've done some fast work, because she was standing at the front of the crowd as if this was *her* village now, and Iggs had better respect it.

"What is going on?" she continued, lifting her tall horns higher still. "Why is the ground shaking? And where is our queen?"

"Fighting traitors," Iggs replied, motioning for his nervous soldier to stay back as he climbed up to stand on top of the wooden table where all newly-freed demons were given their first meal.

"Children of Ishtar's Wrath!" he cried in Riverlander, bellowing the words to make sure everyone in the crowd—which was so huge that it filled the stone square and spilled out into the dirt streets beyond—could hear. "Our queen has been betrayed! The war demons she entrusted to lead her army have turned on her!"

A roar of fury rose at his words before Zargrexa silenced the crowd with a wave.

"Why would she trust one of them?" the old village chief demanded when the square was quiet again. "War demons are all traitors! They alone joined Gilgamesh willingly, burning down Paradise and killing their own kind. Our queen knew this. Why would she give them the chance to do it again?"

"Because our queen believes in the Children of Ishtar," Iggs replied gravely. "She swore to set us *all* free, even the traitors. The war demon's treason is their sin, not hers, and we'll make sure they answer for it, because we are Wrath! Of all the clans of the Riverlands, we are the only ones who *never* kneeled, and they will know our fury!"

A great cheer went up, forcing Zargrexa to wave much more vigorously to reestablish order this time.

"How will they know it?" she asked when it finally grew quiet enough for her to speak again. "I don't need a reason to fight war demon scum. Those traitors killed my family and burned my village to the ground. I would have butchered all of them before they had a chance to betray us again if I'd had my way, but our queen ordered us to stay in this place, and her word is the word of Ishtar."

"I know," Iggs said. "That's why I'm giving you a new order."

The old demon's red eyes narrowed to scornful slits. "And who are you to speak in her divine name?"

"I am Iggerux," Iggs said proudly. "First freed and most loyal servant of the Bonfire Queen! I swore on my name to fight for her until all demons are free, and for seven years, that's what I've done. You've all seen me at her side! I helped her build this place." He waved his hand at the towering trees that shaded the village square before turning to smile at Zargrexa. "You just arrived yesterday, so you don't know me beyond a glance yet, but the others will tell you that what I say is true."

The crowd around Zargrexa all began to whisper and nod, but while the old demon was looking at him with a modicum of new respect, her jaw remained stubbornly set.

"Fighting at the queen's side does not give you the authority to speak in her name. Only the eldest and most experienced are allowed to give orders in the queen's stead. You're barely more than a child."

"But I'm still the one she trusted to save her people," Iggs argued, holding his own horns tall and proud. "Our queen ordered me to come here and lead you all to safety, but there is nowhere safe so long as the war demon traitors control Gilgamesh's sorcery. They've barricaded themselves inside the room that controls the doors to our fortress. So long as they hold that position, we're sitting ducks for Gilgamesh's punishment, which is why I've come before you now. I'm not here to speak in the queen's name. I'm here to ask your help in fulfilling the final order she gave me to keep her people safe!"

Zargrexa looked mollified by that logic, and Iggs seized his chance.

"We are the children of Wrath!" he cried, throwing out his arms. "The daughters of Ishtar fight for all demons, but Bex is *our* queen! No one can fight for her as we do, so fight with me now. Help me defeat the traitors who would see her fall and prove once and for all that Wrath is forever loyal!"

A great shout went up again at this, but unlike before, Zargrexa was shouting with it.

"Well said, servant of the queen!" she cried, grinning from ear to ear. "I was not willing to leave if it meant defying her will, but if the Queen of Wrath asked you for help, that's as good as asking all of us. We will follow you. Now, tell us where to fight!"

Iggs slumped in relief. "Thank you," he said.

Zargrexa waved the words away. "Killing war demons is its own reward. I only objected because the queen ordered us to stay put, but if you're willing to take responsibility"—she paused until Iggs nodded—"then I gladly bow my horns to you."

She did so by the barest fraction, but Iggs was still floored. These were extraordinary times, but an elder bowing her horns to him was a miracle Iggs had never thought he'd live to see. He was still processing it when he realized there were now thousands of demons waiting for him to tell them what to do.

That almost killed the whole thing right there. Iggs had spent the last seven years working in a four-person crew. Before that, he'd been a soldier and a cowherd. He was used to fighting. Even arguing with stuffy old demons like Zargrexa had become pretty normal, but actually standing up and giving orders? That was a wholly new, wholly terrifying front.

If things hadn't been so dire, he would've dropped his horns straight to the floor and told Zargrexa she could have her command back. But if Iggs had one goal in this life, it was to prove to Bex that she hadn't wasted her fire when she'd burned herself to save him. He'd sworn a thousand times that he would always be and do whatever his queen needed. Right now, she needed this, so Iggs sucked it up and lifted his horns high, standing tall on the table as he did his best to copy Bex's calm, commanding tone.

"Our first priority is to take back the control room," he told them. "I'll need fifty of the strongest demons here to come with me. The rest of you will go to the training grounds and take back our weapons from the war demon traitors. This demon will guide you."

He pointed at the lust demon soldier who'd followed him all this way, causing the poor demon to tremble in panic.

"Wait, what's going on?" they yelled at Iggs as a bunch of wrath demons left the crowd and started toward him. "You're all speaking ancient gibberish!"

"I need you to lead these people back to the training area and help them retake the weapons depot," Iggs explained in English. "You don't have to fight with them. Just point them at the war demons, and they'll do the rest."

"Guiding and pointing I can do," the soldier said, looking extremely relieved now that they knew what was going on. "Hey! Over here! Follow me!"

They were shouting in English, but some things didn't need translation. A crowd of wrath demons was already forming at the exit, their red eyes gleaming with excitement at the thought of finally hitting back at the war demons who'd burned their homes, which was a big part of why Iggs had decided to send them. Technically, Bex had ordered him to get their people to safety but Iggs had never met a wrath demon who'd rather run than fight. There was nowhere to run to, anyway, but if they could retake the control room and save their weapons stockpile, then maybe their rebellion wasn't over after all.

That certainly appealed to Iggs's wrath demon nature more than cowering in the basement. He sent the demons off with a grin, calling encouragement as they ran down the tunnel after their lust demon guide. When he was certain everyone was moving, he turned back around to start picking his own team, only to discover they'd already picked themselves.

Just as he'd asked, fifty wrath demons had stepped forward to volunteer for retaking the control room. This included Zargrexa, who was standing proudly at the head of the pack.

"Wait," Iggs blurted before he could think better of it, "*you're* coming?"

"Of course I'm coming," the old demon snapped, reaching up to smack Iggs across the horns just like his gran used to. "Weren't you listening earlier? Those war demon traitors killed everyone I loved and burned my home to the ground! If you think I'm not taking that blood back with my own claws, you're an embarrassment to our clan."

"Yes, village chief," Iggs said, ducking his horns at once.

The old lady nodded sharply before turning to wave her hand at the salty-looking band of demons standing behind her.

"These are all survivors like myself who have no one left to mourn for them. We may not be the youngest or the strongest, but loss has made us the sharpest. We are ready to give everything for our queen. You will not find us lacking."

"I'm sure I won't," Iggs said, nodding his head to each of the demons, none of whom looked like someone he'd want to get into a fight with, whatever Zargrexa said. "Follow me, then. We don't have a lot of time."

The village chief motioned for Iggs to lead the way, yelling at the others in Riverlander to keep up or face the flames of the Bonfire Queen.

They didn't have to go far. As the command center for the entire Anchor, the control room was located in the middle of the stretched space. This put it only two floors below the wrath demons' village, an easy jaunt now that the panicked crowds had finished fleeing to the lower levels.

Iggs was relieved that everyone had finally evacuated, but now that the stairs were empty, it was easier to see all the cracks the war demons' treason had put in his Free Market. Each one filled Iggs with a fury that had nothing to do with the war. That had been raging for eons, but this was *his* fortress. He was the one who'd convinced Bex to stay here, dammit. The Anchor was supposed to be somewhere they could start over, a place where demons like him could have a home again. Now, the war demons had smashed it just like they'd smashed Iggs's actual village, and he was so mad he would've ignited if he could've.

"Iggs."

The name sounded right in his ear, nearly causing Iggs to pitch face-first down the stairs. By the time he recovered his balance, Nemini was running right beside him.

"Where in the Hells did you come from?!"

He was so surprised, he didn't even realize he'd asked the question in Riverlander until Nemini answered in kind.

"Far away," she said, keeping her yellow eyes on her feet as they raced down the stairs. "Bex asked me to do something, but it didn't work. We both knew it wouldn't, but..."

"You tried anyway," Iggs finished for her.

Nemini nodded, letting out such a heavy breath that even her snakes looked deflated.

"She's fighting the Princess of War on the walls of Heaven right now," the void demon went on. "I know the outcome of a single duel means nothing in the grand scheme of the universe, but that's a bad match."

"Nonsense," Iggs said stubbornly. "Bex can beat anyone. That's why she's Ishtar's Sword."

Nemini's mouth pressed into a hard line. "War has broken many swords."

Iggs's face fell into a scowl. He didn't know if the void demon was just being her usual pessimistic self or if she actually thought Bex would lose. He was debating whether or not it'd be worth the effort to try to get a straight answer out of her when Nemini put a finger to her lips and pointed at the landing below them. The one with a security door set into the carved wall and a big red sign that read *Authorized Personnel Only*.

Iggs nodded and came to an immediate stop. All the demons running behind him stopped, too, their faces wary. Iggs motioned for them to stay put and crept the rest of the way down alone, tiptoeing over the elegant stairwell's cracked stone to press his ear against the metal door.

What he heard was not good. Though it was called "the control room," the office containing the network of interlocking cuneiform tablets that dictated the use of the Anchor's magic was really more of a suite. You couldn't even get to the actual controls without passing through the giant conference room where the sorcerers who'd run this place used to hold their meetings.

The beige walls were still covered in diagrams of the Gordian knot that had been their office. Those carefully-labeled drawings were what had helped Iggs and his team of former Anchor slaves figure out how to build their current demon-friendly Anchor. But while they'd changed almost everything else, the control room itself had remained untouched, which meant there was still a large meeting room on the other side of the door. A room that, if Iggs's ears were correct, was jammed full of war demons.

Cursing under his breath, Iggs crept back to the others waiting on the staircase.

"Entry's packed," he reported in a whisper. "We're going to have to go through an army to get to our target. Fortunately for us, we don't actually have to take out the whole place. We've just got to get our hands on the main control tablet long enough to reopen all the doors." He glanced at Nemini, who was perched like a bird on the brass railing beside him. "Do you think you can do your shadow-step thingy to get past the blockade and undo whatever nonsense they used to lock us in here?"

"As much as anyone is able to do anything," the void demon replied flatly. "But I've never used the control room before."

"That part's easy," Iggs assured her. "Or at least, it'll be easy after you read the 'Door Control' section of the manual I wrote."

Nemini gave him a long, slow blink. "You wrote a manual?"

"Of course," Iggs said proudly. "RTFM is the first rule of how not to suck at stuff, and Gilgamesh's sorcery bullshit doesn't exactly have an intuitive interface."

His fellow wrath demons blinked at the sudden avalanche of foreign slang interjected into the sacred language of the Riverlands, but Nemini just nodded.

"I can do it, then, but you'll have to create a distraction for me." She flicked her yellow eyes back to the packed room. "Nothing only exists when no one's looking."

"A distraction we can do," Iggs promised. "Let me get everyone into position, and then you just say the word."

He turned and crept back down the stairs, motioning over his shoulder for the other wrath demons to follow him this time. When they were all standing by the walls on either side of the doorway, Iggs looked back to see if Nemini was ready, but the banister was empty. He was looking all over the stairwell for her when a quiet voice whispered like a memory in his ear.

"The word."

He almost blew the whole thing by yelping in surprise. Shaking his head at creepy void demons and their creepy habits, Iggs balled his hands into fists and pulled himself to his full height. He focused on his anger as he did so, reaching for the wrath that had smoldered in his heart since the moment five thousand years ago when he and every other wrath demon had felt their queen fall. He might not actually burn like Bex did, but that didn't stop him from catching the ember and holding it tight, willing his fury hotter and hotter, bigger and bigger. Finally, when he'd gotten big enough that his horns were touching the stairwell's tall ceiling, Iggerux turned and lashed out with his now-giant fist to bash the metal security door off its hinges.

Straight into a war demon's face.

The sight filled Iggs with satisfaction. He'd known the room was packed with the big bronze bastards, but he hadn't expected them to be stupid enough to stand in the doorway. That was a welcome stroke of luck, but when Iggs marched into the room to start slamming heads, the war demon army he'd expected was not standing ready to meet him. They were on their knees on the floor, sitting with their heads down and their four arms held up in surrender.

The sight was so shocking that even the fully-transformed Iggs stopped cold. The other wrath demons were still charging behind him, unable to see around Iggs's giant back. They would've plowed straight into the kneeling demons if Iggs hadn't caught them at the last second, holding his fellow wrath demons back as the biggest war demon in the room—the one Iggs had just kicked in the face with the door—pushed himself off the floor to resume his position of surrender.

The other wrath demons fell silent when they saw it. For a long moment, no one made a sound, and then Iggs pulled his huge red body up straight as he asked, "What are you doing?"

The transformed war demon took a shuddering breath. "We are surrendering."

"Why?" Iggs demanded.

It was a simple question, but the war demon took a long time to answer. Fully ten seconds went by before he finally raised his face—General Kirok's tear-streaked face, Iggs realized with a start—and said, "Because we are sorry."

Those words brought Iggs's rage back hot and sharp.

"You're *sorry*?" he roared, baring his fangs. "You *betrayed* us! Your war demons shot their own squadmates in the *back*! It's the same treasonous bullshit you pulled during the war, and—"

"And that's why we are sorry," General Kirok interrupted, looking up at him with so much sorrow that even Iggs's wrath faltered. "We never wanted to betray you. This rebellion was our hope, too. We thought this was our chance to finally escape the shame of slavery, but we were wrong. There is no escape for us."

"What do you mean?" Iggs asked. Not angrily this time. He was too confused to be furious now. He just wanted the truth. "You were Bex's general. If you didn't want to be slaves anymore, why did you do this?"

"Because I couldn't tell her no," General Kirok explained desperately. "Taking over the control room wasn't our idea! We didn't even know the attack was coming until the queen spoke in our heads and ordered us to shoot our fellow soldiers."

"The queen?" Iggs repeated incredulously. "*Impossible.* Bex would never—"

"Not *your* queen," the general snapped, regaining a bit of his old pompousness as he let the implied *you idiot* hang unspoken in the air. "The other queen." He gritted his white teeth behind his bronze lips. "*Our* queen."

"You don't have a queen anymore!" Iggs yelled. "No one does, except—"

"What do you know?" Kirok bellowed. "You wrath demons will never understand our suffering because your queen never faltered in her duty! Even after Gilgamesh killed her, the Bonfire of Wrath never stopped fighting. That's why I agreed to stay and train her circus. I knew a bunch of lust, sorrow, and greed demons could never be soldiers, but I tried to whip them into shape anyway because your queen asked me to. She never abandoned the Children of Ishtar, but *our* queen—"

He stopped suddenly, grabbing his throat. Iggs had never experienced the phenomenon himself because he'd never had anything bad to say about Bex, but he recognized it the same way he'd recognize when someone was suffocating. The general had run into what happened when a demon spoke against his own queen. Even when his bronze face turned green from lack of breath, though, General Kirok was a soldier to the end, and he did not surrender.

"The Queen of War threw us away," he gasped, his eyes bulging from the sheer, willful fury it took a demon to speak those words. "She was the one who forced us to do this, right before she left us to die." He raised his bulging eyes to the roof, which was starting to crack above their heads. "She left us to *die!*"

The other war demons rumbled in agreement, but Iggs still didn't understand.

"How is that possible?" he demanded. "The Queen of War is dead. They all are. Only Bex—"

"How could she be dead?" the war demon demanded, his breath finally bursting back into him now that he'd stopped blaspheming against his queen. "War was never defeated. Unlike her sacred sisters, she surrendered to Gilgamesh willingly. Do you really think the Eternal King would let a prize that glorious die?"

He looked Iggs straight in the eye, daring him to argue, but Iggs didn't take that bet. He was too busy processing the implications of what the general had just said, what it could mean for all of them if—

Iggs lurched backward, grabbing the frame of the door he'd just kicked down as he bellowed. *"Nemini!"*

Since he was still transformed, the void demon's name came out in a roar. Iggs was about to bellow it again when Nemini suddenly stepped into view from the corner where he hadn't been looking.

"I'm not done yet," she said, her face set in a slight scowl, which was the angriest she got. "Just because time is infinite doesn't mean it doesn't have an order, and your manual is useless since the war demon smashed all the cuneiform tablets that control the—"

Her annoyed explanation cut off as Iggs grabbed her shoulders.

"You have to get to Bex," he said, ignoring the oblivion that started seeping into his fingers the second he touched her. "You said she was fighting the Princess of War, right? And that that's a match she doesn't win?"

"I did say that," Nemini whispered, dropping her eyes. "But I can't go there. It's too close to Heaven, and I am nothing. Nothing can't—"

"I don't care about that!" Iggs roared, dropping to his knees to make her look at him. "You're always saying you're nothing and that nothing matters, but you're *something* to us, dammit! Bex has always been

363

there for you just like she's always been there for all of us, but you're the only one who can get to her now." He bowed his horns to her as his hands began to shake. "Please, Nemini, the Queen of War is alive and Bex doesn't know. You have to go tell her. You have to go *help* her!"

He was begging by the end, but the void demon was quiet for so long that Iggs thought she was ignoring him. Even her nothingness wasn't seeping into his hands anymore. It was as if she'd pulled away entirely, which made Iggs angrier than anything else she could have done. He was about to curse her name and run upstairs to help his queen himself when he felt the soft brush of Nemini's hand—her actual hand, not the void inside—land on his lowered head.

"I probably can't change anything," she warned. "But it's been a long time since anyone bowed their horns to me. I'd forgotten how motivating it can be."

"Then you'll help?" Iggs asked hopefully.

"As much as nothing can help," she said, dropping her eyes again. "It won't be much. Everything that was strong or useful in me was broken long ago, but I..."

She trailed off, clutching her bony hands into fists as her snakes writhed on her head. "I don't want Bex to die," she whispered at last. "Even if I can't change anything, even if my efforts come to nothing, I still want to try."

"Then do it," Iggs said, letting go of her shoulders.

Nemini's head shot up. For three full breaths, she stared straight through him, and then her face broke into a smile. Not a smirk or a curve of the lips but a real, honest-to-Ishtar grin that lit up her face like the light of Paradise.

"I'll do my best," she promised, stepping backward through the wrecked door. "Take care of things here, Iggerux. Don't let our fortress fall."

That was the closest thing to an order Iggs had ever heard Nemini give, but it was the sound of his true name on her lips that made him jerk. Something about the way she said it just now had struck him like a hammer. A tiny, broken one, nothing like what he felt when Bex named him, but *something* was there. Before Iggs could figure out what that was, though, Nemini was gone, vanishing into the empty staircase like the nothing she always insisted that she was.

Chapter 15

The clash of battle rang over the walls of Heaven, drowning out even the roars of the lions. It rang down into the empty void and up, up, up to the highest tips of the golden towers that stood above the snow-white buildings of Gilgamesh's perfectly-ordered Holy City. Every strike rang out like a mountain-sized gong, shaking Adrian's enormous tree to its roots as the Blade of Wrath crashed into the Blade of War.

Bex certainly felt it. Every strike rattled her teeth and made her bones ache, but she kept her focus honed to a diamond point, feeding all her rage and fury into the clean, even, all-consuming torch of her wrath. She was no longer a burned-out shell. She wasn't even the cocky novice she'd been when she'd gone into Limbo and ended up facing her first prince. She was an avenging fury. She was Rebexa the Bonfire, born anew like a phoenix from her own ashes. She was the Queen of Wrath, Sword of Ishtar, wielding the weapon she'd been born to hold. The flash of her fire was so bright, even Bex was blinded as she brought Drox down like an executioner's ax. It was the best she'd ever fought, the most powerful she'd ever been.

And it wasn't working.

Bex didn't know *why*. She was moving so fast she was practically flying, swinging Drox's huge new hacking blade as if it weighed nothing. She attacked from above and below, from the left and the right. Every angle, every opening, every gap was exploited the nanosecond it appeared. But no matter how fast she attacked, the Princess of War was always faster, blocking her onslaught on the seemingly impenetrable wall of Havok's black blade.

Rebexa.

Another swing too fast to see, but the princess ducked it like it was nothing, making Bex want to scream. Dammit, dammit, *dammit!* She just needed one hit! One slip, one mistake, one opening, and the traitor of War would be—

Rebexa!

"*What?*" she snarled through clenched teeth since opening her mouth under these circumstances was asking for a bitten-off tongue.

Something's not right.

Damn straight something wasn't right. She was going full burn, swinging her restored sword with more power than his rickety old blade ever could have withstood. She should've beaten this stupid princess ages ago and gone back to wrecking cannons like she was supposed to, but the white hag simply wouldn't *die.*

Princesses of Gilgamesh never die, Drox reminded her. *That's what makes this so odd. Have you ever seen a princess with a black sword?*

No, but that didn't mean anything. Bex didn't remember ninety-nine percent of the crap she'd fought over her many lifetimes. That was Drox's job.

And I'm telling you this is wrong, her blade insisted. *We've fought a lot of princesses, but they always turn into swords for their princes, and their blades are always white. We've never fought a Princess of Gilgamesh who used her own sword, or whose blade was still black.*

Maybe War was different. Hadn't they fought her before?

No, Drox said in a worried voice. *In the past, the Princess of War only appeared* after *you were defeated by someone else, usually to torture you in an attempt to make you surrender. You always spat in her face and died rather than bow your horns to Gilgamesh, but we've never fought her like this.*

Hearing that made Bex smile. All of her attacks were still failing, but knowing this was the first time they'd made War come down from Heaven to fight her in person felt like an achievement. Bex just wished she was getting more out of it because right now, she felt like a fly attacking a mountain.

It makes no sense, Drox insisted as he slammed into Havok's black blade for what felt like the millionth time. *Princesses become white Blades of Gilgamesh. Even Havok's armor was white, but that is a queen's weapon.*

He had a point there. The Princess of War still had Havok's armored gauntlet over her arm, but the black blade in her white hands could have been Drox's brother. The shape was different—a two-edged blade wide enough to double as a shield rather than a long, one-sided hacking sword—but they were both made from the same shiny black metal.

The hallmark of the Blades of Ishtar, Drox agreed. *That is also Enki's creation, so why is it in a princess's hands? What divine weapon would let itself be wielded by a traitor?*

Bex didn't think it was surprising in the slightest. She'd spent an entire day with Havok, plenty long enough to identify him as a grade-A asshole. He'd probably gone over to the enemy even more eagerly than his queen. The question in Bex's mind was: Why was War a princess? She'd famously never been defeated, so where was her body? What had Gilgamesh done to—

Her thoughts flew apart as the princess's sword slammed into her side. She must have gotten distracted by all the questions because while War had never stopped defending, she'd somehow found the time to slip in an attack. It was just a quick jab, but it was still enough to smack Bex off Adrian's tree. She would've hurtled out of Heaven entirely, but Bex caught herself with a blast of fire at the last second, shooting back up like a flaming comet.

We can't keep wasting time on this, Drox said as Bex landed back at the edge of Adrian's branches. *We'll figure the blade out later. Ignore Havok and go for the princess.*

Bex *had* been going for the princess, but her sword had a good point. Aside from that last hit of opportunity, the Princess of War had been completely on the defensive. If she was hiding behind her sword, that must mean her white body was as breakable as a normal princess's. Bex just had to land a hit, which was what she'd been *trying* to do this whole time. All her normal tactics were failing, though, which meant it was time for something crazy.

With that, Bex stopped attacking and grew very still. She called back the fire that had been powering her blazing speed and held it close instead, squeezing the roaring flames smaller and smaller, hotter and hotter. Even with the great care she was taking not to damage Adrian's tree, the heat rolling off of her was so intense that the wood began to smoke.

That was no good. The last thing Bex wanted was to hurt Adrian's forest, so she clenched her fire even tighter, shaping all that she was into a single white-hot flame that burned like a star in her hands.

Burned in Drox specifically. Her superheated fire spread over her sword's shiny new surface like oil, coating his black blade in a flame so hot and bright, even Bex's burning eyes couldn't look straight at him. Then, when her sword was shining like a star's core, Bex dug her feet into the creaking branches of Adrian's tree and swung, slamming her flaming sword into the princess's dark one like a hammer.

As always, Havok stopped Drox's blow. This time, though, the sheer force of all that concentrated fire pushed him and his princess back along the branches, which was where Bex took her chance. The moment she saw the princess move, she let go of her sword and reached in with both of her white-hot hands to grab War's left arm. The one that wasn't covered in Havok's armor.

This was where all her previous experience paid off. War's sword might be unbreakable, but a princess was still a princess. Her body was carved from the same ivory as all the others, which meant Bex already knew exactly how much heat it took to crack her. The glowing hands she'd wrapped around the Princess of War's arm were already twice that hot, but Bex wasn't taking any chances. She went in with every joule of energy she could generate, pouring her fire into the princess's arm just like she'd poured it into the prince back in Adrian's clearing until, at last, the white carving cracked.

Not just cracked. *Exploded.* The princess's entire left arm shattered like a porcelain grenade. The force wave nearly threw Bex off the tree again before Adrian's branches caught her. By the time he set her back on solid wood, the Princess of War was on her knees, staring at her destroyed arm with a look of utter horror.

"*You broke it!*" she screamed.

"Occupational hazard," Bex replied with a smirk, holding out her arm to catch Drox as his black blade flew back into her hands. "You out of everyone should know that all's fair in love and—"

The rest of her gloating was drowned out by the princess's roar of fury.

"*You have no idea what you've destroyed!*" she wailed as she surged to her feet. "This is my original idol, the first ever made! My glorious king carved it with his own hands, and you *broke* it!"

"I'll break your face next," Bex promised, but the princess wasn't listening.

"He made it just for me so I could be beautiful," she sobbed. "Of course *you* would break it. Wrath breaks everything it touches, but perhaps it's better this way. You're the one who refuses to let this war die. It's only fitting that you should be forced to look upon its true face."

"What are you talking about?" Bex asked nervously.

"Your own words," the princess replied, glaring at her with mismatched eyes full of hate. "You're the one who told me long ago, as you pushed me into that pit, that war is never pretty."

Before Bex could even figure out how to ask what that meant, a deafening *crack* rang out across the battlements of Heaven. That was nothing new, but the destructive sound hadn't come from swords or cannons this time. It came from the princess, filling the air with the sound of a thousand dropped porcelain vases as her lovely, doll-like body shattered even more explosively than her arm had. Once again, the blast nearly blew Bex off the tree, but when Adrian's oak set her back on her feet this time, she was no longer facing the Princess of War.

Ishtar have mercy, Drox whispered.

Bex would've said the same if she'd had the presence of mind for words, but she didn't. Every bit of sense she had, including the instinct to run away, had been blown out of her head by the shock of the figure standing in front of her. The towering, terrifying, four-armed woman with a ring of protective horns sitting on her head like a crown and a full suit of plate armor as white as the bones of those who fell in her wake. The *not*-dead, *not*-kneeling, *not*-conquered, very-much-alive Queen of War.

If Bex hadn't been a queen herself, the sight would have sent her to her knees. She still staggered a little, though not because she was awed. The feeling overwhelming Bex now was confusion because that wasn't the sister she remembered.

Every other time she'd seen a princess, or at least a princess's hand, Bex had known instantly and instinctively that this was a fellow daughter of Ishtar. The same was true for the Queen of War. That was absolutely her sister, but while Bex had no memories of what the Queen of War looked like, she was absolutely certain that this wasn't it.

"What the—" She stopped to swallow, hands shaking on her black sword as she lowered it. "What did Gilgamesh *do* to you?"

"You mean this?" the Queen of War asked, pointing her armored hand at the ruin that should have been her face.

Like all war demons, her skin was made of bronze. But though her features had clearly been lovely once, her shining skin was now misshapen and pitted. It looked like she'd been dunked in acid and then beaten with a hammer. But before Bex could unleash her rage at Gilgamesh for doing this to her sister, even one she disliked as much as War, the queen shook her head.

"This wasn't him."

"How could it not be him?" Bex demanded, forgetting their enmity as she marched toward her sister in righteous fury. "Who but Gilgamesh could do *that* to a queen's face?"

"The one who made it," War replied as her scarred lips pulled into a misshapen sneer. "You were always her favorite. Her precious, obedient sword. You were *so* dutiful, *so* good, you never let yourself see

373

what our mother was really like, not even when she did it right in front of your face."

"No," Bex said, shaking her head. "That's not possible. Ishtar is our goddess, our *mother*. She would never do that to—"

"*Shut up!*" War screamed, swinging her sword wildly. "How dare you deny what happened? How *dare* you still defend her after what she did to us?"

"What did she do?" Bex cried, scrambling out of the way. "I reincarnate, remember? I don't know any of this!"

"What does that matter?" the queen demanded, chasing her. "You denied it even when it was happening right under your nose. It was easy for you because you were Wrath! Your sin was hardly a sin at all. People praised you for your rages, called you strong and brave! Even Mother made you her sword, but I was always evil!"

"Maybe if you hadn't betrayed us to Gilgamesh, people wouldn't call you that!" Bex yelled as she threw herself out of the way with a blast of fire.

"*I* wasn't the one who broke faith first," War snarled, whirling to follow her. "Mother got that ball rolling. She betrayed all of us when she made her queens, her own *children*, eat mankind's sins. She forced us to take their evils into our own bodies, to make ourselves filthy so the precious humans who worshiped her could be reborn clean and pure. We *all* suffered her betrayal! But I was betrayed the most."

She lifted her upper right arm and ripped off her gauntlet—the same white armored gauntlet Havok had used to block Drox's strikes—to show Bex her hand, or at least what Bex assumed was her hand. The queen's bronze skin was so corroded that it was hard to tell, but the rotted stalks that must have once been fingers still curled in rage.

"War is the worst of humanity's sins," the queen said with ancient bitterness. "It is the culmination of all their evils, the place where pride, greed, envy, hate, sorrow, fear, lust, pride, and wrath combine and fester like trash in a midden. War is where good people look away from atrocity, where the old and powerful send the young and vulnerable to die for their greed. It's where conquerors rape the conquered and whole countries are set on fire for a king's pride. It's where mothers lose their children and children lose their mothers. It is the greatest poison the mortal world has ever created, and Ishtar was the one who made me drink it."

"It was our sacred duty," Bex argued, lowering her sword. "We all ate their sins."

"Not like I did," War spat, reaching her ruined hand up to touch her scarred face. "Not even a daughter of the gods could handle that much evil. All my demons suffered for it, but I was at the top. Every sin they consumed was concentrated up into me. Humanity's toxicity pitted my flesh and hollowed my bones, but I was divine. No matter how much I suffered, I could not die. For thousands of years, I knew only pain, and when it finally grew too much, when I finally broke and turned my fury, my *wrath* on the one who'd made me to be this way, Ishtar threw me into a pit so that my screams wouldn't taint her perfect Paradise."

The queen's eyes—still mismatched gold and mirrored silver—flicked back to Bex with a fresh flash of hate. "You were there when she did it. Ishtar's Sword at Ishtar's side, smirking like a spoiled brat as our mother cast me down into the dark. I would have lain there screaming forever had Gilgamesh not come to Paradise and found me. He was the one who pulled me out of the hell our blessed mother damned me to, so you tell me, *sister*, do you think I'm a traitor now?"

"Yes," Bex said without hesitation. "I don't remember any of that, so I can't say if you were betrayed by the gods or not, but I've seen with my own eyes how you betrayed your people."

She stabbed her finger down at the blasted top of the Anchor Market she could still barely see through the gaps in Adrian's tree.

"The war demons you were made to protect suffered in Gilgamesh's Hells just like the rest of our people. I *know* they suffered, because I freed them from it. The war demons I've named wept tears of joy just like every other demon, because *no one* deserves to live in slavery. If the story you just told me is true, then you should understand that better than anybody, and yet you're here, stopping me from setting things right! How can you fight for Gilgamesh when he's spent the last five thousand years grinding our people—*your* people—under his boot? *That* is treason, sister, and I will fight you for it forever."

The Queen of War's ruined face pulled into a disgusted sneer. "Poor little brainwashed Bexa," she spat as she put her armored gauntlet back on. "No matter how many clean slates you were given, you could never stop being Ishtar's loyal dog. It's pathetic, really, but that farce is over now. There's no more second chances, no more mercy. This time, it's the end."

"You're bluffing," Bex said, keeping her eyes on all four of her sister's arms as the Queen of War raised her sword. "You've made it clear how much you hate my guts, but if you kill me, all my demons become hollow shells. Your precious King Gilgamesh didn't trap the entire population of Wrath in Limbo for five thousand years to risk turning them into void demons now. That's why his stupid princes are always trying to make me bow and why you decided to bombard my Anchor instead of having this fight earlier. You didn't even come out until I started breaking Gilgamesh's infrastructure, which means I've got your number." Her lips curled into a fang-toothed grin. "You've been ordered not to kill me."

"Don't presume to know the mind of the Eternal King," the Queen of War replied haughtily. "The only reason we tried to make you submit before is because killing you was pointless. Every time we smacked you down, you just popped back up again like a weed. Hunting you was pointless and wasteful, and my glorious king has no tolerance for waste. But that's not how things are anymore, is it?"

She leaned forward, using her towering height to loom over Bex like a falling tower.

"I know your secret," she whispered. "You told it to me yourself when you tried to recruit my Havok for your doomed crusade. You have no more reincarnations. This is your very last life, which means

I'm finally free to do what I should have done five thousand years ago."

Be wary, Drox cautioned as Bex stepped backward. *She's—*

Her sword didn't even get to finish before the Queen of War attacked. The only reason Bex was able to avoid getting skewered was because the queen moved exactly like her sword did. Thanks to Bex's obsession with beating Havok, she'd already practiced this fight a hundred times. But while the queen's habits were the same as her weapon's, War was even faster, her four arms lashing out like switchblades to rip Bex in half.

Drox was the only reason she didn't succeed. The Blade of Wrath moved of its own volition, bashing away War's attack before Bex's brain could finish processing what was happening. This bought her the precious seconds she needed to leap away, but she still wasn't fast enough. The Queen of War was already on top of her again, swinging Havok's sword with her top two hands while the bottom two punched at Bex's sides, coming in like armored hammers to turn her ribs to powder.

Bex saved herself by a hair. Trusting Drox to block the sword strike, she switched her focus to her left foot, transferring all her fire to blast a kick straight into the queen's knee. This ended up hurting her foot more than her enemy, but at least the flash distracted the Queen of War long enough for Bex to launch an attack of her own.

They'd cut Havok's armor before, so Bex felt confident as she slung a line of razor-sharp fire straight at the queen's chest. Her swing hadn't even made it six inches, though, before the Queen of War dropped low and spun, slamming her armored leg into Bex's to knock her off her feet.

The punt sent her flying over the white walls of Heaven. For a breathless moment, Bex saw the whole of Gilgamesh's Holy City spread out beneath her. That was better than being kicked into the void, but Bex hadn't actually had a chance to take a look at Heaven's capital yet. Most of it looked exactly like she'd expected—elegant white buildings arranged along gold-paved streets that ran like a starburst out of the giant white-and-gold tower that marked Heaven's center—but there were no people. Even during an attack, Bex would've thought she'd spot the famous Heavenly denizens cowering behind their silk-curtained windows, but the whole city looked deserted. There wasn't a soul to be seen. There were, however, lots of constructs.

They'd been so still she hadn't noticed them at first. Now that she was flying over their heads, though, Bex realized that what she'd thought were gold-paved streets were actually *white* streets packed with Heaven's golden war machines. They raised their heads as she flew over, their intricate gold eyes whirring as they locked on, and then all their giant arms came up as one to shoot a wave of gleaming arrows straight at her face.

Bex swore and flipped herself over, sweeping Drox around just in time to knock the volley out of the air. That kept her from getting pincushioned, but she was far out over the city now. So far that she could see the spire of Gilgamesh's fortress—the heart of Heaven itself—rising like a cliff in front of her. That was all she had time to notice before she started to fall.

Use your fire! Drox roared.

Bex scrambled to obey, pulling her sword back into his ring as she slammed her flaming—and now empty—hands together to blast herself back into the sky. This kept her from crashing into the middle of Gilgamesh's construct army, but she was still far away from the walls and even farther from Adrian's tree, which was the only place in this whole cursed afterlife where she could safely put her feet down. She was working out the angle she'd need to blast herself to get going in the right direction again when the sword smashed into her unguarded back.

That was almost the end. The blow crashed into her like a falling building, but Bex was still a queen. Even a direct hit from a divine blade wasn't enough to kill her instantly, though it did send her crashing like a meteor into the sea of constructs, who were busy reloading for their next volley.

Ironically, this ended up being her salvation. Bex couldn't set foot in Paradise without the ground cracking like rotten wood beneath her, but Gilgamesh's war constructs were another story. *Those* Bex could step on just fine, a fact she learned for certain when she landed on their heads.

The impact cratered the street and broke the constructs to pieces. It broke Bex as well, but her fire was burning as hot as a jet engine now, knitting her cracked bones and sundered muscles back together in seconds. Not two heartbeats after she crashed down,

Bex was pushing herself out of the wreckage, throwing pieces of smashed constructs out of her way as she rolled to her feet and started running.

Now, this was more like it. Bex couldn't set foot on the actual street, but Heaven was packed with so many soldiers that she didn't need to. She ran across the enemy itself, leaping from construct to construct like a mouse jumping between golden rocks. She hadn't spotted the Queen of War yet in the chaos, but Bex knew she was after her, just like she knew she couldn't win. She'd already thrown everything she had at that fight and only managed to land one consequential hit, and that was when War had been a princess with only two arms.

Now that the queen was back in her real, Ishtar-given body, Bex knew she didn't stand a chance. Even at her best, War was better, but while that was a bitter pill to swallow, Bex hadn't come to Heaven to duel her sister. She was here to stop the bombardment from killing her people, which meant she needed to stop wasting time on losing fights and get back to breaking cannons.

At least they weren't hard to spot. Gilgamesh's lions were right in front of her, gleaming high atop the city's battlements like big golden targets. She'd just pulled Drox back into her hand to wing a slash of fire at them when her sword's voice roared through her head.

LEFT!

Bex was still trying to figure out if the attack was coming from the left or if Drox wanted her to dodge left when the Queen of War tackled her. They landed in a tumble of flying fists and flashing swords. Where Bex could only swing one at a time, though, the Queen of War was pounding her with both, throwing punches with her lower arms while her upper ones tried to chop Bex's head off.

Since Bex only had enough arms to block one, she chose to protect her head. This meant her torso got pummeled, but Bex had already accepted that the Queen of War was the superior fighter, so she didn't waste time being mad about it. For once in her life, her skills were not at fault. Other than a few slips in reaction time, her footwork, swordwork, and fire had all been at the absolute top of their game. Even Drox hadn't had a single criticism, which would've made Bex crow with pride if any of that had mattered.

Alas, it didn't. Bex was fighting the best fight of any of her lives, but the Queen of War was still pounding her into the flattened body of a crumpled construct. She was going to get flattened, too, if she let this keep up, so Bex decided to stop defending and focus everything on finding a way out.

Just like Havok, the Queen of War didn't seem to care about her fire, so Bex ignored heat and went for volume, sending her flames out as wide as she could to create a fireball that blew them both into the sky. As usual, the Queen of War righted herself almost immediately. Unlike her, though, Bex had expected to go flying, which meant, for once, that she was faster.

It was a tiny sliver of an advantage, but Bex used it to the hilt, firing another blast to launch herself back toward the city walls. Since she'd already blown them both sky-high, she made it to the top of the battlements in seconds, but Bex didn't bother trying to land. The white stones would just crack the moment she put a foot down, so she swung her sword instead, taking out another golden lion seconds before it fired.

The giant cannon was a *much* easier target than the Queen of War. The stupid construct didn't even get to turn its head before Drox's fiery slash cut it in half. The blowback launched Bex into the air again, buying her time to turn and swing another slash at the next cannon in the line.

Fast as a machine gun, Bex spun through the air, launching flaming whips from her sword at the lions below. By the third spin, she was going so fast she couldn't even see what she was aiming at, but it wasn't hard to hit a bunch of giant immobile targets sitting in a line. She knocked the lions over like tin cans, throwing herself higher and higher with each blast because never stopping meant she didn't have to worry about the fall.

It wasn't the sort of plan that had an ending, but so long as it was going, Bex was unstoppable. She blew over the Holy City like a tornado, sending out wave after wave of fire until the whole left side of the city wall was drenched in it. She was about to blast over to start on the right when something shot off the ground to stab her through the chest.

She'd known her run couldn't last forever, but the suddenness of the stop still caught Bex by surprise. She looked down at the heavy black sword sticking through her chest, then down farther still at the queen on the battlements who'd thrown it. Her sister yanked her arm down as she watched, recalling her sword back to her hand.

Since Bex was still skewered, this meant she came, too. War was even good enough to tilt Havok's black blade down, locking him between Bex's ribs as she yanked the flaming Bonfire of Wrath out of the sky. She pulled her sword back into his ring at the last second, dropping Bex like a shot bird onto the battlements at her feet.

As always, the white stones started cracking immediately. Bex was actually helping by pushing down in the hope she'd drop out of Paradise before her sister grabbed her, but it didn't work. War's armored hand was already wrapping around her throat to lift Bex off the ground.

"Did you think that just because I couldn't fly, you were out of my grasp?" she growled, hauling Bex up in front of her like a broken doll. "Arrogant child! Nowhere is safe from War."

Bex's response to that was to slam her horns into her sister's face. It was the obvious move with their heads so close together, but—ironically, considering the sin she'd been made to consume—War hadn't been in the trenches as much as Bex had. For all that she claimed to hate Ishtar, she was still a noble queen, and she wasn't prepared for the brutality as Bex lurched forward, crushing her own throat against War's gauntlet to stab her foot-long horns into the hollow beneath the queen's chin.

Unlike all of Bex's other strikes, *that* one got through. Drox might be a divine blade, but he was still a product of Enki. Bex's horns, on the other hand, were the crown placed on her head by Ishtar herself. They cut through the Queen of War's armor—both Havok's bone-white plates and the pitted bronze of the queen's own skin—to stab deep into her neck. She was still choking on her own black blood when Bex ripped herself free.

And immediately started falling again.

She danced from foot to foot, cursing up a storm. Her stupid sister had yanked her back to the top of the wall, where the cannons were. The ones Bex had already scorched, thank Ishtar, so at least she didn't have to worry about getting blasted, but there was nowhere to stand. Anu's banishment was still in effect, turning what should have been a clear, open expanse of stone into one gigantic pitfall. She couldn't even hop on top of the wrecked lions since the waves of fire she'd used to destroy them had melted their corpses into boiling lakes of molten gold. Even Bex would burn if she tried to stand on that, which meant the only safe place left was Adrian's tree.

Fortunately, it wasn't far away. She could already see the oak's branches sticking up over the wall just a few hundred feet down the battlements as she started to run, moving her feet so fast that the ground didn't have time to crack beneath them. She leaped as soon as she was in range, landing on the tree hard enough to make it sway, but when Bex grabbed the nearest limb to tell her witch that the cannons were slagged and it was time to go, what she saw made her black blood run cold.

The oak was still sturdy under her feet, but it didn't look right. Bex had been staring at Gilgamesh's stupid city for so long, she thought her eyes were playing tricks on her, but a few blinks later, she realized there was no mistake. Adrian's oak tree was *white*. Not snow white, or mold white, or cloud white, or any other white found in nature. His tree was as white as the wall behind her, as white as the vault where she'd killed Enki. Princess white. *Quintessence* white. Bex was still trying to figure out how that was possible when a pair of hands wrapped around her bloody horns from behind.

"Got you."

The Queen of War's hate-filled voice was growling right next to her ear, but Bex couldn't even turn her head with her horns locked up like that. She was stabbing Drox blindly behind her in an attempt to make the other queen let go when a third hand grabbed her sword blade. She was trying to yank it back when the Queen of War's own sword dropped like a falling ax to slice through Bex's right arm just above the wrist.

She screamed when it hit, sagging against the Queen of War's grip on her horns as she grabbed the bleeding stump with her left hand. Her fire cauterized the wound instantly, and Bex said a quick prayer of thanks to Ishtar that the Queen of War's sword was still black. No white Blade of Gilgamesh meant that the injury would heal on its own eventually. Not that "eventually" helped much when she was down one arm and the Queen of War still had her by the horns.

Kicking at her captor with a string of curses, Bex reached out with her remaining hand to call Drox. She wasn't nearly as good with her left arm as her right, but it wasn't hard to hit someone who was holding you in front of them. Bex was already tensing her muscles for the upswing that would cut the Queen of War's arms off at the elbow for maximum karmic payback, but for the first time in memory, her sword didn't fly to her hand. When Bex arched her flaming body around to see why, War's armored foot was planted on top of him, keeping the furiously-rattling Drox from his queen through sheer brute strength.

The moment she saw it, Bex's rage flared out of control. She'd been keeping a tight hold on her fire to make sure she'd have enough oomph left to get out of here, but the sight of her sword—*her* Drox, her other half—writhing under that traitor's boot was the last straw. The Queen of Wrath exploded, engulfing all of them in a pillar of white-hot flame.

The heat was so intense, even War's armor began to crack. Bex could actually see the queen's bronze flesh melting beneath her protective plating, but while the pain had to be intense, her sister ignored it, keeping a tight hold on Bex's horns with her top two hands as she began to twist. The pressure built slowly but inexorably, grinding against Bex like an army against a besieged fortress until, with a crumble of bone and a sickening *crack*, she ripped the horns, the very crown of Wrath, right off Bex's head.

Chapter 16

"**T**hat magic-drunk idiot," Boston muttered, watching from the branches of Adrian's heart tree as Malik dumped yet another barrel of foul-smelling white poison onto his witch.

When the sorcerer left to get the next drum, Boston dropped out of his perch, landing silently at the edge of the hole where Adrian was lying on his side, curled around his root-bound heart in the fetal position. "Adrian!" he hissed, keeping a careful eye on Malik, who was still walking toward the barrels. "*Adrian!*"

No response.

Cursing under his breath, Boston hopped into the hole next to him, landing with a *squish* in the quintessence-soaked mud. Adrian's clothes were soaked with it as well, the familiar black bleached an ugly, unnatural white by the liquid magic that dripped from everything. His skin, however, was radiant with the stuff. The mud under Boston's paws was actually getting drier as Adrian's body sucked up the glowing quintessence like a sponge. But while Malik seemed delighted by that every time he came over with another barrel, Adrian's face was pinched with pain. His eyes were darting wildly behind their closed lids, and his cheek was burning hot when Boston batted it with his paw, making up the familiar's mind.

"That's it," he said with absolute authority. "I'm putting a stop to this."

The statement was purely for his own conscience since his witch was clearly insensible. Even lost in a delusional fever state, however, Adrian must have found the idea of stopping too unacceptable to bear, because before Boston could leap back out of the hole to make good on his threat, his eyes cracked open.

"No," he begged in a weak voice. "I can't quit yet. I'm Bex's only support up there. She's fighting so hard. She needs—"

"She needs you to not die," Boston snapped. "We all do, which is why I'm pulling the plug. It's a familiar's sworn obligation to put his paw down when his witch goes too far, and this is *too far*, Adrian! Just look at what you're doing to your tree."

He moved his furry head out of the way so that Adrian could see the ghostly, unnatural white that was creeping up his heart tree's branches.

"You might not have enough sense to stop before you kill yourself, but I do," Boston said as he leaped out of the hole. "You can yell at me all you want later, but I'm ending this right now."

Adrian reached out feebly, but Boston was already gone, changing into his jaguar-size form as he burst out of the shelter of the fir tree's low branches and skidded to a stop in front of Malik, who was already carrying the next barrel of quintessence across the clearing toward them.

"*Stop!*"

He spoke with the authority of the forest, causing the ground to shake. Any normal human would have frozen in his tracks, but Malik just smiled that obnoxious, know-it-all smile of his and kept walking.

"Is that my son's request?"

"It's not a request," Boston growled, showing his fangs. "Adrian's body and his Blackwood are both at their limits. You will not dump any more of that poison on either of them!"

"I'm just doing what he wants," Malik said as he continued to carry the barrel forward. "My son can make his own decisions, and he asked for this. What kind of father would I be if I didn't help him?"

"A *father* should care about his son's life!" Boston roared, digging his claws into the roots that were rising up to help him. "Your sludge is killing him! You might be too power-drunk to see it, but I am Adrian's familiar! I swore an oath before the Great Blackwood that I would be his reason when he had none!" He crouched low and turned his body sideways, making himself into a wall between this man and his witch. "You will not get another drop of Gilgamesh's toxic magic near him!"

Malik set down his barrel with a shake of his head. "That's not your decision to make."

Boston was unlocking his fangs to explain to this idiot that making decisions when his witch was incapacitated was a familiar's most important duty when Malik flicked the fingers on his right hand, and an invisible wall of force slammed into Boston like a car.

If he hadn't been in his big form, it would have punted him into the inlet, but Boston was built like a brick in this shape, and he had the forest on his side.

The trees caught him before he could fly out of the clearing, breaking his fall and giving Boston's paws something to launch off of when he turned around and threw himself back at Malik. He was about to tackle the sorcerer to the ground when Malik raised one finger, freezing Boston in midair.

"Your concern is noted," he said as Boston struggled against the giant, invisible fist Malik's magic had closed around him. "I am truly touched to see that my son is so well cared for, but I'm afraid I can't permit you to interfere." He turned back to the heart tree that was slowly turning white above them. "Adrian has finally discovered his true talent. What kind of father would I be if I allowed anything to get in his way?"

"You're killing him!" Boston gasped, struggling against the invisible force that held him frozen above Malik's head. "You're killing his forest! Even if he survives, he'll never forgive—"

Malik pinched his fingers together, and the pressure that was holding Boston suspended in the air tightened like a knot to seal the familiar's mouth shut.

"That's enough of that," the sorcerer said as he reached down to pick up the quintessence barrel— which had to weigh several hundred pounds—with one hand. "I won't kill you because that would damage Adrian and my new relationship, but I can't tolerate any interruptions at this critical stage. I'm sure you understand. Now, if you'll excuse me."

He moved the hand he'd used to catch Boston to the side as if he were putting the captured familiar on an invisible shelf. Boston had never seen any magic like it. Malik hadn't spoken a word of sorcery, but even though he was no longer holding the fist he'd used to catch him, Boston still couldn't move or make a sound. He could barely even breathe as Malik ducked underneath him, carrying the drum of quintessence to the hole under the heart tree, where he upended it over Adrian, dumping all fifty gallons at once.

Stuck so high in the air, Boston had a perfect view of the white poison washing over his witch. But while he couldn't get to him, couldn't move, couldn't even growl, there was still one path that could never be blocked. One connection Boston would always be a part of.

He reached for it now with everything he had, calling out through the roots that connected all Blackwoods with the magic he'd been training just as long as Adrian. He didn't expect to get anything back—even in a magical forest, signals took time to travel—but the Blackwood must have been waiting for him to call because the moment Boston reached out, a hand reached back. Three hands, moving as one. That was all Boston had time to make out before the forest behind him opened like a mouth, and three witches stepped out.

"*Stop.*"

They spoke in a single voice, and all the forest spoke with them, filling Adrian's small grove with the magic of the great wild places. The sorcery trapping Boston crumpled under its power, dropping him into the muddy grass as the Three Old Wives of the Blackwood marched forward to confront Malik, who was still holding the empty barrel over Adrian's head.

"Stop," they said again, sending the word echoing through the past, present, and future. "This was not our bargain."

"It was not," Malik agreed, setting the barrel down as he turned to give the three greatest witches in the world the same charming, say-nothing smile he showed to everyone. "But I'm not the one who broke it. I said I would leave Adrian in your care for as long as he wanted to be a witch. You're the ones who conspired to hide his true potential. All I did was answer a call for help. Help *you* refused to give him." His charming smile grew cutting. "How could a father refuse such a heartfelt plea? Especially when you're the ones who drove him into my arms."

"You took advantage of his desperation!" Agatha snarled, her blue eyes shining with fury as she broke rank with her sisters. "He didn't come to you willingly. He was driven there by desperation caused by circumstances *you* created!"

"And yet I was still the one he chose," Malik said, paying no attention to the dark forest that was closing in around him like teeth. "He could have run back to the Blackwood's shelter at any time, but my sons have never liked hiding. You knew that, and yet you deliberately let me think he was a coward." The sorcerer shook his head with a *tsk*. "You hid him from me, Agatha. Who's breaking the bargain now?"

"You will never have him!" Agatha cried, her voice echoing with the power of the present, the moment when a witch's fury is most potent. "Adrian is a Blackwood, one of us! You have no claim over him!"

"Really?" Malik said, glancing over his shoulder. "Doesn't look that way to me."

Boston didn't see how he could say that with a straight face when the whole forest was twisting with the witches' anger, but when he looked at Agatha to see why the Old Wife of the Flesh hadn't turned this trespasser into a toadstool yet, her pale face was the color of ash. Her sisters looked the same, all three of them staring in horror at the Douglas fir Malik had just drawn their attention to. The towering spire of Adrian's heart tree, which was now pure white from trunk to tip.

"It seems that Adrian has made his choice," Malik said as the horrible whiteness began to spread across the ground toward the rest of the forest. "Once again, you have failed to keep my son out of my grasp, but I was very impressed by the effort. I suggest you and your sisters take advantage of that by returning to your witchwood while I'm still in a benevolent mood. It would be the greatest shame if I was forced to do something unpleasant to my favorite woman in the world."

Magic rose as he spoke, a hard, bright, heavy power that crushed the writhing forest into stillness. Even Boston was slammed to the ground. He thought he was going to be squashed like a bug when Agatha shoved back, bucking the crushing weight just long enough to grab her son's familiar and vanish them all back into the Blackwood's roots.

When the witches were gone, Malik waved the crushing pressure away and walked over to pick up another barrel of quintessence. He ended up grabbing two, carrying the enormous drums as easily as two teacups back to the fir tree, where he proceeded to empty them over his son, who was still lying motionless as a corpse in the heart of a forest that was rapidly turning white.

Adrian was pretty sure he'd gone too far this time.

One second, he'd been inside his oak tree, desperately trying to give Bex somewhere to stand while she fought the princess-turned-terrifying-demon. The next, he was standing in nothing. Very, very white nothing. It wasn't painful or uncomfortable, but he couldn't feel his forest or his body anymore, and that was an enormous problem. He'd been speaking absolutely literally when he'd told Boston that he was Bex's only support. If he didn't get back to his tree this instant, the oak was going to crumble beneath the endless flow of time, and then he'd have let Bex down in the truest, most final sense of the word.

That was absolutely unacceptable. Adrian hadn't come this far to fail at the finish line, especially not when Bex was doing her part so spectacularly. The sight of her fighting the four-armed, armored Queen of War had been the most terrifying, most wondrous thing he'd ever seen. Even when she'd gotten kicked into the Holy City itself, she'd flown right back out like a flaming comet and started cutting down lion cannons from the *sky*.

Just the memory made him grin. Great Forest, he loved that woman. His mother had warned him many, many times that witches had a bad habit of being attracted to powerful, dangerous things. Moths to flame was her usual metaphor, which felt uncomfortably apt for this situation, but in Adrian's defense, what wasn't to love? How could he not be attracted to someone so bright and glorious and, best of all, effective? Bex had taken everything Heaven threw at her and returned it in magnificent fire. He *had* to get back to her, if only so he didn't miss the moment when she won.

With that, Adrian broke into a sprint, keeping Bex's image firmly in his mind's eye as he ran across the endless white nothing. He still didn't know what this place was, but given the feel of the magic pulsing around him, he was ready to hazard a guess. The liquid quintessence must have formed a pool beneath his tree, and by reaching so far in his desperation to help Bex, Adrian had fallen right out of his roots into the deep end.

That wasn't *so* bad. Unlike solid quintessence, which gave him a headache and made him feel out of control whenever he bit off more than he could chew, liquid quintessence suited his body fantastically. From the moment Malik had poured the first barrel over his head, Adrian had felt like he could do anything, and then he *had*. He'd grown a tree all the way to the afterlife!

If he could do that, nothing was out of reach, including getting out of here. He just had to find the root he'd accidentally stumbled out of. Since he was currently disembodied, the easiest way to do that was to follow his connection to the forest. Still a tricky task when all his senses were stuffed with white, but while Adrian was admittedly not the best at Soul witchcraft, he wasn't *that* bad. The Blackwood was his heart by every definition. He should be able to find it blind, but when he reached for the memories of his beautiful grove nestled in the islands of the Puget Sound, what came back was a night full of fire.

Adrian jolted, banging his chin on the paving stones he was suddenly face down on top of. This wasn't right. He should be back under his heart tree, or at least inside his Blackwood, but this didn't look like a forest at all. He was lying on his stomach in the middle of what appeared to be an ancient road. A very bloody road. *So* bloody that Adrian could actually see his reflection in the dark-red pools.

The sight stopped him cold. The ash-smeared face staring back at him looked like his, but it was too old. There were scars he didn't remember getting, and this was definitely *not* his memory. As a Witch of the Present, Adrian had been taught not to dwell on the past, but he was certain he'd never been face down on a blood-soaked road in the middle of a burning city before. He was worrying he actually *was* that bad at Soul witchcraft and had wandered into his future by mistake when a familiar voice spoke above him.

"Look up, worm."

Adrian jolted again. The words sounded strange and the tone was terrifying, but there was still no doubt in his mind. That was Bex's voice!

The realization made Adrian slump in relief. He must have snapped back to her battle in Heaven. *That* was why the city was on fire! But when Adrian lifted his head to see how much of the fight he'd missed, he realized he was wrong. Excessively, horrifically, terrifyingly wrong.

The road he was lying in the middle of was *not* part of Gilgamesh's Holy City. Adrian didn't know where it was, but the burning buildings were neither white nor grand. They were small and made from mud bricks held together with straw. Terrified oxen ran braying down stone-paved streets in front of them, and the still bodies on the ground were dressed in simple, unfamiliar clothes that had clearly been made by hand.

It looked like he'd been dropped into a history-book illustration about life in ancient Mesopotamia on a *very* bad day. Everything he could see was on fire, including the woman standing over him.

Adrian shrank back down against the bloody stones. He'd seen Bex in her full glory plenty of times now, but he'd never seen her like this. The burning queen in front of him looked like a true demon with her gigantic black sword and her towering horns as she sneered down at him from an impressive distance.

Too impressive. The Bex he knew was five foot two in boots. This burning woman was well over six feet, and every inch was terrifying. Especially her face, which was looking down on Adrian with such a contemptuous sneer, he almost missed the corpses lying at her feet.

There were two. One was gigantic: a slaughtered bull so big that its chest rose higher than the reed-mat roofs of the burning buildings. But while that should've been the shocker, Adrian's eyes were stuck on the second corpse trapped beneath the terrifying new Bex's burning feet. The human-sized body of a large man dressed in bloody furs, his handsome, black-bearded face frozen forever in a final terrified scream.

Brother!

Adrian jumped. The shouted word had come from inside him like an intrusive thought. He didn't know why—Adrian had no brothers that he was aware of—but the desperate cry must have broken some kind of floodgate, because his mind was suddenly filled with a sea of raging, violent emotions. He still had no idea who the dead man was, but Adrian knew for certain that he'd been precious and loved. A best friend, a brother truer than the bonds of blood. The only one who'd understood him, fought alongside him, laughed with him at things no one else could laugh at. A glassy-eyed corpse was all that was left of the most important person in his world.

And that demon had killed him.

"Don't look at me like that," the tall new Bex commanded from her perch on his beloved brother's back. "You brought this on yourself. For reasons I cannot comprehend, the divine Ishtar singled you out among all mortals to be her consort. Such divine favor should have been the honor of your pathetically short life, but you turned down my holy mother and shamed her in front of all the gods. Even after you humiliated her, though, the Divine Ishtar's mercy was endless. She sent her own sacred bull"—she jerked her tall horns at the giant corpse lying behind her—"to be the instrument of your destruction. A truly pious man would have bowed his head and given thanks for the honor of such an extravagant execution, but your barbarian defied the flawless judgment of the gods."

She stomped her flaming foot on the bearded man's corpse, and something inside Adrian clenched.

"This uncultured *pig*," she growled as her boot came down again. "This *insult* to the enlightened culture you were given your gifts to build. You should have sent him back to the howling wilderness you pulled him out of! That would have been the intelligent choice, but *no*. You took him in like a feral dog, and like a feral dog, he ran wild."

She bared her flaming fangs at Adrian, who was still lying on his stomach in the bloody street. "Your *animal* slew a cherished weapon of the gods! He stopped the punishment meant for you alone, and for that sin, he has been executed."

She lifted her black sword to show him the bright-red blood that still boiled along its smoking edge, and something inside Adrian clenched again.

"You're lucky the Executioning Blade of Ishtar swings at her will," Bex said in a deadly voice. "If it followed *my* will, you'd be dead as well. But despite all sense, my blessed mother still holds you in her favor, which means you get one more chance."

She pointed her bloody sword at the ground between them. "Bow," she growled. "Crawl on the ground like the worm you are and beg the gods' forgiveness. Tell me I was right to kill the uncultured wild man you so stupidly took in. Show me how humbly you wish to return to Holy Ishtar's side, and perhaps I will not cut you in half and burn your precious Uruk to the ground."

The clenching knot in Adrian's chest squeezed tighter with every word. Part of him couldn't understand why Bex was being so horrible, but the rest of him, the man whose past these memories actually belonged to, wasn't surprised at all.

The daughter was the same as the mother. All the creatures of Paradise were arrogant, cruel, fickle beasts who made laws only so they could stomp on those who broke them. It was the same behavior he'd put up with all his life, because what else could you do but play along when infinitely greater powers declared you their favorite toy? He'd endured the gods' favor because he could not escape it and because their gifts uplifted his kingdom, but this was too far. His own suffering he could swallow, but to kill his brother? Butcher the brave, wild, free Enkidu, whose only sin was to stand beside him?

That, he could not tolerate. *That,* he would kill them for. All of them. He would burn their precious Paradise, slaughter all of Ishtar's children just as her haughty daughter had slaughtered his Enkidu. He would destroy them with his bare hands if he had to, he—

"What is this?" the Queen of Wrath asked, interrupting his murderous thoughts with the tip of her burning sword as she pressed it against his cheek. "Is the silver-tongued king finally at a loss for words?" She shook her horned head. "I never did understand what the gods saw in you, but it is my duty to see their will done, so let me give you a hint. The phrase you're looking for is 'forgive me.'"

When the man did not repeat the words immediately, Bex's burning arm lashed out, grabbing his head and shoving it into the street with gods-given strength.

"'Forgive me, Holy Ishtar,'" she recited as she ground his face into the bloody stone. "'I am but a selfish maggot who is utterly unworthy of your sacred attention. Have mercy on my stupidity and spare your beloved daughter the trouble of incinerating me and all my filthy people.'"

She stopped there, releasing her grip on the man's head so he could recite the groveling prayer she'd just made up for him, but the king said nothing. He just lay there on the ground, staring at the coagulating blood that had once belonged to his best friend in all the world. When it was clear he wasn't going to speak, the Queen of Wrath stood back up with a sigh.

"That was an unwise decision," she informed him. "I'm sorely tempted to make it your last, but Ishtar does favor you unreasonably..."

She trailed off, tapping her sword painfully against his head, and then she sighed.

"Better to wait," she muttered, her burning brows pulling into a scowl as she eyed her downed prey. "Unlike you, I'm not foolish enough to risk my mother's anger. I'm sure I'll be back tomorrow with orders to destroy you and your entire kingdom, but until then, enjoy your last dawn."

She spat on the bloody ground by his hands, and then she vanished, leaping back into Paradise with a blast of fire and a clang of holy bells. When the demon was gone, the king pushed himself slowly to his feet, picked up what was left of his brother's broken body, and started walking.

He walked out of his burning city, under the grand lion gates built with the knowledge taught to him by Enki. He walked past his kneeling soldiers, who were still frantically praying for mercy the cold, haughty gods would never grant. He walked through the fertile fields and rich vineyards the Queen of Wrath had promised to burn. Walked and walked until he'd carried his brother's body all the way back into the mountains where they'd first met, up a winding goat path to a peak crowned with a dead tree where a crow was perching, her round, black eyes glistening with tears.

"*No!*" she cried, flying to the ground. She transformed as she landed, becoming a pale, wild warrior of a woman with dark hair as tangled as the roots of her forest and horror on her bloodless face as she snatched the body from the king's arms.

"My son!" she wailed. "My beautiful, wild Enkidu! No, no, *no!*"

She pressed her weeping face against the dead man's bloody chest with a sob, and then her fingers curled back into deadly talons as she whirled on the king.

"Who has done this?!"

"Who do you think?" he answered in a voice that, though still mortal, shook the mountain with its fury. "They punished him as they punish all of us: cruelly and unfairly. They claim they do it for the betterment of all, but the only ones they uplift are themselves. We're nothing but their pet project, toys to be broken and discarded the moment we no longer entertain."

The woman's black eyes narrowed in disgust. "And yet you played along."

"I did," the king agreed angrily, "and that was my mistake. I let myself be used so I could take their gifts and actually do something to improve my people's lot. I thought I was being a good king, sacrificing so that my kingdom could flourish, but I was a fool. I played the gods' games, but he's the one who paid the price."

He reached out to touch his dead brother's beloved face, and the woman bent over her son again with another sob.

"What will you do?"

"What I should have done from the beginning," the king promised, clenching his bloody hands. "Your son did not die in vain, Morrigan. Because of him, I have finally learned what I should have known all along: the gods have never been good. They have never been wise, never been benevolent, and they have *never* been on our side. They have always been and will always be our tyrants, and I swear on your son's blood that I will bring them down. I will take the knowledge they gave me and use it against them, cut them with their own weapons and burn their Paradise to ash! I will strike them again and again until they are beaten at my feet as I was beaten tonight. And when they know *exactly* who has done this and why, I will show them the same mercy they showed our Enkidu when I take their immortal lives."

"Then I wish you luck," the Morrigan whispered, clutching her beloved child's body as she rose into the night on raven wings. "If you would accept one more blessing, go with mine. Kill them all, Gilgamesh, and let my son's death be avenged."

The king raised his bloody fist in acknowledgment and turned on his heel, marching back down the mountain to rally his soldiers for war.

Chapter 17

Adrian woke with a gasp, sitting up in the ditch beneath his fir tree with his heart pounding beside him in its knot of roots. All of that was right and normal, but the rest of what he was seeing made no sense. He was definitely back in his forest, but everywhere he looked was white. The roots, the dirt, his tree, even his witch clothes were bleached as white as the nothingness he'd been running through before he'd stumbled into that horrible dream, which was absolutely the wrong color for a Blackwood to be.

Carefully, slowly, Adrian picked his way out of the snow-white mud and climbed over the white roots until he was crouching beneath the white branches of his heart tree. He called for Boston as he went, but his familiar didn't answer. There was no birdsong, either, or wind or motor noise from the boats that puttered around Bainbridge at all hours. Just silence as pure and unrelenting as his forest's new monochrome color palette, making Adrian's stomach shrink to the size of a pin as he finally pushed out of the thick fir branches to see his father waiting.

The sight almost sent him running back in. Despite the white and the silence and everything else, Adrian had still held out hope that his bad dream had been exactly that: a hallucinatory vision caused by his ineptitude at Soul witchcraft and too much quintessence. He wanted nothing more than to have imagined the whole, terrible experience in a drug-induced fit, but he wasn't drugged. He actually felt amazing, perfectly awake and aware, with no soreness or tiredness or weakness of any sort. Even his senses felt sharper, painting him a flawless picture of the handsome older man dressed in dazzling golden armor who was waiting for him in the clearing with Malik's familiar smile on his face.

"Hello, my prince."

Adrian didn't answer. He was too busy staring at the sorcerer's face, the one that had always looked like an older version of his own. The same one he'd seen reflected back at him in the bloody street.

"It wasn't a dream," Adrian whispered, clenching his fists. "It was you. It was always *you!*"

"I'm sorry for the deception," King Gilgamesh replied, not looking sorry in the slightest. "But it was necessary to allow us to have a proper conversation. As fond as I am of your mother, she has a bad habit of prejudicing my sons against me."

"Probably because you're the reason we're the only witches left," Adrian snarled, forgetting his fear in his rage. "You're the one the Spider got his power from! You're the cause of *everything* that's happened!"

"All the more reason for you to stop yelling and hear me out," Gilgamesh replied calmly, motioning behind him, where a second golden-dressed man was setting up an elegant wooden folding table and two chairs in front of Adrian's porch.

"Come," the king said as he strolled across the unnatural white grass. "You've proven yourself to be a clever, reasonable sort of person in the past. Wrestle that up again, and let's sit down and discuss this like civilized men."

He finished with the same open smile that Malik had thrown at him dozens of times, but it no longer looked charming. That was still his father's face and his father's voice, but nothing about the golden king felt friendly or familiar as he sat down at the table and accepted an ornate porcelain cup that the other man—the other *prince*, Adrian realized with a shudder—had filled with tea.

"This is your brother, by the way," Gilgamesh said casually, waving his teacup at the golden-armored figure who was currently pouring a second cup of tea from an ornate iron pot. "Alexander, my eldest."

Adrian's eyes flicked to the prince like a terrified animal's. He was so shaken, it took him several seconds to realize that this was the same one-eyed prince he'd seen in the Boston Anchor, the one the dirty prince from the chain desert had deferred to. He didn't know if Gilgamesh had told his other sons about the infiltration, but the eldest prince was certainly looking at Adrian as if he was a traitor. He might only have one left, but his lone mirrored eye was as sharp as a dagger as he set the teacup he'd just finished filling down in front of the table's empty seat. The sheer malice was enough to make Adrian take a step back, but Gilgamesh just waved it away.

"Don't mind him," the king said dismissively. "My crown prince comes by his suspicious nature honestly. He's also a son of the Blackwood, and he knows exactly how treacherous you witches can be. He thinks I should've killed you the first night you landed on my beach, but I keep telling him that would have been a waste, and there's nothing I hate so much as waste."

He chuckled as if that were an old joke and motioned again at the empty chair across from him, but Adrian hadn't moved a muscle. It was finally starting to dawn on him just how badly he'd been played. He'd known Malik's sudden intrusion into his life was suspicious from the beginning, but he'd ignored the warning flags because he was desperate for help and even more desperate to believe he had a father who wanted to give it.

"How are you even here?" he asked bitterly. "I always heard Gilgamesh was so bloated on quintessence that he could no longer leave Heaven."

"There's a lot of false rumors about me that I've found beneficial to ignore," his father replied sagely. "It's much easier to avoid notice when people think it's impossible for you to be there, and I enjoy having a place of my own. I've always been a man of varied interests, and I could hardly invite an Old Wife of the Blackwood to dally with me in Heaven, could I?"

He winked as he finished, and Adrian looked away in disgust. He couldn't believe his mother had put up with this, but then, he was in no place to judge. He'd also fallen for Gilgamesh's beautiful island and charming traps, though at least now he understood why the Eternal King had spared the Blackwood.

Given how old some of Gilgamesh's princes were rumored to be, this was clearly a long-standing arrangement. But while Adrian was impressed that his mother had figured out a way to ensure their coven's survival, he was not following in her footsteps. It might be bleached white with quintessence, but this was still his Blackwood. He didn't feel Boston anywhere, either, which meant he was free to be reckless. But when Adrian reached for the forest magic that lived in his rootbound heart, a mass of quintessence got in his way, driving him back like a snapping lion.

"Now, now," chided Gilgamesh, wagging his finger at Adrian with one hand while he sipped his tea with the other. "None of that. You're a powerful witch, which is a large part of why we're having this conversation, but you can no longer use your craft against me."

"Why not?" Adrian demanded, shaking in fear and rage as the quintessence lion in his chest drove him away again. "What did you do to me?!"

"Nothing you didn't ask for," his father replied. "You wanted power, so I gave it. I gave you all the quintessence you could ever need, enough to turn your forest into this."

He waved at the paper-white canopy over their heads with that all-knowing smile Adrian was starting to hate.

"I was told once by a knowledgeable source that the heart of a witch is the Blackwood, and the heart of the Blackwood is a witch," the king continued. "If this is an accurate representation of what your heart looks like now, I'd say we're in bed together pretty solidly. I normally have to take my sons to Heaven and submerge them in a sarcophagus for a full year to achieve this level of saturation, but you dove right in."

He chuckled and took another sip of his tea. "You're as proper a prince now as ever I could ask, though I will miss the novelty of having a child with my eyes."

The way he said that turned Adrian's blood to ice. He scrambled through the pockets of his enchanted coat, which had been dyed as white as everything else. Thankfully, unlike the witchcraft Adrian had reached for earlier, his coat still worked. It took a few tries because he was so upset, but when his fingers finally located his breakables pocket, the compact mirror he used for scrying spells was right where he'd left it.

Adrian yanked it out with a jerk, prying the plastic shell open and holding it up in front of his face to see what he'd been dreading.

"No," he whispered, reaching up to pull his eyelid back, but seeing more of his eyeball didn't change anything. The rings of his irises were still mirrored silver. A prince's eyes, in *his* face. Between that and the quintessence seal over his heart, Adrian's body didn't even feel like his own anymore. He was struggling to process that in a way that didn't end in a panic attack when something hard grabbed his shoulder.

Adrian snapped his head away from his mirror to see the eldest prince standing beside him with his golden-gloved hand clamped on Adrian's shoulder. He marched the witch to the empty chair, pushing him down with a strength Adrian couldn't possibly match. When he was properly seated across the table, his father set his teacup aside and leaned his elbows on the polished wooden surface with a sigh.

411

"I know you're feeling hard done-by at the moment," he said, looking at Adrian with the same earnest expression he'd worn the first night they'd met. "But other than my name and a few other unimportant details, everything I've told you has been the truth. I *am* your father, I *was* a sorcerer of Uruk, and you truly are the only one I believe can fix the mess this world is in. That's why I showed you my memories just now. I wanted you to understand who I am and why it is that I do what I do."

"Why you..." Adrian's voice trailed off with a furious breath. "You conquered Paradise and enslaved all demonkind! I don't care how badly the gods treated you. You hurt people who didn't deserve it! You hurt *my* people, all the witches whose forests you burned before you stopped at the Blackwood. You've spent five thousand years ruthlessly purging every form of magic that's not your own. You've killed hundreds of thousands of innocent people and enslaved millions more. Your warlocks terrorized my coven for centuries, and now you want me to have sympathy? To *forgive* you?"

"Absolutely not," Gilgamesh said. "I'm well aware that my actions are unforgivable, but that's the price of being king. Ask your own Coward Queen, and she'll agree that doing what must be done no matter the cost is the cost of a crown. I would never presume to ask forgiveness for my sins, but I do want you to understand *why* I committed them. It's not because I'm a villain who delights in destruction. Just the opposite. As I've told you several times now, I *hate* war. It's wasteful and distracting, but I had no other means by which to solve my problem. Not until you."

He'd been saying that since they met. Adrian had always assumed it was flattery, but King Gilgamesh no longer needed to butter him up. If he was still saying the same things now, he must really mean it, so the only question left was, "Why?"

"Because you're the one who did the impossible," his father said, looking down at his scarred, golden-ringed fingers where they rested on the table.

"Remember when I told you that I purged humanity's magic because its presence made it impossible to keep the gods in their graves? Well, I'm afraid the actual situation is a bit more complicated. There's a lot of technical details I won't bore you with, but the primary problem is the chains."

Adrian frowned. "You mean the sin iron chains we were trying to cut?"

"The very ones," the king said, sitting back in his chair. "Tricky stuff, sin iron. It's the heaviest, densest, strongest material known to man or god, but due to certain unavoidable factors in its manufacturing process, it's extremely prone to metal fatigue. The more a chain moves, the more microscopic cracks appear on its surface, resulting in erosion and structural weakness."

"Sounds like a bad material to make a chain out of," Adrian said.

"It is *horrible* for chains," Gilgamesh agreed. "But sin iron is the only substance capable of stopping the Wheel of Rebirth. That's why I had to eliminate all

413

other forms of magic. Power drawn from the great cycles shakes the entire world. If I let all the witches and shamans and so forth keep rocking the boat, chains would be breaking all over the place, and the wheel would be completely uncontrollable."

He said that as if he expected Adrian to praise him for his feat of engineering, but the witch just crossed his arms tighter over his white-dyed chest.

"Maybe you should have thought of that before you tried to chain one of the great cycles," he said, ignoring his untouched cup of tea as he glared across the table at his father. "I know you have reason to hate the gods, but no personal grievance gives you the right to cut the rest of us off from the cycle of rebirth."

"That would be true," the king admitted, "*if* we were actually meant to be reborn."

"What are you talking about?" Adrian demanded. "Of *course* we're meant to be reborn. How could there be a cycle of rebirth if we weren't meant to turn with it?"

"Because it didn't get there naturally," Gilgamesh said, giving him an impatient look. "Come on, Adrian, you're smarter than this. When have you ever seen a spoked wheel in nature?"

Never, admittedly, but... "It's a great cycle!"

"And they were gods," his father countered. "Meddling with things that shouldn't be meddled with is what they do. I know the Morrigan told you that because she complains about it to everyone, usually while trying to meddle herself. The complete inability to keep one's hands to oneself is a universal divine trait, but Ishtar, Anu, and the rest of their ilk took it even further. They weren't content to merely meddle in mortal lives. They took over our deaths as well."

"I know they created Paradise," Adrian said, "but—"

"It's so much bigger than that," Gilgamesh interrupted. "Human souls used to be washed away by the river of time just like everything else in the universe. You felt the force of it yourself on your way to my Holy City, but the gods were different. They were *true* immortals, untouched by time, and they viewed our ability to die as a tragedy. They were so upset that their human favorites were fated to end, they changed the very foundation of our existence. They built a wheel to catch us before we washed away, and a Paradise to purge our sins so that we could be reborn in a form they found more suitable."

He clenched his scarred fists on the table. "Don't you see? They weren't just meddling with our lives. The gods of Paradise changed the very nature of what it meant to be human. They're the ones who defined what a sin *is*. They didn't create Paradise to cleanse our souls out of the goodness of their hearts. They were *pruning* us, trimming off the unsightly bits and grafting on new parts to create something that better fit what they wanted us to be. They were destroying us death by death to breed a more pleasing, more cultured, more *obedient* human. I would know, too, because I was their greatest success."

He unclenched his fists to place a hand on his golden-armored chest. "I didn't become King of Uruk merely because my father was king before me. My soul was placed in this body specifically by Anu, God of

Wisdom and Kings, so that I would grow up to become his ideal ruler. That is why I was brought to Paradise as a child, to learn from the gods. My kingdom was their prototype, a grand experiment to see if humans could truly be domesticated, and it almost worked. I was their obedient dog, happy to lie at his divine master's feet and eat their scraps. I might have stayed that way forever had I not met Enkidu."

Adrian winced. Even if he hadn't seen the scene in the burning city, the mournful way Gilgamesh spoke that name would have told him everything he needed to know.

"He was more than just my friend," the Eternal King went on, his voice dragging like every syllable was a wound. "He was my awakening, the living embodiment of everything the gods had taken from us—freedom, hedonism, raw emotion, the ability to let go and simply live. His mother, the Morrigan, had warned her wild peoples away from civilized lands specifically to keep them from being caught in the gods' wheel, but from the moment I met him, Enkidu befriended me without hesitation. He had no guile, no manners, no respect for my crown or fear of my magic. The only thing he cared about was *me*, the person known as Gilgamesh, not the king."

He dropped his hand with a sigh. "He completely changed my life. We shared no blood, but he was my brother in every way that counted. No one before or since has ever been so wholly and truly my friend. There was no battle he wouldn't fight, no enemy who could intimidate his foolhardy bravery. He would have given his life for me in a heartbeat, which was why I begged him not to get involved. I wanted my friend alive, but it didn't matter in the end. The gods killed him the moment he got in their way. They didn't even care."

He sounded so bitter by the end, Adrian almost felt sorry for him.

"That was the moment I realized the gods could never be reasoned with," Gilgamesh said, looking at him again. "They made me to be a civilized king, so I always assumed they were civilized as well, but I was wrong. The gods only wanted *us* to be civil. *We* were the ones who were expected to be lawful and reasonable, while they did whatever they wanted. Even Ishtar, the supposedly merciful mother of the Riverlands, thought nothing of sending a giant bull to destroy my kingdom after I refused to sleep with her. We were less than animals to them, so I took the knowledge they'd given me to make me a better servant, and I struck them down with it. I killed the callous, tyrannical gods. I killed their monsters, imprisoned their demon soldiers, stole their tools, and, in doing so, set all humanity free."

A smile spread over his face. "You might not approve of my methods, but the only reason this world—*your* world—is no longer the gods' playground is because I fought to make it that way. For five thousand years, I've done whatever was necessary to keep the deathless gods in their graves. Every evil you've laid at my feet—the enslavement of the demons, the creation of the Hells, the destruction of witches— was done in service of that greatest good."

"That doesn't make it right," Adrian said in a frustrated voice. "I don't care how noble your intentions were. You enslaved an entire race. Everyone I hold dear is in danger right now *because of you*. You hold up your bloody hands and claim they make you a hero, but you're no better than the gods you overthrew."

"Then help me change things," his father said, pinning Adrian in place with blue-gray eyes that gleamed like knives. "I've spent the majority of my life doing whatever was necessary to keep the gods down. No matter how foul or bloody or distasteful the work was, I did it, because I knew there was no cruelty I could commit that was worse than what would happen if the gods came back. For five thousand years, that has been my only goal, and yet for all my power, all I've built, the best I've been able to do is hold the line. The foe has never actually been defeated. I thought I'd be stuck in this stalemate forever, and then I found *you*."

The king leaned across the table toward his son. "You're the breakthrough I've been waiting eons for. With you at my side, I can finally end this—the war, the Hells, the purges, all of it! Your precious Rebexa will never have to fight again, and all you have to do is help me."

He finished with a dazzling smile, but Adrian was leaning back so far that his chair was in danger of tipping over. He knew better than to trust anything that came out of the mouth of the man who'd been the world's enemy since the dawn of recorded time, but his father looked truly excited, and that gave Adrian hope. He was still certain this was all a trap, but the fact that Gilgamesh was even willing to suggest an end to the endless war was enough to make Adrian open to hearing him out.

"All right," he said as he set his chair back on all four legs. "What exactly would this help entail?"

Gilgamesh lifted his hand, snapping his fingers impatiently until his eldest son handed him a black chest the size of a shoebox. It wasn't until the king set it down on the table between them, though, that Adrian realized the box was made entirely of sin iron. Very thick, very *old* sin iron that flaked away on the king's hands as he undid the latch and opened the lid to reveal a pile of what appeared to be broken stones.

"What are those?" Adrian asked, because it seriously looked like his father had just presented him with a chest full of dirty black gravel. Some of the pieces were no longer than pebbles. Others were as big as Adrian's thumb. Every chunk had some smooth sides and at least one jagged edge. This gave them the look of broken shards, like someone had shattered a stone statue and then swept the rubble into a box. He was still trying to figure it out when Gilgamesh reached in and carefully pinched one of the largest chunks between his fingers.

"This is all that remains of the once-magnificent Queen of Pride," he said, passing the broken piece to Adrian, who took it with trembling fingers. "Aside from the Queen of Wrath, whose story you already know, she's the only daughter of Ishtar who died during the war. Contrary to the official history, however, I wasn't the one who killed her. She did that to herself, choosing to shatter her own horns rather than bow them to me."

"Sounds like a fitting way for the Queen of Pride to go out," Adrian said, staring at the ancient piece of broken horn, which still felt as warm as Bex's had when she'd let him touch them. "But why are you showing these to me?"

"Because I want you to fix them."

Adrian's head snapped up to see his father smiling.

"You're the one who does the impossible," Gilgamesh reminded him. "You brought the Bonfire of Wrath back from the ashes before you even knew what she was. That was what caught my interest initially, but then I discovered you were also an instinctual sorcerer. It took my other princes years to master teleportation, but you got it on your very first try. Like all the sons I had with Agatha, you were able to handle massive amounts of quintessence, but you didn't just endure the power like the others. You *thrived* upon it. Such a feat would already be enough to catapult you to the very top of Heaven, but you took it even farther, blending your knowledge of witchcraft and sorcery into something entirely new. Even I couldn't grow a tree through the gap between life and death, but *you did.*"

He slammed his hands down on the table, making both his sons jump. "*That* is impressive, Adrian," he announced with a grin wide enough to show all his too-white teeth. "If I'd known leaving one of my sons in the Blackwood would have such powerful results, I'd have done it eons ago. I was an absolute fool to write you off as a sop to Agatha, but I've never been happier to make a mistake, because look how marvelously you turned out! You're the lucky break I've been waiting millennia for, and I just know you're going to be the one who finally helps me figure this out."

"Figure *what* out?" Adrian demanded, placing the fragment of the poor dead queen's horn back in its box. "Why do you need the Queen of Pride's horns fixed? Are you trying to heal the void demons?"

The Eternal King laughed. "Those old fossils? Absolutely not. Even if the damage the Queen of Pride's shattering did to their psyches was fixable, I wouldn't bother. The last thing I want is to put more of Ishtar's soldiers back on the field. No, no, no. I need these horns repaired because I've got a plan to fix the god problem for good, but I'm going to need all nine queens to do it, and I can't have that if one of them is in pieces."

"You'll never have it at all," Adrian said. "Even if I did agree to do this *and* actually managed to pull it off, you'd still only have eight queens, because Bex will never surrender."

"That is my concern," Gilgamesh said, waving his words away. "The only queen you need to worry about is this one." He tapped his finger on the box of broken pieces. "This is the reason I came to find you, the why behind everything I've done. I know you're predisposed to hate me, but you already put aside your prejudices once for Malik. If you can overlook my sorcery, I'm sure you can overlook the rest, because we're going to do great things, Adrian. If we work together, we can make this world a better, safer, *freer* place for everyone who lives in it. That's my promise to you, and as a show of my good faith, I'm willing to start with the Blackwood."

Adrian's eyes went wide, and his father gave him a wink.

"I'm a famously thrifty king," he said. "But considering this could be the alliance that finally ends the war I've become very, *very* sick of, I am prepared to be uncharacteristically generous. If you agree to help me put the Queen of Pride's horns back together, I will grant full amnesty to the witches of the Blackwood. No more hiding in trees, no more sending children to the warlocks, no more restricted movement. Your forests will become an official part of my kingdom with all the privileges that guarantees. I'll even put you in charge so you can decide how best to meet your coven's needs. This could be the beginning of a grand new era of witchcraft, so what do you say? Is that not a fair offer?"

It was better than fair. Being officially recognized meant that their coven could finally stop living in fear. Witches would be able to leave their groves again, and boys born in the Blackwood could grow up in the forest without being torn from their families. All the problems he'd left home to fix could be eliminated right now with a single word. But while that was *extraordinarily* tempting, Adrian was no longer just a witch, and he had a lot more than just the Blackwood depending on him.

"The demons, too," he said. "Full amnesty for the Blackwood *and* you empty the Hells and Limbo. No more slave bands, no more warlocks, no more kick demons. Also, the Queen of Wrath gets a full pardon. Do that, and I'll help you right now."

That was a lot to ask for, but Adrian saw no reason to dream small. If the man who'd overthrown the gods was coming to *him* for help, why shouldn't he ask for the moon? The Great Forest knew he'd never get a chance like this again, but while Gilgamesh had seemed eager to offer him the Blackwood, the moment demons were mentioned, the smile fell off his face.

"I know you've been raised to see me as an all-powerful enemy," the king said testily, "but as successful as I've been, I'm still just a man. There are things that even I can't do, number one of which is releasing the demons from the Hells. They're a critical part of the plan I'm bringing you in to help with. If I have to let them go to get you on board, we might as well not do this at all."

"How is that their problem?" Adrian demanded, crossing his arms stubbornly. "You put the demons into the Hells. You can let them out."

"How about a compromise?" Gilgamesh suggested. "I can't free them yet because that will ruin the whole system I'm building. If you help me make that system successful, though, I won't need the demons anymore. I'll be happy to set them free after that. You wouldn't *believe* how expensive running nine separate Hells can be, especially when only seven of them are functional. I'd be more than happy to cut all of that off my balance sheet, but only after I secure a replacement."

"Which is what?" Adrian asked, curious despite himself. "You keep saying you have a plan, but you still haven't told me what it is. I'm not even sure what you're trying to accomplish, other than ending the war."

"That is a far more complicated matter than we have time to discuss at the moment," the king replied dismissively. "I'd say you'll just have to trust me, but I already know I won't get that, so let's keep our focus on the terms of your surrender."

Adrian jerked so hard he knocked over his untouched cup of tea. "I never said I was surrendering!"

"Come now, Adrian," his father said with an indulgent smile. "Surely, you must understand there's no getting out of this. You're a prince, eyes and all. I could put you on the ground with a snap of my fingers"—he held his hand up menacingly—"but that would be highly counterproductive. I have plenty of fawning subjects. What I need is the Adrian I saw in action tonight: the brilliant sorcerer witch who isn't afraid to break the rules. Men like that aren't found on their knees. That's why I'm trying so hard to meet you halfway, but my patience is not infinite."

He leaned closer, and Adrian leaned away before he realized what he was doing. He couldn't say what had changed. Gilgamesh's face was the same as ever, but any resemblance to the cheerful, clever father he'd come to rely on was now completely gone. The man sitting across the table could no longer even be mistaken for Malik. For the first time since this whole mess had started, Gilgamesh looked like exactly what he was: the Eternal King of Heaven, slayer of the gods, and he was done being generous.

"You have one more chance to do this on your terms," Gilgamesh said, holding out his teacup for Crown Prince Alexander to refill. "Make me an offer—a *real* offer I might actually accept, not a wild demand— and I will give it my consideration. If you cannot be reasonable, I have many cells in Heaven where you can reconsider your priorities. I've waited eons for this, Adrian. I don't mind waiting a little more, but this is the only time I will be entertaining requests. If we have to have this conversation again, your cooperation will be on my terms, not yours, so I suggest you make it count."

He took a sip of his tea as he finished, watching his son with the blue-gray eyes Adrian no longer possessed. For his part, Adrian was fighting not to panic. He'd known he was screwed from the moment he woke up in a white forest, but he hadn't felt truly afraid until right now.

Not for himself, either. Adrian wasn't sure how long he'd spent in Gilgamesh's memories, but he'd been out of his tree for at least ten minutes. He still didn't think Bex would lose, but the oak he'd grown to Heaven had to be a dry rot-riddled piece of dust by now, which meant she had no ground to stand on. He'd fallen for Gilgamesh's trap, but she was the one who'd been left stranded. Still, Adrian didn't believe for a second that Bex was dead. She was still fighting, he was certain of it, which meant his job wasn't over. Gilgamesh had called it a surrender, but suddenly,

Adrian knew exactly how he was going to turn this around, and all it would cost was him.

"Okay," he said, putting up his hands. "Here are my conditions. I want the Blackwood amnesty you offered the first time, but I also want you to stop the bombardment on the Seattle Anchor. You don't have to let anyone go, just don't kill them, *and* I want you to let the Queen of Wrath leave Heaven and return to her people unharmed. Meet those terms, and I'll surrender."

The Eternal King drummed his fingers on the table as he thought it over.

"I agree to all but the last," he said after several minutes. "The Blackwoods and the Seattle demons I can lose, but I already told you my plan requires all nine demon queens."

"Then we don't have an agreement," Adrian said, crossing his arms stubbornly over his chest. "I'll rot in a cell for the rest of eternity before I sell Bex out."

The Eternal King's eyes narrowed, and for a moment, Adrian thought that was it. Then the smile returned to Gilgamesh's face like it had never left.

"Alexander," he said as he rose to his feet, "is the situation we discussed earlier still the same?"

"Yes, my king," the Crown Prince replied. "All awaits your command."

"Excellent," replied Gilgamesh, rubbing his hands together before he turned to offer the right one to his youngest son.

"You are a loyal man, Adrian Blackwood," he said solemnly. "You've seen my history, so you know how deeply I admire that. That's why I'm going to

426

show you one more thing before letting you decide to put us at odds forever. It will only take a moment, and if you still feel the same way when it's over, you can go right back to rotting for all eternity."

Adrian didn't appreciate having his words turned around on him, but he also wasn't actually looking forward to dying in a cell. He knew this had to be a trap, but everything had been a trap since Sharif had flown into his forest. If nothing else, a change in location might open new opportunities for escape.

That would have to be good enough. Rising from his seat, Adrian jogged back to his heart tree to grab his witch hat. The delay made Gilgamesh scowl, but that hat had been a gift from his aunt Muriel. Even though it was bent and stained with quintessence, Adrian wasn't about to leave it behind. He shook the dirt off and slapped it on his head. Only then, when he was back to feeling somewhat like a proper witch, did Adrian reach out and take his father's hand.

The change happened in an instant. Adrian was so used to teleporting by this point, he didn't even flinch at the now-familiar *clang* and swing. But while the noise and the movement were expected, *where* his father teleported them to was a complete shock.

It was so high up in the thin blue sky, Adrian didn't even recognize the cliff he was standing on as a tower until he saw the city stretched out below. It was the same white skyline he'd caught glimpses of from his tree, the Holy City of Heaven. But while everything still looked exactly as he remembered from before the world had gone white, one critical element was different.

There was no more fire burning in the sky. The only light now came from the white glow of Heaven itself. And at the farthest edge of it, crumpled on top of the bleached-white skeleton of his dead tree like a burned-out match, was Bex.

She was so small and bent that Adrian could barely see her from this distance. He'd only spotted her because the giant, four-armed, armored demon she'd been fighting was standing right next to her, looming over the snuffed-out queen with two long objects clutched like trophies in her upper set of hands. It wasn't until she turned around and raised them to the golden tower in salute, though, that Adrian realized the war demon was holding Bex's *horns*.

The shock nearly knocked him off the tower. He grabbed the balcony's golden railing, pulling himself as far out over the empty edge as he could without falling to his death, but it didn't change what he saw. Bex's tall, graceful horns were still in that hateful woman's fists, and the longer he looked at them, the more terrified Adrian became.

"She's not dead yet," his father said, making him jump. When Adrian whirled around, Gilgamesh was standing right beside him, watching the grim spectacle with a satisfied smirk.

"Removing a queen's horns doesn't kill them," he informed his son conversationally. "Ishtar's daughters are just as frustratingly hard to kill as their mother, but Rebexa the Bonfire has always been the worst. This is actually the third time we've ripped her horns off, but she always manages to die and take them back when her body is reborn." He sighed. "I thought we'd have to keep running this circle until she was ground down so far that her horns fell off under their own weight, but then you came along."

He flashed Adrian a beaming smile. "Thanks to you filling her up with the mortal flames of life, Ishtar is no longer able to throw her fallen sword back into the fight. This is the Queen of Wrath's very last incarnation. When she goes out this time, that's the end, but her horns—her *crown*—belongs to Ishtar. That's the part of her that can truly never die, so you see, Adrian, I've already won. Everything I need from Ishtar's most troublesome daughter is already in my hands, but you don't care about queens or crowns. I saw it in your eyes just now when you said you'd rather spend your life in a cell than betray her. You care about Ishtar's daughter, not her queen. Once again, I respect that loyalty, so here is my final offer."

He reached out his golden-armored arm and pointed at the tiny black dot kneeling on the horizon. "Agree to repair the Queen of Pride's horns, and I will spare your beloved's life. She won't be a queen anymore, but that never made her happy, did it? Serving the gods has never been a joy for anyone except the gods themselves. Think of it that way and you're actually doing her a favor. Didn't she always want to be free?"

"Not like this," Adrian said, squeezing the golden banister until it creaked beneath his fingers. "Bex would never want this."

"She no longer has a choice," Gilgamesh said as he lowered his arm. "But you do. Join me and save your Bex's life, or let her die as Rebexa and I take her horns anyway."

Adrian opened his mouth, but his father cut him off.

"Considering how many of my other sons she's killed, the fact that I'm even making this offer is a sign of just how highly I hold you in my esteem. But this leniency will be tendered only once, so think very carefully about the next thing that comes out of your mouth."

There was no need for threats. Adrian hated it, he hated all of this, but he'd known his choice from the moment he'd seen Bex on her knees.

"I'll do it," he said. "I'll help you. Just don't kill her."

"Done," Gilgamesh replied immediately, shoving Adrian away from the railing as he stepped up to take his place.

"Denizens of Heaven," he announced in a voice that, though seemingly no louder than the one he'd spoken with just now, somehow managed to boom across every inch of the Holy City. "It is with great joy that I announce the arrival of my newest son, Prince Adrian. In celebration of this blessed event, the witches of the Blackwood are no longer considered heretics in the eyes of Heaven, but are instead welcomed into the divine light of our benevolence. Furthermore, as a mark of my son's fathomless compassion, the defensive campaign against the demon rebellion in Seattle is henceforth suspended, and their cowardly queen's life shall be spared. Be in awe at the benevolence of your prince, and give thanks

430

for the divine wisdom that has brought us peace on this day."

He nodded at the silent city and turned back to Adrian, who was staring in shock.

"There," the king said, brushing his hands together as if he were dusting the whole matter away. "Everything you asked for has been granted, which means your surrender is now complete." He motioned toward the tower behind them. "Shall we get going? We have much to do."

Adrian was too shocked to answer, but it seemed his cooperation was no longer a question. His father had already linked their arms together, forcing his son to march with him through the enormous golden doors and into the palace of Heaven.

Chapter 18

Bex was falling.

Not physically. Her body was still where the Queen of War had knocked it down, kneeling on Adrian's dead tree at the edge of the Holy City's battlements. She could feel the pain of her chopped-off hand and the throb of her broken horns. She could see her black blood like a stain on the branches that shouldn't have been white and hear the silence of Drox's blade where he lay still, even though the Queen of War was no longer stomping him down.

It was all there in front of her like a picture from someone else's life, but Bex was no longer part of it. She was hurtling backward, falling down the endless pit that had opened inside her the moment her horns came off. She wasn't even sure how long she'd been falling. It felt like eternity, but the Queen of War's punctured neck was still bleeding when all of Heaven was filled with the peal of golden bells.

The clamor was so loud, Bex felt it in her chest, but she couldn't make herself look up. Beside her, she was vaguely aware of the Queen of War lifting her severed horns like trophies, but she didn't turn her head to see for sure. It all just seemed so unimportant compared to the yawning nothingness that had opened inside her. Even when the booming voice started speaking—a man's condescending tone Bex was certain she'd never heard before, but which still sounded so familiar—she didn't pay it any mind until he spoke two words that actually caught her attention.

Prince Adrian.

Even when she was falling into the void, that was enough to make Bex pause. Slowly, painfully, she forced her eyes up, looking across the white city to the glittering spire at its heart. A shining, vertical palace of towers with two figures standing on a balcony near the very top.

It was impossible to make out faces from so far away, but that didn't matter. Even on the other side of the Holy City, even after falling into an endless void, Bex still recognized him. He was even wearing his witch hat. The tip was bent and the color was wrong, but that was undoubtedly Adrian up there on Heaven's tower, and standing beside him like a golden spider was a man she'd never seen before in this life but would never not know.

Gilgamesh.

Despite the empty pit she'd become, the sight still filled Bex with rage. Baring her bloody teeth, she reached for her fire, but there was no more of that. Not even ashes remained in the hole left behind by the loss of her horns.

Horrified, Bex reached for her sword next only to come up empty again. The place inside her where Drox lived had also been ripped away, leaving her alone. She couldn't feel him, couldn't speak to him, couldn't do anything but watch as the Queen of War picked his still blade up off the ground and pressed his hilt into a pale severed hand.

Bex's severed hand.

"There we are," War said as the Blade of Wrath vanished, becoming a ring on his queen's lifeless finger. Her traitorous sister gave the black band a twist to make sure he was settled properly, then she turned to the figure who'd just appeared beside her with a crash of golden bells. A golden-armored man with an ornate patch over his missing eye. Her prince.

"Well done," he said as the Queen of War handed over Bex's severed hand and horns. "You accomplished everything we asked with minimal losses, *and* the Blade of Wrath is back to its original strength." He looked impressed. "I confess I'm surprised by that last one. I didn't think she'd go so far."

"I did," the Queen of War said, looking down at Bex. "There's no line my sister won't cross to win. That's why she always loses." Her scarred lips peeled back from her teeth in a sneer. "She's just another of Ishtar's charging bulls."

The prince chuckled and tucked the prizes under his arm. "I have to get these to my father. I trust I can leave the rest to you?"

The Queen of War bowed her towering head. "Of course, my prince. It will be my pleasure."

If she hadn't still been plummeting through nothingness, the hateful delight in that last sentence would've made Bex shiver. As things were, though, she couldn't do anything but slump over her knees as the one-eyed prince vanished with another crash of bells, leaving Bex alone once again with the Queen of War.

"I suppose you think you get to live now."

Bex blinked in confusion. That wasn't what she'd been thinking at all. Her sister must not have expected an answer, though, because she just kept talking.

"The Eternal King is a very good liar," she said as she reached down to grab Bex's black hair. "His silver tongue fooled the gods themselves, but he's always kept his word to me. He told me he'd get me out of the foul pit our mother shoved me into, and he did. He said if I ordered my war demons to fight for him, he'd free me from their incessant whining, and he did. He even said he'd make sure I got revenge against you someday, and here we are."

The Queen of War bent down from her towering height until she and Bex were face to scarred face.

"That's why I follow him," she told her sister quietly. "I betrayed Ishtar because of what she did, but I joined Gilgamesh because he did what no one else has ever done. He gave me what I wanted. He gave me beauty, gave me freedom, gave me revenge. Now, he's given me you, even after promising his son he'd let you live." She dropped her voice to a chilling whisper. "*That* is a king who's worthy of loyalty. *That* is a man I'll follow to the ends of the earth. He brings me happiness, and by his grace, I'm about to be very happy indeed."

She gave Bex a shove, sending the hornless, handless, no-longer-queen sprawling on her back. She was still sluggishly trying to get back up when the Blade of War's heavy edge landed against the skin of her exposed throat.

"Goodbye, Bexa," the Queen of War said sweetly. "And if you see her on your way to oblivion, give my regards to Mother."

Bex swallowed against the blade. She knew she needed to fight, push back, do *something*, but her body felt like a sock puppet with the hand removed. All the vital parts were gone, leaving just an empty shell of biology, a body that was only still alive because its heart hadn't stopped beating.

The Queen of War was about to take care of that. She pressed her sword down millimeter by millimeter, her mismatched eyes gleaming in joyful triumph as the black blood began to spill across Bex's neck. She was just about to cut into her windpipe when Bex felt something bite into her back.

It was several somethings, actually. Bex had no idea what was happening, but it felt like a hundred tiny vipers had just sunk their fangs into her. That was all her flailing brain had time to process before she was yanked away.

She felt her sister's sword jerk in response, but Bex was no longer beneath it. She was flying along the ground like a wind, whisked into the Queen of War's own shadow. Bex was still reeling from the motion when a pair of strong hands grabbed her by the shoulders and yanked her in the other direction. The world went dark for a moment, and then Bex found herself twenty feet away, lying on the stone battlements behind the melted remains of one of the slagged lions with a familiar dark-skinned face hovering over hers.

"Shh," Nemini whispered, pressing a finger to her lips as her yellow eyes flicked over to the Queen of War, who was still staring at the black bloodstain on Adrian's white tree where Bex had just been.

For three long heartbeats, all was silent, and then the Queen of War threw back her head with a scream. It was a guttural howl, a true bellow of rage that would've done the Queen of Wrath proud. The scream went on and on, and then the Queen of War raised her four arms and threw her sword at the ground.

Bex's first thought was that she was destroying the tree, but it turned out she was wrong. War wasn't attacking Adrian's oak, at least not directly. She'd thrown her sword down for a different purpose because as the black blade fell, it changed, turning back into a ring before wrapping itself in a snowball of white, bony plates.

The Queen of War's armor vanished at the same time, the heavy protections falling off her body like shed scales. The whole process took less than five seconds, and then there were two figures standing on the dead tree: the scarred Queen of War, her pitted bronze skin covered only by a thin, white-linen wrap, and Havok, his armored body whole and unbroken, like he'd never been cut. For several moments, the two of them stared silently at each other, and then the Queen of War and her sword split to begin methodically searching the tree and the battlements.

Even in her emptiness, that was enough to make Bex shudder. The wrecked lion Nemini had pulled her behind wasn't exactly good cover. All War or her sword had to do was walk a few feet down the wall, and the jig would be up. Bex couldn't even move her body enough to wiggle deeper into the lion's shadow. It was absolutely hopeless, but just when she thought everything was over yet again, War and Havok walked right past them.

Bex blinked in surprise. Her murderous sister was standing only five feet away, but her mismatched eyes slid over Bex and Nemini like she couldn't see them at all. It felt like a miracle, and it wasn't the only one. Now that Bex was no longer facing imminent death, she realized the floor she was lying on wasn't cracking like an eggshell under her weight. For the first time since she'd come to Heaven, the stone battlements felt as solid as they looked, which was just weird enough to make her croak out the first word she'd managed since everything ended.

"How?"

"Because you're like me now," Nemini whispered, her yellow eyes flicking up to Bex's broken horns. "Rebexa is the enemy of Heaven. She's the one Anu's crown banished, the one War and her sword are looking for. But you're not Rebexa anymore, are you?"

That should have been the bomb drop of Bex's life, but the moment Nemini told her, she realized she already knew. She hadn't had time to categorize everything she'd lost yet, but Bex felt the hole where her name should've been the same way she felt the absence of her fire and her sword. Together, they made a chasm she could never escape, but just as Bex was about to crumble into the void again, she looked at

Nemini—*actually* looked—and what she saw shocked her right back together.

Nemini's head was no longer covered in snakes. The black serpents that normally formed her hair were still crawling under Bex's back, the source of all the little bites that had dragged her to safety. But while Bex was very grateful for that, her eyes were locked on Nemini's *actual* hair: a soft, dense, black cloud that swirled around the broken stubs of what must have once been an incredible set of horns.

"Nemini," she whispered, barely able to speak, "what happened to your—"

The void demon pressed her finger down on Bex's lips, cutting her words off with a touch, but not an empty one. For the first time ever, Nemini's hand felt warm against Bex's skin. There was no pull of the void, no yawning emptiness. It was just a finger, soft at the joints and calloused at the tip.

That raised a thousand questions, but Bex didn't dare say a word. Even though they couldn't see them, the Queen of War and Havok were getting uncomfortably close. Too close for Nemini, apparently.

"Let's go," she whispered, moving her finger.

"Go where?" Bex whispered back.

The broken demon reached down to let the black snakes that were still hiding under Bex slither back up her arm. When they'd resumed their normal position on top of her head, she answered.

"Where everything goes in the end."

The quiet words were still brushing over her ears when Nemini wrapped her arms around Bex's waist and lurched sideways, dragging them both off the wall.

They fell from Heaven like stones, plummeting past the white battlements and the crumbling trunk of Adrian's white tree. Bex caught one last glimpse of the Queen of War's furious face before they dropped below the foundations of Heaven, and the waterfall of time washed over them again.

Everything was lost after that. Bex barely managed to keep hold of Nemini as they spun together through the dark. If they'd been trying to get back to Heaven, it would have been impossible, but they were falling with the flow instead of against it now. All that roaring pressure just helped them escape faster, washing the two nameless demons down, down, down until they landed with a splash in the familiar, freezing water of the Rivers of Death.

It was the water that finally ripped them apart. For several terrifying seconds, Bex tumbled out of control in the river's churning depths. She thought she was about to be washed away for good when Nemini's strong hands grabbed her again, dragging Bex out of the rapids onto a sandy riverbank.

That's what it felt like, at least. It was so dark here that even Bex's eyes couldn't see anything, though it took her several seconds to realize that was because they were no longer glowing.

The despair that followed that thought almost kicked her down the hole again. Even when she'd been reduced to ash, Bex's eyes had always burned a little. No more than banked coals, but there'd always been *something* there. Now, though, everything was gone.

For the first time in her existence, Bex's bonfire was completely out, leaving her cold and empty, like a hollow charred log washed up on the riverbank.

It was hard to say how long she lay like that. She could feel the river silt beneath her fingers, see the black void above their heads without a single trace of the white Heaven they'd fallen out of, but Bex couldn't bring herself to care. She was falling again, plummeting into the nothingness that seemed to be all she had left. She might have kept falling forever had Nemini not touched her hand.

"It's okay," she whispered, her warm fingers curling around Bex's cold one. "I'm with you. You don't have to fall alone."

There was comfort in those words. Even though Bex couldn't feel it, she could hear it in Nemini's voice, which no longer sounded emotionless, but warm and welcoming as a fire. It was the only fire Bex had now, and she went toward it instinctively, crawling out of the emptiness bit by bit until she found herself lying in the cold sand of the black riverbank with Nemini sitting beside her, holding her hand.

"Sorry," she whispered.

"Don't be," Nemini said, squeezing tighter. "Are you back, or do you need more time?"

"I think I'm okay for now," Bex said, reaching up to rub her face with her other hand only to discover she couldn't, because that was the hand War had cut off.

She lowered her stump back to the sand with a sigh, closing her eyes against the wetness welling inside them.

441

"Where are we?" she asked, more to have something to distract her than because she cared.

"Death," Nemini replied, her clothes rustling in a way Bex could only assume meant she was looking around since it was too dark here to actually see. "The actual death, not the afterlife interpretation."

Bex wasn't sure what that meant, but she was too exhausted to demand a better explanation.

"Does that mean it's over?" she asked instead.

"Only if you want it to be," Nemini said, letting go of Bex's hand to dig her fingers into the cold silt between them.

"This is where I fell, too," she whispered, her soft voice barely audible over the endless roar of the river. "I don't remember how it happened. Unlike you, my horns were broken, not removed. I'm not sure if that makes it worse since I've never had them ripped off to compare, but I know I lost some time. One minute, I was in Paradise. The next, I was lying right where you are, staring up at nothing."

"That sounds horrible," Bex said, pushing into a sitting position. She didn't actually want to move, but even when she was empty, Bex never could stand to be lying down when someone else was over her.

"It wasn't horrible, actually," Nemini replied, her voice oddly light in the dark. "As I've told you many times, there is freedom in the void. This is the place where I learned that."

Bex turned toward her in the dark, and even though it was impossible to see anything in this blackness, she swore Nemini smiled.

"All my life, I had to be what others made me," the hornless demon told her quietly. "Everything I did was measured by outside expectations. Even when I died, I did it to spite someone else. No part of me was ever my own, but lying here in the dark, I didn't have to be anything to anyone. I didn't have to listen, didn't have to meet any standards. I could simply *be*."

Bex wished she felt that. The process sounded so peaceful when Nemini described it, but when Bex looked at the void, all she could see was what she'd lost.

"How do you do it?" she whispered, covering her eyes with her handless right arm in a desperate effort to make it *stop*. "How do you see freedom instead of everything that's gone?"

"It gets easier," Nemini promised. "Perspective helps. Even enormous losses appear small compared to the endless expanse of the universe."

Bex didn't find that as comforting as Nemini did. She was curling into a ball in a desperate effort to get away from all the blackness when she felt Nemini's snakes brush against her cheek.

"I'm sorry."

"For what?" Bex asked. "They're the ones who did this. You saved me."

"But I meant to do it earlier," Nemini confessed, her normally neutral voice heavy with regret. "I was in position before you lost your horns, but I couldn't pull you through the shadows until you became nothing."

Bex heaved a long sigh and sank deeper into the cold river sand. "It's not your fault," she said. "If you'd come out earlier, we'd both be dead. The Queen of War was just too strong. I knew that the moment we started fighting, but I still had to try."

"You always try," Nemini agreed, scooting closer. "That's why we follow you."

She'd clearly meant that to be comforting, but all Bex heard was condemnation. She'd gotten cocky and gambled her very last life on a long shot, but she wasn't the only one who'd lost. Their whole rebellion would suffer for her stupidity. She almost wished Nemini had left her to die. At least that way, she wouldn't have to be around to watch everything she loved get stomped into oblivion. But just as Bex was sinking into her deepest despair yet again, Nemini wrapped her arms around her and pulled her into her lap.

"What are you doing?"

"What you did for me," Nemini whispered, holding Bex like a child in the dark. "It was right here," she whispered, petting Bex's hair. "Maybe not this exact river, but it was in this place. I was lying on my back, enjoying being nothing, when I saw a light. There'd never been a light here before, so I sat up and saw you walking down the river."

It was impossible to see her face in the dark, but that didn't matter. Bex could hear the wonder like a shimmer in Nemini's voice.

"You were on fire," she whispered, "shining like a star. You tried to talk to me, but I was too broken back then to understand words. I had no idea what you were saying and no way to give you an answer, but it didn't matter. You still picked me up just like this and carried me back to the world of the living."

"Was that a good thing?" Bex asked nervously. "You said you liked being here."

"I did," Nemini replied, hugging her close. "But I liked being rescued, too. I can always be nothing, but being something to someone is special and rare. It took several of your lives before I put myself back together enough to tell you that, but even though you forgot me every time you died, you never left me behind. No matter how silent or useless I was to you, you always picked me up and took me with you again. That's why I never left your side even though the war was pointless and we never won. I'd already lost everything, so I didn't care about victory, but I *did* care about you."

She leaned closer, pressing their faces together until Bex could feel Nemini's smile.

"You're the one I chose," she whispered. "When everything was lost and nothing mattered, you're what I decided to care about. Not because I had to, but because I wanted to. You were *my* choice, and you've never let me down. That's why I'm not going to let you down now."

It was on the tip of Bex's tongue to say Nemini had never let her down either. The void demon had saved her bacon countless times, including right now. She was only alive because of Nemini's bravery and quick thinking, but Bex had the feeling that wasn't what this was about.

"How would you let me down?" she whispered.

"By not telling you the truth," Nemini said, setting Bex back on the sand so that they were sitting face-to-face in the dark.

445

"A queen's horns are the source of her authority," she said gravely. "They are her crown and her name, the mark of Ishtar's blessing, but they can also be her shackles. What War did to you was a grave and unforgivable sin, but could also be seen as a blessing, because for the first time in your existence, you don't have to be the Bonfire. You don't have to be anything at all. You can be nothing, like me, and since we're both nothing together, you won't have to do it alone. I'll stay with you whatever you decide, but I wanted you to know that there *is* a choice, because no one else will tell you."

Bex let out a breath as her body settled deeper into the cold river sand. A few hours ago, Nemini's words would have made her furious. Now, though, all she felt was grateful. So, so grateful that someone understood.

All her life—the one she could remember and all the ones she couldn't—Bex had lived for her demons. Being queen was the air she breathed, the point around which everything else revolved. And while the loss of that still felt like her heart was being ripped out, Bex was finally able to look beyond the pain, and what she found out there was that Nemini wasn't wrong. There *was* peace in the void. There *was* freedom in nothingness because for the first time in her existence, Bex wasn't Rebexa.

She didn't have to fight anymore. She'd already lost, which meant the war was no longer her sole responsibility. If she never moved from this spot again, the world would keep turning without her. She could finally stop being angry. Finally stop hurting, stop dying. All she had to do was nothing. Just sit here and let everything else drift away into the void. The end of all her suffering was right in front of her, a life of peace right at her fingertips. All she had to do was let go, and yet...

And yet...

"You can't do it, can you?"

There was no way Nemini could see, but Bex still shook her head.

"Just because I didn't get a choice doesn't mean I didn't choose this," she said, squeezing her one remaining hand into a fist. "Even when my fire was nearly gone and no one remembered what my horns meant anymore, I was still the Queen of Wrath. I don't need my name to be me, but there are lots of demons who *do* need Rebexa. Good people who've fought just as hard as I have."

Bex looked back up at the dark, which didn't seem nearly so scary now. "It's nice to know that freedom's out there, but I can't sit here and enjoy it while everyone else is still struggling, so I guess I'd better get back in there."

"I knew you'd say that," Nemini replied, but her voice wasn't triumphant or resigned. She was simply stating fact in her usual monotone, and that was enough to make Bex grin.

"Yeah, well, I've always been a stubborn piece of work," she agreed proudly. "And starting over from nothing *is* what I'm best at. Also, someone's gotta bust Adrian out of Heaven, and we're the only ones who know he's there."

"Are you sure?" Nemini asked. "He's a prince now."

"I don't care," Bex said stubbornly. "I don't know what happened between his tree falling apart and him standing on that balcony with Gilgamesh, but I *know* Adrian didn't betray us." She clenched her hand tight. "We're getting him back. Him and my horns and Drox. We're going to take back everything Gilgamesh stole from us, and then we're bringing Heaven down."

Those were insanely cocky words from someone who'd just fallen out of Heaven like a piece of trash, but Bex refused to take them back. At this point, hope was all she had, but Adrian had always made her hope for impossible things, so Bex pushed herself up out of the cold sand. Nemini rose up right behind her, rustling in the dark as she reached into her pockets.

"I thought that was how you'd feel," she said as the rustling stopped. "That's why I brought this."

Light blossomed in the darkness. For a moment, Bex thought Nemini had done some kind of unknown magic. Then she saw that the glow was coming from a rectangle clutched in the void demon's hand.

"You brought your *phone*?"

"Of course," Nemini said, tapping her finger against the screen. "The new ones you bought us might be cheap, but they're very water-resistant. Signal's not bad, either, since death is so much closer to the living world than Heaven."

"I can't believe it works at all," Bex said, staring in awe.

Nemini shrugged and started tapping out a message to Iggs. Despite what she'd just said about signal, the bars looked *very* low to Bex. It must've been enough, though, because the message went out. Iggs's reply came back a few seconds later, promising to meet them at the door.

"Just like that, huh?" Bex said, looking around at the empty black-silt riverbank, which she could now see clearly thanks to the glow of Nemini's phone. "Maybe we should have evacuated to here."

Nemini shook her head. "The lands of death are not a haven for the living. The rivers don't even have shores for most people. The only reason we were able to sit like this is because we're both alive and dead."

That would explain why Bex hadn't felt anything but water the last time she'd fallen in. Even if the riverbanks had been accessible, Bex didn't think she could've gotten thousands of terrified demons to jump into an ice-cold torrent of death. Now that she was no longer wrapped in the balm of endless nothingness, just standing next to all that raging, unnatural water was making Bex jumpy. Fortunately, the walk wasn't far.

They must have dropped straight down because Bex spotted the light from the door Iggs opened almost immediately. That light was also how she saw that the darkness beyond the door wasn't just one river. There were tons of them out here, a whole braided stream system of banks, sandbars, and rivulets. All the waterways were gushing like mountain rivers during the spring flood season, but even weakened by the loss of her fire and missing her hand, Bex was able to jump over them easily.

That did a lot for her confidence. Being unable to move after losing her horns had hit hard, but while her magic was thoroughly hollowed out, there was nothing wrong with her body. She was tired, and her missing hand burned like a brand, but she didn't feel any weaker than she had before Adrian had put her in the bonfire. Better, actually, since she didn't have a never-healing wound in her side anymore. It was still a huge drop in power, but Bex had lived like this for seven years. She knew how to work without her fire, and that knowledge gave her courage as she stepped up to the raging edge of the last and largest of the rivers.

The water roaring beneath the jagged end of the chain she'd cut was every bit as huge, black, and cold as she remembered. The door Iggs had opened was a good fifty feet away. It was also much higher than their position on the bank, hanging twenty feet above the raging water like a lantern. That wouldn't have been a problem yesterday, but now that she had no fire to help blast her across, Bex was having serious concerns about the jump.

"Do you want me to carry you?" Nemini offered.

"Nah, I got it," Bex said, walking back up the bank. "Just let me get a running start."

Nemini nodded and stepped out of the way, giving the former Queen of Wrath plenty of room as she began to sprint, digging her feet into the soft silt and pumping her arms for extra speed. When her bloody running shoes were almost to the water's edge, Bex kicked off the ground and leaped into the air, using all that was left of her strength to launch herself over the deadly water and into Iggs's arms.

She hit his big red body like a cannonball. As always, though, her demon didn't budge.

"*Bex!*" he cried, hugging her so hard her ribs creaked. "I'm so glad you're alive!"

"I'm glad I'm alive, too," was what Bex wanted to say, but Iggs was squeezing her so tight she couldn't speak.

"I felt you vanish," he told her in a desperate voice. "We all felt it, then the cannons stopped firing, and everything got so quiet, and... and..." He squeezed even harder. "*I thought you were dead!*"

Bex would be if he didn't let up. Iggs was in his true form, which was strong enough to crush a tank. She was gently smacking his arm to get his attention when Iggs finally pulled his head back.

And saw her missing horns.

He dropped her at once, slapping a hand over his mouth as his red eyes got bigger and bigger.

"My queen..." he said at last, reaching out like he was going to touch her shoulder only to close his hand back into a fist instead. "What happened to you?"

Bex took a long breath. There were a lot of answers to that question. In the end, though, she went with the simplest.

"I was defeated," she said, lifting her chin to face it. "But thanks to Nemini, it doesn't have to be forever. We can come back from this. We *always* come back."

Iggs normally ate stuff like that up, but the haunted look on his face didn't go away. He just kept staring at Bex as if she was a stranger, his giant red body shaking like he was about to fall apart. Looking up at the demon she could no longer truly call hers, Bex felt the same way, but there was nothing she could do about it. There was nowhere left to go but forward, so forward was where she went.

"What's the situation?"

Iggs jumped at the question, and a horrible feeling began to clench in Bex's chest. She'd asked for the information out of habit, but she wasn't Iggs's queen anymore. She wasn't *anyone's* queen. No one here had to do a thing she said. But just as Bex was starting to panic over how she was going to keep everyone together if no one listened to her anymore, Iggs launched into his report.

"The bombardments started decreasing half an hour ago. Five minutes after that, the attacks stopped entirely. Nothing's blown up since. The Market's bombed to powder, but other than some cracks and the control room, which was smashed before this started, all the lower floors are still intact."

If he hadn't been looking at her so intensely, Bex would have doubled over in relief. He was watching, though, so she kept her back straight and her voice calm, determined to act like a queen even if she wasn't technically qualified to be one anymore.

"And my demons?"

"Safe," Iggs assured her, looking genuinely happy for the first time since he'd spotted her missing horns. "We couldn't do anything for the ones who got killed during the initial attack or the war demons' betrayal, but everyone who made it to the shelters is alive."

Bex smiled in relief. "Not a total disaster, then. Are we still locked in?"

"Like fish in a barrel," Iggs said as he stepped aside to let Bex walk past him into the cratered wasteland that had been the world's first demon-run Free Market.

Even knowing what to expect, the destruction was shocking. Gilgamesh's golden statue was untouched, of course, but everything else was destroyed. Adrian's tree had finally collapsed into splinters, and Bex couldn't even see the RV anymore. The sky was still missing as well, giving her a perfect view of Heaven's white city, which was still floating above them like the moon.

It did look smaller, though. It was hard to tell with no references, but Bex would've sworn the city was moving away from them, sailing off into the dark like a ship going out to sea. As it got farther, Bex realized she could actually see the chains running up to it. The black lines were invisible in the dark, but they stood out like stray threads against the whiteness of Heaven's foundations where it met the cliff all the rivers poured into. It was the same sight she'd seen from the golden bridge, but from a different angle. Looking up from the ground, Bex could clearly see the place where all the chains came together at the base of the Holy City's walls, tying Heaven to Earth like a glittering white balloon.

If Adrian had been here, he'd have been losing his mind over that, but he wasn't. He was up there, trapped in the enemy's stronghold. So were Drox and her horns, and Bex wasn't going to rest until she got back every single one.

"Let's go find Lys and start making a new plan," she said as she turned her back on Heaven and started marching through the gray dust that was all that remained of their Market. "Is our army still full of traitors?"

"Actually," Iggs said, catching up with her in a single step thanks to his long legs, "that's the part of this that turned out kind of good. The war demons *did* betray us, but not because they wanted to. Get this! The Queen of War is—"

"Alive," Bex finished, pressing the stump of her severed hand against her leg. "I found that out the hard way."

Iggs shot her a worried look, and Bex shook her head. "It's gratifying to know that Kirok and the others didn't sell us out on purpose. So long as they have their horns, though, we can't guarantee it won't happen again. I think our best move at this point is to keep the war demons away from anything mission-critical until we figure out how to get out of..."

Her voice trailed off. It was hard to tell when there was a gaping emptiness where her fire used to be, but Bex swore she could feel magic rising in the air. Very *familiar* magic that smelled like the forest, but that couldn't be right. Adrian's giant oak tree had already collapsed. There wasn't even a proper stump left, just a bunch of jagged wood and mangled roots. Bex had already moved her eyes off it to keep searching when a flash of movement brought them back just in time to see the ball of roots start twisting like a nest of snakes.

They burrowed into the blasted dirt as she watched, churning up the powdery soil as they shot out in every direction. Within seconds, every inch of the destroyed Market was filled with roots, including the ground under Bex's feet. She could feel them wiggling like worms through her soggy sneakers, but it was the magic that really had her attention.

It'd been rising the whole time, expanding and unfurling like a leaf in the summer sun. When it was finally fully opened, a forest burst out of the ground.

It exploded before Bex's eyes, filling the entire blasted disk of the Anchor before she could finish her gasp. It wasn't just any forest, either. This was a deep woodland complete with giant trees, mossy glens, rings of mushrooms, and golden fireflies dancing over the little streams that were suddenly everywhere. It was nothing like when Adrian had made his Blackwood, because these trees hadn't grown. They'd popped out of the ground like springs, like someone had grabbed a fully grown forest from somewhere else and just shoved it up through the dirt.

Wherever it had come from, the wood was everywhere. Bex couldn't even see the empty sky anymore thanks to the canopy of green leaves growing over her head like a ceiling. Owls and bats fluttered between the branches, and the air grew heavy with moisture as the trees began to breathe.

There was a lot of breathing going on, actually. Now that she'd recovered from the initial shock, Bex could feel the whole spontaneous forest expanding and contracting like a pair of lungs. It reminded her of the pulses she'd felt when Adrian had buried his heart in the ground, except these fluxes were even bigger. Each one pushed the rich, wild power of the forest higher, growing the magic denser and thicker until, like water being forced out of the air when the humidity got too high, the magic condensed into three women dressed in black standing right in front of her.

Bex jumped out of the way, her hands—hand—coming up before she could think. Drox's blade didn't appear in it, of course, but that turned out to be a good thing. Now that she wasn't acting on instinct, Bex realized she recognized the woman in the center of the trio. It was Adrian's mom, and she looked *terrifying*.

They all did. Maybe it was because Adrian had been her first, but Bex had never found witches particularly scary. These women, however, looked like the fury of nature incarnate. The white-haired crone with the bone-handled scythe especially looked like she'd come straight out of the darkest of medieval fairy tales to gobble up children.

Bex kept her eyes on that one since the oldest was usually the leader, but it was the third witch—a young, pretty, black-haired girl with an intense blue-eyed scowl that could have cut glass—who stepped forward.

"Greetings, no-longer-Queen of Wrath," she said in a measured, dreamy voice, keeping a light hand on Boston, whom Bex had just now realized was perched on the young witch's shoulder.

"I am Muriel," the girl went on, "Old Wife of the Soul, Witch of the Future. For many years, I have foreseen this day, and so it is with a mix of joy and sorrow that I come before you and your demons to offer the aid of the Blackwood."

"Is that so?" Bex asked after a long, shocked silence. "We're in no position to turn down help, but... Are you sure? We're at war with Gilgamesh for real now, and I thought the Blackwood didn't do that."

Muriel's pretty face pulled into a scowl even more terrifying than her sisters'.

"That was in the past," she said sharply, "before the self-proclaimed King of Heaven decided to steal what he never should have touched. A witch of our coven has been taken and his grove defiled. For his sake and the sake of everything that is to come, all the old pacts are broken. The time for hiding is over. The Blackwood goes to war! And I have foreseen that you will be its greatest ally against the storm that is to come."

Bex didn't see how a hornless ex-queen with no sword was going to be anyone's "greatest ally," but she wasn't about to argue against her own miraculous salvation.

"Any enemy of Gilgamesh's is a friend of ours," she said instead, holding out her one remaining hand. "On behalf of the free demons of Seattle, we are happy to accept the Blackwood's aid. Thank you."

"It is we who should be thanking you," Muriel said as she shook Bex's black-stained fingers. "This war affects us all, but you've been left to hold the front line by yourself for far too long. It is because of your efforts that our plans had time to grow to fruition. Now,

Gilgamesh shall know a witch's vengeance, and you shall be there to enjoy it."

Bex couldn't think of a single thing she'd like better, but as much as she wanted to believe in what the witch was saying, there was a problem.

"How?" she asked, pointing up at the retreating Holy City, whose light was still shining through the forest's thick canopy like the moon. "I wasn't in my right mind during Gilgamesh's big announcement, but I'm pretty sure Adrian gave himself up to save the rest of us. How are we getting vengeance out of that?"

The Witch of the Future's lips curled into a wicked smile. "The weapon you don't recognize as a weapon is the most dangerous of all," she said, waving her hand at the old-growth forest that hadn't been there three minutes ago. "Where one tree grows, so do we all. Gilgamesh didn't take a prisoner. He brought a wild seed into his garden, and we all know how those take over."

She finished with a chuckle, as if this was all a big inside joke, but Bex's teeth were clenched so hard they ached.

"Why does it sound like you knew this was going to happen?"

"I could hardly be the Witch of the Future if I was surprised," Muriel replied, reaching out to touch Bex's arm just above the stump of her severed hand. "Your concern speaks well of you, Child of Ishtar, but you have no need to fear. We raised Adrian to be a hearty hybrid. He'll grow well wherever he is planted, though I do have a question for you."

Bex arched her eyebrows as the witch leaned closer.

"When you saw him last, was Adrian still wearing his hat?"

"Yes," Bex replied at once. The end of her trip to Heaven was a painful blur, but she clearly recalled seeing Adrian on the balcony. "He was definitely wearing his hat," she said. "It was the only reason I recognized him from so far away."

"Then all is on the right path," Muriel said, clapping her pale hands in delight. "By the time Gilgamesh realizes he's being overrun, it'll be too late."

She looked supremely happy at that, but Bex didn't like how openly Adrian's family seemed to be using him as a plant. She wasn't even sure if the witch was speaking literally or figuratively. Given the nature of his family's magic, Bex wouldn't have been surprised if Adrian sprouted actual roots, but there was no point getting mad about it. She could worry about Adrian until she'd worried herself down to a nubbin, but she couldn't *do* anything to help him until they got out of here. His family was offering to do just that, so Bex forced herself to stop being suspicious and focus on the disaster at hand.

"I need to get my demons out of this Anchor," she said, getting back into queen-mode, since that was more comfortable than thinking about all the variables she couldn't control. "You teleported in. Can you teleport us out?"

"That's what we're here for," Muriel said, turning back to her sisters, who were already opening a tunnel into the mossy forest floor. It looked like a rabbit burrow, but it was tall enough for Iggs to walk into comfortably, and the moment it was finished, a flood of women wearing the same black hat and coat that Adrian always did came pouring into the Anchor.

"Gather your people and bring them under the trees," Muriel instructed as the witches hurried past. "This forest is a piece of the Great Blackwood. Once all your demons are safe beneath its boughs, our coven will work together to move it back to its original position in Massachusetts. My sisters and I must return to our heart grove to make sure Heaven doesn't see what we're about to do, but Boston will be here if you have questions."

"Happy to help," Adrian's familiar said as he leaped off the witch's shoulder onto Bex, who was so surprised she nearly knocked him back off. She'd never been this close to Adrian's cat before. Not surprisingly, he smelled like his witch, which made her empty chest clench up a little before she forced herself to get a grip.

"Thanks for everything your coven is doing," she whispered to Boston as the three terrifying Old Wives disappeared down the tunnel. "But will this actually work? Not to poke a sore spot, but Gilgamesh has never had a problem killing witches before."

"That's because the other covens didn't have centuries to prepare," the familiar replied with his usual authority. "We couldn't stop Gilgamesh from taking Adrian, but not even the gods themselves can remove a witch's heart once it's been given to the forest. No matter what they do to him up there, he'll always be a Blackwood, and the Blackwood takes care of its own." He bared his teeth with a growl that sounded more like a panther than a house cat. "We'll get him back."

"We'll get him back," Bex promised, placing her shaking hand on Boston's fur as she glanced around for her demons.

As expected, Iggs's jaw was on the ground as he tried not to gawk at all the pretty witches. Nemini was right beside him, perched on a fallen log as she kept a silent watch over all the newcomers. No one else had made it up to the market yet, so Bex borrowed Nemini's phone to tell Lys the good news. She was still typing out a message when the lust demon in question burst through the trees to her right, tackling Bex to the mossy ground with a shout of pure relieved delight.

Epilogue

Adrian had to get out of here.

He was finally alone, sitting in the white bedroom his father had given him high up in the gilded citadel that stood at the center of Heaven. According to Gilgamesh, he was supposed to be resting and recovering from his ordeal, but Adrian didn't think for a second that his father actually cared for his well-being. He'd been put away, set aside for safekeeping like all the other tools in his father's workshop, while Gilgamesh dealt with more pressing kingly business. He'd made it clear that fixing the Queen of Pride was his top priority, though, which meant he'd be back soon.

Fortunately, Adrian had always been an efficient witch. The moment his smiling father locked him in here, he'd shoved all the fancy furniture out of the way and started scratching a sending spell into the stone floor with the jagged edge of the golden lamp he'd broken off the wall. Normally, for a spell like this, he'd make the circle out of wood from his forest and use blood as the connecting element, but the stuff in Adrian's veins was still as white as quintessence from the overdose that had gotten him into this mess, so he made do with a lock of his hair instead. He'd just about gotten everything ready to send the message to Boston when someone knocked on his door.

He shoved all the furniture back into place, tossing the rug over his almost-finished sending circle just in time as the door opened to reveal a princess. It was the tall one with the mismatched eyes that Bex had been fighting, which was a shock. The last time Adrian had seen her, she'd been a gigantic, scarred, four-armed demon. But she must've had a spare princess body shoved in a closet somewhere, because the woman standing at his doorway looked just as creepy and doll-like as the rest of them. She bowed when she saw Adrian staring, folding her hands—one bone white, one covered in a glove—demurely in front of her carved dress.

"Most illustrious Prince of Heaven."

Adrian didn't bother hiding his wince at the ridiculous title. He was supposed to be playing along, though, so he didn't say anything rude or try to stop the princess as she stepped into his room.

"Forgive the interruption of your repose," she said, though the tone of her voice made it sound more like an order than an apology. "Your glorious father, ever may his wisdom shine upon us, values your continued good health most greatly. I promise I will not intrude long upon your solemnity, but I come bearing a gift from his most holy majesty."

"What sort of gift could Gilgamesh have for me?" Adrian asked once he'd finished translating all that flowery garbage.

"The only one worthy of a prince," she said, giving him a smile that looked more cruel than beautiful. "A princess."

Adrian stepped back in alarm, but it was too late. The princess had already reached out her hand to someone he couldn't see who was still in the hall.

463

Another white hand grabbed hers a moment later, and Adrian felt his heart take a nosedive all the way back in the Blackwood as a second white woman stepped into his room.

One who looked exactly like Bex.

Even though she was standing right in front of him, Adrian couldn't believe what his eyes were seeing. That was Bex's face and body, her lovely shy smile and alert stance, but everything else about her was wrong. Her shiny black hair was now the color of chalk, and her eyes—the lovely, fiery eyes he'd always found so fascinating—were gone completely, replaced with the cold interlocking golden rings all the constructs of Heaven shared. Her skin, which had always been fair, was now as hard and colorless as the leviathan bone his father had been carving when Adrian had visited him in his workshop. Carving into *her*, Adrian realized with a shock. He was still trying to process that when the new princess rushed forward.

"*Adrian!*" she cried in Bex's voice as she threw her arms around him. "I'm so happy you're safe!"

He stumbled under the assault, grabbing the construct's white shoulders to push her away only to find that he couldn't. This new fake Bex was even stronger than the real one, and she'd latched on to him like a bear trap.

"I'm so happy," she said again, burying her face in his chest just like the real Bex had the night they'd taken the Anchor. "I thought it was all over until I heard the king speak. You saved my life!"

She hugged him even tighter, bruising his sides with her hard, cold arms.

"Oh, Adrian, I've been such a fool. I hurt so many people fighting the gods' stupid war. Now that you've brought me here, though, I can finally see the truth. Ishtar never loved me. I was just her tool. We were *all* her tools, but Gilgamesh set me free. He'll set us *all* free, the whole world!"

She pulled back to look up at him with glittering golden eyes. "Thank you so much for joining him. If you hadn't accepted your father, I'd still be trapped in Ishtar's web. Now, though, thanks to the glory of my new king, I'm free to do what *I* want. I don't have to be my people's slave anymore, which means we can finally be together! Look, I even brought you a sword."

Her white doll face broke into a grin as she stepped back and yanked the white glove off her hand, holding it up to show Adrian the ring on her third finger. Drox's black ring, on Bex's severed hand.

"Isn't it amazing?" the princess who looked like Bex cried, shoving the ring at him. "Aren't you happy?"

Adrian didn't reply. His mind was full of words, but he didn't dare speak any of them. He just stood there perfectly still, not even daring to breathe while the fake Bex rubbed her hornless head against him like a cat. He was fighting to keep himself together when the Princess of War finally broke the silence.

"I'll leave you two to get reacquainted," she said as she stepped back into the hall. "Remember, Prince Adrian, all things are possible for those who stand high in the Eternal King's esteem. He has already been extremely generous. Continue to please him, and your rewards shall be greater still. This palace can truly be Heaven for those who earn the Eternal King's favor.

Fail to meet his expectations, however, and your fall shall be precipitous. Never forget that your divine father is also king of the Hells. It would be most unfortunate if you did anything to squander his good opinion of you."

"My prince would never be so stupid," the fake Bex declared, moving to Adrian's side with a lift of her head that was so like the real one's it made his heart clench. "He'll beat all his stupid brothers to become Gilgamesh's eternal favorite. If I were you, sister, I'd tell your prince to start packing up his office, because *my* Prince Adrian will rise to become the Crown Prince of all Heaven."

It was hard to tell on her carved face, but Adrian swore the Princess of War's jaw ticked at that.

"So glad to see you're back to yourself, sister," she replied in a tight voice Adrian would never have identified as glad. "Rest well, Prince Adrian. Your princess will inform you when your divine father requires your presence again."

Adrian tried to say something, but the Crown Princess had already closed the door, locking him inside his luxurious new prison with the monstrous thing that was not Bex.

Thank you for reading!

Thank you for reading *Hell to Pay*!

If you enjoyed the latest chapter of Bex and Adrian's story, I hope you'll consider leaving a review. Reviews, good or bad, are vital to every author's career, and I'd be extremely grateful if you'd take a moment to write one for me.

The series will continue for two more books to reach its grand conclusion. The fourth book in the *Tear Down Heaven* series is already out and the last book launches early 2026.

You can be the first to know when it drops by signing up for my new release mailing list! (Over at rachelaaron.net) List members always get first dibs on my books, and I only email when I've got something new, so there's zero spam. Signing up is free and easy, so come join the fun!

Again, thank you so, *so* much for being my reader. There would be no books without you. Thank you from the bottom of my heart, and I'll see you in the next story!

Yours sincerely,
Rachel Aaron

Want More Books?

Tear Down Heaven is only the latest addition to the Rachel Aaron library. I have plenty more titles of all sorts for you to enjoy, including five finished series! Keep paging forward to see my top picks for new readers or visit rachelaaron.net for the full list, and, as always, thank you for reading!

Nice Dragons Finish Last

"Super fun, fast-paced urban fantasy full of heart, and plenty of magic, charm and humor to spare, this self-published gem was one of my favorite discoveries this year!" - **The Midnight Garden**

"A deliriously smart and funny beginning to a new urban fantasy series about dragons in the ruins of Detroit...inventive, uproariously clever, and completely un-put-down-able!" - **SF Signal**

As the smallest dragon in the Heartstriker clan, Julius survives by a simple code: stay quiet, don't cause trouble, and keep out of the way of bigger dragons. But this meek behavior doesn't cut it in a family of ambitious predators, and his mother, Bethesda the Heartstriker, has finally reached the end of her patience.

Now, sealed in human form and banished to the DFZ--a vertical metropolis built on the ruins of Old Detroit--Julius has one month to prove to his mother that he can be a ruthless dragon or lose his true shape forever. But in a city of modern mages and vengeful spirits where dragons are seen as monsters to be exterminated, he's going to need some serious help to survive this test.

He just hopes humans are more trustworthy than dragons.

My first and most popular DFZ series, complete at 5 books.
Available in **audio, print, eBook, and Kindle Unlimited!**

By a Silver Thread

"By A Silver Thread *is exquisitely trademark Rachel Aaron. Immensely readable & instantly engaging, with new characters that you can't help loving. The inclusion of fairy lore just leveled up the already fascinating world of the DFZ. So good, so fun!*" - **Novel Notations**

"*A superb return to the world of the DFZ. This is a heroic story that is in parts heartwarming, in parts mysterious and just a fantastic read all the way.*" - **Fantasy Book Critic**

In the world's most magical metropolis where spirits run noodle shops and cash-strapped dragons stage photo-ops for tourists, people still think fairies are nothing but stories, and that's exactly how the fairies like it. It's a lot easier to feast on humanity's dreams when no one believes you exist. But while this arrangement works splendidly for most fair folk, Lola isn't one of the lucky ones.

She's a changeling, a fairy monster made just human enough to dupe unsuspecting parents while fairies steal their real child. The magic that sustains her was never meant to last past the initial theft, leaving Lola without a future. But thanks to Victor Conrath, a very powerful--and very illegal--blood mage, she was given the means to cheat death.

For a price.

Now the only changeling ever to make it to adulthood, Lola has served the blood mage faithfully, if reluctantly, for twenty years. Her unique ability to slip through wards and change her shape to look like anyone has helped make Victor a legend in the DFZ's illegal-magic underground. It's not a great life, but at least the work is stable... until her master vanishes without a trace.

With only a handful left of the pills that keep her human, Lola must find Victor before she turns back into the fairy monster she was always meant to be. But with a whole SWAT team of federal paladins hunting her as a blood-mage accomplice, an Urban Legend on a silent black motorcycle who won't leave her alone, and a mysterious fairy king with the power to make the entire city dream, Lola's chances of getting out of this alive are as slender as a silver thread.

The newest standalone series set in the DFZ, complete at 3 books!
Available now in ebook, print, KU, and audio!

About the Author

Rachel Aaron is the author of almost thirty novels both self-published and through Orbit Books. When she's not holed up in her writing cave, she lives a nerdy, bookish life in the suburbs of Denver, CO with her perpetual-motion son, long-suffering husband, and mountains of books. To learn more about Rachel and read samples of all her work, visit rachelaaron.net!

Cover Illustration by Luisa Preissler
Cover Design by Rachel Aaron
Editing provided by Red Adept Editing

As ever, this book would not be as good without my beta reader Linda Hall, the keenest typo-hunter of all time.

www.ingramcontent.com/pod-product-compliance
Lightning Source LLC
Chambersburg PA
CBHW061537190726
48289CB00004B/1073